WHAT THE #@&% IS THAT?

ALSO EDITED BY
JOHN JOSEPH ADAMS &
DOUGLAS COHEN

Oz Reimagined

ALSO EDITED BY
JOHN JOSEPH ADAMS

The Apocalypse Triptych, Vol. 1: The End is Nigh
The Apocalypse Triptych, Vol. 2: The End is Now
The Apocalypse Triptych, Vol. 3: The End Has Come
Armored
Best American Science Fiction and Fantasy
Dead Man's Hand
Epic: Legends of Fantasy
The Improbable Adventures of Sherlock Holmes
The Living Dead
The Living Dead 2
Loosed Upon the World: The Saga Anthology of Climate Fiction
The Mad Scientist's Guide to World Domination
Operation Arcana
Press Start to Play
Wastelands
Wastelands 2

ALSO EDITED BY
DOUGLAS COHEN

Realms of Fantasy: A Retrospective

WHAT THE #@&% IS THAT?

THE SAGA ANTHOLOGY
OF THE MONSTROUS
AND THE MACABRE

EDITED BY JOHN JOSEPH ADAMS
AND DOUGLAS COHEN

SAGA  PRESS

LONDON SYDNEY NEW YORK TORONTO NEW DELHI

SAGA PRESS
AN IMPRINT OF SIMON & SCHUSTER, INC.

1230 AVENUE OF THE AMERICAS, NEW YORK, NEW YORK 10020

FOR CTHULHU

IÄ! IÄ! CTHULHU FHTAGN!

CONTENTS

INTRODUCTION

DOUGLAS COHEN

Explaining how this project came to be is a story unto itself. Back in 2007, Harper Perennial Modern Classics published a book called *Tales of H. P. Lovecraft*, which reprinted a number of tales penned by H. P. Lovecraft, one of the most influential horror writers of all time. The book's cover featured an illustration of Lovecraft's most famous creation, the iconic monster known as Cthulhu.

Fast forward to 2012. While scrolling through Facebook one day, I came across an Internet meme[1] featuring the cover art from the aforementioned *Tales of H. P. Lovecraft*. The book's original design elements had been stripped away and replaced with *new* design elements—so instead of the original title, the meme's creator had replaced it with the title *What the Fuck Is That*. And whereas on the original cover, Stephen King had provided a real promotional quote that called H. P. Lovecraft "The twentieth century's greatest practitioner of the classic horror tale," in the meme version, King's quote now read: "I don't know what the fuck is going on." And so on.

So I had a good laugh, never imagining this gag cover was based on a real one. I did know what (the fuck) "that" was though—it was clearly everyone's favorite tentacled beastie, Cthulhu. This particular meme proved

---

1 Wikipedia defines an Internet meme as "an activity, concept, catchphrase or piece of media which spreads, often as mimicry, from person to person via the Internet." It's as good a definition as any for our purposes.

funny enough that over the next few months, I came across it several more times, as the online community continued sharing and linking to it across various social media.

Then one day, months later, I again came across our intrepid meme on yet another social media site. While reading the accompanying comments, someone opined how this meme would make a great poster. I thought so too, but I chimed in with a different possibility: "Forget that. Make it the cover to a horror anthology. Twenty stories, and in every story one character is guaranteed to say, 'What the fuck is that?'" I'd written this as a joke, but the ensuing comments were so enthusiastic that I realized I had stumbled onto a legitimate idea for a horror anthology.

Sometimes, good ideas come from mediocre jokes.

Since the "that" in the title and artwork referred to and depicted Cthulhu, I thought that this obviously should be an anthology set in the universe of the Cthulhu mythos, and since the book was inspired by the Internet, my initial plan was to fund the project via Kickstarter[2].

I had never run a Kickstarter campaign before, but I knew from talking with colleagues that there is a lot that goes into them. So rather than go in flying blind, I decided to bring a collaborator onto the project, someone with previous Kickstarter experience I could learn from.

Enter Jaym Gates[3], good friend and editorial colleague . . . and as you're probably figuring, wise in the ways of Kickstarter. So, I pitched her the idea, and in short order I had recruited a coeditor. From there we did as coeditors do, slinging ideas and questions back and forth, and the anthology gradually started assuming a more definitive shape.

One possibility we had discussed was to possibly incorporate the original artwork from the meme into the anthology. The problem was we had no idea who had done the artwork; the meme's creator didn't credit the artist, and

---

2　Kickstarter is an online platform that relies on public crowdfunding for entrepreneurs in various fields to achieve the financial backing for their creative projects. Publishing projects are no exception, and around the time I was initially developing this book, anthologies were starting to find success on this platform.

3　If you've noticed that this book is actually coedited by John Joseph Adams, not Jaym Gates . . . very observant! I'm getting to that. Be patient!

at the time I didn't know what book cover the meme was actually based on.

Then one night I stumbled upon this nifty online tool called Google Image Search. When I uploaded the meme through this search engine, my efforts were rewarded by revealing a book called (you guessed it) *Tales of H. P. Lovecraft*, featuring the exact same artwork as in the meme. From there it was a simple matter to finally uncover the artist's identity.

That's when my jaw dropped.

The artist was none other than Mike Mignola. If you're familiar with the movie and comic *Hellboy*, you are familiar with the work of Mignola. I could practically hear the steam whistling from my ears as the gears in my brain started churning. A quirky anthology based on a silly meme owed everything to a cover illustration for a real book by *Mike Mignola*? It was all too perfect.

The project had suddenly developed new tentacles. The cover illustration of a book reprinting a bunch of horror stories had inspired a meme. Now we could take that meme and do what the Internet so often does with memes: reinvent it. Only, in our case we would be bringing it back to the printed page, this time in a book filled with *original* horror stories. And while I knew it would be a long shot, who better to provide an original illustration than the artist who unwittingly started it all[4]? (*How* we might get him was an obstacle for another day!)

Sometimes, good ideas come from blind luck.

Then, in keeping with this introduction's emerging theme, something unexpected happened as the project progressed: my coeditor, Jaym, had to step down. Her reasons were more than solid and I wished her nothing but the best, but I was still of the opinion that a coeditor savvy to Kickstarter would benefit the book tremendously. Enter John Joseph Adams, a good friend and previous coeditor of mine. Of course, with John's participation, I understood there would be changes—you don't invite a new coeditor aboard without accepting their creative input. John

---

4   Technically speaking, I suppose H. P. Lovecraft started it all back in 1928 when he first published "The Call of Cthulhu" in *Weird Tales* magazine. But I digress. . . .

suggested some additional authors for recruitment, excellent writers who hadn't occurred to me before. But John's involvement went far deeper, and the end result is that this project is every bit his as much as it is mine.

For example, there is the matter of the title. *What the Fuck Is That?*—the title of the meme—made for a fun title, one that grabbed your attention. And it *did* represent the theme of the anthology. But did we really want a curse word in the title? Would it be too much? *What the Hell Is That?* was safer, but did the anthology lose something in the bargain, perhaps too much? So John said, "What if, instead of "What the Fuck Is That?" we just use the *F* in 'Fuck' and put three symbols afterward, like they do in comic strips?" I loved this idea . . . only I misheard him, and I thought he suggested we replace *all* the letters in the word with symbols . . . giving us a title of *What the #@&% Is That?*

Sometimes, good ideas come from misunderstandings.

Employing these symbols (or "grawlix[5]," as they're called) also created an unexpected side benefit: the exact wording of the phrase "What the fuck is that?" was no longer mandatory, nor would any other phrase be (at least not exactly). So, instead, we asked the authors to use the phrase "What the #@&% is that?" at least once in their stories and to substitute the grawlix with whatever word (or words) they wished, "fuck" included.

Sometimes, good ideas come from weird, random bull#@&%.

Another important change had to do with Cthulhu. While I initially envisioned that each of the stories would be about Cthulhu, John suggested we make it more diverse, allowing for *all sorts* of monsters. And as it happened, John was not alone in thinking this. Enter Joe Monti, editorial director of Simon & Schuster's Saga Press. Shortly after joining me as coeditor, John received an e-mail from Joe, wondering if he had any horror anthologies to pitch. (Yes, timing is indeed everything.) When Joe learned about the anthology, he expressed an interest in acquiring it . . . but like John, he wondered if perhaps the theme could cover *all monsters* . . .

---

5 The word "grawlix" was coined by American cartoonist Mort Walker, and it refers to the typographical symbols employed in dialogue balloons that represent profanities.

Long story short, we agreed to sell the anthology to Saga with a focus on all monsters (beings in the Cthulhu mythos included). In explaining the anthology's premise to Joe, we explained its evolution, including how we hoped Mike Mignola could be recruited to do a new cover . . . and as it happened, Joe had a lead that could maybe bring this about. Several months later, the final puzzle piece fell into place when we learned that Mignola had indeed agreed to illustrate the cover. (Go ahead, look at it again. Ain't it *grand*?)

So, there you have it. Although there were many trials and tribulations along the way that caused the book to morph and evolve over the course of its development, essentially we ended up with (almost) exactly what we intended from the start: twenty stories, and in every story one character is guaranteed to say, "What the #@&% is that?"

So, now that you've heard the story-behind-the-stories, it's time to take a backseat while you enjoy the twisted imaginations of our authors . . . and maybe, *just maybe* you will learn what the #@&% that is . . .

MOBILITY

LAIRD BARRON

Life is hard in forty million B.C. beneath the apple-green heavens. Something is always trying to eat the monkeys. A shadow ripples across the forest canopy to confirm this fact. The monkeys screech and scatter among the lush treetops. The black shape veers out of the sun in pursuit. It closes the gap at an astonishing rate.

Branches slap together and howlers howl. The shadow snatches a few of the slower troop (rending treetops as well) and glides away, trailing pitiful monkey screams.

The forest is still. Eventually, birds trill and buzz in a thousand tongues. The monkeys also call to one another and the survivors make their way back to the central group for commiseration. The troop settles. The monkeys return to cracking nuts and eating fruit and picking each other's nits. One watches the cloudless apple-green skies, although the memory of why soon fades.

Bryan murdered a squirrel a few hours into his eleventh birthday. Uncle So-and-So handed him a pump-action air rifle for a birthday present and the kid shot the first animal he saw. Which happened to be a semi-tame gray squirrel nibbling an acorn on the sidewalk in front of Bryan's house. He pumped the action twenty or thirty times, aimed with his tongue sticking out, and squeezed the trigger. Lucky (?) shot blew that squirrel's eyeball to jelly. A little kid laboriously pedaling a tricycle witnessed the slaughter with a vacuous smirk. This was the brat who'd recently learned how to burn ants with a magnifying glass.

Bryan felt surprised and a little bit sick for a few minutes. The family cat, Heathcliff, also known as the Black Death, swooped in and nabbed the squirrel's corpse and Bryan forgot the whole thing.

The universe would have its vengeance. It had begun to wreak it eons before Bryan was ever born.

Snow fell on Providence all afternoon. Made a mucky slush of the walk from school. Bryan ordered baked tuna at the grill where Lovecraft had eaten whenever *Weird Tales* sent a check, which was sufficiently infrequent to qualify as a special occasion. Came back to bite both of them in the ass.

Bryan stood a shade under six feet. Burly Scandinavian stock. Curly hair and precisely trimmed beard, colored blond out of a bottle. Forty-five years made him as good as any vintage LP. He didn't smile, but he didn't *not* smile, either. He'd worn his lucky cardigan to dinner. Black and white, separated by a jagged divide, animals fighting, the two wolves of the soul from Native American folklore locking jaws. He'd worn a knit cap, black. He'd worn black-and-white knit gloves to match the sweater. He'd worn glasses, rimless. Not necessary, yet the coeds liked the look. The glasses said *philosopher, poet-wunderkind*; he was a professor of Pawhunk Community College Nonfiction Writing Department these past four years, so it seemed appropriate. He'd worn a gold band, although it signified nothing since he'd never married and never planned to (God help him if Angie ever twigged to the truth). Merely a prop from his community theater stint. The coeds *liked* men with wedding bands. The band said, *I could fuck you if I wanted to, but I'm not gonna try, because well, look.* He'd worn buckskin pants. And moccasins. With fringe.

Angie, his eye-rolling girlfriend of a decade, served as the English

Chair at Brown, and good for her, although he routinely mentioned she could do better and tried to ignore how her eyebrows shot up. Late that autumn, after much subtle manipulation on Bryan's part, they celebrated her thirty-fourth birthday with a cruise to Nova Scotia. Serendipity! He wanted to research a nonfiction crime author who lived there, anyway. Angie toured thrift shops and outlet malls while he spent the weekend plying the down-on-his-luck author, one Buford Creely, with booze and picking (pickling?) the fellow's brain about a sensational murder case from the 1960s and '70s. Thirty-nine missing persons, a secret grotto littered with skulls piled into pyramids, and skulls on stakes. Unsolved, cops baffled, movie-of-the-week fodder. The kind of lurid material the faculty at Pawhunk frowned upon yet were stuck with in the infrequent event one of its professors girded his loins and took a stab at publishing.

The vacation arrangement worked out great, although Angie seemed moody after they returned to his apartment in Providence. Meanwhile, Bryan was positively energized and stoked to sequester himself in the spare bedroom (his den) for a week or two to go at a new essay, which is exactly what he did.

This was the first evening they'd been together during that hectic stretch.

"Eat up, sport," she said, watching him put away another fork-load of the tuna. "You'll need your strength tonight."

"Oh, boy!"

She smiled, pure flint. "Got some bad news. Skylark Tooms passed away. Remember her?"

"Rich, attractive. Dad was a clothing designer or . . . ?"

"She died in an industrial accident the other day. Burned alive. Like this damned steak."

"I'm sorry your friend is dead." Through a mouthful.

"Friend, no. We weren't close since school. It's been on the news. A whole port town was destroyed. Train derailment. Chemicals. Nobody can get close."

"Awful, awful." Another chunk of delectable, flaky salmon glazed in garlic and lemon. This bite almost lodged in his throat. It left a metallic aftertaste. Bryan's eyes smarted and he quickly sipped water to ease the lump in its passage.

"I'm over it. A shock, is all." Angie appeared oblivious to his struggle, utterly consumed with her own concerns.

Bryan recovered. He signaled the waiter and ordered crème brûlée and a cup of black coffee. Delicious. "Did you want something?" he said, dabbing his lips with a cloth napkin, vaguely piqued she hadn't offered to do it for him like when they first dated. She'd acted the part of a depraved concubine then.

She smiled and shook her head.

After dinner, he called a cab to save them from another slog through the gloppy streets. Back at his place, he put *Boys in the Trees* on the stereo (antiquing for the win!) and broke out a bottle of kinda good wine. Angie watched from her perch on the arm of the leather couch, where he'd begged her pretty please not to sit a million and one times. Her manic-pixie haircut, thick-rimmed glasses, and red lipstick seemed brutally severe. However, she rocked an angora sweater and tartan skirt combo, and that made up for the rest.

He wiped his sweaty face with his sleeve. He pried the cork loose, poured half a glass, and drank it while sorting his phone messages. Three—two from Mom, and the last from that drunken author Creely. Mom said, *I love you; why don't you ever return my calls*; Creely said, *Get in touch soonest; you got my number,* and hung up. From all the hooting and yelling in the background, the author sounded like he'd used a payphone at the local tavern.

Bryan's stomach felt the slightest bit queasy. He burped and the metallic taste returned. He did himself up with another quarter glass of cabernet sauvignon, glanced over his shoulder, and saw that Angie remained poised and smiling as if she'd slipped on a reasonably lifelike mask of herself in one of her better moods. Ah, yes, he should pour her a stout one, keep her in that happy place.

Angie accepted the too-full glass without comment. She balanced it on her thigh.

"Your engagement ring," he said. "You're not wearing it."

"I'm not?" Again with the flinty smile.

His stomach burbled. He made his apologies and beelined for the bathroom. His reflection in the mirror was an ashen nightmare. He dropped his trousers and sat on the commode, head in his hands.

Angie knocked on the door. "FYI, I don't fancy you anymore, Bryan. Ten years in Chinese Hell should be considered time served. It's your turn on the spit."

Bryan would've retorted, but at that moment, his guts began to convulsively evacuate their contents. He groaned.

She continued in a pleasant voice, quite unlike her customary tone. "Do you recall that dream I mentioned? The one where I was a knight traveling the land on a fearless steed and lopping heads with a talking broadsword? Probably not. That's the problem, Professor. Had it again last night. I am now convinced time has come to cut bait and pursue other life opportunities. You always say I can do better. Kudos. Kudos, you heartless motherfucker!"

His vision contracted. His breath whistled. He clutched his tightening chest and toppled face-first onto the tiles. The descent took forever.

"Don't be melodramatic. Whining isn't manly. I mean, hell, Bry. I'm the one who should be pissed. Ten goddamned years." She sighed, and if Bryan hadn't simultaneously been suffocating and shitting himself, he might've imagined her pressed against the panel, wistfully tracing the grain with her nail, enacting the breakup scene that comes at the end of act two of every chick flick. "FYI, I've already met someone, so please do fuck right off and don't pester me with calls. We're flying to the Caribbean in a few hours."

Bryan clawed at the door in a doomed gesture. He vomited. Angie's engagement ring rode the sluice from his guts and floated in a puddle of bile and salmon under his nose. He blacked out and had a vision of lying helpless among reeds while giant herons pecked his liver to itty bits.

Angie, clad in a shiny chainmail bikini, leaned upon her equally shiny broadsword and smiled contemptuously. She stroked the pommel with her thumb and said, "Who's sticking it to whom now, you silly bitch?"

"Collapsed lung," the beefy nurse said with supreme indifference. "You aspirated a shitload of vomit. Not good, bro."

Bryan woke, after a fashion, in a hospital bed with the monotone report in progress. Tubes clogged his nose and throat. Cottony wooziness softened the interior of his skull. No, aspirating a shitload of vomit did not sound good at all, he had to agree. He closed his eyes and had a foggy recollection of his eleven-year-old self standing in the drive, pellet rifle in hand while the squirrel twitched its last. The tops of the sycamore (sequoia?) trees rustled and monkeys screeched fearfully. A shadow blotted the sun. A ten-foot-tall Martian descended from the belly of the mother saucer on a cold white beam. The Martian took his eleven-year-old self's pulse while brandishing a shiny chromatic blaster in the other hand. *Nice shooting, Tex,* the Martian said via telepathy. We hate those *damned things where I come from.* Heathcliff snatched the squirrel and darted away. The Martian telepathically laughed with savage gusto and Bryan's nose bled.

"Go back to sleep," the beefy nurse said, and snapped his fingers.

Bryan went back to sleep.

A few days and several sketchy diagnoses later, the beefy nurse said, "That's a wrap. You're officially mended. There's your clothes." He turned the light off as he left the room.

Darkness shifted to light. Bryan hobbled into his apartment on a set of cheap hospital crutches with no memory of how he'd arrived. His muscles and nervous system remained mysteriously at odds, causing spastic tics and farcical nightmares starring aggrieved monkeys and an endless green hell of jungle. His reinflated lung felt seared and scarred. He wheezed at the slightest exertion.

The weekend dripped through his veins and cocooned him in a gray malaise that precluded research, much less actual writing. He possessed trace memories of whatever had flickered ceaselessly across the television screen. His condition remained so moribund, he only left five or six increasingly strident messages on Angie's answering machine. Between stretches of torpor, he obsessed about her and his new rival, picturing them on a Caribbean beach sipping rum and laughing at his misfortune.

On Monday, Frank Mandibole, a former college chum and infrequent confidant, rang. Mandibole said the situation sounded intolerable and that he'd be over right away with proper medicine. The man arrived within moments. He pranced through the door and laid his hand on Bryan's forehead. "Gracious! Not a moment too soon. Let's take a ride, get some fresh air in your lungs. Hang around sucking in Providence, you'll eventually go the way of Uncle Howard."

"I feel half-dead, Frank."

"It's Tom. To-om! I don't go by Frank anymore. Try to focus on the positive. We'll throw a few things in a bag and *wheee* all the way to Mom and Dad's house for some R and R."

Bryan didn't argue the point. While generally the same height and composition as his old self, Mandibole no longer precisely resembled the "Frank" of school days. He'd trimmed his hair and shaved off the mustache. His skin gleamed the way a doll's skin does. In fact, his features (and helmet hair) were decidedly action-figure plastic. There'd been rumors of an accident. Obviously, he'd had work done. He wore a black-and-white cardigan that also seemed annoyingly familiar, yet not.

Bryan lacked the strength to protest the car ride. Anyway, how much worse could it be than lying around his apartment sloughing into eternity?

They hopped onto the interstate and cruised south, then west, into the wild lands of the Empire State. Mandibole's car had a rusty pink paint job. Compactly European, a tin can on bicycle wheels. Bryan didn't recognize the make or model, nor could he decipher the faded pennant on the radio antenna. Polka music burped and barked over the radio, interspersed with commentary that sounded Russian.

Mandibole said, "I've a theory regarding your illness. You're not superstitious—you gave up bowing to altars and thumping holy tomes, yes? Hang with me for a second. What if you're punishing yourself sub-consciously?"

"Punishing myself for what?"

"For bailing on the Mormons. Unresolved guilt."

"All my guilt is resolved. I'm a confirmed atheist. Happily." Bryan mas-saged the swollen glands in his neck. Bundled in a parka, scarf, mittens, snow pants, and snow boots he still shivered. The landscape stretched brown and bare on either side of the highway.

"Uh-huh. When I first met you, I knew something was amiss. Absolutely knew it. You were kind of head-shy. Ponder this: Leaving the fold, run-ning off to college . . . screwing, smoking, educating. Kicking indoctrina-tion takes a stout heart and a dedicated support system. Nobody helped you, did they? You packed your bags and split the family homestead in the dead of night with nary a kiss-my-ass to anyone. Cold turkey off the LDS teat. Traumatic, right?"

"Of course, Fra—I mean Tom. I had a few dark days."

"Surely that left a scar."

"Not likely."

"Be realistic, friend. Unplugging from a cult is tricky. People who detach from rigid, hierarchal religious organizations are prone to depression, alcoholism, suicide, you name it. Botch the deprogramming and, well . . . Exhibit A in my passenger seat."

"Really, that's not related to my situation."

"If you say so."

"Getting away from the church meant getting away from my dad. That's a net gain, I assure you." A sense of déjà vu overcame Bryan. He recalled vivid fragments of this very conversation from years before—he and

Mandibole tossing darts at a college pub, blitzed on draft beer and sharing life stories. He tried to recall Mandibole's tale and drew a blank. The main thing that stuck in his mind was that his friend had been blond, taller, and cheerfully evasive.

"Daddy issues. Revealing, although not the nut of your predicament. *My* father worked for the FBI." Mandibole adjusted his glasses. Thick and square, straight from a 1960s NASA control room. "He vetted the suicide letter Hoover's boy sent to Martin Luther King."

"Suicide letter?"

"*The* suicide letter. The feds wrote a note detailing the reverend's alleged infidelities and gave him thirty-four days to 'do the right thing.' By which they meant blow his brains out. My dad proofread the letter, made revisions, and got it up to snuff."

The music changed and broadcasters argued in Spanish. Fields and barrens ceded to hills and forest. Sunlight ebbed. Mandibole made several turns that propelled them along dilapidated roads through increasingly rustic habitations. After the last town had disappeared from the rearview for the better portion of an hour, he pulled into a yard before a quaintly ramshackle two-story house. Some of the windows were boarded. The gutters were stuffed with twigs. A squirrel sat amid the twigs and glared. Bare-limbed trees encroached upon the yard, their roots exposed in the muddy soil. Patches of snow glowed like bone.

"This is the summer house. Mom and Dad lived here until 2010. I bolt here every few months and hibernate." Mandibole climbed out. He snatched up a stone and drilled the squirrel in the head. The creature fell, boneless, into the bushes. He chuckled and came around to Bryan's side. "Easy does it, pal. Bit of a climb, I'm afraid. Now, now, struggling only makes this more embarrassing. You're a bag of bones! Don't they feed you at the hospital?"

Bryan gave in and allowed himself to be carried like a bride along a flagstone path, up nine rickety wooden steps, across a covered porch, and into a foyer. The house smelled of dampness, algae, and unidentifiable spices. Tall ceilings and narrow passages, with nooks and crannies galore. Antique black-and-white portraits full of crabby subjects. The whole scene—Mandibole, the house and environs—could've been drawn by Gorey. Mandibole propped Bryan against the wall. He swooped around like a bat, flicking on lamps here and there. This pallid light pushed back the gloom and held it in tenuous abeyance. He hauled Bryan's suitcase and overnight bag in and stacked them near a dusty player piano.

"Kitchen's that way. Parlor's over there. The couch folds out into a bed. I advise against the stairs in your delicate condition. The cellar is absolutely off-limits. Phone is in the hall. Sometimes it works. No Internet, sorry."

Bryan summoned the strength to speak. "Why does the mailbox say SMITH?"

"Eh? I didn't mean this place belonged to *my* parents. Here are your crutches. Okay? Okay! Got to run. Make yourself at home."

"Wait, you're leaving? I thought—"

"Hell yes, I'm leaving. I wouldn't stay in this creepy shithole for a million bucks. Weather is supposed to be warm tomorrow. You'll find the garden to be the tonic to cure your ills." Mandibole adjusted his fedora and ducked through the door. He called, "Remember, don't go down into the cellar. The amontillado isn't worth a broken neck."

As the motor's whine receded, Bryan tried to piece things together. Why had he agreed to lay up here in the boonies? He *hadn't*, not in so many words. Life caught him in a bore tide and swept him to this peculiar shore. He thumped his way into the kitchen and wearily rummaged through the tall pine cabinets and a deep, dark pantry. Dark because the light bulb was dead. Plenty of canned goods and pilot bread. Who ate pilot bread these days? He heated tomato soup and rustled a bit of not-too-moldy cheddar and a loaf of bread from the buzzing refrigerator. The fridge was an old, decrepit model: lime green exterior, pale and fluorescent-lighted interior. Spartan other than the cheese, a bottle of murky milk, and dubious items sealed in plastic containers. There were half a dozen eggs nestled on a side rack—four cream-colored hen's eggs, a pale blue pigeon egg, and a crusty black petrified egg. He took the lump of cheese and closed the unit, killed the pale, deathly light and the strident buzzing.

Yes, yes, soup and grilled cheese. He slumped at the kitchen table and ate every damned bite in defiance of his queasy guts. Ten minutes later, he puked onto the sixty-year-old linoleum. *Ting!* went Angie's damned engagement ring as it rolled across the floor and into the shadows of the sink cupboards. Novocain numbness filled his mouth. He located his cell phone and tried to dial Angie. *Tried*, because the moment it powered on, the screen went into video mode and there she was on a beach blanket, taking it doggy style from an oiled dude in sunglasses and a ponytail. Bryan cursed. He stabbed impotently at the face plate until it went black.

Those movies where the emaciated, shipwrecked hero staggers along a beach, step by agonizing step? Such was Bryan's voyage into the parlor. He collapsed onto the sofa and surrendered to a tidal surf of terrors thudding against the break-wall of his conscious mind.

The administrative secretary at Pawhunk CC called him, or maybe he imagined it. Either way: "You're fired."

"I'm on sick leave!"

"We don't honor sick leave. Fired, squirrel-killer. Don't bother cleaning out your desk. We burned your shit."

Tom Mandibole emerged from the shadows and tiptoed across the parlor. His plastic features had altered to mimic those of Bryan's father circa Bryan's childhood.

Mandibole knelt in an uncannily mechanical series of motions. "If you devour the raw heart of an enemy, you gain his courage. But! If you consume his living brain, you acquire his memories. My gods, the Smiths were fusty!" He smiled and ran his wormy tongue up Bryan's left nostril, kept wriggling deeper.

Bryan gazed in terror at an enormous black form detaching from the sun. If words were possible, he would've cried, *What the hell is that?* Instead, he screamed and screamed.

* * * *

The house seemed much cheerier by daylight. Its crooked edges were blunted, its remnant shadows less sinister. In some respects, the place reminded him of his childhood home—Mom in her flour-dusted apron, Pastor Tallen on the step wagging his finger, and the serial puppy murders, ritual suicides, and forced sodomy. Reminded him of how Dad sometimes hid under the bed while wearing Mom's nylon stocking over his face, and the homemade blood transfusion kit he unpacked when they played Something Scary.

Bryan managed to gain his feet after a bitter contest with the crutches, which were carved from the antlers of a stag. Their tips dug grooves in the floor as he maneuvered down the hall. His muscles ached, his head ached, and pain knifed him in the bowels. His breath gurgled and his throat constricted. His hands twitched with palsy.

Greatest blow to his vanity came from a direct, hard look into the mirror. Formerly shot with gray when left uncolored, his hair and beard were bleached white as dirty snow. Could this explain Angie's unceremonious decampment? Had it been his hair all along? Bryan made a mental list of his symptoms and feebly attempted to correlate them with various diseases. Epidemiology wasn't his area of expertise, and thus he could only speculate as to whether he'd contracted AIDS, syphilis, hepatitis C, or something worse. It could always be something worse. He didn't speculate for long, however. Walking from parlor to bathroom and back again taxed him to the core. The notion of peeling off his musty, sweat-sticky clothes and taking a hot shower made him want to vomit again. That reminded him: another sandwich?

Crazed, scotch-guzzling has-been author Buford Creely awaited him in the kitchen when, after hours or days had dragged past, Bryan made it there.

"You gonna die if you don't eat, kid." Creely slurred so it sounded like *eat a kid*. He wore a brown tweed jacket. His eyes were possum-red and glazed with cataracts from staring at crime scene photographs for too many years. The evil of the abyss and so forth. "Fuck it. You ate last week.

We gotta do somethin' about your nerves. Gotta do somethin'. C'mere, squirrel-killer. You're fresh outta agency."

Bryan contemplated fleeing. He immediately lost his balance and fell. His right-hand crutch spun across the floor. He feebly brandished the other at Creely. "How did—why?" Each word was a tooth pulled with tweezers.

"Eh, your dad sent me. Your old man, remember him? Was him did all them slasher killin's back when. The Headless Horseman of Halifax. Didn't have the heart to break it to you earlier. Frank said you deserved the truth. Frank abhors a lie."

"Not Frank. Tom . . ."

"Who in blazes is Tom?" Creely knelt and cradled Bryan in his bony-flabby arms, lifted him to the kitchen table, and set him there. "Relax. I know what you need. Hospital didn't help, did it?"

Bryan shook his head.

"Right, you need *real* medicine. Old medicine. See, kid, you can barely move. Gotta drop some weight." Creely smiled a boozy, reassuring smile as he unbuttoned Bryan's shirt and removed it with the tenderness of a father undressing his son. "On three, roll to your left." He counted and then turned Bryan over. "That hurt?"

"Yes!" Bryan said it as more of a protest rather than an assertion of fact. The fear of further pain or, worse, humiliation provoked his anxiety. "Mr. Creely, Buford . . . You have to be careful. The spine is delicate."

"Nothin' to worry about, kid. You're already beyond fucked. Good news is, my family learned acupuncture from the Chinese. Fix you right up, yes indeed." The old man banged cupboard doors and rummaged through shelf drawers.

Bryan mouthed the word *acupuncture* in horror with his cheek pressed against the tablecloth. In an act of great willpower, he lifted his head and looked over his shoulder. What he saw did not prove comforting. "Are those knitting needles?"

"Stifle yourself. Hold real still." Creely raised both arms and then hammered them downward.

The twin bolts of agony ripping through Bryan's lower back had a psychoactive effect. He departed his body. The kitchen windows transmitted a pristine white glow. White gradually dulled to rose, then crimson, then black. The blackness absorbed him. He sailed on a cosmic breeze until a pinprick of pale white radiance flickered ahead. The flickering candle flame steadied and grew. Angie and her lover fucked on a white sand beach bordered by a black gulf of water. The man glanced at him: Mandibole wearing a shiny white shirt and a huge, cruel grin. Angie turned her head—also Mandibole's superciliously grinning face. Bryan's eyes popped open. Returned to the shabby, dim kitchen, he tried to scream but couldn't suck in sufficient air.

"Huh," Creely said. "Well, hell. Whoops, I guess." The author's footsteps clipped rapidly away. The front door slammed.

Blood pooled around Bryan's hips and dripped from the edge of the table. Enough blood that he felt as if he were partially afloat in a kiddie pool. He tried to lift himself and realized the darning needles had gone clean through the small of his back and into the wood of the table. He cried.

Snow fell against the windows, and after a while, it grew dark.

Light engulfed the room and gushed into his eyes.

"Ten years! Nary a tear. But now that you're nailed to a table, look at the waterworks. I mean, really." Angie circled. She had dressed in white-and-black earmuffs, a white-and-black pea coat, black pants, and white Wellingtons. "What a mess, what a bloody mess. Proud to wallow in your own gore, I suppose. Really showed me, haven't you?"

"Please help me."

"Addition by subtraction. Are you ready for that, squirrel-killer?"

"Angie. Please." Bryan's right arm refused to work. He feebly pawed with his left, supplicating a goddess of torment.

"Fine. Fine, Bryan. This doesn't mean we're back together." She sighed and yanked the needles free. "Oh, you asshole. This coat is ruined."

Air, and everything else, hissed out of him.

* * * *

Winter had slinked into the mountains. A warm breeze shushed through the treetops and awakened Bryan by thawing his frozen, glaciated innerscape sufficiently for a stray thought to escape the merciless grip of entropy. Pine sap, grass, and perfume tickled his nose. He opened his eyes. Angie hunkered before him, pristine but for several drops of blood on her coat and galoshes.

"You're in a bad way," she said.

He'd been stripped naked. From the blackened thighs down, his body resembled an unearthed Egyptian mummy, or one of the petrified corpses of climbers that adorn the slopes of Everest. His feet had ballooned and split at the joints. The nails were gone. Pus seeped. He felt absolutely nothing. Oh, inside he screamed unceasingly, but it didn't hurt.

"Call an ambulance," he said. *Barely* said. His lips cracked. Possibly he'd only projected the thought at her.

"Are you crazy? The ambulance drivers around here are surely not. They wouldn't come within a mile of this creepy shithole for a million bucks. Nope, it's home remedy or death. Worse than death, actually."

"Ambulance," he repeated. How shiny and plastic her hair flowed in the light like mud, how shiny and plastic her lovely face seen through a muddy filter. Differently familiar, it provoked queasiness.

"Gangrene," she said. "On its way to your heart. My opinion is, your heart's *already* rotten. Nonetheless, I've a filial duty as your ex-fiancée. You made me call you Daddy often enough." Angie hefted a serrated cleaver. A relic from some Civil War surgeon's grim bag of atrocity tools. She poked his leg. "These have to come off. That's how you regain mobility. Give to get, sweetheart. I'll do the first, as a favor. After that, you're on your own." She set the teeth of the blade against his left thigh and began sawing. His flesh made small corkscrew piles on the floor. Only a dim tugging sensation reached his brain. He screamed anyway.

The femur cracked. Sweat dripped from the tip of her nose as she made several final strokes, gesticulating with the frenetic grace of a concert violinist. "Done!" Angie shoved the severed limb aside and wiped her brow. "Easy-peasy. You're a total dipshit with tools, I know, I know. Just . . . Do your best." She pressed the cleaver into his hands and, despite his cries of protest, assisted with getting a groove started. "Keep going, Bry. That gangrene will eat your innards if you fail. Ciao, stumpy."

He persisted, albeit sloppily, after she kissed his forehead and left. His hands, both of them swollen and plum dark, operated independent of his delirious mind. There was something childishly compelling about the repetitive action of sawing—almost akin to the morbid pleasure in shooting a woodland critter or dismembering a bug, except he *was* the woodland creature in this instance; he *was* the bug. Amputation would free him from the trap, this sundew house.

Plop went the right leg onto the deck. Birds twittered encouragement.

Yes, this seemed a slight improvement. He dragged himself, hand over hand, inside and through the kitchen into the parlor. His body felt light, although the journey took several days if the rotating carousel of sun and moon could be trusted as a guide. He left a red trail through the parlor and to the box television. He clicked the television on and then rested. Some kernel within his dimming soul craved information from the outside world. It yearned for even the sterile contact of cathode rays. He crawled to the couch and lifted himself onto its bleached flower-pattern cushions. The TV played in jittery black and white. Static snarled. *Davey and Goliath. The Muppet Show. Mr. Rogers. Lamb Chop.* The actors spoke in Russian or Spanish or Slavic or the *click-click buzz* of hunting insects.

A dark-haired toddler pedaled a red tricycle into the room. The child wheeled close to the couch and stopped. His shiny hair and plastic features glowed with roly-poly good health.

"I know you," Bryan said in a perfectly clear voice. His breathing came easily. Still woozy, still full of pustulant anxiety (and pus), yet he grudgingly admitted that the compulsory mutilation had alleviated the worst symptoms of whatever disease gripped him. "Yes, you were there. I know you."

"As I know you," the child said.

"Wait. Who are you?"

"But you know. Feel better?"

"Yes. It's a miracle."

"Leeching is good for the soul. You aren't really better. Daddy said it's only temporary. You've got the gang-green."

The putrefaction of Bryan's hands had corrupted his arms to the elbows. He'd done his best to ignore this latest incursion of rot and enjoy the cartoons. Now the meddling kid had ruined everything. "What am I supposed to do? It's in my arms, for fuck's sake."

"Everything must go." The boy rolled over to the couch and handed Bryan a serrated penknife. "Daddy says to do a good job. Bye!"

The sky darkened and clotted and the windows became opaque with purple. Bryan sniffled bitter tears. He gripped the toy knife between his thumb and index finger and made the first, tiny cut. Better still.

Months oozed past. Years. Once his traitorous limb was severed, he dropped the knife and took a few breaths. Yes, better. Lighter. Addition by subtraction made increasing sense with a come-to-Jesus shock of epiphany. The next stage presented a challenge to his transcendence. Not wildly intelligent, but plenty clever, went Bryan's family motto as mumbled by drunk Dad.

He raised his remaining bicep to his mouth and bit in. Angel food cake, food of the gods.

"I am impressed. Truly." Mandibole retrieved Bryan's severed arms and studied them. "My grandfather trapped wolves along the Yukon. Leg-hold traps with nasty teeth. Those wolves, ah my. Rebellious critters chomped their own legs to get free. Humans really are animals with a fancy operating system, aren't you?"

Bryan concentrated on *Sesame Street*. He frowned when Mandibole clicked the screen dead.

The man dressed in a soot-tarnished three-piece suit. His profile could have been Bryan's father's during his prime belt-buckle-swinging days.

He clucked his tongue at the filth and grime: the holes in the ceiling, the windows melted to slag with age, mushroom beds where carpet once spread, the wasp nests, and termite-riddled beams.

"This joint sure went to seed," Mandibole said. "Stupid me. You're Bryan the Amazing Torso. I can hardly expect you to push a broom. You can't even wipe your own ass. Entropy. There's a secret to life. Entropy. Our dads are the gods of our puny universes, and yet even they are powerless beneath the cloddish tread of enervation and heat death."

"I'm at peace." Bryan's belly distended with a feast of his own muscle and marrow. Perfectly sated for the coming ages and divested of humdrum, mortal concerns such as fear and happiness.

Mandibole threw back his head and laughed. His helmet hair didn't stir, nor did his eyelashes flicker. "Not so fast, chum. Are you blind? The rot is in your chest. It's creeping toward your brain. We must act fast, else you're a goner. Or worse."

Bryan waggled his stumps with bewilderment. His serenity evaporated, replaced by petulant misery. "What do you expect of me, Dad? I can't chew my own damned throat."

"A bit more commitment would be nice. No matter." Mandibole leaned over and retrieved the rusty penknife. "I used to tie your shoes. In for a penny."

"Wait," Bryan said, too late. Despite years of accreted cynicism, he was profoundly surprised at how much blood remained, albeit momentarily, in his body.

Mandibole finished the job by twisting Bryan's skull until it popped free. He whistled as he carried his trophy into a lush garden amok with brambles and bushes. He offered Bryan's head to the dark and ominous tree that lorded it over the smaller plants of the kingdom. The tips of its thorny branches pierced Bryan's ears and lifted him until he hung like a piece of bleeding pomegranate, a gaping manikin skull.

Constellations drifted and the sky became green. The house went under the burgeoning jungle. Heat and steam and green, endless green.

The pomegranates in the great tree possessed distorted faces. The newer heads, raw and brash, could speak at first. A wrinkled and ruddy soul dangling next to Bryan said, "Ezra Tooms, goddamn you cretins! Ezra Malachi Tooms! I'm a rich man! A powerful man!"

A howler monkey descended from its leafy berth and plucked that shouting fruit-head and promptly chewed it to gushing smithereens. Such were the risks of making a scene in paradise. Not that it mattered. Sooner or later, the animal would crap, the seeds would grow, and in a hundred years or so, Mr. Tooms would again blossom on the vine, on this tree or another, sadder and infinitely wiser.

Later, as happened every epoch or two, the sun divided and a vast, Godlike hand extended with greedy eagerness. The monkeys gibbered and screamed and fled in all directions while the hand made itself a claw and tore loose swathes of canopy. Hundreds of monkeys, and squirrels, and bright-plumed birds tumbled toward the sky and became tiny silhouettes inhaled by the sticky maw of a child leaning over the colossal handlebars of his trike.

Bryan could do nothing except exult in this recurring terror. Tears of red juice trickled from his bulging eyes. He was gravid with seeds and they stifled his mindless protest. Whenever he screamed, red seeds dripped from his mouth, splattered upon the soil, and found purchase.

Over time, inconceivably deep geological time, the sentient fruit of his tree and the trees of the surrounding jungle multiplied. Each became a perfect version of himself, howling and gibbering in a mute, eternal chorus. Eventually, he grew to accept it. His multiplicities spread inexorably across the infinite and took root everywhere.

—*For Michael Cisco*

FOSSIL HEART

AMANDA DOWNUM

Nan Walker doesn't mean to fall asleep. She never does. But tonight the creak of the ceiling fan lulls her. Evie curls warm against her side, one long leg thrown over hers. Nan's eyes sag, her fingers relax, and her worn paperback slides onto the bed. Sleep strokes gentle hands across her eyes.

The nightmare waits, constant, unchanging: *muddy water, stale wet air. The car shudders in the torrent as the flood rushes past outside. Debris scrapes the doors and windows. Chelsea's hand clutches hers, cool and clammy, already starting to slip. A child's fear paralyzes her, warring with the adult knowledge that she has to change it, change anything, but she's already too late—*

The dream—the memory—slips and shatters. Eyes flash in the darkness—the monsters coming for her.

Nan wakes to thunder, to the hot press of flesh and a weight on her chest that steals her breath. Her spine is full of razor wire. She thrashes, trapped and tangled, and strikes fur with one flailing hand. Evie's fat white cat *murr*s indignantly and leaps away, digging a parting claw into Nan's stomach.

Nan swallows nausea. Her pulse pounds in her throat. Only a moment's inattention, but the night is different, deeper. Rain drums the roof and Evie has rolled to the far side of the bed, taking the covers with her. Nan fumbles for the clock; her novel slides to the floor with a muffled thump. The clock face is black, the ceiling fan still; the power is out. Rainlight and storm-shadows shift across the ceiling.

Eyes flash in the darkness by the door and she's sure the monsters have come. Then lightning splits the night open, revealing Winnie the cat. Thunder shakes the house. Nan falls back on her sweaty pillow, waiting for her heart to slow and her stomach to settle, for the pain in her back to dim to its usual nagging awareness.

Evie stirs beside her, one hand clenching in the sheets. She mumbles something incoherent and kicks. Her foot settles against Nan's shin and she stills again. The familiar touch steadies Nan, too. Everything's all right, she tells herself. It's just a storm. She leans in, pressing her shoulder gently against Evie's, grounding herself in human warmth.

When the pins and needles in her fingers fade, she slides out of bed and grabs her phone and cigarettes off the nightstand. Four in the morning. She lost five hours. Not so bad. Nothing, really—normal people lose more than that every night. But normal people can sleep, can rest, can dream of something besides the same moment over and over again.

Moisture slicks her skin as she pads across the sticky floor, her own rank fear-sweat and the storm's paper-curling miasma. The screen door creaks as she steps onto the porch. The cool autumn night laps over her and she sighs. Goosebumps crawl up her legs and her breasts tighten under her damp tank top. The power is out all down the block, no electricity but the lightning seething in the clouds. Rain pounds the roof, rattles the gutters, and rushes to the ground in shining cascades.

It can't wash her away. She's safe here in this house on the hill. The water can rise but it can't reach her. Not this time.

She sinks onto the porch swing and lights a cigarette. Smoke clears the sleep taste from her tongue, the sour metal fear taste. She wants a drink. Water all around her, but her tongue feels swollen between her teeth. A cockroach scuttles across the weathered boards and Nan pulls up her feet to let it pass. The swing squeals softly.

Somewhere, in some other reality, there's a Nan who sleeps soundly. Who sleeps at all. A Nan who isn't afraid of storms and rushing water and the constant crushing weight of failure.

She closes her eyes to the sound of rain on shingles, the wet rattle of oak and magnolia leaves. Rain on muddy earth. The drone and buzz of insects searching for the stolen porch light. The smell of rain, of damp wood and cigarette smoke and her own salt sweat. Start with this, she tells herself. *You lost five hours—take them back.*

She was here earlier, alone on the porch. She can do this. Her pulse jumps at the thought, and she forces herself to ignore it. Ignore the rain, too; it wasn't here. She reaches for the pain, the angry fire that licks her spine, lets it swim up from her subconscious and arc along her nerves. Her constant, her anchor.

Colors pulse behind her eyes, spinning fractals and kaleidoscope swirls. The world unravels along invisible seams and Nan falls into the void.

Darkness burns around her, shot through with stars. A million points of light, each one a moment, a possibility. She hangs on a precipice, tide rushing past her. The depth and vastness will swallow her if she lets them. She could float there forever, without pain, without fear. . . .

Ananda Walker.

The monsters are always waiting. Long, sleek beasts, all bone-sharp jaws and cutting angles, their words razors and broken glass. *Thirsty. Stay. Soon.*

Teeth close into her flesh. Electric tongues spark against her skin. Nan fights a scream, searching for the right spark. A pinprick hole in the black. She reaches for it, reaches through, and pulls herself out the other side.

She opens her eyes, muscles spasming. Her jaw snaps. Teeth graze her cheek and the taste of red and copper spools across her tongue.

Overhead, a moth beats against the grimy globe of the porch light. Streetlamps bleed sodium halos through the sticky air. A car speeds down Locust Street, tires humming on dry asphalt.

Nan gasps. Her cigarette snaps in a numb hand, scattering orange sparks and flecks of tobacco across the porch. Adrenaline sings through her. She did it. Five hours. The most she's ever rewound.

She looks at her hand, at the shadow of teeth marks already fading around her wrist. No blood, no broken skin, just chill and weakness.

Soon. Waiting. A greater darkness flickers in the shadows below the porch, there and gone in an eyeblink. *Hungry.*

The screen door opens and Evie steps out.

Nan swallows nauseous spit; the stutter of perception makes the queasiness worse. Tension throbs in her neck and jaw. The roar of her pulse is as loud as the coming storm.

She counts silently: sixty seconds later, the screen door creaks open and Evie steps out. "Nan? It's eleven—I'm going to bed."

"I'll be there in a second." Her voice only trembles a little.

Evie frowns, cocking her head. "Weren't you wearing pants a minute ago?"

Nan looks down at her bare legs. She was, before. The first time. The past overwritten. Her heart speeds again.

"It's hot," she says, standing up. Her left calf twitches with an incipient cramp.

Evie's frown deepens. "Are you all right?"

"My back." It's not entirely a lie. Nan takes Evie's hand and pulls her close, kissing her neck and breathing in the clean smell of her skin: salt-and-honey soap and sweet citrus shampoo.

Evie laughs as Nan's lips brush her collarbone. "Maybe we should take this inside." She pauses and leans in. "You smell like rain."

"A storm's on its way."

That earns her a different frown. Not the crazy girlfriend who wanders around in her underwear frown, but the crazy girlfriend who predicts the future. Who thinks she can change the past.

Nan kisses Evie again and leads her into the air-conditioned house.

"Five hours," Evie says later, stroking her fingers through Nan's short hair. The storm hasn't hit yet, but the wind picks up and thunder growls in the distance. The room smells of sweat and musk and hot wax. Candlelight dances across the walls, votives of St. Peter and Mary and all the others that crowd the little shelf Evie refuses to call an altar.

Nan nods, her head pillowed on Evie's stomach, her cheek sticking to the soft curve of the other woman's belly. She concentrates on the murmur of Evie's heart, the weight of her fingers. The now. This moment with no pain, no fear, no past, no monsters. The river of time waits to sweep her away, but she won't let it.

It can't last, but she can pretend.

"Hey," Evie murmurs as comfort threatens to lull Nan to sleep again. "Love you."

"I love you. But do you believe me?"

Evie sighs. "It would be easier if I didn't, but I do."

"I *am* crazy."

"You surely are." She strokes Nan's hair. "But I dreamed about the black dog again last night."

Nan shivers. "I'm getting closer. I could only manage five minutes before."

"Five minutes is a long way from fourteen years."

"I can do it. I'm sure I can now."

"But are you sure you should? You see monsters, Nan. Don't you think that means you ought to stop?"

She flexes her left hand. Only a faint chill lingers in her bones. She's told Evie about the monsters, the hounds, but not about how they feed. "I can't."

Evie's fingers still. *You mean you won't. Don't lie to yourself.* It's not mind reading; she hears the words leave Evie's lips. Precognition. *Déjà vu.* But Evie chooses a different path.

"What's that word you told me about the stars? The light we see that doesn't exist anymore?"

"Fossil light?"

"Yes." She sighs again, and Nan's head rises and falls with her breath. "That's you. You're not really here. And I'm afraid by the time I find you, you'll be gone."

* * * *

The first time Nan rewrote the past, she was dying.

A bottle of Xanax and a bottle of tequila, determined to stop it once and for all. The lost time, the panic attacks, the nightmares. The eerie precognition that left her stumbling away from people who hadn't moved yet, dodging parked cars, answering unasked questions. Slipping grades, doctors' warnings. Another lost job, another girlfriend walking out on her. Everyone tired of dealing with crazy, broken Nan.

She was sick of living with it. Sick of living.

She was sick of dying before long, huddled on the bathroom floor with the stench of vomit thick in the air. Her cheap phone smashed to pieces against the linoleum—no more calls for help. Maybe she should have hanged herself instead. All she wanted was sleep, but an empty place unfolded inside her, sucking her down. The empty place that never healed after Chelsea died.

Chelsea always believed people would find each other again on the other side. If that was a lie, it was the sweetest Nan had ever heard.

It should have been her all those years ago, her instead of Chelsea. Her with Chelsea. Why hadn't she died too, if this was all she had to live for? To live through.

She remembered Chelsea's hand in hers. Cold and damp and clutching tight, before her best friend's fingers went limp and slipped away.

The precise instant was lost. When she realized there was nothing she could do, that her parents weren't coming back and there was no one to help them, she'd shut her eyes and tried to get through, pushing as hard as she could against that awful moment. Trying to fast-forward through the pain as if it were a song she didn't like.

The emptiness opened, welcoming her inside.

But as she fell, Nan snapped awake to find herself back in the drowning car. Muddy water rising all around her, her back throbbing where she'd slammed against the door when the station wagon slid off the flooded bridge into the rushing, rain-swollen creek. The flood roared past, pulling at the car, pinning the doors. Debris scraped like claws against metal.

And Chelsea. Chelsea trapped in the back seat, seatbelt locked tight. Brown eyes wide and shot with panic as the water rose higher around her head, closing over her black braids and purple plastic barrettes.

Best friends since second grade, blood sisters by needle-pricked thumbs since the age of twelve, an awkward sugar-sticky first kiss on Nan's thirteenth birthday. A world of possibilities stretching out before them with only the certainty that they would be together. And now Nan watched those possibilities wither and fall away one by one with every millimeter of rising water.

The other Nan, the poisoned, dying Nan, clawed her way up from the dark. This wasn't a dream: she was back. The body that ached so fiercely wasn't a child's. She could change it, change anything, and maybe she could save them both.

Chelsea's dimming eyes flashed open, blazing like cut glass. *Thirsty.*

It was the first time Nan remembered hearing the monsters, their words like scalpels, but the sound was as familiar as childhood lullabies. Teeth pierced her flesh, sharp as the doctors' needles that took the pain away. She screamed in panic and recoiled.

With a sickening wrench, she fell back through the dark, back into the now.

She opened her eyes to warped linoleum tiles, the bathtub slick and steady against her back and her spine throbbing like the injury was fresh. The amber bottles sat on the floor in front of her, full of liquor and little blue pills, but she still felt sick and poisoned. White-knuckled fingers clamped tight around her phone.

This time, she called for help.

Four in the morning again, the long way round this time. The power is still out, so Nan takes a cold shower by candlelight. Modafinil keeps sleep at bay, but maybe she'll walk to the corner store and get some lousy coffee and be back in time to wake Evie at five.

Even candlelight can't flatter her reflection. The face in the mirror is worn and whittled thin. Only twenty-seven, but she looks ten years older. Hollow cheeks, indelible bruises around her eyes, threads of gray in her spiky brown hair. Lack of sleep, maybe, or drinking—though she drinks less when she's on her meds. Or maybe all the time slips take their toll, all those moments lived twice. She's moving faster than the rest of the world, rushing toward the end.

She won't go without a fight.

She leans against the doorway, watching Evie curled in tangled sheets. Guttering candles kiss her chestnut skin, limning her with gold. Midnight curls splay across the pillow.

The suicide-that-wasn't and all the possibilities it opened were enough to keep Nan going. To scale back the booze and pills, to keep track of the slips and lost time, the nightmares and flashes of precognition, and especially the monsters. It kept her alive long enough to meet Evie, and she can never regret that, no matter how bad things have been since or will yet be.

Evie, who spends all day with the sick and broken and dying and comes home to light candles to powers she refuses to name. Who invests her time and training and student loans in medicine but carries magic close and silent in her heart. Her brushes with the weird aren't the same as Nan's, but they're enough to let her listen. To accept if not understand.

Chelsea is a shadow between them. Nan's therapists tell her to let go, to move on, to make peace, but how can she when every careless moment tugs her back? She lost three years to a haze of drugs and doctors and quiet rooms, but even that couldn't keep the past away forever.

Evie deserves more than Nan can offer. But to fix herself may mean losing everything she has now.

She turns back to the medicine cabinet and reaches for her fluoxetine. As she counts out forty milligrams in green-and-white pills, eyes flash in the angled mirror. The bottle slips from cold fingers, bounces off the counter, and sprays pills across the floor with a machine-gun rattle.

So thirsty. She feels its attention shift, past her to the bedroom. *Sweet.*

"No!" Her hands clench on the edge of the counter. If feeding the monsters is the price she pays for what she does, so be it. But not Evie. "Don't you fucking touch her," she hisses.

Teeth like shards of ice blaze in a grin. *You touch her.*

Nan slams the mirror shut, rattling glass and bottles. Behind her, the doorway is empty except for a soft chuffing laughter fading in her head.

Tension builds that week, simmering, implacable. Evie is scared, hurt, and Nan doesn't know what to say to make it better. Knows, but isn't willing to lie. She hears the things Evie almost says but holds back. Unlike so many others, Evie considers her options before she acts, doesn't always take the easiest, obvious path. It was a balm when they first met: someone Nan couldn't always predict, a journey whose end she didn't know from the start. But now it leaves her off-center and shaky, fighting not to react to things unsaid.

She could make it easier. Lock herself into the now and turn her eyes away from the probabilities and possibilities constantly unfurling. After so many years, she's learned to turn the volume down. Instead, she stretches herself wide, searching, riffling through cracks whenever she sees them. The night of the storm left her with a sense of momentum, a cold weight of anticipation in her stomach. She doesn't dare lose herself to complacency again.

She sees the next storm coming on a dead television. A roiling mass of green sweeping across the state. Flooding, devastation, death. Reports of destruction that hasn't yet occurred scroll past her, and she knows bone-deep that one of those deaths could be hers.

This is her chance.

She comes back to herself in Evie's cramped living room. The lamplight is wrong, crystalline and fractured as if she were tripping. The monsters, her monsters, wait in the corners. Sharp lines, cutting angles, nothing of softness.

Impatient. Yearning. So thirsty for destruction. A lean shape slinks around her, flickering in and out of her vision. *Come with us, Ananda Walker. We'll show you.*

Jaws close on her right wrist. Needles of ice pass through meat and bone. A rough, sparking tongue laps at the wound. Nan feels some part of her draining away, but she can't name it. Behind her eyes, the void begins to unfold, the threshold to uncounted worlds.

"Nan?"

Glass shatters.

"Nan? Are you—" Evie lets out a strangled shriek. Nan spins to see a glass slip from Evie's long brown hand. It falls so slowly. So easy to move between heartbeats and catch it. Gravity resists for an instant as she moves it from its downward path, then it's safe on the counter.

Evie stands frozen, hazel eyes wide. Tall and rawboned, the proud arch of her nose slightly off-center, an asymmetry that leaves her more arresting than simple prettiness could. Nan is often struck by her beauty, her strength, but now she marvels at the life in her. The blood jumping beneath her skin, the dampness of her parted lips, the film of moisture shining on her dark-flecked irises. So sweet.

She looks for her reflection in Evie's eyes and sees only a dark, angular shadow.

The light softens. Cut-glass shadows melt back to normal. Evie recoils, catching her hip against a little table. A vase teeters and falls to the floor.

Glass shatters.

"What the hell was that?" Evie's eyes flash white as she looks from Nan to the empty corners and back again. She shakes her head sharply, curls rasping against her scrubs. "Those things— You were—"

The room stifles with potential, none of it pleasant. Some inevitabilities can be dodged only so long.

"How long have you been feeding them?" Evie demands.

"Since the beginning, I think. I didn't realize it at first." Nan lifts her hands in a useless shrug; the right is still numb. "I didn't want to scare you."

"I've dreamed of the black dogs ever since I met you. I thought I could protect you from them. But all this time, you've invited them in. And you don't want to scare me."

"Evie—"

"Look at yourself!" She catches Nan's wrist, presses palm to palm. Her touch burns. Nan's skin, always paler, is spectral now in comparison. Bone and tendon and veins stand stark, any softness she's ever had melted away. "They're stealing your life."

Nan draws breath to answer, but there's no answer to give.

"I'm living with a ghost," Evie whispers. "Because you won't stop living with yours."

And now the dam cracks, and the things she holds back come rushing out. Evie points at the desk, at the carved wooden box where Nan keeps her old photos, yellowing reminders of the days when she had a family, a life, when she had Chelsea. "Do you think I can't see? Those could be my baby pictures. I look just like her. How the hell is that supposed to make me feel?"

Not quite, Nan almost says. *Her eyes were darker. She didn't have that little mole. She wouldn't be so tall.* She smothers each thought in turn— she's not that crazy.

"Am I just a placeholder?" Evie goes on. "The next best thing until you"—*finally kill yourself*—"bring Chelsea back?"

"No." Nan's chest aches around the word. Her own anger rises in turn, even though she knows it's just defensive hurt. "What about me? You want to protect me? To rescue me? Am I just another project to you? Another broken bird to nurse? Don't you get enough of that at work?"

Evie laughs harshly. "Maybe neither of us knows how to have a healthy relationship."

"I know I love you. But that's not enough to fix me."

"Nothing will ever be enough if you don't let go of this!"

"Do you think I haven't tried? I can't let go. I'll never be enough for anyone. For myself. Something is wrong with me, Evie." It's her turn to laugh now, just as rough and ugly. "A lot of things. But something is broken, and I have to try to fix it."

"Bad things happen. Terrible things. They break us in a hundred ways. We can repair ourselves, but we can't change the past."

I can.

She catches Evie in her arms. "Hey," she whispers. After a second's stiff resistance, Evie hugs her back.

"Hey. Love you."

They hold each other in the dark. It's not enough.

"Pardon my language, lady, but you're fucking crazy." The cabbie glances at her in the rearview mirror. He takes one big-knuckled hand off the wheel to gesture at the rain sheeting down the windshield, the furious *squick-ick squick-ick* of the wipers. "Which makes me equally crazy, too. We're going to fucking drown."

"No," Nan murmurs as images flicker and scroll through her vision. "You won't."

Texas is drowning, though, or it will be soon. Every path that branches from this *now* ends in destruction somewhere, unavoidable. Whether it will be hers Nan doesn't know, but she won't get another chance like this.

She left Evie sleeping, walked out on everything, and called a cab to the bus station.

"I love you," she whispered. *"I love you, but I have to do this."*

The driver glares at her. She leans her head against the window and doesn't meet his eyes. Every drop of water glistens with potential, a million worlds falling all around her, but she doesn't look. The gutters surge, trees and buildings and the few other cars on the road swallowed alike by gray. Her stomach is sour from too much coffee, cup after cup every chance she had on top of the Modafinil to make sure she didn't fall asleep on the Greyhound. Her eyelids feel like sandpaper, and a muscle has been jumping in her left cheek for the past hour. No idea what time it is, but that hardly matters anymore.

"Crazy," the cabbie mutters again. A gold saint's medallion sways from the rearview mirror, flashing in the gray light. It reminds her of Evie's candles, and she looks away. She's too tired to cry, too dry.

"That's what all the doctors tell me." An old joke, but her mouth can't force a smile, and the words fall flat and humorless. The din of rain and windshield wipers replaces conversation, and she's grateful.

They leave offices and shopping centers behind. Hills rise through the blinding rain ahead. She hasn't been back to Austin in years, but she remembers. Karst topography, limestone and granite cloaked in thin soil, green with live oak and cedar scrub. Hot and dry most of the year, perfect for flash flooding. Which everyone knows, but every time the rains roll in, someone is stupid or unlucky enough to drown. People like Nan's parents. And Chelsea.

Nan should have died too. How had she lived without Chelsea? Best friend, sister, first love, even if she hadn't realized that at the time. Every plan they had ever made had included both of them. Chelsea, always the precocious one, had taken all the steps she could think of to keep the connection. Blood mingled on pricked fingertips; brown hair and black braided together in friendship bracelets; their names written together with Chelsea's mom's fancy fountain pen, smudged and sloppy cursive script offered to a candleflame. Maybe it worked too well.

If that day had played out any other way. If Chelsea had taken the front seat instead of Nan. If Nan had been trapped in the broken seatbelt while water filled her lungs. Chelsea had been the clever one; she would have figured something out. And if she hadn't, if Nan had paid that price so her friend could live, Chelsea would have been the strong one. She would have survived and thrived and carried Nan's memory forward into a life worth living, instead of wasting everything.

Maybe Chelsea would have met Evie.

Soon, the monster whispers from the angled sliver of the rearview mirror.

"Did you say something?" the cabbie asks.

"No," she says. "We're almost there."

"Look, I know this is none of my business, but this isn't a suicide thing, is it?"

Nan catches his eye in the mirror. "No." She manages a smile this time. "It's not a suicide thing."

"All right, then," he says reluctantly. "This is it."

He turns off the main road onto the narrow lane that leads to the park. Scraps of color break the gloom, orange and black balloons tied to a post, dangling in tatters from their ribbons. Markers for a party come and gone, or thwarted by the storm.

The creek is already flooding, sluicing over the grass and blacktop. The driver curses as wings of white water flare on either side of the car. Nan's stomach turns over as they hydroplane. The cab slues to the left, spray tracing its turn. The cabbie hits the brakes and slaps his hazards on.

"What the fuck was that?"

Nan looks up in time to see sleek black shapes move at the edge of the headlights. She might mistake them for dogs if she didn't know better. "Don't worry. They won't bother you. I can make it from here."

"Are you sure, lady?"

"Yes." The conviction in her voice surprises her. She tugs her wallet out and hands him all the cash she has. She doubts she'll need it again. "Thank you."

He shakes his head. "Try not to drown."

"I'll do my best." She opens the door into the deluge.

Two steps and she's soaked to the skin. Three and her boots squelch. Four and the lights of the cab fade into the gloom. She spares a moment's distraction to reassure herself that he'll probably make it home tonight.

Would you do anything differently if you knew he wouldn't?

"No." Rain fills her mouth, sour with the salt and grime sluicing off her skin but better than the lingering taste of bad coffee. The moisture makes her realize how thirsty she is.

Implacable. Indifferent. You'd make a good hunter.

She doesn't look at the hound straight on but tracks it from the corner of her eye. "You didn't used to talk so much."

Hard for us to interact with your world, for the angles to intersect the curve. But you slip further and further into ours. A pause, broken by thunder. It won't work. Not like you hope.

"I know that." The first time Nan has admitted it, but she does know. All her experiments warned her, a missing pair of jeans the final piece of data. Her now always overwrites the before. Whether it's five minutes or fourteen years. She'll never be young with Chelsea again. All the futures they could have shared have long since burnt out. Her might-have-beens with Evie smolder behind her.

The monster gives a soft *whuff*. *You give up your mate for your sister, even if it means giving up both of them.*

"Evie will be better off without me. I'll give up everything to let Chelsea have a future. She'll do something with hers."

You don't know that. You cannot.

"No, I can't. But I wish it. I hope it. I'd pray if I knew how."

The water reaches her knees now, weeds and branches catching on her jeans with every step. The weight of wet denim and soaked boots drags at her. The creek is somewhere in front of her, only yards away. Not that its boundaries mean anything now. To her right is the low bridge, whose flimsy guardrail hadn't been able to stop her parents' car from sailing downstream.

You are ridiculous creatures. But hope is sweet. Hope, love, despair—we drink them all.

Another step toward the bridge. Mud shifts beneath her, sucking at her boots. She reaches for the pain in her spine. Only a few more strides—

Headlights flash behind her, the sound of tires and engine lost to the storm. The cab, Nan thinks, and then the realization hits her.

"Nan!" Evie is a dark blur in the rain, but her voice carries. "Nan, don't! I won't let you do this alone."

"I have to!" she shouts back. "Evie, go!"

The water surges around her thighs. She can't see the car, but she hears Evie's shout, watches the headlights slide sideways.

Time slips. Slows. Raindrops hang in midair, crystalline and iridescent. The roar of the storm dims to a sound like hollow breathing. The hound slinks across the water, its faceted claws carving slices out of the frozen surface.

Forward or back?

"If I go back, if I change it, she'll never come here in the first place. I'll save her either way."

She can change the past, and erase herself from it. Or she can try to salvage the life she has instead of longing for something that never existed. All the things she dreamt of with Chelsea, she could find with Evie. No— they could find new dreams together. But she knows better even as she tries to convince herself. She'll never be free of her past, not that way.

She dives for the bridge.

Time resumes as the water envelops her. The surge crushes her, scathes her with debris. Her outstretched arm catches the guardrail. Metal bites skin. Bitter froth fills her mouth and nose.

A seam opens. The station wagon stutters in and out of focus. Almost there. Muscles strain and stretch. Her fingers slip. The cold breath of the hounds chills her neck. Waiting to drink the last of her down.

Her grip gives way. Nan reaches.

Warm flesh closes around her wrist, hauling her back. She screams in pain and frustration and inhales a mouthful of water.

Evie holds her close, braced against the storm's fury. "You can't do this," she says, lips moving against Nan's ear. "But I can."

She lets go, and Nan's scream is lost as water closes over her head.

The car tilts, shuddering in the surge, caught in a tangle of tree branches. Nan leans over the passenger seat, stretching her hand toward Chelsea. Her back screams, and every movement is agony. Her breath comes in high, keening sobs.

Chelsea struggles against the broken seatbelt as water rises higher around her head. It laps against her chin now, closing on her mouth. Her lips part as if she means to speak, but instead she spits and coughs. Her dark eyes widen.

A shadow moves across the windshield. Nan glances back, and shrieks as the glass spiderwebs under a blow. Another impact and a thousand glittering fragments rain into the car, stinging her outflung hand.

A woman crouches on the slanting hood of the car. Dark curls writhe around her face, and her clothes are plastered to her skin. Shadows move behind her, like a pack of rib-sprung black dogs.

The woman shoves broken glass aside, shoves Nan aside, and reaches into the back seat. Muscles strain as she tugs on the seatbelt; the tendons in her neck leap taut. Joints pop. Fabric pops. The tongue snaps free. The woman falls back as Chelsea clings to the driver's seat and gulps sticky wet air.

The woman looks at Nan with sad, dark-flecked hazel eyes. She raises a bleeding hand, brushes Nan's face with warm fingers. Her lips move, but Nan can't hear over the roar of water and her own pulse.

Then the dogs surge through the broken windshield, closing skeletal jaws in the woman's clothes, in her flesh. She doesn't scream as they drag her out into the storm.

Nan screams for her, grabs for her, but she's too slow. Then Chelsea squirms out of the back and into her arms, wet and chilled and shaking. They hold each other tight, sobbing, as the flood rages on.

Nan Walker sits on her porch swing, a cigarette smoldering in one hand and her phone warming in the other, watching heavy pewter storm clouds slide across the sky. The wind rises, whipping fallen oak leaves across the lawn. The smell of ozone prickles her nose.

"Are you listening to me at all?" Chelsea asks, five hundred miles away.

"Sorry." Chains squeal as she shifts her weight. A column of ash falls to the floor, disintegrating in the breeze. "A storm's on its way."

WHAT THE #@&% IS THAT?

Chelsea makes a soft noise, equal parts sympathy and disapproval. She pretends Nan's fear of storms is a childhood foible to be outgrown, but Nan doubts her nightmares have stopped, though it's been years since they shared a bed. "Anyway, I said I might come back to Texas next month. For Vangie's birthday. She'll be four."

"I know." She's seen Chelsea's daughter more often than Chelsea has, but she doesn't mention that. Evangeline's grandmother doesn't talk about Aunt Nan's visits. Chelsea's mom knows about the fallouts and makeups and the slowly widening gyre of two people who love each other but can't live together, but she's too polite to talk about that, either. "Shall I come down?"

The sky darkens during Chelsea's silence. A fat drop of rain splatters on the steps. Thunder growls in the distance and Nan shudders.

"Sure," Chelsea says at last, trying too hard for nonchalance. "Vangie would like that."

A shadow flickers at the corner of Nan's eye. She glances up to catch a lean black shape moving at the edge of the yard. A dog, maybe, but so thin. It's gone before she's certain it was there at all. Her scalp prickles. Chelsea dreams of storms even if she won't admit it; the black dogs are Nan's alone.

"You're still not listening," Chelsea says with a sigh.

"The connection's bad. Must be the weather. Call me back later. Or else I'll see you soon."

"Yeah. I'll see you."

A familiar ache opens in Nan's chest, the absence of something she can't quite name. She used to think Chelsea was the only thing to fill that void. She's not sure anymore.

"Hey," she says before she ends the call. "Love you."

THOSE GADDAM COOKIES

SCOTT SIGLER

Nobody could bake like Bubbah.

The scent filled Jamel's nose, his mouth, and his lungs. He didn't just *smell* it, he *felt* it, an instantly peaceful sensation that whirled in his brain and chest.

Chocolate-chip macadamia cookies . . . his favorite.

Walking down the corridor toward Bubbah's quarters was like walking through a cloud of joy. It made Jamel happy for two reasons: First, if Bubbah was making cookies, that meant he was okay. Sick, maybe, perhaps feeling under the weather from an extended exo-shift and soaking up a little too much raw radiation outside the hull, but not so sick he couldn't perform alchemical magic with sugar, flour, eggs, and butter.

Since the load-in at Rhea, Bubbah had missed the last three shifts. Missing a shift in itself wasn't a big deal, not with ten people in Jamel's crew. That built-in redundancy of having ten bodies for jobs that took eight provided flexibility for people calling in sick, either because they *were* ill or because they just needed to burn a sick day. But three in a row?

Bubbah had called in the first time; he hadn't the second. The second time, Jamel had called him to find out if he was showing up for the shift or not—Bubbah had said he still felt like crap. The third time, Bubbah hadn't called in, and he also hadn't answered Jamel's calls. With that shift complete, Jamel and Inaya, another member of the crew, decided to pay a visit to Bubbah's cabin and make sure everything was A1.

The second reason the smell made Jamel happy, of course, was that he would soon be noshing on the very same cookies that he smelled. Those little chocolate chip bits of magic had made Jamel realize—after twenty-five years of blissful ignorance—that his own mother couldn't cook for shit.

And maybe . . . maybe Bubbah had scored some milk, too, and if so, the universe would rejoice.

"Gaddam, Jam," Inaya said. Her eyes were closed and a smile tugged at her crinkled cheeks. She walked with one hand lightly touching the wall. "You smell that?"

"Fuck yes, I do," Jamel said, although the loud rumbling of his belly was answer enough.

Inaya kept walking, eyes closed, fingertips sliding along the wall. After four years aboard the *Suraa Horse* she could probably walk every inch of the ship blindfolded with her hands cuffed behind her back. Jamel could do exactly that. He knew because he'd done it. Sometimes, space travel is crazy-boring. Finding ways to entertain oneself was as important as actually being able to do the job.

"You think he's really sick?" Inaya asked. "Or is he having another *emotional episode*?"

She didn't hide her disgust. Inaya liked Bubbah, everyone in the crew did, but the man ran at the mouth talking about his feelings of inadequacy, wondering if he'd made the right decisions in life, bemoaning the fact that he was thirty-five and still only a level-two maintenance tech.

Jamel liked Bubbah, too—in fact, Bubbah was probably his closest friend on the ship—but Jamel shared Inaya's disdain for the man's constant whining. Exo-work was a hard job for hard people: *feelings* weren't something that merited attention.

Inaya sniffed deep again.

"He missed three shifts, but he's baking," she said. "I know he's your boy and all, Jam, but if he's just faking, you have to do something about it."

Jamel shrugged. "Maybe he had that corridor crud that was going around after we laid up at Iapetus. I caught it. Had the shits for three days."

"Information I did not need," Inaya said. "I wonder if he's been binge-ing all this time."

"And nary a purge to be found, I'll bet."

Inaya laughed, finally opening her eyes.

"That's mean," she said.

Jamel knew it was and felt bad for saying it. He didn't want to talk poorly about Bubbah, but sometimes, looking out for the man was so damn frustrating.

"Well, you laughed at it," Jamel said.

"Because I'm an awful person. We all know this. I expect better of you, crew leader. Let's hope he hasn't put on so much they have to adjust his EVA suit again."

Jamel made a reactive *mmm-hmmm* noise of agreement.

Bubbah had weight issues. He also had self-esteem issues, which were connected to his weight issues. And to deal with the self-esteem issues, he overate, creating a vicious circle that gradually added inches to his waistline. The one-size-fits-all EVA suits turned out to be not so much with the one size, at least not where Bubbah was concerned.

They reached his cabin. Just a wheel-out door, same as twenty others in Corridor B. Inaya rapped her knuckles on the door. The knock left a tiny streak of blood, a dash of red on white.

Jamel tilted his head to look at her hand. "You cut or something?"

She glanced quickly at the knuckles on her right hand; Jamel saw they were dry and cracked. Inaya covered her right hand with her left.

"Stupid psoriasis," she said quietly. "Thanks, Mom."

Inaya pulled a small tube from her pocket, squirted the white lotion into her palm, then rubbed it into her cracked skin. It made some of the dryness vanish, but Jamel could still see angry red lines that carved her hands up like tiny riverbeds running through long-dry hills.

"That stuff a prescription?"

She nodded. "For all the damn good it does. You know our dispensary is for shit. I'll get it looked at when we get to Europa."

Jamel nodded and let it go. Dry skin was a problem for a lot of people on the ship, especially those who spent twelve-hour shifts in EVA suits. He didn't have that problem himself, but then again, he was just a bit over half Inaya's age.

She didn't *look* fifty, that was for sure. She didn't feel like it, either, especially in his bed late into off-shift hours, but all the jogging and lifting and yoga couldn't keep the years at bay. Genetics was genetics. Inaya hated any reminder that she was that much older than the young kids she hung with.

They stood there awkwardly for a moment, Jamel staying quiet because anytime Inaya's age came up, it created a conversational vacuum. She chased away the silence with a swift kick to Bubbah's door.

"Hey, fat-ass," she yelled. "Answer the damn door."

Bubbah didn't.

Inaya crossed her arms. It seemed like she wanted to stay mad, but her nose crinkled once, twice, and the anger faded from her face.

"Gad*dam*, that smells divine," she said. "He's not answering. Open it up."

Jamel shook his head. "Privacy regs, man."

"Whatever," she said, rolling her eyes. "I know you know his code, so get to getting. The brownies still smell warm."

He looked at her, surprised.

"Brownies?"

She gestured to Bubbah's door as if it was made from the very delicious confection she was talking about.

"Yes, *brownies*. You said you smelled it."

"I smell *cookies*," Jamel said. "Chocolate chip macadamia."

Inaya huffed. "Maybe your sense of smell isn't as good as mine."

Jamel sniffed again. No question: cookies. Didn't smell anything at all like Bubbah's brownies, which were also to die for. Those were Inaya's favorite, he knew. Maybe her age also affected her sense of smell? Just one more reason Jamel was not looking forward to getting older.

He waited a little bit longer, but still, Bubbah didn't answer.

"Ah, screw it," Jamel said. "We're worried about his safety, right? Possible medical emergency, right?"

"Of course. He might have slipped on some melted butter and bonked that head of his. Don't worry, Jam; I'll back your story if the commander crawls up your ass."

Still, Jamel hesitated. He already had one privacy strike against him, courtesy of a drunken night at the crew lounge and misreading the signals given off by Camilla Bolden. He'd followed her back to her cabin, his alcohol-soaked brain convinced that she wanted him as much as he wanted her. She'd asked him to leave her be but he hadn't heard, or maybe hadn't *wanted* to hear. Putting his foot in her door to stop it from shutting had been the final straw. Frank and Jenny Anne from security had come, cuffed him, taken him to the hold. Commander Shobatzi didn't fuck around with stuff like that. A week's worth of correctional courses, a month's worth of cleaning toilets, and the threat of a second offense costing him his crew leader position were enough to teach him to drink less, pay attention more. On top of that, he'd had to face Camilla again the next day. He'd manned up and apologized to her; she hadn't accepted. Their interactions remained icy, at best, even six months later.

"Jesus, Jam," Inaya said. "Open the fucking door or we have to report this to the commander anyway."

She was right about that. Bubbah hadn't come to work, hadn't contacted his supervisor, and now he wouldn't answer his door. Technically, this *was* a potential medical, or a possibility of one, so Jamel was in the clear as far as entering went.

He punched Bubbah's code into the door pad. The pad let out a slight *beep*, then the door hissed open. When it did, the smell that had filled the corridor boiled out like steam, like an engulfing, loving, invisible cloud.

Jamel had never smelled cookies that good. He'd never smelled *anything* that good.

"Spank my ass with a wooden spoon," Inaya said. She closed her eyes and inhaled. "Fatso has outdone himself this time."Jamel started to agree with her, then remembered that she was smelling *brownies*, not *cookies*. There was something weird about that, something off he couldn't nail down. It was . . . it was a little frightening.

Why would he be afraid of a scent?

The two crew members walked into Bubbah's small living room.

It was trashed.

Spacers never had a lot of room to call their own. They had it better than terrestrial ship crews, to be sure, but still, the tiny living space didn't leave a lot of decorating options. Living room, a tiny galley big enough for one person, bedroom, and head. When that was all the area you had, shelves, pictures, and hanging monitors became your best friends, your link to the life that existed outside of the ship. If you had a life outside, that was, which Bubbah did not—most of his hanging pictures showed photos of his best cooking creations. He had knickknacks from his many ports of call—just like Jamel did, just like everyone did—little talismans that were breadcrumbs the galaxy gave to you to remember your path.

Frames, monitors, and breadcrumbs alike were scattered all over the floor. Someone had moved the couch, making it stick out at a shallow angle from the wall.

And there was blood.

Streaks of it on the walls, across the floor, staining the couch, dried up on the galley counter. It looked like someone had suffered a small but significant cut, then thrown themselves about the place in melodramatic agony.

"Holy shit," Inaya said.

Jamel nodded. Bubbah had to be hurt. Or drunk. *Way* drunker than Jamel had been when he'd tried to force his way into Camilla's room. Maybe hurt and drunk both, as those two things tended to go hand in hand.

But that smell, that wonderful, spirit-soothing, stomach-fluttering smell . . .

Jamel looked to the galley; he saw no cookies. That filled him with an instant and powerful sense of despair. Had Bubbah hidden them? Had he *eaten them all* like a motherfucking selfish fat-ass pig?

Inaya walked to the galley counter, leaned over it, looked at the tiny kitchen even though she could easily see everything in there from the front door. Her hands curled into fists, which she punched knuckles-down on the countertop—the hard *clonk* surprised Jamel, made him wince.

"No *brownies*," she said. "Where the *fuck* are the fucking *gaddam brownies*?"

Cookies, not brownies—Jamel was getting tired of this old hag's bull-shit and getting tired of it right quick.

She turned toward him, finger pointed at his face, her lip twisted by a snarl.

"Shut that door," she said. "He's not getting out of here until we find out what's up."

Jamel nodded, reached back, and touched the door panel. The door swung shut. In an almost instant afterthought, he grabbed the wheel at the door's center and spun it shut, sealing the cabin.

Wait, what was he doing? Stop Bubbah from getting out? There was only the tiny bedroom and the bathroom left; it wasn't like Bubbah could escape through some secret maze.

"Inaya, calm down," Jamel said. "There's blood all over the place. He must be hurt."

Her eyes narrowed and her nostrils flared, not with anger but with *need*, the need for whatever it was she smelled. She blinked, seemed to pause even though she was standing still. Her pointed finger relaxed. Her hand slowly dropped to her side.

"I . . . yeah, all right," she said. "Calm down . . . right. He must be in his bedroom."

She turned toward the closed door that led into the bedroom and the head, and when she did, Jamel took two quick steps forward, almost sprinting before he stopped so fast, he stumbled. He shook his head to clear away the panicked thought that she might *get there first* and she might *get all the cookies and there wouldn't be any left for him.*

What the hell was going on? He needed to get out of there, go get security or at least call for help.

But what if he did that and it turned out there actually *were* cookies? He wouldn't get any. Any at all.

And they smelled *so good.*

"He's got to be in there," Jamel said quietly, as if a loud noise might spook Inaya. "We go in together?"

Her eyes narrowed again, a hateful look that showed her age far more than the cracked hands and dry skin, more than the wrinkles at the corners of her mouth. She looked like she wanted to kill someone—kill *Jamel*—then the look melted away.

"Together," she said. "We check on him *together*? You promise?"

A negotiation of sorts, a deal. Inaya, pleading yet firm at the same time. If Jamel didn't agree, would she come at him? She was strong, with long, lean muscles hardened from decades of twelve-hour shifts, but he had forty pounds on her, and a fight wouldn't last long. If he got the first shot in, it would be over almost immediately, then he would get the cookies, get *all* the cookies. Maybe he should just kill her now, kill her before she could attack him, *kill her* got to *kill that greedy bitch* and—

Jamel punched himself in the mouth so hard, he felt a tooth crack. The pain flared in his face and on his knuckles, enough to overpower the strange, sudden thoughts of murdering Inaya.

He had to leave. He had to stay.

Inaya stared at him, not at all surprised by his actions. Maybe she understood his sudden, overpowering need.

"Together," he said. They hurried the few steps to the bedroom door, stepping over broken frames and treading on the scattered, blood-spotted mementos of Bubbah's career in space.

Jamel and Inaya stood at the bedroom door. Unlike the door that led to the corridor, there was no wheel, no locks. Locks weren't allowed on internal rooms.

Pain screeched from deep inside Jamel's broken tooth, like the dispensary robot had gone haywire and jammed a wide-gauge needle straight into the nerve. Jamel looked at Inaya.

"Go ahead," he said.

She licked her lips. She sniffed, meaning it to be only a quick intake of air but then changing it, inhaling deeply, her eyes fluttering half shut.

Jamel needed her to hurry. A few more seconds and the pain wouldn't stop him anymore; he'd have to elbow her in the throat, break her windpipe, put her down so she couldn't get any of what was his and *only* his.

Inaya looked at the panel on the bedroom door, then put her hand to it. The door slid open: Jamel's eyes snapped closed. He had no control over his body because the odor bulldozed him, roiled out of the bedroom and forced its way into his body, his atoms, his very *being*, so powerful he couldn't think about anything else; he could only surrender to it, succumb to it. Beyond the smell of food, beyond anything he'd ever known, beyond love, beyond breathing, beyond *life*. A caressing tidal wave enveloping him and lifting him.

He smelled *heaven*.

Jamel opened his eyes.

The door was only a meter from the foot of the bed, from Bubbah's feet. Bubbah's naked feet. His bloody, naked feet. His naked legs. His bloody, fat, naked legs. Fat, naked, bloody arms. The obscenely bloated belly rose so high that Jamel couldn't see Bubbah's face.

Reaching up from Bubbah's stomach were long, thin, willowy rods, the thickness somewhere between wire and grass. Supple, waving so slightly in a wind that did not exist, just enough motion to hold your eyes, to make you watch. Their deep red color seemed to absorb the overhead light, soak it up, diffuse it, and cast it out again in what might be a glow, might be a reflection. And at the top of each of those stems, clustered like black-copper berries the size of the end of Jamel's thumb, strange shapes—spheres made of flat facets.

The stems flowed in that phantom breeze, slowly, hypnotically. The triangular facets caught the light in a staccato shimmer, one side flashing, then the next, then the next, then back . . . pulsing, repeating, a metronome of light and movement.

The smell . . . so *overwhelming*. There were cookies in here, somewhere, the best cookies ever made . . . and Jamel would find them.

Bubbah didn't move. He was asleep. Peaceful and content, relaxing on his bed as he should because this was his room even though he was fucking bogarting those gaddam cookies and Jamel was going to fix that problem ASAP.

Jamel glanced at Inaya. She still had her eyes closed, her head tilted back, that grin quivering on her face . . . her throat, exposed . . . It would be so easy to kill her, to throw an elbow and crush her trachea and leave her suffocating, gagging for air that would not come. Jamel could take her out, keep all the food for himself because it wasn't just food; it was *everything*.

It was the universe.

It was creation.

Inaya opened her eyes; the moment was gone.

She didn't look at Jamel. She looked at Bubbah. She looked at the reddish stems and the round-but-not-round black-copper berries.

"Jamel," she said, "what the *fuck* is that?"

He didn't want to look, because looking made the smell *more*, made it drive fishhooks into his soul and reel him closer.

But look he did.

Bubbah, all peaceful and shit, just sleeping, and that *smell*, and—

Jamel felt the punch before he knew he'd thrown it. He'd hit himself a second time, harder than the last, maybe harder than he'd ever hit another human being before. The pain swelled and blossomed and stun-shocked his brain into another place.

A place of reality.

He stared at the fat man.

Bubbah wasn't sleeping. Bubba was dead.

His belly had swollen to three times its original size. Swollen far past where it had been on even his worst days, puffed up like a balloon. No, not a balloon, like a *muffin* made of brittle gelatin or fragile red foam, because great, ragged fissures split that belly, split it *deep*, but the dome of hard flesh didn't deflate. In those fissures, Jamel saw organs, frozen and shattered, fossilized remains embedded in the bloodless strata of Bubbah's body.

The willowy reeds grew up from *inside* those fissures, like trees reaching from a canyon's darkest depths and stretching toward a sun's primal, life-giving force.

They weren't plants. They were something else.

Something horrible.

And then Jamel understood.

He didn't smell cookies; he smelled *the berries*. The berries were tricking his brain into thinking they smelled like something else.

Inaya pointed at one of the berries, her fingertip gently following its swaying path.

"It's beautiful," she said. Her voice sounded hollow, a hiss and a breath pretending to make words that only someone standing right next to her could hear. Her voice might as well have been the invisible breeze that made the red stems sway.

Jamel felt blood coursing across his lips, down his chin. He'd punched himself in the nose and done a bang-up job of it.

His nose . . . It was clogged. He couldn't smell anything. But the memory of that scent, it pulled at him. Like the best lover he'd ever had—Romona, the one who lit him up from the inside out, who knew just what to say, just how to touch, just what buttons to push, that did him so good, he just wanted to float in a fuck-coma for days—his body knew that smell and wanted whatever had caused it even if it wasn't real.

He knew he had only moments before his resolve faltered.

What was this thing? An infection of some kind, obviously. A parasite? A predator? A fungus? Where had Bubbah contracted it? Was the incubation period days or weeks? Or possibly *months*—if so, Bubbah could have been infected at any of seven or eight different work sites.

Which meant others in the crew might have the same thing.

"Inaya, come on. We have to get the hell out of here."

Jamel grabbed her arm, pulled at her to guide her out of the room.

She faced him, snarled, and ripped her arm away all in the same motion. She *growled*, an ancient sound culled from the ancestors of her ancestors, from a time before man walked erect. The sound made him take a step away.

Inaya rushed at Bubbah's corpse. She reached out, grabbed a handful of the round-but-not-round berries

—that smell like cookies that have to BE cookies that ARE cookies the food of the gods and the things that MADE the gods—

and she shoved them into her mouth, swallowing instantly.

—she'll get them all there won't be any left for me!

He launched himself at her, slammed a solid shoulder into her so hard, she flew into the wall. Out on her feet, Inaya slumped down, leaving a streak of blood to mark her path.

—psoriasis psoriasis psoriasis you old bitch the cookies are mine—

Jamel's hands reached, his fingers closed. He felt the berries in his palm. He twisted his wrist. The berries *popped* free with a tiny sound of escaping air.

And then they were in his mouth.

He chewed madly, feeling the *crunch* and the *splat* of the juice inside, his mind exploding in an anticipated orgasm of flavor and textures and perfection.

He swallowed it, *all* of it, before he realized the berries didn't taste like cookies at all.

They weren't berries. They were *seeds*.

A primitive fear crashed across his mind. He turned to run, but as he did, he breathed out sharply through his nose, clearing the clog of blood, and he took an accidental breath in.

He smelled *it*.

Jamel turned back to his sleeping friend.

There were still some cookies left.

And now he didn't have to share them with anybody.

They were all *his*.

THE SOUND OF HER LAUGHTER

SIMON R. GREEN

Two things for you to remember: First, that even the closest of married couples still keep secrets from each other. And second, that we all have pasts we don't talk about.

Alan and Cora Tye had been married for almost a year, and Alan could honestly say he'd never been so happy. He still loved her smile, the way she looked at him, the way she always clung to his arm when they were out in public together. They were in London that day. They'd been to see the musical *Chess* and were waiting to catch a train home from Paddington station. Alan kept humming the song "I Know Him So Well." For some reason, Cora found that endlessly amusing. She hung on his arm and giggled happily but didn't laugh. She never did—just one of the little quirks that endeared her to him.

They'd been waiting at Paddington for some time. The wide concourse was packed with people, crammed almost shoulder to shoulder in places, because of a major signals failure. All trains were stopped, the destinations boards were blank, and no one was going anywhere. The station staff had gone into hiding to avoid admitting they didn't have a clue as to what was going on. People stood around with grim mouths and stressed eyes, listening to the occasional blurred announcement from the overhead loudspeakers, and queuing endlessly at the fast food outlets.

Because queuing, eating, and then complaining to each other about what they'd just eaten at least helped pass the time. Alan and Cora decided they weren't really hungry. Alan had a strong suspicion the fast food would end up justifying its name, sweeping through these people so quickly, it would elbow its way out the back door the next day.

He was vaguely aware of another distorted announcement but was caught completely off guard when Cora's head suddenly came up and her eyes widened. Her head whipped around as she looked for the overhead loudspeaker, her arm tightening fiercely on his.

"What was *that*?"

"What?" said Alan. "What was what? I wasn't listening. . . ."

"That announcement!" said Cora. "I was expecting a platform allocation, or an arriving train, but all I heard was a name. Just a name."

Alan looked at her doubtfully. "Are you sure? I didn't hear . . ."

"I did," Cora said firmly. "Clear and distinct: Elena Marsh."

And then she stopped, as she saw the look on Alan's face. An old, cold hand had just squeezed Alan's heart, hard. He felt like he'd been hit. He shook his head slowly, to clear it. Cora squeezed in close beside him.

"You know that name, don't you?"

"Yes," said Alan. "I knew an Elena Marsh once."

"Who was she? What did she mean to you?"

"She was the woman I used to love, before I met you," said Alan.

Cora let go of his arm and stepped back so she could look directly into his face. "You never mentioned her before."

"I'd moved on," said Alan. "Sometimes, the past needs to stay in the past. So you can move on."

Cora considered that carefully. "Did you really love her?"

Alan nodded slowly. "For a while."

"Why did you break it off?"

He shrugged uncomfortably. "Because she became . . . unstable. It was her work. It drove her crazy."

Cora saw the genuine pain in his face. She moved back in beside him, slipping her arm companionably through his and squeezing up against his side, to show he was forgiven . . . for the moment.

"But why did I hear her name out of nowhere, over a station loudspeaker?" she said. "A name I never heard before but that meant so much to you? There must be a reason!"

"I'm not so sure you did hear a name," said Alan. "It was probably just some sound that your mind interpreted as a name. Just . . . coincidence."

Cora shook her head. "I just happened to hear a name that no one else heard? A name that means so much to you? I don't think so, sweetie. This has to mean something!"

There was another announcement. Everyone stopped to listen, and then a whole section of the crowd surged forward, heading for a particular platform. A train had come in at last. Alan and Cora went with them. Thinking only about getting home, at last.

Later, sitting at their ease in their comfortable lounge, Cora hit Alan with question after question about Elena Marsh. He tried to hide behind his book and fob her off with grunts and monosyllabic answers, but she was having none of that. She sat curled up in her favorite chair, a small thing in a big armchair, hugging her knees to her chest. Cora was small and petite, with long blond hair, big blue eyes, and a pale pink mouth that always seemed to be smiling. Alan frequently wondered what he'd done right to win such a prize.

"Why did you never mention this Elena before?" said Cora, pressing the subject relentlessly.

"I wanted to forget her," said Alan.

"Why?"

"I left her . . . walked out on her when her work led her out of the more extreme borderlands of science and into mad thoughts and bad places."

"What kind of work?" said Cora.

"She worked at a privately funded think tank," said Alan. He closed his book and put it down, admitting defeat. "That's where we met. Elena was a scientific researcher, and I was in administration. It was one of those places where radical thinkers were encouraged to experiment outside the box. Trouble was, some of the scientists ended up so far outside it, they couldn't get back in again. Elena isn't the only one that place ruined."

"What happened to her?" said Cora, peering unblinkingly at him over bony knees hugged tightly to her chest.

"Elena was researching into—and then became obsessed with—immortality," said Alan. "Not philosophy; she was looking for a practical means to a practical end. You see, Elena was afraid of dying."

"Isn't everyone?" said Cora.

"Not like Elena," said Alan. "The whole idea of death simply . . . offended her. That her life could be arbitrarily cut short for any number of reasons before she was finished with it made her incandescently angry. She considered death a basic design fault in life and was determined to put it right . . . by force, if necessary." He paused, picking his words carefully, as he tried to put across an argument he wasn't sure he'd ever properly understood. "Elena ended up becoming convinced that it might be possible to live on, maybe even forever, through the transmigration of souls."

"Souls?" said Cora. "I thought you said she was a scientist?"

"I told you," said Alan. "Her work drove her crazy."

Cora looked at him for a long moment. "Did she . . . ever get anywhere? With her work?"

"Of course not!" said Alan. "And her failure to achieve anything practical drove her out of her mind. I had to get out before she drove me crazy too."

"And then you found me," said Cora.

"Yes," said Alan. He smiled at her. "And you were everything I ever wanted."

Cora got up out of her chair, hurried over, and curled up in his lap, in his arms. She cuddled up against his chest and laid her head on his shoulder. He breathed in the perfume from her hair and was quietly content.

"So," Cora said finally. "Where is Elena now?"

"I don't know, and I don't want to know," Alan said firmly.

But Cora wasn't ready to let it go. She had become intrigued, and

Alan knew her well enough to know when something caught hold of her imagination, she would never let go of it until she was satisfied. She kissed him quickly on the forehead, jumped up out of his lap, and went looking for her laptop. She sat down at the table, fired up her computer, and went to work searching the Net. Her short, stubby fingers stabbed determinedly at the keyboard as she searched through site after site, in pursuit of the elusive Elena Marsh.

In the end, Alan gave up on his book and went to help her. Because he knew he wouldn't get any peace until he did. They sat side by side at the table, taking it in turns to suggest things and work the keyboard. Alan was able to narrow down the many Elena Marshes on offer through biographical details, personal reminiscences, and finally the name of the think tank itself: the Tiresias Institute. It turned out the think tank had been shut down some time before. No official reason given. Cora was able to dig up an old video file showing Elena at an Institute staff party. It was time-stamped eighteen months before, and Alan leaned forward in his chair despite himself as Elena filled the screen. She was tall and dark-haired, tight-bodied and packed full of nervous energy. She had a drink in one hand and a roll-up in the other, and she was laughing loudly. Alan flinched, and a cold shudder ran through him. He remembered that laugh, that fierce, crazy laugh. One of the things he prized most in Cora was that she never laughed like that. Never laughed at all.

And then they discovered why the Institute closed. There had been a scandal. A scientist committed suicide in the main lab. And, of course, it was Elena. There weren't many details; she had taken poison, there were no signs of foul play, nothing to show anyone else was involved. No photo of the body was available, for which Alan was quietly grateful. Cora slipped her arm through his.

"You poor sweetie. Your old girlfriend is dead. How do you feel?"

"Sad, mostly," said Alan. He felt oddly numb. "That she died so young. That she wasted her life, and all the things she could have done and been, because she was so obsessed with death. Does it say whether she left a note?"

"Let me check. . . . Yes! A mysterious note, in fact, found lying beside the body. There's a hell of a lot of discussion threads about it."

"Really?" said Alan. "Why?"

"Because it's a riddle!" Cora leaned forward till her nose was almost touching the screen, scowling at the image. "It says . . . 'Death is not the end. I have found an answer. Come and look for it. You'll find what I discovered above the sea, under the fish.'" Cora sat back in her chair. "What the hell does that mean? How can you be above the sea but still under the fish?"

Alan sat there for a long moment, quietly amazed. "I think I know," he said finally. "I think I know what that means."

Cora turned sharply around on her chair to look at him. "Really? You clever old sweetie! What does it mean?"

"Elena and I once spent a holiday weekend in Devon, at an old cottage," said Alan. "Dolphin Cottage is set high on a rocky outcrop overlooking the Devon coast. It was one of the last times we were really happy together."

"Then that's where the answer must be!" said Cora. "We have to go there!"

"I'm not sure I want to go," said Alan. "Not sure I want to know. Whatever she discovered, it drove her to suicide."

"We have to go," said Cora. "Because I want to know all there is to know about the woman I replaced in your life."

They drove down to Devon. The journey took hours. Dolphin Cottage wasn't on any map, so the satnav couldn't help. Alan found he only remembered part of the way, so Cora spent most of the trip hunched over a series of maps. They didn't talk much. Almost against his will, Alan was remembering more and more about Elena. Her crazy laugh and her fiercely passionate mind. Especially when it came to her work. He never did say a proper good-bye to her, because he just couldn't face another angry scene with that woman. She never wanted to let go of anything she considered hers. Like him. Alan had always been a little surprised, and quietly relieved, that she'd never come after him. Of course, now he knew why.

He couldn't understand why someone so afraid of dying would end up taking her own life. It didn't make sense. But then, people can always surprise you.

When they finally reached the old cottage, standing alone on its gray rocky clifftop, the last of the day's light was fading away. The cottage looked much as Alan remembered, so much so he was actually reluctant to knock on the door, in case Elena answered it. Or her ghost. In the end, Cora had to knock for him. The cottage's current owner turned out to be a stooped old man with a crooked back, long stringy gray hair, and a coolly polite manner. Johnny Hilton was dressed very casually, and seemed happy enough to greet unexpected visitors.

"I bought this cottage last year, at auction," he said. "Never heard of this Elena Marsh . . . or this mysterious message of hers. But I suppose you can come inside and look around, if you want."

The interior was dark and gloomy, all small rooms and low ceilings. Nothing like the light and airy holiday cottage Alan remembered. Cora stuck close to his side as he looked uncertainly about him.

"The message," she said, prompting him. "You said you understood how something could be above the waters but under the fish? I saw the coastline below, so obviously that's the water. And Dolphin Cottage is the fish. But how . . ."

"There's a concealed door," said Alan. "It leads down to a cellar. Is the door still there, Mister Hilton?"

"Johnny, please. I never looked for any hidden door. Point it out to me and we'll go take a look."

The door was still there, hidden away behind a tall bookcase with dusty, empty shelves. Alan and Johnny manhandled the bookcase out of the way easily enough while Cora bounced up and down on her toes with excitement. The door wasn't locked. It opened to reveal a narrow stone stairway dropping away into darkness. Alan and Cora had to wait while

Johnny went to look for a flashlight. When he came back, Alan insisted on taking the flashlight and leading the way down. He was still bothered by the idea of ghosts. Things left over, from the past.

They ended up in a stone cellar some distance underneath the cottage; it was crammed full of strange machines and unfamiliar equipment. Alan moved slowly forward, peering about him. Johnny found a light switch by the door and harsh fluorescent light filled the cellar, illuminating odd shapes and weird technology that Alan didn't even recognize, let alone understand. None of it made any sense to him, and some of it actually hurt his eyes when he looked at it. And two chairs stood side by side. Topped with gleaming steel helmets.

"I don't remember any of this," he said. "None of this was here the last time. . . ."

And then someone struck him down from behind; and he was unconscious before he hit the floor.

When Alan woke up, he was sitting in one of the chairs. His head ached, but when he tried to raise a hand to it, he found he couldn't. He'd been strapped firmly in place with heavy leather restraints. And he could feel, even if he couldn't see, that the steel helmet had been placed on his head. He looked around and there was Cora, strapping Johnny Hilton into the other chair. She looked around suddenly, caught him looking at her, and laughed at him. An old, cold, and very familiar hand gripped Alan's heart. He knew that fierce, crazy laugh. He remembered it.

"My God," he said. "You're not Cora. You're Elena."

"Got it in one," she said. And just like that, she didn't sound like Cora anymore. She turned away from him to carefully lower the steel helmet onto Johnny's head. She fussed over it, taking her time, before turning back to Alan again. "Yes. I'm Elena. You really should have stuck around to see me finish my work. The wonderful machines I created at Tiresias, with the help of my colleague here, Professor John Hilton. Turned out I was right all along; with a little technological assistance, the transfer of minds, if not souls, is perfectly feasible. Immortality at last, and in an entirely practical manner."

She moved away from the chairs to stand before a control panel. "Johnny helped me transform my theories into hard science. He has a marvelous mind. He made all of this possible."

"How long?" said Alan. "How long have you been . . ."

"I put my mind into Cora's body before you ever met her," said Elena. "I found a face and a body I knew you wouldn't be able to resist, and then I took it for myself. And went after you. Alan, darling, did you really think I'd just let you go? Let you walk away from me? You never met Cora. It's always been me. You've been married to me all along."

A sick horror surged through Alan. His whole marriage had been a lie. The woman he'd thought he was sharing his life and his bed with had been someone else entirely. Cora never laughed because inside, Elena was laughing at him all the time. And because . . . he'd know her laugh. Alan couldn't believe he never once suspected that his new love . . . was the old love he'd run away from.

"What happened to the real Cora?" he said finally.

"She's gone," Elena said easily. "I poisoned my old body before the transfer, so she had nowhere to go. And now you're going too. Although I was so desperate to get you back, although I went through all this just so I could have you . . . I hate to say it, Alan, but you turned out to be such a disappointment. Now, Johnny here has a far superior mind. And once I put that mind into your body, I'll have everything I ever wanted."

"I loved you," said Alan.

"Of course," said Elena. "You always did."

"How long have you been planning this?"

"Months."

"Why wait so long?"

"It took time to understand you and give up hoping you'd become what I wanted you to be," said Elena. "And then it took time for Johnny to calibrate the machinery. But finally everything was ready, and all I had to do was fake hearing my own name on a loudspeaker so I could start the ball rolling."

Her hands moved steadily, almost casually, across the control panels. And all Alan could do was watch her helplessly, unable to move a muscle inside the leather restraints. There was a flash of unbearably bright light, filling his head from the inside out, and then he was somewhere else.

When he could see again, he was standing in an unnatural place made up of mists and broken ground. Everywhere he looked, the world seemed vague and indistinct. Gray mists swirled slowly around him, full of bodiless voices, calling out. Mourning, angry, desperate . . . Here and there, shadows moved through the mists, searching for . . . something. Not all of the shapes seemed entirely human.

Johnny Hilton appeared suddenly out of the mists in front of Alan. He didn't look old or crippled anymore. Alan braced himself, but Johnny didn't even try to fight him. Instead, he tried to go around him. And Alan just knew Johnny was heading for his abandoned body so he could climb inside it. And be Alan for Elena. Alan grabbed hold of Johnny, and the body felt perfectly normal under his hands. Johnny fought fiercely to break free, but Alan hung on grimly. He wrestled the other man to the ground and held him there. Not because he was stronger than Johnny, or a better fighter, but because he wanted to live more. Because he wanted his revenge on Elena. He pinned Johnny to the ground, pushing his face into the broken earth . . . and then wondered what he should do next.

He looked up, and there was Cora, standing before him. Smiling at him. And it only took Alan a moment to recognize this was the real Cora. He started to think about what that meant, about her and the place he was in now, and then he made himself stop thinking. Cora drifted forward, out of the mists, becoming more real and more solid the closer she got, until finally she knelt down beside Alan and Johnny. She nodded to Alan, and he nodded back. He understood. He let go of Johnny and stood up, and Cora put her arms around Johnny. He cried out at her touch and tried to fight her, but she held him where he was. She had been in the gray place so much longer, and it had made her so much stronger. Alan backed slowly away. Cora laughed quietly. It sounded nothing like Elena's laugh.

Alan woke up in his own body, still strapped helplessly in his chair, but still himself. He watched Elena as she bent over Johnny. He was convulsing and crying out in his chair while Elena laughed at him. And then he died. Elena stepped back from him and shrugged briefly. She looked across at Alan, and smiled as she saw he was watching her.

"I didn't expect your old body to die, but it doesn't matter. I'm a little disappointed that Alan didn't end up trapped in your crippled old body, but then . . . You can't have everything."

Alan just nodded, not trusting his voice to sound like Johnny. Elena came over and quickly removed the steel helmet from his head before freeing him from the leather restraints. Alan stepped carefully out of the chair and stretched slowly. Pulling on his body again, like an old pair of gloves. And then he looked round quickly, at something behind Elena.

"What the fuck was *that*?"

Elena turned to look, and Alan struck her down from behind.

He stood over her unconscious body for a while, thinking many things. And then he picked her up and strapped her into the chair he'd just vacated. He put the helmet on her head, and moved away to stand before the control panels. He was pretty sure he knew what to do. He'd watched Elena do it, and it seemed straightforward enough. Elena woke up in her chair, struggled fiercely for a moment, and then glared at Alan.

"It's you!" she said. "Not Johnny!"

"No," said Alan. "Not Johnny."

"You can't do this to me!"

"I think you'll find I can."

Elena looked at Johnny's dead body, still slumped in its chair. "You can't use the machine on me with him dead. There's nowhere for me to go."

"That's the idea," said Alan.

"You can't kill me," said Elena. "I'm your wife. You love me."

"You're not the woman I married," said Alan. "I loved Cora."

"You never even met Cora! It was always me! You loved me. . . ."

"No," said Alan. "I loved the woman . . . I thought you were. And then I found out you weren't her at all and never were." He smiled briefly. Coldly. "Isn't that why most marriages break up?"

His hands moved steadily across the controls while Elena fought and writhed in her chair . . . until the light went out of her eyes and she was still.

"For you, Cora," said Alan.

And just for a moment, he thought he heard the sound of her laughter.

DOWN IN THE DEEP
AND THE DARK

DESIRINA BOSKOVICH

It's a crisp Friday in autumn, the day before my brother Aaron's wedding, a week before Halloween. Aaron and his bride Kristina have planned a getaway in Eureka Springs, Arkansas, among the forested hills of the Ozarks. Eureka Springs is a tiny tourist town, once a mining empire and luxury resort, now reduced to a faded Victorian Era strip of generic art galleries and pottery shops, Vegas-style wedding parlors, and after-dark ghost tours. We're staying at the Hidden Springs Inn: a grand historic resort, known for both its picturesque weddings and its rumored hauntings.

I've been appointed maid of honor, which would be great except I hate weddings, and dresses, and "vision boards," and to be perfectly honest I'm not crazy about the bride. Neither are my parents, though they're mostly hung up on the fact that she has a kid whose father isn't in the picture, and *Aaron, we love you dear, but aren't you taking on an awful lot of responsibility?*

Me, my mom, my dad, and my eighty-seven-year-old grandmother enjoy an appropriately nightmarish plane ride together. (It's nearly Halloween, after all!) Gran curses joyfully at security and farts in the aisles and torments the flight attendants, while my parents pretend not to know her. Then there's an hour-long drive, on a winding two-lane highway flickering in and out of steep, rocky hillside. My dad takes the curves too hard and my mom white-knuckles it all the way, gasping at every glimpse of the valley below.

By the time we reach the hotel, all I can think about is the fact that it's 5 p.m. and I need a fucking drink.

Kyle, my brother's best friend and best man, is already at the bar and three beers deep. "Hey, Hillary," he says, grinning broadly. We have always disliked each other, especially since an unfortunate incident that took place about a year ago. (We got too drunk. Mistakes were made.) He's cocky, obnoxious, the quintessential bro, and he would be really stupid if not for the fact that he's actually pretty smart.

While I'm ordering a whiskey and Diet Coke and trying to ignore him, he decides to bound right over and force me into this over-the-top fake hug. "Hillary! I left like a hundred messages on your answering machine. You never called me back." (He's being sarcastic. I think the joke is that he never called. Actually, I'm not sure what the joke is, but I'm pretty sure that I'm its punch line.)

"I'm filing a restraining order," I say, and sip my drink, already certain this weekend is going to be the worst.

"How about this hotel, huh?" Kyle says. "Freaky. It's like some Jack Nicholson shit."

"It used to be an insane asylum," I say. "And a sanatorium for people with incurable diseases. That was after it was a luxury resort for people with more money than God."

I'd read about it, a bit. The Hidden Springs Inn was built in the 1880s when the town was a bustling metropolis, a luxury oasis for the millionaires who'd made their fortune on the backs of dead bodies now lost and buried inside the mines. Then the economy faltered, the veins dried up, and the town faded. The grand old hotel, with its sweeping ballrooms and crystal chandeliers, was repurposed as a hospital with experimental aims. Later—much later—after it became gauche to ship the mentally disturbed off to unsupervised prisons where they'd sit chained in their own feces, a renewed interest in history led preservationists to rebuild the old hotel. Though never restored to its former glory, at least it clung to a shabby dignity . . . and its tourist trade.

"I hope I see one of the *sexy* ghosts," Kyle says. "You know, the ones who died in their lingerie and now they have to wander the halls with their tits eternally hanging out."

Luckily, right then Aaron arrives and sits between us, intent on keeping the peace.

Aaron is a wonderful brother, and a wonderful person; accomplished, talented, attractive, nice. Maybe a little *too* nice, like the kind of nice that doesn't really pick up on the fact that people who call you their knight in shining armor might actually see you as an easy mark.

Kristina had been a single mom since seventeen—her people didn't believe in averting such things in the usual way. Her parents helped raise the kid, by spoiling him within an inch of his life, while Kristina earned a certificate in sports therapy and massage. They met after Aaron suffered an injury on the football field, which sounds serious until you find out that the football field was actually a casual Thanksgiving get-together and the injury was a tweak in his lower back. His angel appeared with scented oils to nurse him back to health. Less than two years later, here we are at the wedding. It's either a fairy-tale ending or an embarrassing cliché.

My parents won't say anything too pointed, because they practice courtesy as if it were a cult, but they don't really have to. Aaron's not dumb; he just pretends to be.

Still, I know, from the subtle hints they've dropped, and some less-than-subtle comments delivered on the harrowing journey here, that if in these final moments Aaron were to suffer cold feet, they wouldn't be overly disappointed. And, as maid of honor and trusted older sister, should I find myself in position to sow a few fast-growing seeds of nagging doubt . . . well, who would they be to cast blame?

We've been catching up for a while when Kristina arrives in a dress and heels and greets me with way too many air kisses and *oh my gods*. And then she's like, "Aaron, honeybear, did you ask?"

"Sorry, pumpkin," Aaron says. "I forgot. Hil, would you mind watching Gabriel for a few hours? We've got dinner with both sets of parents."

Somehow, I manage to both (a) not choke on my drink and (b) gracefully agree. "Sure thing. Let me tab out and I'll be right up."

Kyle snickers at me mockingly. He knows that I really hate children. Even more than I hate weddings. Or him.

As I ride the elevator up to the third floor, I give myself a pep talk. Gabriel is bratty, but how bad can it be? It's just a couple hours. Just a couple hours of sticky little hands, nonstop nose-picking, and endless six-year-old monologue, voiced like nails on a blackboard.

Kristina and Aaron point me to a stack of kids' DVDs, then head out. At Gabriel's request, I put on the most uninteresting film in history. While it plays, he warbles nonstop, just enjoying the sound of his own piercing voice. Then he demands fruit snacks and goldfish crackers, and a second movie to follow the first.

Finally, he settles down. His breathing slows, his eyes drift closed, and I think maybe, if I stay very still, he'll actually go to sleep.

Next thing I know, I'm waking up in a dark room and the credits are playing and my mouth feels like the inside of a wool sweater that's been in the back of a closet for years.

And Gabriel isn't here.

I panic and start searching the room even though it's obvious there's nowhere he could hide; I check inside the bathtub, yank away the drapes. Then I come to my senses and dash out into the hall, calling his name.

I power-walk my way up the corridor and around the corner, hoping I can find him before anyone else does.

The hallway smells of must and mildew. The dark floral carpet is patterned with odd blotches and mysterious stains, and feels weirdly spongy underfoot. The signage is inadequate; brass room numbers are affixed

WHAT THE #@&% IS THAT?

to the dark-painted doors, but several of the numerals are missing. The corridors, routed and rerouted several times in the past century and a half, suddenly feel like a maze.

Maybe it's the counterintuitive geography. Or maybe it's my sleep-bleary fear. But a minute into my mad scramble, I'm completely lost, standing in a corridor I don't recognize.

Up ahead, on the left, I notice another hallway, jutting diagonally to the left. This makes no sense; I must have circled two or three times by now. But I run toward it.

It turns into a dead end, with two doors on the right-hand side and three on the left. Gabriel is standing there, staring intently at the twisted paisley patterns on an empty stretch of wall.

"Gabriel?"

He doesn't respond. I approach slowly, wondering if he's sleepwalking, suddenly even more afraid. Do I try to wake him? This whole thing is giving me the creeps. The skin on the back of my neck is prickling and I feel as if I'm being watched.

I rest my hand on his shoulder, dreading the moment he recoils, or screams, or goes catatonic. Instead, he turns and looks at me. His eyes are droopy, but he's definitely awake.

"Hello, Aunt Hillary," he says politely, which is the weirdest part of all.

"Um. Whatcha doing there, partner?"

"I had to let the little boy out."

"You mean yourself? You let yourself out of the room after I fell asleep?"

"No. Not me. The other little boy. He's been locked in that room a really, really long time. That's why he was crying. So I had to let him out."

"Um, okay," I say, ready to not be having this conversation. "That's . . . freaky. Why don't we go back to the room now?"

He ignores me and keeps on staring at the wall. "I thought we were going to play, but then he ran inside. And now he won't come out."

"Um . . . ," I say again. "Inside where?"

He shrugs, then gestures at the wallpaper. "That door there."

"There isn't a door there," I say, but I can't help but glance up and down the hallway as I do, because I'm noticing three doors behind us, and two doors to the right, and we're standing exactly where the third door would be, *if there was one*. And I have this awful feeling. It isn't rational, but it's powerful all the same.

"He said people always think that," Gabriel informs me. "It's not the kind of door you can see with your eyes, but that doesn't mean anything. It's still a door. And I can see it just fine."

"Okay," I say, really sharply this time. "That's enough. This isn't funny anymore. We're going back to the room."

"No," he says, but I don't care; I've had enough. I grab his arm and pull him toward the end of the corridor. Then he melts down into full-on tantrum, so I'm forced to hoist him into my arms and carry him.

To my surprise, I wasn't lost at all; the hotel room is right around the corner.

Of course, I've locked us out of the room, and my key, my phone, and my wallet are all inside. So I carry him to the elevator and down to the lobby.

As soon as we step off the elevator, we run into the bride and groom and both sets of parents, returning from dinner. Kristina runs over and scoops up her kid, whose tantrum has disintegrated into sniffles. He tells her the whole story, garbled and teary so none of it makes any sense, not that it made much sense to begin with. I play it off like he had a nightmare. Kristina's mother, Lydia, who's obviously drunk more gin and tonics than strictly necessary, offers to take over for the night. Gratefully, I hand off Gabriel, and since I'm several drinks behind, head back to the bar.

"To the future!" my brother toasts with a flourish.

Best drink up.

At 2 a.m., I'm woken by a woman screaming. I leap out of bed, yank on a hoodie, and dash out into the hallway; this time, I remember my key.

My mom and dad are out there, plus Aaron and Kristina. "That was my mom, screaming," Kristina is insisting, anxious and confused. "She has Gabriel. I can't remember the room number. Thirty-six? Thirty-nine? Oh my God, I hope they're okay. . . ."

It's room thirty-nine. We pile in; Lydia is sitting up in bed, disheveled and pasty in her pink satin dressing gown. She appears to be hyperventilating. Gabriel is lying in the other bed, flat on his back; his eyes are open but he's looking away. Kristina's dad hangs off to one side, awkward and frumpy in his old-man pajamas.

"What's wrong? What's the matter?" Aaron and Kristina crowd around Lydia.

It takes her a while to get the words out; she's gulping and gasping and sobbing a little. "Something woke me up. Like I felt something. I opened my eyes and Gabriel was standing right above me, except it wasn't him, really." She pauses to collect herself. "He was all *changed*; his eyes were big, and he was holding a knife. Just looking down at me, laughing, holding that knife."

"It was only a dream," Aaron tells her. "A bad nightmare. It's fine."

"So, can we all go back to bed now?" my dad says, so patiently that he's obviously annoyed.

"But then I sat up," Lydia says, gesturing wildly, "and he was laying in his own bed the whole time, like he never even moved."

"You just imagined it, Mama," Kristina says, sagging into a visible exhaustion. Aaron massages her shoulders.

"But I didn't," Lydia insists. "I know what I saw. It was so real." She starts to cry.

"There, there," my mom says, and sits beside Lydia; for her, this is not an insignificant show of affection.

"But let's be *reasonable*," my dad says, in that tone I detest. "If there *was* an awful little boy holding a knife, he'd still be here. He wouldn't just disappear into thin air."

That tone, that logic—I think maybe it's part of the reason I never let myself get all emotional, not like Kristina or her mother.

"But there's not an awful little boy," my dad continues. "There's just Gabriel, in his own bed, falling back to sleep. . . ." but his voice trails off because we all instinctively look over at Gabriel and he's not actually falling back to sleep. Instead, he's sitting up and staring intently at the television, which isn't on. His mouth is moving, and he's mumbling something too faint to understand.

There's a long moment. "He's just overtired," Kristina says uncertainly. "The wedding," my mother agrees. "For a little boy. It's a lot of stress." "It was so real," Lydia repeats again, faltering and sad.

"We'll take the little trooper back to our room," Aaron says. "You all get some sleep." He scoops Gabriel up into his arms, and I think maybe I'm the only one who notices that Gabriel seems to be lost in another world.

I wake early to dim light filtering through the gap between the blackout curtains and someone pounding at the door. It's Aaron, telling me that Gabriel is missing again, and they don't know where he is.

Kristina is standing in the hallway, wrapped in Aaron's flannel shirt, crying and fidgeting. Aaron is trying and failing to be Mr. Fix-It. Everyone is texting and calling and knocking on random doors. Gran emerges, demanding to know what the goddamn never-ending racket is about, and what the damn hell was happening last night, anyway? Kyle shuffles—hung over and shirtless—into the fray, awake only because Aaron dragged him out of bed. Lydia is recounting her nightmare, or hallucination, to anyone who will listen. My parents are clearly thinking that this is Aaron's future in a nutshell: a nonstop parade of petty disasters and emotional displays.

Finally, someone thinks to alert the manager, who promises to alert the staff. Five minutes later, Aaron gets a phone call. "Sssh, it's him," he says, pointing at his phone. (Meanwhile, everyone argues over where we should look next, and if a kidnapping is a likely scenario, and how far could a sleepy six-year-old get, really?) "Hello? Oh! Great. We'll be right down."

Gabriel is outside. A groundskeeper found him.

We crowd our way onto the elevator, through the lobby, and onto the hotel grounds: a complex maze of shaped hedges, moss-covered benches, and unkempt flowerbeds gone to seed. The Hidden Springs Inn sits high on a ridge; dense fog saturates the autumn leaves below. Up here, it's misty and cool.

We catch a glimpse of the manager standing by a haphazard arrangement of cracked statuary, where he seems to be locked in an intense conversation with the groundskeeper. Gabriel fidgets on a nearby bench.

Kristina takes off running and soon enfolds Gabriel in a flurry of hugging and scolding. The rest of us edge closer to the manager and the groundskeeper, who are having a fight.

The manager is late forties or so but seems younger; dapper in his suit, which is perfect for a wedding, not so appropriate for a muddy hillside at sunrise. The groundskeeper is burly and gruff, and his standard-issue coveralls are stained with mud . . . and . . . is that blood?

"I'm telling you," he says, with an aggressively pointed finger. "Not my job description. Not even close."

"Now, let's all just calm down here. . . ."

"I'll do you one better," retorts the groundskeeper. "I quit." He rips off his gardening gloves and tosses them onto the ground. Next, he's going for the back brace.

"What on God's green Earth is that *smell*?" my mother wants to know.

Kyle catches sight of it first. The look on his face as he points: it's naked as a scared animal. I've never seen him like that, far below the swagger and front. This scares me the most . . . until I see what he's pointing at. A little ways down the slope, arranged on the damp grass in a sloppy approximation of a circle, are half a dozen freshly eviscerated carcasses, the stinking meat and hot blood and unraveled organs of a chipmunk, two bunny rabbits, a handful of squirrels.

I walk over, as if in a dream; I don't want to, but somehow I'm compelled. And the feeling is exactly the feeling I had yesterday, standing in that weird half-a-hallway. There's something very near me, so close it could tap me on the shoulder, except there's nothing at all but the damp morning air, and the stench of death, and Kristina's mother, screaming again.

Behind me, Kristina is yelling at the manager. "I just want to know . . . could someone explain . . . why does my son have *blood* on his clothes?" Gabriel stands beside her, perfectly calm, still wearing the cowboy pajamas he wore to bed. They do appear to have some stains.

"You people have no idea," the groundskeeper rebukes us all, and for an instant, what I see flickering in his eyes is even worse than the carnage here on the hillside. "No clue." Shaking his head, he turns hard on his heel and strides away. The manager throws up his hands. The groundskeeper disappears into the mist.

"Um, why don't we all head inside?" the manager says briskly. "Can I offer you breakfast on the house! Oh, what a romantic weekend for a wedding!"

The breakfast buffet is jarringly cheery. Soon, everyone is milling around, loading their plates with leaden pancakes and grease-laden sausage links. I grab a cup of coffee and sit across from Kyle.

"To what do I owe the pleasure?" he inquires jokily, but I can tell his heart's not there.

"Something weird happened last night," I say. "I don't know why I'm telling you." But actually I do: It's not like I can tell my brother, or Kristina, not right now. My parents would tell me I'm being crazy. I have no idea what Kristina's parents would say. And of all the happy couple's friends and acquaintances gathered here, Kyle is the only one I actually know, and not just in the Biblical sense.

So I tell him about the hidden half-hallway, and the missing door, and the creepy conversation I had with Gabriel, who was probably just being a kid, but come on, right? And then I fill him in on the 2 a.m. incident, which he somehow slept through, that lucky son of a bitch.

"You're not just pulling some stupid prank to get me back or something?" Kyle asks, and I can't tell if he's concerned that I am, or concerned that I'm not.

"You think I snuck out this morning and slaughtered a dozen fucking woodland creatures just to fuck with you?"

"Hmm," Kyle says, like he's not sure either way. I can see why he'd be concerned; if this was a prank, it would be beyond epic. He'd definitely have to acknowledge my superiority from here on out.

"I'm not fucking with you."

"Will you show me that hallway? My room's on that floor and I have no idea what you're talking about."

"Sure."

He snags an extra handful of bacon and together we head upstairs, pretending not to notice the family's too-interested looks.

"Or maybe," Kyle says speculatively as we ride the elevator, "maybe this is some kind of ploy to interrupt the wedding. You guys can't be too happy about this whole thing either."

Not entirely sure what to say to that, so I settle for "It's not a ploy."

But once we're on the third floor, I can't find that hallway anymore. I can still picture the wallpaper in my mind, the twisted, scrolling paisley with its slight metallic sheen, oddly textured to the touch. I can see the five doors, unmarked. I can remember the way it jutted off, up on the left. But it's not here, and there's no way it could be here; the geography simply doesn't make sense.

Kyle keeps looking at me like he's waiting for me to let him in on the joke. "You're kinda freaking me out, Hil," he says finally. "Like . . . what's really going on with you right now?"

"Fuck it," I say. "Never mind."

But I'm totally freaking out too.

By 11 a.m., I'm at the salon with Kristina, and both moms, and all Kristina's giggly bridesmaids. (Gran wisely sat this one out, opining that she's eighty-seven years old and knows better than to try to make a silk purse from a sow's ear.) The ladies talk everything over, and then talk everything over again, and by the time we get to updos, it's decided that

Gabriel is acting out because he's excited to finally have a real dad, and Lydia is suffering from exhaustion after helping her lovely daughter plan this incredible wedding . . . and who knows what was up with that crabby groundskeeper? Solutions: some one-on-one time for Aaron and Gabriel, another glass of champagne for the mother of the bride, and no one mentions the unavoidable conclusion that our cherubic six-year-old was outside slaughtering tiny animals in the hours before dawn.

I'm the only one who isn't participating in the conversation. It's because I know things that they don't know, and I'm almost certain this isn't over.

My mother and Kristina chalk my sullen attitude up to the fact that I hate pedicures, and fancy chignons, and the prospect of wearing a floor-length purple satin dress. (This is true.) They lecture me about how it wouldn't hurt me to pull myself together and take some pride in my appearance for a change. I should be grateful! I might look pretty for a day! "Ever since we let her join that softball team . . . ," my mother begins, and since I'm deep in the land of sorority girls, debutantes, and ladies who lunch, I don't even try to explain how offensive all this is. By this point, my hair is sculpted and shellacked and my fingernails are polished pink.

By the time we're gathered back in the hotel lobby, a few hours have passed. We're met by Aaron—laid-back, easygoing Aaron, who looks rather unhappy and tense.

"I've just been talking with the caterer. The manager was supposed to let them in a while ago so they could start the prep. Except he isn't there. He isn't anywhere. He seems to have just . . . left?"

"That's ridiculous," my mother says. "He's got a job to do. He can't just *leave.*"

"The front desk is empty too. I've been looking everywhere for someone who works here. So far, I've only been able to find a maid, but there's a bit of a language barrier, and, like, I just don't know what's going on. . . ."

Mystifyingly, one of the bridesmaids perceives this as a good moment to share her opinion that if *those people* are going to live here, they should really learn to speak English. Biting my tongue and wishing all these people would just go fall into the Hidden Spring, wherever it is, I volunteer to go look for the manager, or an assistant manager, or a bartender, or, really, anyone with the keys to the kitchen. Though really, the bartender would be nice.

But I walk right past the front desk and no one even tries to stop me; the door to the manager's office is open, the computer still on, the lights bright overhead. Loose papers are scattered everywhere and a ring of keys sits on the desk.

Outside, the fog is thickening, and the lights are flickering overhead.

By 4 p.m., an odd kind of darkness is settling in outside, the first edge of a storm. The lights are faltering more frequently now and everyone is reassuring each other that it's normal for an old building like this one, surely there's a generator, there's simply no way the power could go out. The bride is having a meltdown. The mothers send me to the lobby to keep an eye out for the florist, who is supposed to be delivering a truckload of bouquets.

The ancient elevator is creaking and moaning its way down when the lights go out, then blink back on. The elevator shudders, lurches, plummets half a floor, then jerks to a stop. The lights die.

I'm standing in pitch dark, trapped in an elevator in America's most haunted hotel, wearing a floor-length satin dress and eggplant-colored heels and trying not to hyperventilate.

Somehow, I can't bring myself to sit down.

"Hello?" I yell out tentatively, but of course there's no response.

And then, sing-songing out of darkness, is a voice I almost, maybe, kind of recognize. Like Gabriel's voice but different; it's shrill and grating on the surface, but a rusty, rasping shadow is gathering beneath. "Hello," the voice says back.

In the edges around the voice I can hear my own ragged breathing, rattling jagged in my chest.

"It doesn't like to be locked in the dark," the voice observes. "They didn't like it either. They made it go away."

I want to scream and scream, but I can't seem to make a sound.

"They didn't like that little boy. They didn't know what happened to him, down in the deep and the dark and the cave, but they knew he wasn't the same. So they locked him in the dark and they disappeared the door. You're not the same, are you?"

It starts laughing and the laugh is horrible.

"You know a little boy who's not the same. It won't be the same, not after this. It just needs more time to eat."

I'm aware of a sick, soupy feeling in the air, and a smell like rotting meat. There's no oxygen anywhere, and I wheeze and gasp. I want to reach out my fingertips and *feel*; is there anything here with me, really? But I can't move.

"It doesn't like to be locked in the dark," the voice repeats.

Then the voice is gone and the stench is gone and the lights flicker back on. The cage is empty; I'm alone. Slowly, achingly, the elevator begins lurching down toward the lobby once more. Somehow, I've managed not to piss myself.

The lobby is empty. I trip and stagger my way over to one of the unwieldy antique couches, spraining an ankle in those unbearable heels. I sink down and rest my forehead on an overstuffed pillow.

It occurs to me that I have the ammunition now to bring the wedding to a halt, just like my parents hoped.

Or maybe I'm just having some kind of breakdown.

Dress gathered in one fist, I tiptoe barefoot to the abandoned bar and snag myself a high-class bottle of scotch.

I wait for an hour, but the florists never show up.

Kyle is gripping my shoulder, shaking me awake. "On your feet, soldier. The wedding's about to begin."

I blink and rub the upholstery pattern emblazoned on my cheek.

"But there's something I have to tell you."

"Okay?"

"Gabriel is missing again. Kristina and Aaron don't know. Your parents were supposed to be watching him, but they can't quite remember when they saw him last."

Surely, they wouldn't . . .

"We decided it would be best to just go ahead. He's just trying to get attention, they say. Just . . . don't say anything to Kristina. Aaron told me she's stressed to the max and a hairsbreadth away from calling it off."

"Isn't that what we wanted?" I stupidly remark.

"You know what, though?" Kyle tells me, serious now. "He really loves her. I think he even really loves that snotty kid."

Kyle's right, of course; whatever else they are, Aaron and Kristina are madly in love. If I'm being honest, it's been disgustingly obvious all along.

We walk together across the hotel grounds, past the spot where the tiny, lifeless animals had been, but they're already gone.

We reach the picturesque white chapel at the edge of the woods and pause together at the side entrance. "In an hour, this will be over," Kyle says. "And maybe, the labors of the caterers notwithstanding, it might be best to make like that useless manager and get the hell outta Dodge."

Suddenly, I remember a nightmare. "I got trapped on the elevator . . . ," I begin, but then Lydia is opening the door, yanking us in, and scolding us for being late when the whole wedding party is poised and waiting to begin.

The chapel is stuffy and hot and dimly lit. Yawns ripple across the audience like a breeze through cobwebs. *Love is eternal,* intones the minister. Kristina and Aaron are gazing deeply into each other's eyes. Outside, the light has failed and wind is rattling the windows. *It cannot be overpowered by fire or flood; it is stronger than death and even death is no escape. It can conquer the tomb and reach beyond the grave.*

Someone coughs.

It will eat you alive. Till death do you part, and a long time after . . .

Louder and fiercer than the rattling at the windows, there's a creaking and banging at the door. The door flails open. The wind blows in.

*. . . I pronounce you man and wife. . . .*We're standing at the front of the chapel, so we see him first. Him, it, no longer sure? The thing that was once Gabriel, grown and changed. The too-tight skin stretching and tearing over the rapidly expanding frame, the fingers curling like talons, the glossy black shadows for eyes, the mouth dropping open like twilight and the entrance to a cave.

Behind it are the tiny animals, bloodied and eviscerated, heads twisted at odd angles, but standing, marching with animatronic force. Larger animals, still dripping blood. A couple humans, or once humans, their necks broken, their limbs askew, their eyes black shadows too. One bears a striking resemblance to the caterer (but with half her head bashed in).

One by one, the audience begins to shift and turn, alerted to the fact that something unspeakable is happening behind them.

Gran breaks the silence and her scratchy voice reverberates throughout the chapel: "What the fucking Christ on a cracker is *that*?!" Kristina drops her bouquet.

The thing begins to laugh. Like a spider, it furls and unfurls its limbs: it plucks Aunt Becky from the nearest row, and as she screams and writhes, it snaps her neck like a twig and runs its talon like a knife down her torso and slurps the viscera from the cavity around her heart. She becomes one of them.

You'd think everyone would start running and screaming, but no one moves an inch.

Then there's a shout from behind. This is where everything gets fast and crazy and chaotic and slow: Behind the thing and its army of reanimated corpses is a crowd of people, pressing their way through to us. It's drizzling now and they're standing in the rain. They're wearing masks and holding torches and pitchforks. Literal pitchforks. Among them is someone who looks like the groundskeeper, though with the mask, I can't be sure. A woman is shouting orders.

"We've come to take it away," she says. It turns to her with death in its eyes and murder in its limbs. She thrusts the torch forward and utters something in an ancient tongue. Her companions form a tight circle, pointing their pitchforks and humming incantations.

Kristina is running down the aisle, tripping on the fringes of her wedding dress. "But that's my *son*," she says.

"Mommy," the thing says. "It doesn't like to be locked in the dark."

"Your son is gone," the masked woman says. "The demon plants itself like a seed in an egg. The egg is the nourishment it uses to keep itself alive until it has enough strength to hatch. Soon, very soon, the shell will crack." She and her compatriots prod it and poke it forward, trapping it in their circle of pitchforks and fire.

The rest of us follow, while Kristina tries to get closer and Aaron tries to hold her back. The zombie squirrels march implacably under feet, following their master. The minister dons a mask.

"What are you doing with him? Where are you taking him?" Lydia is demanding. I'll say one thing for her, she always takes her daughter's side.

"We're taking it back to the crypt," the masked woman says. "It's eternal. It cannot be destroyed. Obliterate the shell and it simply moves to another host. It can only be contained." She pauses for a while. "I don't know how you found the door."

We are not walking back to the hotel, as I'd imagined (me and my guilty secret, the hidden hallway, the invisible door). We're taking a door at the back of the church, a door I didn't know was there. We go down a steep flight of uneven steps—followed by the entire wedding party and half the guests—while Lydia pushes as close as she dares and says, "Well, what I want to know is who do you think you are and what gives you the right?"

"We protect you," they say. "We always have."

We're walking down the lost hallway: the dark, unmarked doors, the hypnotic paper with its twisted swirls.

"The door must be physical and metaphysical," the woman explains. "The door must be locked with a key and the key must be lost. The door must be paved over. The door must also be lost."

The impossible, invisible door opens on a cell, a dark musty cell that stinks of death and rot, lined with cinderblocks and iron and lead.

"It is bloodthirsty but simple," the woman says. "Simple but cunning. It comes from a time before time, a place before places, when language was powerful magic written into the substrata of the world."

The man that might be the groundskeeper says, "If we can lose the door for another generation, we've done our jobs. We can go with God in peace."

Kristina is crying and pleading. "You can't put him in there," she sobs. "Not in there. He hates to be alone. He's afraid of the dark."

"We must," they say, and push and prod him toward the darkness.

"Mommy," it says. "It didn't mean to, Mommy. It didn't mean to open the door."

"Then me, too," Kristina says. "He can't be alone. I'll go in there with him."

"Forever?"

"Yes. Forever."

For the first time, I see her, really *see* her. I understand in a rush how cruel and unfair I've been, judging her shallow and provincial when I was the one all along. I want to say I'm sorry, but it doesn't matter, and it's much too late.

"Me, too," Aaron says, and steps forward, and pulls Kristina into his arms. "Together. We'll go in there together. I won't let you do this alone."

"Are you people fucking kidding me?" Gran demands, and her scratchy voice rattles through the hallway. "You're going to let these Halloween assholes run the show? You think we can't take 'em? We got ourselves a whole goddamn wedding."

Just like that, a brawl breaks out. They have fire and pitchforks and ancient magic; we have hysteria and passion and paranoia, and the bride's cousin Ron, who came to the chapel packing heat.

The thing has itself, its useless, eager, bloodied army, and its vicious desire to survive. In the chaos, it feasts on another extended relative. Now it looks almost nothing like a boy.

With the gun and the fire and the crowded hallway, we battle each other to an impasse in two minutes flat. There is crying and sobbing and gunshot wounds, and Gran has been knocked over, trampled, bruised, and bloody. But amidst the struggle, the thing has gotten past us. Or maybe it opened itself a door?

It's gone. Perhaps it is about to hatch.

A shout goes up among the masked order when they realize what's happened. We follow them as they run up the stairs, into the chapel, out into the storm.

"We've got to find it. Call in anyone and everyone you can," the woman instructs her people. "We'll put together a search party. We'll search until it's found."

She turns to us with contempt in her eyes. "Look for it. Look for it everywhere. You have no idea what you've done."

I notice then that Kristina and Aaron are missing too.

Two hours later, maybe three, maybe four. Kyle and I have been stumbling through the woods for what seems like an eternity, maybe longer, maybe less, looking for any sign. Kyle's holding a flashlight; its beam has begun to falter. I'm holding his hand. Wet leaves and rough branches are slapping us, scratching us. We're slipping and falling in the mud. Unspeakable noises whine from the dark.

"What's that . . . over there?" Kyle asks.

So tired we can hardly move, but knowing we must, we trudge forward. Snagged on a sharp branch is a flutter of white—a scrap from Kristina's veil.

A little farther ahead, what looks like one of Aaron's shoes.

And then dropping open before us is the entrance to a cave. Pitch black. Reeking death.

The cave is a tunnel. We walk through darkness: forward, forward, down, and down. The tunnel opens into a yawning cavern, too high and too deep and too endless to be real.

Far off, beyond the gulf, is an immense stone throne. The bride and the groom kneel before it. There are fires burning, primal and fierce. The horde is larger and stronger than before.

The prince sits upon its throne. It has ruled before. It could rule again.

Simple and cunning, it fixes us with bright, burning eyes. *We are ignorant,* it says. *We are selfish and monstrous and violent and cruel. We belong to the dark.*

Beyond lies the hidden spring, where death bubbles forth from one of the many secret mouths of hell.

Kyle and I kneel weeping before it. It has seen us and known us for what we are.

ONLY UNCLENCH YOUR HAND

ISABEL YAP

They're killing chickens again in the backyard. Last time, a headless chicken ran in and danced blood puddles around my feet. I can't relax, anyway, because of another thrumming headache, so I grab a textbook and decide to get a few pages in by the river. As I make my way down the rocky path I hear Tito Benjo laugh and Aling Dinday scream for the chickens to stay still. I should be used to noise, from Manila, but here in the province, every sound is amplified. In a village this small, you can hear everything for miles.

It would be good for my review, Mom and Dad said. No distractions. When you get home, you'll be all set to pass the entrance tests. So, after graduation and three weeks of rest and sleep, Tito Benjo picked me up and drove me out here. They were right, mostly—I can barely get a cell phone signal, let alone a few bars of Wi-Fi, and even then I have to work out of the village carinderia. But I finished my study plan, with time to review. Besides, I'll be heading home in a week. I hold up my arm to block out the sun, and see a mosquito latched onto my elbow. When I swat it, blood smears across my palm. "Damn bug."

"Damn bug," someone echoes behind me, the English exaggerated. I turn around, grinning, and seize Edna by the armpits. She shrieks as I lift her into the air. "No, Ate Macky! Bloody hands!"

I laugh, put her down, and wipe my hand on my shorts. Edna is the daughter of Aling Dinday and Manong Edgar, the caretakers of Tito Benjo's farm. I think she's nine, though she's tiny enough to be six. She's one of the few people in the village who humor me, who don't mind the English I mix with fumbling Tagalog, or the short hair and comfy clothes that get me mistaken for a boy. If not for her company, it would have been a pretty lonely summer. I might never even have set foot outside Tito Benjo's property.

"Where are you going? Studying?"

"I want to. But my head hurts."

Edna makes a monkey face—wide eyes, jutted lower lip. "If you have a headache, you should see Mang Okat."

"Who?"

"Mang *Okat*," she says, tugging my arm. "Our healer."

"It's fine," I say. "I get these headaches pretty often." I don't mention that they've gotten worse, or that they only started this summer, when I decided to pursue law. I don't mention that I think faith healings are whack, fit only for TV specials and sensational news.

"He can fix it!" she says, still tugging. Because I like Edna, and my brain hurts, and I don't think I can concentrate anyway, I let her drag me off.

Edna bounds up the steps to Mang Okat's house, which to my city-girl sensibilities looks kinda like a hut. "Manong! I brought someone new for you!"

"New?" He peers out. His weathered, wrinkled face unfolds into a grin. "Ahh-ahh! Ser Benjo's niece, the Manileña!"

"Hello, po," I say, ducking my head as I enter. He gestures for me to sit on a plastic chair by the window. I can't refuse. Edna perches on a bench across from us.

"What's the problem?"

"She has a headache," Edna says.

"Yes, po," I answer, helplessly. Mom got my head checked out when I first complained—but the brain scan they took showed nothing. Take some painkillers, they said, but I've already had my quota for the day. I decide to just go along with it, since it can't possibly get worse. Mang Okat slaps his hand on my forehead. It's greasy and smells of herbs.

"Hmm-hmm." He turns to his table, which is covered in vegetables and herbs and jars of—potions, I guess, or liquids that are supposedly potions. He turns back, holding a glass filled with water in one hand, and a small bamboo tube in the other. There's a black stone in the glass. "Stay still," he instructs, holding the glass against my head. I glance at Edna, but she just smiles back. Mang Okat dips the tube into the glass and starts blowing into it, making the water bubble. He hovers the glass back and forth and around my head. I feel profoundly weird. To distract myself, I watch the movement of a bug across the floor—it looks like a giant fly, but it doesn't have wings. Some kind of beetle. It skitters from one wooden plank to another, then races up the window ledge and disappears over the edge.

At once, the pain in my head evaporates. It's a sudden, sweet relief that extends from my forehead down to my shoulders—I didn't realize how heavily the ache had been sitting on me. "Better?" Mang Okat asks.

I nod. My breath comes languid, heavy; I feel like having the best sleep ever.

He holds out the glass. The water has turned murky green, with solid particles floating in it. "This was inside you," he says, before dumping the water out in a plastic bucket.

"Thank you," I say, rather awed.

Edna beams. "Told you so!"

I fish in my pocket and pull out a crumpled fifty-peso bill. "Here, Manong." I hold it out.

He waves it off, brow wrinkling.

"No, please," I say.

"Oh, just take it, Tay," someone says from the door.

"Ate Senya! I thought you were still in Manila!" Edna launches off the bench and wraps around the legs of the woman coming in. She looks a little older than me. Her mouth is set in a tired smile, and she has severe eyebags. She's wearing a yellow tank top stained with sweat so that I can see her bra through it, and a sky blue skirt. She wipes her face with the back of her hand while setting down a woven bag of groceries.

"I came back three days ago," Senya laughs. She pats Edna's head because Edna is still wrapped around her like a leech. This makes me feel oddly jealous.

"Welcome back, anak," Mang Okat says.

"Tay, you should stop healing for free. And besides, I think the Manileña has some cash to spare." She grins—probably to show she's just ribbing me—but it stings a little, even if I'm used to it. After a brief pause, Mang Okat takes the bill from my fingers. He passes Senya, gives her a quick kiss on the cheek, then holds out his hand. She gives him a pack of cigarettes, and he stumps out of the house.

She looks at the bucket against the wall, mouth quirked.

"Your dad is pretty amazing," I say, suddenly defensive. Quack powers or not, there's no denying the fact that I feel a million times better.

"I know," she answers softly. "I'm glad he was able to help. Don't you have any paracetamol, though? I bet it's more effective."

I decide not to argue, and shrug. My longing for a nap is overwhelming.

"Ate Senya, be nice. I like Ate Macky," Edna says.

"I'm always nice." She crouches down to whisper something in Edna's ear, and they giggle. Feeling left out, I glance out the window. There's a cockroach creeping on the ledge. It scuttles down the wall, across the floor, toward Senya. She doesn't pay attention, even when it crawls between her feet, disappearing somewhere under her skirt. It crawls out again on the other side and drops down between the planks of wood.

Edna has to go to the market with Aling Dinday the next day, so I take my backpack and decide to try my luck with the carinderia Wi-Fi. My head feels so light and clear, I practically skip down the road. Manong Edgar waves at me from where he's knee-deep in a bunch of Tito Benjo's goats. I wave back.

The lady at the carinderia knows me by now. She fills a paper boat with greasy chicken skin, squirting banana ketchup on top, and hands it to me with a bottle of Coke. I settle in at my favorite table, waving away the flies that cluster in bunches, hoping for scraps off people's plates. I'm holding up my MiFi, searching for a signal, when I hear glass shattering.

"Fuck you!" a man shouts, and someone shouts back, "Let go of me!"

The Carinderia Lady makes a face at the street, but she stays where she is, waving her flyswatter back and forth. I dash outside. Mang Okat's daughter—Senya—is trying to wrench her arm away from some shirtless dude in low-hanging shorts. Bits of beer bottle litter the ground around them. A trickle of blood drips down his face, but my eyes fix on the knife he is holding. Senya is gripping the jagged edge of a beer bottle, but the knife will be faster, more precise.

"Hey!" I default to English in my anger. "Let her go!" The man turns, eyes blown to their whites, lip curled. He glares at me, calculating. I'm lean and empty-handed and not that near—but I'm the niece of Tito Benjo, the governor, the landowner, and you don't fuck with politicians.

He releases Senya's arm and stalks off, still clutching his knife. The look of searing hate he throws at her, then at me, makes me want to run after him and beat his head with a stick—but I don't. Senya rubs her arm, looking at me warily.

After he disappears around a corner, she says, "You didn't need to do that. I can take care of myself, Miss Macky."

The formality surprises me, that she thinks of me that way too. "I know, I just—what a dick."

Senya manages a huff of laughter. She comes over, still rubbing her arm. We walk to my table.

"You're . . . funny, you know that?"

I smile. "You want some chicken skin?"

She shakes her head but takes a seat. There's a brief pause where I sense the Carinderia Lady watching us, but Senya glances at her, and the Carinderia Lady suddenly starts talking on her cell phone. My cheeks grow hot. If she's gossiping, it's not that different from what I have to deal with in Manila—the casually tossed-out *tomboy*, the more piercing *lesbo*. I've got my friends, my humor, and enough self-preservation to not let it get to me most of the time. It's not supposed to fucking *matter*, how I dress and who or what I like. But I can't escape the blabbering mouths, not even out here.

I tap my fingers on my laptop. My MiFi has absolutely no signal. "Did you know that guy?" I ask finally.

"I told him I didn't want to see him." She rubs one finger down my bottle of Coke, still cold from the icebox. A ring of water from the condensation stains the plastic tablecloth. "I don't know how to get the message across. I forget about him till I'm back here."

"What do you do in Manila?"

"I study. Nursing. I'm old," she adds quickly. "It took Itay and me a while to save enough. He wants me to get work in a hospital abroad, after. That'll make it worth it. But if I do end up going . . . Well, Itay does okay for himself, but . . ." A brief sadness crosses her face, and I remember Mang Okat kissing her cheek, her exasperation at his work. Then her eyes fix on the textbooks I've piled next to my computer. She picks one up. "Law?"

I nod, unable to ignore the way her eyebrows tighten. "Hopefully."

She sighs. "Corporate, right? Or something like that?"

"I haven't decided yet." I haven't even gotten in.

She dips her finger in the ring of condensation and drags it around the tablecloth. "Doesn't matter, I guess." I keep quiet while she continues. "Miss Macky, you and Ser Benjo and your family back home in Manila, you'll probably be okay. People like him"—she jerks her head at the road—"they won't bother you. They won't try. Random bastards won't try. If anything happens, someone would at least try to solve it."

"That's not true," I say. "Even stars and athletes and people from— people with power—sometimes they get attacked. Sometimes, their cases don't get solved too. Look at—uh, Nida Blanca."

"You don't understand," she says, with a tired smile. "It's different here. We just get used to it. Besides, if what you're saying is true—why would you ever want to study something so useless?" She looks up from her water-tracing.

My mouth feels dry. I take a sip from my Coke. "I want to help," I say— but it's true; I'm probably not going into criminal law. Too much shit, too much stress. I'm not cut out to become a burning Defender of Justice. It's too easy to get disillusioned, or at least that's what my parents tell me, and they've both been practicing for years. "Same reason you're doing nursing, right?"

Senya nods, slowly, but with more deliberation than I could ever muster.

I stay at the carinderia until evening, when the flickering fluorescent no longer helps. There's still a faint streak of pink way in the distance, but I use the camera flash of my phone to light my path as I walk back to Tito Benjo's, because there are no streetlights and too many potholes.

Halfway there, I hear violent retching somewhere ahead of me on the dark path. The local alcohol is cheap and goes straight to one's liver. Tito Benjo asks me to drink with him every now and then; it's pretty awful, but I wouldn't dare turn my host down. I scoot to the other side of the road and hold my phone-light up. A man is doubled over; the wet chunks of his dinner splatter the ground while he heaves. Disgusted, I try to edge past him, but my light catches the mess he has made on the ground, and I see . . . tiny black balls of . . . what looks like hair stained red with blood. He vomits again. More dark balls splat on the ground, with shiny pink things that look like slugs or tongues. The man glances up, panting. "You," he manages, one hand gripping his bare stomach.

I see a knife handle poking out of his shorts, and remember—but even if he's a fucker, if he's barfing out his intestines, I have to do—*something*. "Do you—" I ask, but he spits, wipes his mouth, and staggers away. I cringe, relieved and grossed out. Already, a trail of ants has caught the mess and is sifting through the vomit. Feeling sick, I run the rest of the way back.

Tito Benjo laughs.

"Puking out hairballs? Like a cat?"

"Tito, I'm serious."

"Must have eaten something awful for dinner." Tito Benjo shrugs. "That kid—he's usually up to no good, always sleazing, but he's never actually *done* anything."

I remember his searing look of hate. "He carries a knife around."

"Lots of people do, here. You can't stop them. They're usually blunt." He waves it away. "How are your studies going?"

"Okay, I guess."

"If you don't pass your exam, I'll be in trouble with your mom. Ha-ha!"

I grin, because Tito Benjo laughs far too much, and I peck him on the cheek, excusing myself for the evening. Tito Benjo's house has concrete walls. There's no gate, but there are locks on the doors. The path is long and the farm surrounds us and no one would dare. I think of Mang Okat and Senya in her hut, Edna and her parents in their own hut, and that drunken man raving through the night, with a knife in his shorts and the smell of vomit and blood hanging off him.

Edna appears in our kitchen the next day while I'm ladling out tinola soup. "Mama says you're going back at the end of this week?"

"Yep."

"You didn't tell me!"

There are so few kids in this village; I realize that I'm a rare friend of Edna's too. "I'm sorry! I thought you knew." I pass her a bowl of soup. "I'll come back next summer," I say—but I won't have an exam to pass then, and I'll probably have summer class. "I'll *try* to come back next summer."

"Try, okay?"

I nod. We sip our soup.

"Ate Senya said we could visit her house later. She's making mais con hielo."

"Oh, good," I blurt out. I suddenly remember the blood and puke spilling from that dude's mouth—but that path was very dark, even with my phone-light on. He probably *did* just eat and drink too much, and anyway, I was still learning about all the weird local delicacies.

"So you wanna go?"

"Uh—er—" I was relieved that he hadn't gotten to them—I had been secretly scared about that all night—but that didn't really mean I wanted to go.

"It's *mais con hielo.*"

"Okay, okay."

On our way to Mang Okat's, I find my eyes trailing the ground, both hoping and not hoping to find proof of last night's encounter. A part of the road has vomit, but in the daylight, the color is more watermelon pink, nothing like blood at all. There are no hairballs. Edna skips over the trail of ants creeping across the mess; if she finds nothing weird, then neither do I.

Senya is crushing ice in plastic cups when we arrive. She hands us both knives so we can help. It's a burning day, and the ice is already half melted by the time we pour condensed milk and corn kernels into it. We don't talk much, sitting on the steps of her house, eating our frozen treats. There's one moment when I act ridiculous, closing my eyes. I don't hear cars or smell pollution or feel like someone's about to snatch my phone out of my pocket—it's another one of those times where the province feels peaceful, otherworldly, and I'm glad it's not Manila. I'm glad the freeways don't extend to here; I'm glad I don't feel the need to take a selfie with the cup in my hands and give it the appropriate hashtag.

Edna sings a song in Batangenyo, which I vaguely understand as being about a river, and Senya joins in during the chorus, winding her hair into a braid over her shoulder.

Mang Okat emerges from the trees blocking our view of the path. We're already standing to greet him when he shouts for help. He's dragging something—someone.

I get to him first and let him drape the arm of the person he's carrying over my shoulders. I don't ask, just move. Senya and Edna watch as we climb up the short steps and deposit the person on Mang Okat's narrow wooden bed. The man stirs, moans. There are open sores all down his arms and over his chest: cuts and scrapes that gleam raw, wet, and weeping. The wounds are all colors, a grisly sunburst spectrum of red-yellow-orange-purple-black, some graying at the edges.

Mang Okat picks a bottle off his workbench, full of wood chips and herbs suspended in oil. A strong smell of rum leaks when he opens it. He pours the liquid over the patient's chest, smearing it into the wounds. The patient makes a gargling noise, inhuman-sounding.

"Tay, do you need help?" Senya asks.

Mang Okat glances up and shakes his head. His eyes linger on mine briefly, but I can't decipher the look in them—something almost like fear. "I think you girls should go."

It takes effort for me to walk away. I can't tear my eyes from the sight of the man, or stop noticing the smell of his skin, warm and slick with fluid from his wounds. There are weeping sores even on the soles of his feet, and before I turn around completely, I see a black bug crawl—out of his wound, or next to it?

"Ate Macky," Edna calls. I sprint down the steps.

We reach the river. I lean over the bank, knees against my chest, willing myself not to retch. The thought of vomiting makes me think of the man from the previous night again. I stare at the water, watch my reflection stare back.

"Who was it?" Edna asks.

"I didn't see," Senya says. I turn to look at her. She sits cross-legged, fingers twiddling the grass. "I don't think even Itay can fix that kind of curse."

"Curse?" I ask, stomach bunching as I stand. "That was a curse? It looks like he got—*I don't know*—sliced by tons of invisible knives."

Edna and Senya look at each other, then back at me, almost pityingly.

"It's a mambabarang," Senya says. "I guess you wouldn't encounter that in Manila."

"Mambabarang? What the fuck is that?"

"They curse people," Edna answers. I forget that I shouldn't curse around kids, but she doesn't seem to care. She's pulling up little blades of grass. "They're like . . . the opposite of Mang Okat. You can bring them money, or things they want, and they'll curse your enemies. Or sometimes they'll curse people just because." I wonder why she won't look at me as she says it.

"Witches?"

Edna shrugs. Her little face is dull, and I realize it's not that unusual here. My ignorance is—if not annoying, puzzling. "They can be boys, too."

"What the hell? There's someone like that in the village and you just— haven't they ever tried catching the person?"

"The mambabarang won't get caught," Senya says, still with that gentle voice. "It's not like there's only one. If they were found out, the village would murder them, or at least—send them away. They're careful. They won't let others talk."

I think of Mang Okat's glance. I remember that the man yesterday gave me the same look, after he'd hurled and started walking away—and heaviness sprouts in my chest. *Was it him?* But I already know it was.

"It's not me," I say.

There's a moment of silence. Then Senya laughs, doubled over, shrill and gasping. It's the loudest sound I've heard her make. Her laughter makes me feel ridiculous, but I crack a smile, because if she thinks it's impossible, it must be.

"Of course not, Miss Macky," she says. "You'll use the law instead, right?"

I stare at her, mouth open, fighting the urge to slap her—I'm trying, in my own way. Her gaze levels mine. "You wouldn't do a thing like that," she says, back to her soft voice, like something escaping a dream. *You wouldn't dare*, her eyes say, *and anyway, why would you ever need to?*

Tito Benjo and I eat in the carinderia that evening, because Aling Dinday isn't feeling well and can't make us dinner. I push around the stewed goat on my plate, while Tito Benjo watches a basketball game on the over-saturated TV. I am about to ask if I can go home when Edna crashes into our table. The dim light shows tears streaked across her face. "Ate Macky! Governor! Itay is—Itay is—"

We run, with Tito Benjo puffing behind us. Edna stops in the goat field outside the house. I don't need light to know that there's blood every-where. I smell it rising from the grass, and when I kneel down beside Manong Edgar and cradle his head, I feel it, slick between my fingers.

"Who—" I ask, but Edna is shaking her head—she doesn't know, she doesn't know.

"I'll get the car," Tito Benjo says, voice pinched. He charges off.

"Is he still alive?" Edna asks. I hold my hand over his nose, expecting the worst. He's breathing, just barely.

"Edna!" Aling Dinday appears at the edge of the field, with Mang Okat and Senya behind her, all of them panting. When they reach us, Mang Okat kneels across me, and Senya pulls Edna into her arms. "Manong, manong, please," Aling Dinday breathes, clutching Mang Okat's hand. She isn't sobbing, but her voice wobbles.

"He needs a hospital," Mang Okat says. "This isn't something my heal-ing will work on."

Aling Dinday draws in a heavy breath, just as Tito Benjo's car comes up the road. He brings it right up to the fence, then hurries over. Carefully, he and Mang Okat lift Manong Edgar to the car. Aling Dinday wipes her eyes and climbs in after them.

"You stay and watch Edna," Tito Benjo says. I nod, hands still wet with blood, shaking, shaken.

* * * *

I try to sleep, with Edna curled up beside me, tears streaming out of her eyes while she half dozes.

Why Manong Edgar? Someone drunk? High? Someone with revenge on his mind?

You don't understand. It's different here. We just get used to it.

For no reason? I pull my blanket up to my chin and let my heart drum me to sleep.

"Ate Macky," Edna whispers. I jerk upright. It's still dark outside. The moon hovers outside our window, bloated, dull silver.

"What is it?"

"Come on." Edna stands from where she was crouched next to my bed. "We've got to hurry." She starts out the door.

I trip out of bed, pull on my slippers, and follow her. She walks down the path, steady and sure, and crosses the goat fields into a thicket of trees—the forest outside our farm. I'm afraid I'll lose her in the darkness, so I walk faster, until I'm in step with her. After minutes of nothing, I see a dim fire blazing ahead—the glow of several candles, beneath a balete tree with dead, drooping branches. I blink to focus. Someone is crouched before the candle flame, wearing a sky blue skirt, hair hanging wild over her shoulders.

She sees us and holds a finger to her lips as we come closer. Her eyes are hazy, half-lidded. Edna pulls me to sit down beside her.

Senya holds out her hand. There are fat beetles on it, the same kind I'd seen in her house. I am not afraid of bugs, but the revulsion inside me is so strong that I gag. Her finger skims their shells, and she makes a clucking sound in the back of her throat. Then she drops them onto her lap, and they rove around in lazy circles. She withdraws something from her shirt pocket—it's a needle, with white thread running through it, ghostly in the moonlight.

She picks up a bug and pierces it with the thread. I dig my fingers into my palm. She pierces the bug, again and again. There is no sound, but with each movement of Senya's stabbing hand I feel like covering my ears, like there's screaming in my skull. Screaming, laughter, crying, screeching. She does this to the two other bugs, and then sets them down on the floor. Instead of curling up or twitching to death, the bugs appear to be unharmed. They begin moving in a line, pale thread strung between their black bodies, and that's when I notice the cloth doll lying next to the candles.

The bugs burrow their way into it. Senya watches, hands folded in her lap. We all watch. The doll flops back and forth as the bugs tear their way through it. Then, from the same holes they bore in, the bugs burrow their way out. Senya whispers to them—or to us, or to the candle flame?—and their black shapes move into the darkness, through blades of grass, thread trailing behind them. The sounds in my head slowly die away.

Senya sighs. It's the first human sound I've heard in what feels like forever. She looks drained, the bags under her eyes alarming, her mouth drawn into a deep-set curve. Edna reaches out her hand toward Senya, and Senya takes it. After a moment, Edna reaches out a hand to me, and I reach out for Senya's, closing the circle. Her fingers are slim and cool in my grasp.

We stay like that, waiting in the dark, while the candle burns and the village twists and seethes around us. It feels like a long time before the screaming starts, but it could have been minutes. In a village this small, every sound is amplified.

There are tears running down Edna's face, but she just squeezes my hand tighter, and the fury in her eyes is matched only by the serenity of Senya's smile.

I look down at my feet. I imagine the skin along my veins cracking apart, gushing with blood; dark beetles crawling out, making their way up my shins, my legs, eating their way into my belly. Pouring out of me, trailing my insides with them, slick with blood. I think of the man holding his knife toward Senya. I think of Manong Edgar in the goat field,

WHAT THE #@&% IS THAT?

singing to himself, waving at me. I curl my toes and hold their hands, and we wait until the screams stop; we wait until we are satisfied.

My shirt is crusty when I wake up, from Edna's tears and snot. She's rolled away from me and is facing the opposite wall. I can't remember when we came back. I can't remember if we ever left.

I fumble for my phone. No messages. I hold it outside the window, trying to get a signal, and after a few minutes, there's a ping: *Tell Edna Mang Edgar will make it. Tks.*

They come home two days later, after the village has found and buried the drunken ass that did it. Manong Edgar's head is heavily bandaged, but his laughter when he sees Edna, despite being weaker, is full of warmth.

I stop by Mang Okat's house my last day in town. Edna's sulking, but I've promised to make it up to her by bringing a souvenir from Manila next time. Mang Okat and Senya are on the steps, shelling boiled peanuts.

"I'm heading back to Manila tonight. Manong, thank you again for your help the other day."

"No more headaches?"

"None. No patients today?"

Mang Okat shakes his head slightly, then stands. "That's right—I have something for you!" He enters his house and rummages around the bottles on his bench.

Senya holds out a handful of shelled peanuts.

"No, thank you," I say.

"Ready for your test?"

"Sort of. I'll feel better when I take it. At least it will be over."

She laughs as Mang Okat emerges and hands me a tiny oil-filled bottle. "Just rub a bit of this on your head when it hurts," he says.

"Thank you, Manong." I fumble through my pocket. He waves me away.

"Just take it," Senya says—to me this time. She stands, puts her bowl of peanuts away, and gives me a quick, awkward hug. "Good luck."

I am halfway down the road when I turn back to face them, bottle clutched in my hand.

Senya gives me a small smile and a wave. I wave back. Something crawls up the side of my neck, perching behind my ear. I pinch it between my fingers, hold it away, let it drop to the ground. I see, briefly, the black thread trailing from its body, before it scuttles off to safety.

LITTLE WIDOW

MARIA DAHVANA HEADLEY

I was fourteen and at a sleepover when the cult drank poison. The sleep-over mom turned on the TV and said, "Oh my lord, Mary, would you look at this? It's the feds is what, and a bomb, right out there where you come from."

But it wasn't the feds, and it wasn't a bomb. It was us. We were destined to die. I watched it burn, and listened to the news call us a cult, which was not what we called ourselves. We called ourselves Heaven's Avengers. I watched it for a while, and then I threw up hamburger casserole.

Miracle didn't have a stoplight. Miracle didn't have a grocery store. Miracle didn't typically attract anything but traffic going the dirty way to some other place. We were on the road to California, and people sorrowing in other states found their way to Disneyland through us. Miracle had no marvels. It was named after a thing that'd happened back in 1913. People got lost—a whole troupe of the religiously devout on a pilgrimage—and then they got found. They came up out of a lake bottom and walked on the water, briefly, before they disappeared again. A cult got started around that notion, and a hundred years later, on the anniversary of the water walk, my cult killed itself.

Now it was trailers and scraggly dogs, and everyone who hadn't been part of the dead cult was an ex-con turned to factory work. An hour away, we had a sugar factory and you could get a company bus. Most of our town worked there, bleaching brown to white.

I watched the compound burning on the news. My mom and dad were in there, and everyone else too, all sleeping on the floor. Nobody'd noticed that we were having problems, or maybe people had—the police had visited us and done a couple of circles with their sirens on, but another cult had lately gunned down half the police force in a little town in Texas. The locals let us be.

We were hippies only in theory. In reality, we were working on an armed takeover of heaven. The Preacher thought if we meditated white knives into our minds, we'd hit heaven as a unified army, slashing. We wanted heaven for ourselves. We didn't see the point of suffering. The plan was to rise up, and so the Preacher put poison in the pop.

A lot of the kids in the town had been born in the cult, and when it committed suicide, there was an epidemic of orphans. The little ones got sent out to the rest of the state, but some of us stayed. We were old enough to be okay. The leftover kids milled around Miracle, grieving and weird, not fitting in. The sleepover had been at the house of a friend who wasn't really, and I wasn't right in the world, not with my long dresses and my uncut hair.

I was married already, but no one except my fellow orphans knew that. I'd been married to the Preacher since I was seven. I was the Littlest Wife, and that was a special role. I brewed tea, and balanced crystals in the palms of my hands, while the rest of the wives did other things. There were fifty of us. All but three were dead now, and we were only alive because we were too young to commit to being killed. Somewhere in the mind of the Preacher, there was a notion of legal.

Our life in Heaven's Avengers was not like some people thought it was. People had ideas about us, that we'd grown up in a sex cult. It was the reverse, except for the Preacher and his army of wives. Most of those were not having intercourse with him. They were just a battalion. The Preacher preached. Once a year, each wife, the of-age wives, spent a night with him, and got a baby or didn't. We were trying to grow Heaven's Avengers. There were only a hundred of us total, though we had some international followers who came to us through our website, and participated long-distance in preaching. So, I was married to him, but I was still a virgin. I was a wedded warrior. There were long traditions of wedded warriors, which most people didn't know about. Armies of women, all married to a chieftain. This is the kind of thing you knew about if you were from Heaven's Avengers.

Back then, I was called Mary out in the world, and the other two were called Rebekah and Ruth, but all three of us were "Sister" on the compound. We knew better than to stay Sister. When everyone died, we chose emergency new names. We looked at a magazine of celebrities and picked by dress color. I chose Natalie, and the other two Sisters, who were both sixteen, chose Reese and Scarlett. Then Reese took out a pair of scissors, cut off my hair, and hacked my dress up from the ground to my knees. She snipped her own hair so short, she could pass for a boy. Scarlett tore her hem into a miniskirt, and chopped her hair into a bob. We were all crying but we looked better.

We got taken in by the Stuarts, and they let us have their old teenagers' bedrooms. The Stuarts had lost two sons in Afghanistan. They didn't care that we were cult kids. There was room in the house for us, and they fed us cereal and scrambled eggs and didn't ask us to go to church.

Mrs. Stuart was a faded-out redhead with white roots, a tight jaw, and a nose that'd been broken four times while bull riding. She chewed tobacco and tended cattle. Mr. Stuart had a motorcycle on the weekends, but during the week, he worked at the factory. They left us alone. We didn't mind. We wanted to be alone. The three of us tried to figure out school. We could read, at least. We were lucky. The littler ones couldn't. No one had taught them. Things had gotten too intense, what with the coming of the War, and schooling had slid.

We could fight with our minds, and that did no one any good in high school. Now we didn't think about white light, nor about knives. We tried not to think about how maybe everyone we knew was warring in heaven now, but Reese sometimes looked up and cried at the sky. She missed her boyfriend, who'd turned eighteen just before the exit. He was a crack shot, and could do a backflip, but I'd never liked him. He hit me in the face once for stealing a piece of gum.

Scarlett was sad about the suiciders too, but not as sad as Reese was. Scarlett had a natural figure for fortune, and knew how to sew. She stitched up a party dress from dishtowels, wriggled into it, and went out to the first school dance of the year wearing shoplifted lipstick. Within a minute, she was leading cheers at the football games, and nobody cared that she was missing some back teeth and had a crooked arm from breaking it during battle training.

Scarlett had strawberry blond hair and unlikely curves, a waist like a funnel. Reese was the reverse. Her body was round, with tiny wrists and ankles. She had curls, tight ones the color of cake batter, and eyes so pale they looked blind. She was smart as a whipsnake, which tricked people. Her albino coloring made people in Miracle think she was mental. She wasn't. She was going somewhere. She was a genius in ways that might scare a person if you didn't know for sure she liked you. Then there was me, Natalie, with a scar where my lip had been prayed back together, my body a unified width from chest to hips, the same turned sideways as front.

My mama was adopted when she was nine from Delhi, and Reese's when she was six from Ethiopia, and they both started as Littlest Wives. We didn't know where Scarlett came from. Her mama'd died of a rattlesnake when she was three, and then her dad dropped her off on the compound, and that's how she ended up married to the Preacher. She was no relation to him. The other two of us were chastely married to our father.

No one really regulated the religious, and so the Preacher had saved a bunch of girls from uncertain futures in countries other than America. By saved I mean saved for first marrying and then suiciding. In theory, this was no one's fault, the fact that no one helped to save any of the older wives from death once Heaven's Avengers decided to suicide, but some part of me had started to wonder if every agency actually just felt like sacrificing a few people every year in lieu of doing their proper jobs. Most of us were brown. Most of the people around us were not. Maybe we'd been purged by lack of social work. I didn't like thinking it, but I thought it anyway, and it put me in a pissed-off place. School was hard. This was why. All us three were suffering badly from the pissed-offs.

No one knew much about us, and we kept it that way. We'd been the Sisters Stuart for a year when the carnival showed up. People called us that without irony. We didn't correct them. Privately, we called each other Little Widow.

The carnival came in a truck and a tent, and it looked like shit, but we were still interested. We liked new things. It set up just outside of Miracle. We hadn't seen television until recently. The fire onscreen was the first time I'd ever watched the news. I didn't know much about fairs, nor about carnivals, and neither did the other two, so we dressed up in our best clothes and walked out over to the grassless ground of the high school football field.

There was a big poster of a girl in a yellow bikini covered in fringe and holding a chicken. I pointed at it. We'd never had bikinis. Reese put her hands on my head and fluttered up my hair. She'd been studying the world. She had a boyfriend again, one with a license to fly a crop duster, and they were having sex. She'd learned how to fly the crop duster, too. She was planning things about the rest of her life.

"Don't worry, Little Widow," she said. "She's not that great."

But I was staring.

"Can we go see her?" I asked.

"She's only a stripper," said Scarlett, and cracked her bubblegum. I didn't know what a stripper was. I thought it had something to do with crows and crops, or maybe threshing.

"I don't care," I said. "I want to see her."

GEEK said the sign, in giant letters. The tent was as yellow as the bikini, and also trimmed in fringe, and outside it, there was a big bearded man with a flat black hat lazing around, looking too warm. His arms were all over tattoos of naked ladies and pirate ships. They weren't good tattoos. We had better.

The women of Heaven's Avengers were artists at tattooing. Each one of us had a small suit of armor under our clothes. It grew with us. I got mine when I was seven, the year I became Littlest Wife. It was an eight-hour tattoo on my solar plexus, and afterwards, it felt like chickenpox mixed with a third-degree burn, both of which I'd also had.

"It's a buck," the man said. "Seventy-five cents if you show me your tits."

Scarlett looked at him coldly. "I have made a covenant with mine eyes," she said. "How then could I gaze at a virgin? Job, 31:1."

"Damn," he said, offended. "I was only messing with you."

"Messing leads to trouble, and trouble leads to regrets," she said, and stabbed him in the eyeballs with her worst white light. She spilled a shower of purse-change into his bucket, and we went in.

"I'm not a virgin," she said, wiping her hand on her skirt. "But, Little Widows, that's what nasty is asking for. He may break out in boils next."

I had no doubt on that. Scarlett was not someone anyone should mess with.

The tent was dark inside. We sat down in folding chairs and stared at the curtains and the stage, a wooden platform with more fringe on it. There were a lot of people in the tent, most of Miracle's population, male category. Us three were the only girls, but no one bothered us about it. No one wanted to talk to us when we were together. They thought they might catch cult like catching flu.

Separately, we were no fuss to anyone, but when we walked down the main road, people crossed it, and anyone who stepped in our sister shadow shook himself. They weren't wrong. When we were together, we were scary on purpose. We were perfectly capable of being regular, but we didn't see the point. Regular might get us nabbed by some other cult, and we weren't in the market for culting. We worried someone would snatch us and then we'd be under the thumb of a plum stealer again. We weren't in the mood for any more of that. We wanted, ultimately, to be normal. As normal as we could be. We were interested in flush toilets and potato chips.

The curtains didn't open, but they started to move, the fringe bobbing around like horses on the gallop, and I leaned forward to check if I could see anyone's feet. This was the best I'd felt in months, since the rest of everyone went to heaven, and Reese and Scarlett felt pretty good too. They were on either side of me, and they each took one of my hands when the curtains shimmied up and the music started playing.

"Step right up," said someone, and a girl came out. No one stepped up, but I felt like stepping. The girl was tanned with braided black hair, and her yellow bikini stood out against her skin like it was made of sun. It was covered with fringe, and it jiggled like a haystack on a flatbed. She was not much older than we were, and in her hands, she had a basket.

"You wanna see the devil dance?" the girl asked the tent, and the tent stamped its feet. Lust in the air in here. We could smell it.

"Well, I'm not the devil," she said. "And I don't dance. I'm a geek."

Nobody stamped for that. No one was quite sure what to do. But beside me, I felt Scarlett smiling.

The girl set the basket on the ground and stalked around it. "Do you know what you're getting into? Do you know why you're here, Miracle? That the name of this little town?"

"Yes," I said, from the back row. "This here's Miracle."

Somebody shushed me, but they turned around, saw Scarlett and Reese, and stopped shushing.

"You ever seen a girl bite off someone's head?"

"No," I said.

"It's a dying art," said the girl casually, and then squatted down and pulled the top off the basket. I leaned forward.

She pulled out a chicken, and looked up at the audience as she put her teeth around its neck. I blinked. Three men got up and out of there. Everyone else stayed still, because there was no way she was going to do what she looked like she was going to do.

The chicken made a whirr, deep in its throat. She took her mouth off it, and it clucked.

"The feathers make it easier," she said. "The feathers make it feel like you're biting down on a pillow, like you're dreaming a great dream of heaven. But you don't want to see me kill a bird, do you, Miracle? I could eat a white dove flying midair. Sometimes, I hold a flock of sparrows in my mouth and spit them out one at a time. That's basic carnival shit. We're all better than that, aren't we? Today, I've got something special for you."

She put the chicken down and it tripped away, over the wood, shedding feathers. The bird had bells around its ankles. It pecked its way out into the audience, jingling and clucking.

She pulled on long yellow leather gauntlets. The Preacher'd thought that fighting angels might require falconry skills, so I knew what they were. She went back into the basket and brought something else out.

There was a quiet gasp in the tent, and then people started to mutter, because the thing she was holding wasn't possible.

"What the fuck is that?" someone said, and then someone else said it back, echoing like the tent had gone box canyon.

The pterodactyl had feathers, so that at first you might mistake it for a crow, but it wasn't. It had a pointy skull with a crest heading backward from it, and membranous wings, each one supported by a long, thorny finger. The feathers were the color of oil on asphalt. The girl held it tightly in her cupped hands, and it struggled slightly, making a high chitter. It had bright black eyes.

"That's a dinosaur," I said to Reese, and Reese said "yep," and Scarlett said "yep," and then we all folded our hands in our laps. It was real. It was a pterodactyl. We knew about dinosaurs. Heaven's Avengers had a book of all the different kinds and the kids got it for a treat sometimes. I'd had it to myself the whole first week I was Littlest Wife.

"This is one of our pterodactyls," the girl said, and looked into the audience, her painted eyebrows up. "Want to check if it's real? You. In the back. Get your hands here."

I was already halfway down the aisle. None of the men of Miracle wanted to touch a dinosaur. A few more were rushing right out, past Scarlett, looking longingly at her, the kind of girl they'd thought they were coming in here to see. They were on the way to carnival food. We'd smelled fried dough on the way in, and seen a cotton candy stand. I wondered if they thought the dinosaur was a lizard dressed up with fake wings. They acted like it would be more interesting to see a naked girl than an extinct reptile, but I'd seen a lot of naked girls in the fifty-wife bathhouse.

I wanted a world full of dinosaurs. I wanted the ground to shake.

"Touch it," she said.

I was on the stage beside her, looking at her fringe, at her hands in their yellow leather, and at the way they pinched into the little dinosaur's scales. She smelled like cigarettes and chocolate. Her lipstick was orange and drawn on with a sharp pencil, the bows of her lips extra pointy. I could see the glue for her fake eyelashes.

In her hands was something as perfect as she was. The pterodactyl was chicken-sized, almost exactly, its body the size of my palms put together, with wings about three feet in span. It was cold to the touch, like a snake, and its down was as soft as angora, but it didn't look like it had much in the way of brain. It did have a lot of teeth. It looked at me and opened its mouth.

"You're going to bite its head off?" I asked her.

"That's the show."

"But what if it's the last one on Earth?"

She beckoned me in and whispered in my ear, all the while shimmying her hips to give the audience something to see.

"We have a lot of them," she said. "They're common as chickens, if you know what you're looking for."

I looked up into the crowd and saw Reese and Scarlett looking back at me.

"Would you like to hold its neck in your teeth?" the girl asked me. The audience shifted uncomfortably. I could hear folding chairs creaking.

"That's one of the cult kids!" someone shouted from the back. Desperate, high voice, voice of an old man. "That's one of the girls that killed themselves! You don't want to give her a chance to kill something else or she'll go wild! They're all crazy from out there!"

"We didn't kill ourselves," Reese said, with dignity.

"Look at us," Scarlett said. "We're absolutely alive."

But both of them were standing up, Reese in her pink starched dress and Scarlett in her flowered curtain fabric. They looked intimidating up there, in the light, with the sawdust in the air. They looked like what the town thought we might be.

I already had the lizardy neck in my mouth, and the girl in the yellow bikini met my eyes and nodded. I bit down hard, and cold blood came into my throat, through the softness and the down, through the dinosaur wings. Rough scales. No resistance. It went limp between my teeth, and I stood in front of Miracle, in my best dress, biting a dinosaur.

I let go of it, and the headless pterodactyl took flight and did a circle around the tent, blood sputtering out like a sprinkler.

People screamed. Most of them were freaking and getting the hell out of the tent. I had no regrets.

The other two Sisters were already out of their seats and down to the stage. People were rushing out, and a grown man vomited, which annoyed me. I pulled some feathers out of my teeth. This was what I'd been trained for. This was what I'd imagined it might be like to fight an angel. We'd been raised for this kind of combat. Who knew what kinds of lizards populated heaven? Who knew that heaven hadn't already been colonized? The girl in yellow was grinning at me, and I wiped blood off my chin.

"That wasn't wise, Little Widow," said Scarlett, and sighed.

"She couldn't help it," said Reese. "You can't spend a life being trained to do battle and think she wouldn't do this." She turned to the carnival geek. "What do you want? You're not normal."

The dinosaur's body dropped out of the air and fell down at my feet. I looked down at the head in my hand and for a moment, it looked like a chicken. Then like a baby. Then like a pile of rubber and feathers. I could taste salt and tar. The prong at the back of its head was soft and malleable, like a rooster's comb.

"What kind of carnival is this?" said Scarlett, and the girl just looked at her.

"We heard about you three," the girl said. "That's why we're here."

"What did you hear?" asked Reese.

"Your people took over some contested land."

My mouth got dry. "Our people?"

"I'm from up there," said the girl in yellow. "I work for your mamas now." She didn't look like an angel. But what did we know? We'd been trained to kill angels, not to like them, and this girl was a girl I liked already.

"I'm Valerie," she said, and shook out her black braids. Her hair was as long as mine had been. "You want to join us?"

This was what we had dreaded. This was a recruitment. Why didn't I mind?

Reese had a very stiff spine. "I have a boyfriend here," she said.

"Do you want out of this town, Sister?" asked Valerie. "You do. It's written all over you. You don't care for him more than you care for yourself. Come help us out in heaven."

"Do you know the Preacher?" Scarlett asked her, suspicious. I was suspicious too. I'd come to the conclusion that Littlest Wife was nothing right. There was a social worker at the school who kept trying to hand me stuffed animals so we could talk about love.

"Know him?" Valerie said, and laughed. "We came down here for him, too. We have him in the back of the cargo truck with Rexie."

We stood there for a moment, in the sawdust, blinking.

This was how we found out that our father had not in fact suicided his way to heaven but had left his own soda undosed. This was how we learned that he'd taken off and stayed alive, letting the rest of Heaven's Avengers fight angels without him. Valerie took us to him.

* * * *

The cage was big, dark, and dirty, full of hay, and the Preacher looked up when Valerie brought us in.

"Sister," he said. "Sister and Sister."

We were quiet for a minute. There he was, worse for the wear, this old man in a dirty shirt with no cult. He'd lost his beard, and his face without it looked skinny and toothy. He looked like the pterodactyl, but not beautiful. I could see where the back of his head might be soft.

I thought about biting through his spine, putting my teeth in and shaking my head. I thought about a frenzy, me and the rest of the Little Widows. We could shred him limb from limb. We could spread his entrails over acres. We could tear him into tiny pieces and strew him about, a sacrifice, a religious act. We knew how to kill a man with the maximum amount of pain. Men were easier to kill than angels.

I heard Scarlett inhale. Normally, we would have sent white light, or I would've balanced some crystals on my hands and prayed the bars away. We were no longer normal.

"You bastard," Scarlett screamed and flew at the cage, rattling it. "You cowardly motherfucker!"

We'd always known how to swear. It was part of our training. We'd figured "damn it" might be useful in a land of the undamned.

"Murderer," Reese hissed, and poked him through the bars with the handle of a muck shovel.

The Preacher looked reduced.

"I didn't mean it," he whimpered. "I never wanted this gig. I inherited Heaven's Avengers from my papa. It was my legacy. What was I supposed to do? I didn't want to die, but dying was the deal."

I spat at him. A fleck of dinosaur blood hit his cheek.

Valerie was looking on in pride, I thought, and so I spat at my husband again.

"I'm not your wife anymore," I said. "Neither are they. No one gets to have that many wives. There's no prize like that in the actual world."

Something moved at the back of the Preacher's cage, and I saw a big orange eyeball open up. Even though I was me, I still felt part of my guts seize up.

"That there's Rexie," said Valerie casually. "She's roosting over a clutch."

The dinosaur clucked and moved her tiny arms a little, looking at the Preacher. I wondered if she was going to eat him. I felt less worried about myself than I might have. The cage looked strong, and the Tyrannosaurus in it looked sleepy.

"How many of those you got?" I asked her.

"Ten. We've been traveling in a caravan. The Preacher's in charge of mucking out their henhouses. Mission from above says we have to do some things to the Earth."

Rexie shuffled herself around. I could see a little heap of eggs underneath her. Her head was maybe ten feet long, and her ears were pinholes. Her fangs were as yellow as Valerie's gloves.

The Preacher looked pitiful beside her, and I was glad.

"It's not my fault, girls," he said. "*You're* alive, and that was all my doing. I saved you. I took mercy on the children. You gotta help me get out of here."

"What are the wages in heaven?" I asked Valerie.

"True believer," she said and grinned. "Room and board. But it's not bad up there."

"Was this a screw-up?" Scarlett asked. "You know dinosaurs are extinct, right?"

Valerie sighed. "The rules are complicated. Geekshow full of pterodactyls. Henhouse full of Rexes. Some of them wanted to come down, and this was how it had to be done."

"Even heaven doesn't have its shit together," Reese said, and rolled her eyes.

"Nowhere does," said Valerie. "But the new administration wanted to get in touch and give you the opt-in. Things are changing."

Even miracles were messes. We'd been helping the mess along since the suicide. We'd never have admitted it to anyone but each other, but we had some skills, the three of us together.

Out behind the carnival was the lake where everyone'd risen up and walked on the water back in 1913. It was a green-algae slime-covered pool, and theory went that it hadn't actually hosted a real miracle. Instead, the miracle had been lake overturn. Poison gases had asphyxiated the original swimming devoted and then brought their bodies back up from the bottom, perfectly preserved. There were photographs of them floating naked and pale after the limbic eruption. All those bodies stayed inviolate for a year, bobbing on top of the great green lake, and that was the everything of Heaven's Avengers. It was why we were where we were, who we were, and what we were. A bunch of dead people. Nobody ever rose, not really, but call it risen and you get worshippers in from all over.

People hallucinated here still, and the lake got the blame, those poisons pushing up into the air.

If the wives were in heaven—and I wondered for a moment about the Rexes; there was something about the look of them that reminded me of my mothers—they'd won, but I wasn't sure I wanted to go up there. I didn't mind being cultless. I liked life among the living.

We joined hands, me, Reese, and Scarlett. We were sisters and wives. We were widows.

"Did you know chickens used to be a remedy for black plague?" Reese said. Reese had worked in the infirmary. She knew a lot about bad ways to heal things. "You'd pluck a chicken's ass and strap it to the bubo, and then the sick person and the chicken would just walk around together."

"Did it work?" I asked, kind of knowing the answer.

"The chicken would get replaced until the chicken and the patient both died. You know what I like about the modern world, Natalie? You know what I like about it, Scarlett? Vaccinations and antibiotics."

"Me too," said Scarlett. "I don't mind being alive."

"We have to vote on him," I said. I had another look into the hen cage and saw Rexie put a claw out in the direction of the Preacher, her mouth opening a little. The eggs shook beneath her, and her orange eyes shone. The Preacher moaned.

WHAT THE #@&% IS THAT?

"Honor thy father," he whined.

"And thy mother. You poisoned the soda," Reese said. "You don't deserve honoring. What if they weren't in heaven? What if they'd just died?"

We thought about that for a moment. The real thoughts. The way our mothers' bodies had been put in the high school gym. They way they'd been covered with sheets. The way the smoke smelled in Miracle, and the way no one cared. The way the town got swarmed with evening news for two weeks.

The way we'd been brought up to take everything down.

No one cares about dead mothers. No one cares about dead women, period; that's what we learned when our cult suicided. The women weren't on the news. Reese's boyfriend was on the news because he was good at sports. Everyone just thought the women were dumb as rocks to fall in with a person such as the Preacher. But we weren't dumb. We were adopted and born into this. We were daughters and wives. We were supposed to be killed, but we knew how to kill, too. Vulnerable softnesses. Skulls and bones.

We were just little girls—that's what people thought about us, the Sisters Stuart. Give any of us a drawing of the human body, and we could map the veins, the likely points for access. Give any of us a list of plants, and we could tell you what the poisons were and how to mix them. We could give you a dose of goldenseal that'd make you hallucinate walking on the surface of a dead green lake, rising up and diving down through the green mire and into the muck, over and over, for the rest of your life. We had kill skills; that's what the Preacher called them. Did we want to use them? Did we want to be known for that for the rest of our lives? We had other plans. Killing wasn't the only thing to do on Earth.

Reese shook her shoulders back and looked at the Preacher. "You're shit out of luck. I'm going to be a pilot."

"I'm going to run the country," said Scarlett. "You're dead officially, and unofficially, you're in a cage with something hungry."

"Join us," said Valerie, but she looked only at me. "Come up to heaven."

My sisters rippled with white light. It wasn't bunk. I didn't want the crystals and the prayers anymore. I didn't want to be good. I wanted to war. I wanted to kill. But I didn't want to die to do it.

"When I was seven," I said to my sisters, "and I was made Littlest Wife, do you remember what happened?"

"All the chickens died of pox," said Reese.

"All the eggs were full of two-headed chicks," said Scarlett.

"And you stood in the middle of the henhouse, with all them dead, and took out the wishbones with your pocketknife," said Reese.

It was a legendary moment in Heaven's Avengers history.

I was a miracle. I was a sign from somewhere that everything would be okay, that we were winning. I was only a kid, but I cut and cut.

I opened up my purse and showed them my collection. I hadn't broken them. They were precious. I had forty-seven. I fetched up the dead pterodactyl and sliced into its sternum with my pearl-handled blade, and within a moment, I had forty-eight. There was a ritual to do. I brought out a packet of matches and a little bit of tobacco. I set a small fire and sprinkled the tobacco on, and then I started breaking bones and wishing.

"Gotta get to the end sometime," said Reese. "Gotta call in the wishes, real and fake."

"Good girl," said Scarlett, and smiled at me.

"It's time to get our vehicle," Reese said, and walked out from the circus grounds, her pale hair shining in the backlights. I was here, breaking bones and making wishes on them, and none of my wishes were pretty. Scarlett took one end and broke a wish with me. Her eyes were shut and so were mine, and we felt that bone give. All bones will give if you ask them.

I looked at the Preacher. We were here together because of him, but that didn't mean he was a good thing. I whistled and the orange eyes opened. Back in the dark, I could see other cages.

Scarlett whistled too. Other orange eyes. The eyes of the hens. We'd both worked in chicken houses. We knew what hens were like. We knew what mothers were like in general.

In the cage where the Preacher was, Rexie shifted. The man was seventy years old and full of sham.

"Sisters," he said, in his supplicating voice. "Sisters of Heaven's Avengers."

"Daughters of a dead guy," said Scarlett. "Wives of a dead guy."

Rexie poked her head out, bending the bars. All over the carnival grounds, dinosaurs emerged from their cages, tottering, that high-kneed bird walk, their chests full of wishbone. Behind us, the lake simmered and a bunch of 1913 ghosts trotted around on the surface of the water. The Preacher looked scared.

The dinosaurs started to tromp harder, thunder-footing, and the Preacher looked even more scared.

"I'm just a simple man," he said, and then tried to make a run for it. Valerie lassoed him and dragged him back by his ankle, him scrabbling all the way.

"And I'm just a cult kid," I said. "You set your henhouse on fire. You made some bad mistakes."

We could hear the humming of a crop duster now, and Scarlett and I whistled louder at the dinosaurs. All over the grounds, pterodactyls pecked and Rexes stamped their feet, and the eggs from the henhouses wobbled and shook. I thought about what would hatch.

Everything. The thought made me so happy, I could hardly stand it. I wanted to yelp and whoop and run around, but I stayed still.

The surface of the lake trembled, and out there in all their glory, ghosts danced on the green, victims of tremors, like these dinosaurs had been back when.

The crop duster landed beside me, Scarlett, and the angel in the yellow bikini. I could see Reese in the pilot's seat, and I said, "Heaven's just a plot of land."

The angel looked at me and grinned.

"I might stay down here myself," Valerie said. "We've got no monopoly on good these days. I got sent like somebody's secretary, down here to recruit. I was thinking I might want to be a truck driver. Maybe I'll run into you out there."

"Might do," I said, and shook her hand. She was an angel in a bathing suit, and I was a kid in a bloody dress. I looked at the rest of the feathery Rexes and figured angels didn't look like most people thought.

Reese leaned out the window of the plane and beckoned us inside; we hopped up, me and Scarlett.

"Little Widow," Scarlett said. "Little Widow."

The Preacher was squatting, a Rex standing over him, looking at him with her head tilted.

Scarlett hung out her window as the crop duster took off, down a little runway in the dirt, past the dinosaurs, and up into the sky. The dinosaurs started to dance, all the hens of the world, a circle of them stepping high, clawfooted, their feathers standing up.

I watched the Preacher get snatched up into the teeth of Rexie, and I watched her rooster come running, a gleaming, green-feathered gigantic. The Preacher's head was in Rexie's mouth, and his body went into the mouth of Rexie's mate. We watched as they wishboned him, tearing him into two sections, one bigger than the other. We watched the angels make certainties of his bones.

The dinosaurs surged up in a roaring wave of feathers and scales, stampeding, a henhouse from heaven, and maybe they were our avenging mamas and maybe they were not. Maybe they were just heaven's livestock. But down here, they'd been livestock too, and so were we. We didn't truck with that anymore. We weren't for breeding. We weren't for feeding. We were our own flying things.

From the cockpit of the crop duster, the three Sisters Stuart smiled as we flew just over the surface of the Earth, low enough to see it, high enough to consider our futures.

"Little Widows," I said, with solemnity. We weren't broken. We were human like everyone else was human. "Now's the time for us to bless the dead."

"Bless them," said Reese.

"Bless them," said Scarlett, and we took each other's hands and blessed.

Below us, Rexes ran rampant, a beautiful flurry of greens and blues and reds, flapping and strutting, eggs hatching in the dirt.

"Bless the dead and keep them dead," I said.

I dropped the head of the pterodactyl out the window, a spinning thing like an axe blade, twisting beaked and toothed to plant itself in the corn.

No one living had ever heard dinosaurs singing before, their trilling lark roars, their falcon wails, but they heard them now, these heavenly lizards, these glorious angels closest to God.

Out we went, my sisters and I in our little crop duster, flying together, us three, up and up, into the clear sky, and out of Miracle.

Out went the dinosaurs, a flock of them from our old town, for a hundred hungry miles, their bellies full of meat cows, sheep, and one old man with no wives left to his name. They ran over blood-drenched ground, singing as they went.

THE BAD HOUR

CHRISTOPHER GOLDEN

The hiss of the hydraulic doors dragged Kat Nellis from an uneasy sleep and she came awake with a thin gasp of hope. Her neck ached from the way she'd been huddled in the corner of the bus seat, her skull canted against the window, but at least the dream had come to an end.

The same fucking dream.

It wasn't an every-night sort of thing, but frequent enough that whenever she went a few days without having it, she began to feel not relief but a creeping sort of dread. Ironic, because what made the dream verge on a nightmare was that same feeling, the inescapable knowledge that something terrible was about to happen.

The dreams were always of Iraq, of the time she'd spent escorting convoys along the worst stretch of highway in the world. In the dream, she would hold her breath as the truck rumbled over ruined pavement, waiting for a tire to smash down on top of a mine or for a broken-down car to explode with a planted IED, or for an old woman or a child on the side of the road to step aside to reveal a suicide bomber. Kat had done hideous things in the war—things that would haunt her waking hours for the rest of her life—but when she slept, it was the dread of the unknown, of *waiting*, that plagued her dreams.

"Come on, honey," the bus driver called back to her. "If you're gettin' off, this is the place. Wish I could get you closer."

Kat stretched her stiff muscles and felt her joints pop as she stood. She'd kept fit in the years since she had left the army, but there were some wounds the human body could heal but never forget. Down in your bones, you would remember. Blown fifteen feet by a roadside explosion, she had survived with little more than some scrapes and bruises and a wrenched back. Kat felt grateful that she still had all of her working parts, that she hadn't been closer to the explosion, but her back had never been the same. She had no shrapnel, no bullets lodged in her body, but her spine always ached, and in warm weather, she had a tinny buzz in her brain that kept her company everywhere she went.

It was autumn now, though. No more buzzing.

She slipped her backpack over her shoulder and walked to the front of the bus. Passengers studied her curiously, wondering why she would be getting off in the middle of nowhere. A seventyish woman in a head scarf squinted at her, and Kat smiled in response, unoffended by the scrutiny.

"How far is it from here?" she asked when she reached the front of the bus.

The October morning breeze blew in through the open door and a man in the first row muttered something, half asleep, and tugged his jacket tighter around his throat as he nestled back in his seat.

"Gotta be eight or ten miles," said the driver. He took out a handkerchief and blew his big red nose, then sniffled as he tucked the rag away. "Sorry I can't run you down there."

"No worries. I could do with the walk."

She stepped down onto the road and the door closed behind her. The bus rumbled away, the morning sun hitting the windows at an angle that turned them black. Kat inhaled deeply, calming herself. The bus was on its way to Montreal, but she had gotten off about twenty miles south of the Canadian border. She stood on the side of Route 118 and glanced around at mountains covered in evergreens and patches of orange and red fall foliage. Most of the leaves that were going to fall this far north had already fallen.

October, Kat thought. She'd grown up in Montana, and though the landscape looked different, the chilly breeze and the slant of autumn light made Vermont feel like home.

Across from the spot where the bus had dropped her, a narrow road led through the trees. The morning sky might be blue, but the trees cast that street into dusky shadow. No sign identified this as King's Hollow Road, and the bus had already pulled away. No way to confirm her location with the driver. A quick check of her phone confirmed her expectation of crappy cell service out here in the middle of mountainous nowhere.

Kat pushed her fingers through her short blond hair, rubbed the sleep from her eyes, and set off into the shadows.

For the first few miles, she doubted she had found King's Hollow Road at all. She passed several farms and spotted a handful of people collecting pumpkins from a field. No cars went by, but she did pass two narrow roads heading off to the southwest. If the bus driver had left her in the right place, this road should take her right into Chesbro, Vermont, if the town still existed.

Not a town, she reminded herself. Chesbro was officially a village, or it had been the last time anyone had noticed there had been a village at the end of King's Hollow Road. She'd had no trouble finding its location on the Internet, confirming its existence on Google Earth and studying three-year-old satellite photos of its small village center. But her Internet searching had turned up virtually nothing else—no local newspaper, no listing of obituaries. Nothing of note had transpired there in the past forty years.

At the bus station in St. Johnsbury, she had found only one person who could tell her anything about the town, an old man who ran the kiosk that sold candy and magazines. The skinny fellow had stroked his beard and told her that there'd been a mill in Chesbro once upon a time, but it had been closed for ages and most of the locals had drifted away. That sort of thing happened more often than people knew. Kat understood that, but the only address she had for Ray Lambeau was in Chesbro. If she intended to find him, that was where she had to begin.

An hour after she'd set out from where the bus had dropped her, Kat rounded a corner and came to a stop on the leaf-strewn pavement. Half a dozen massive concrete blocks had been laid across the road and onto the soft shoulder. The blocks on the left and right had steel hooks set into the concrete, and heavy chains looped from the hooks to enormous pine trees on either side of the road. A dirty signpost reading STOP HERE FOR DELIVERIES had been plinked with bullets, some of which had punched right through the metal. There was no other hint that Chesbro lay ahead—only the certainty that whatever might be down that road, outsiders weren't welcome.

"Fuck it," Kat said, moving between two of the concrete blocks.

She had spent her life going places she wasn't welcome.

The pavement over the next five miles was broken and rutted, weeds growing up from the cracks. Nobody had cut back the trees in years and they had spread into a canopy over the road. Most of the people in the region seemed to have forgotten Chesbro, and the story she'd heard of the whole place being abandoned seemed more plausible with every step. Then she crested a rise in the road and paused to stare at the little village that lay before her.

A white church sat on one end of an idyllic village green with a bandstand at the center. On the other end of the green was a main street with brick buildings, little shops, town hall, and a little diner on a corner. There was even a little theater with a marquee overhanging the sidewalk, the sort of place she had only ever seen in old movies. If not for the large gray building that sat on the edge of a narrow river farther up the road, it would have looked like a New Englander's idea of Heaven. In contrast to her expectations, the village seemed well cared-for, certainly not abandoned.

As she walked toward the green, Kat felt her pulse quicken. Chesbro might not look empty, but it certainly felt that way. She passed several large houses and a brick building that might once have been a bank. Unsettled by the silence, Kat had begun holding her breath, but now she heard the squeak of hinges and saw motion in her peripheral vision. She swung around to see a bearded man in green flannel and blue jeans exiting Chesbro Hardware with a small plastic bag in one hand. The other held a can of paint.

The man's eyes went wide and he dropped the can, which plunked to the ground. His reaction—as if *she* were the ghost—struck her as odd, but not nearly as odd as the way he closed his eyes and took several deep breaths. He pressed his fingers against his wrist as if checking his pulse. When he opened his eyes, he had a wary smile on his face.

"You gave me quite a fright," he said, picking up the paint can and starting toward her. "Looks like I startled you as well."

"That's all right," Kat found herself saying. "I'm guessing you don't get a lot of visitors around here."

The man picked up the paint can, shifted it into the hand holding the plastic bag, and put out his free hand to shake.

"Elliot Bonner," he said. "And that's one way of putting it. If you came down King's Hollow, I'd guess you know we haven't exactly laid out the welcome mat."

Kat shook his rough hand and introduced herself. She stood five foot nine, taller than the average woman, but Bonner was half a foot taller. Another day, somewhere else, she suspected she would have found him quite attractive, but something about the set of his eyes made her uneasy. Elliot Bonner looked worried.

"Sorry," she said. "I'm looking for someone and I guess I was too focused on that to pay much attention."

"Not too late to turn around," Bonner said quietly. "Not yet."

Kat frowned. "Are you being funny? 'Cause I've come a long way and maybe I'm too tired to get the joke."

The man laughed nervously. "Just joshing ya. Who are you looking for? Might be I can help."

"His name's Ray Lambeau. We served together in Iraq. We've been keeping in touch the old-fashioned way for a while, writing letters. Ray said there was no Internet and not much phone service up here. But I haven't heard from him in six months or so, and that didn't seem right. So, here I am."

"Ray," Bonner said, as if the name tasted like shit in his mouth. He sighed, and his smile vanished. "Listen, miss—"

"Kat," she said. "Or Sergeant Nellis."

Bonner narrowed his eyes. Looked her up and down like he was sizing her up, wondering if he could take her in a fight. Kat had seen that look a hundred times before.

"I'm gonna make a suggestion, Sergeant," Bonner said, and he pointed to a split-rail fence on the other side of the road. "If you go and sit there and wait for me, I'll run over to the diner up the street and get you something to eat, packed up all nice for your trip back to the main road. On me. Trust me when I say that accepting my hospitality and my advice would be the smartest decision you ever make."

Something in Bonner's eyes, a frightened animal skittishness, reminded Kat of Iraq in the worst way. The guy felt to her like an IED packed into a broken-down truck on the side of the road, ready to explode if you nudged him wrong.

"I guess I'll find Ray myself," she said, and strode toward the village green.

The diner seemed like the most obvious place to start. This late in the morning, there wouldn't be many customers, but there had to be at least one server and a cook. In a tiny community like this, odds were good they would know pretty much everyone in the village.

Bonner caught up with her as she stepped onto the green, still carrying his purchases from the hardware store.

"Hold up, Sergeant," he said tersely. "You need to listen."

"I don't think so."

An elderly woman came out of some kind of clothing shop a couple of doors up from the diner. She had a fall knit scarf around her neck, and when she spotted Kat and Bonner, she clasped it to her chest like a church lady clutching her pearls. As Kat started to cross the street, she could see the old woman's lips moving in a silent mutter. Fearful, the woman pushed her way back into the shop and Kat heard her calling out to someone inside.

"Damn it," Bonner murmured as he caught her arm from behind.

Kat spun, tore her arm free, and stood ready for a fight. "You want to keep your hands off me."

Bonner held up his hands and exhaled, uttering a small laugh. "I don't want trouble—"

"I didn't come here to make any," Kat said, studying his face. "I'm just looking for my friend."

Bonner's mouth pinched up like he'd been sucking a lemon. He exhaled loudly. "I know how crazy this must seem, but you have to leave right now. For your own safety."

It was Kat's turn to laugh. "Are you threatening me?"

"Please calm down—"

"I'm plenty calm," she said, and meant it. In combat, she'd earned a reputation as an ice queen. "When I'm not calm, you'll know it."

"Lot of that going around," Bonner said.

Kat cocked her head in confusion. Then she heard voices behind her and turned back toward the diner. A waitress in an apron had come outside with a silver-haired man in a brown suit. Other people had come onto the street, and as she glanced around, she noticed a pair of teenagers crossing the village green in her direction. They paused at the bandstand and draped themselves over its railings in classic American teenager poses. Studying her, like there was a show about to start.

"Get her out of here, Elliot," the waitress called from in front of the diner.

Kat could only laugh. What was wrong with these people?

"Look!" she snapped. "I'm trying to find Ray Lambeau. If he's here, I just want to talk to him. If you hate outsiders so much, I'm happy to be on my way as soon as I've talked to Ray."

Bonner grabbed her by the backpack and shoulder, turning her toward the road out of town. "I'm sorry, but you just need to—"

Kat twisted and pulled him toward her even as she hammered a fist into his face. Bonner staggered backward, arms flailing, and went down on his ass.

"I told you not to put your hands on me," she said, a trickle of ice along her spine.

Bonner's lips curled back in anger as he scrambled to his feet. "You little bitch," he said, stalking toward her, fists raised, "all I wanted to do was—"

She stepped in close and hit him with a quick shot to the gut, followed up with a left to the temple, and then a knee in the balls. Bonner roared as he went down.

"Kat, no!" a voice cried out.

She turned to see Ray Lambeau running across the green. Her first thought was that he looked like shit, pale and too thin and with dark circles under his eyes.

"Sarge, please," Ray said, rushing up to her and grabbing her arm. "You don't know what you're doing. You can't be here."

He started hustling her away from Bonner and she let him, startled and hurt by his reaction to her arrival. Her backpack felt much heavier all of a sudden, and she looked over at the hardware store and the beginning of King's Hollow Road and realized that Ray was propelling her back the way she'd come, just the way Bonner had. Corporal Ray Lambeau wanted her out of his hometown.

Behind her, Kat heard cussing and shouts of alarm.

"Kat—" Ray began, his breath warm at her ear.

She shook loose and turned to stare at him, saw the fear in his eyes. "You're all insane. . . ."

"Go," he pleaded with her, shaking his head in frustration as he glanced toward the village green. "Please, just go."

More shouts came from that direction, but she kept her gaze fixed on Ray. His eyes had begun to moisten and he seemed to realize it the same moment she did. Letting out a breath, he struggled to keep his emotions in check the same way Bonner had. Then they both heard a clanking of something metal, followed by the unmistakable sound of someone cocking a rifle.

Ray lowered his head. "Kat, *please* . . ."

She'd been so wrapped up in her hurt and irritation that she had focused entirely on him. Now she turned toward the spectators again and saw that they had lost all interest in the spectacle of her little drama with Ray. They had surrounded Bonner. The man hunched over and a keening wail began to issue from his lips. He dragged his fingers through his hair and tugged at his beard and bent over further, arms folding inward.

One of the spectators stepped forward, a rifle hung in his arms.

"Jesus," Kat whispered.

The teenagers who'd been loitering by the bandstand dragged a net across the grass, its edges weighted with cast-iron pans and a hodgepodge of other metal objects.

All these people had wanted her to leave. For the first time, she wished she had.

"Ray?" Kat said, taking several steps back onto the village green.

People were talking to Bonner the way they would talk to a toddler holding a gun, or a loose dog with a penchant for biting. Nobody wanted to go near him, but the guy with the rifle took a bead and then nudged the teenagers forward.

"Listen—" Kat said.

At the sound of her voice, Bonner whipped around to snarl at her.

She froze, her mind trying to make sense of what she saw. Bonner's mouth opened impossibly wide. Rows of needle-sharp black teeth glistened in the morning light, viscous saliva drooling onto his beard. His skin had turned a bruise-yellow leather, run through with thick crevices and dry cracks in the flesh. His eyes were sickly orange and they fixed on her as he opened those deadly jaws and hissed wetly.

Jaw slack, body numb, Kat flinched and reached for her hip, where she would've had a gun if she were still in the army. Her fingers closed on empty air and she blinked, understanding that all of this was real.

As Bonner took a step toward her, Kat stumbled back.

"Ray," she mumbled, "what the fuck is that?"

Bonner leaped at her. Kat twisted out of the way, let him sail right by, and punched him in the back of the head. As people shouted, she followed through with a blow to the kidney. Ray called to her to get back, but she kicked the back of Bonner's leg and his knee buckled. She felt the familiar sensation of ice sliding into her veins, the calm that always came over her on the battlefield.

She drove a fist into Bonner's skull, then pistoned her arm back for another blow. He turned on one knee and lunged, tackled her around the waist, and drove her to the grass. Kat hit hard, all the air bursting from her lungs. Bonner threw back his head and roared in savage triumph, and she saw those black teeth again. Pink spittle hung in webs from his jaws and dripped onto her face. Kat bucked against him, kidney-punched him again, but Bonner slapped her arms away.

The crack of a rifle shot echoed across the village green and off the main street façades. Bonner jerked. Blood sprayed as the bullet punched through his right side and kept going. Enraged and off-balance, the berserker turned toward the man with the rifle. Kat bucked harder, reached up, and threw him off, scrambling away as Bonner roared again, trying to recover.

The teenage boys were there with the net. They threw it over him and Kat wanted to shout at them, thinking no way could a simple net hold a man so monstrously strong, even with the metal weights tied around its circumference. But Bonner cried out and smacked against the ground. He thrashed once and then was still, wide-eyed and panting like a dog, as if something about the cast-iron pans and other weights caused him pain.

A second passed as they all stared.

Kat turned on Ray. "What the *fuck?* Shit like this does not happen in the real world."

Ray put his hands out. "Kat, calm down—"

"Don't tell me to calm down! Talk to me about this!" She gestured toward Bonner, netted and moaning on the grass. "This isn't just a freak-out. Look at the guy's face! Look at his skin!"

In combat, her ability to remain calm could be eerie. But with the fight over and the reality of what she'd just seen sinking in, panic began to unravel her. Kat could practically feel her self-control shattering.

Ray approached her, hands still up. "Kat, stop. Just breathe and listen to my voice—"

"I'm listening!" She looked over at Bonner again, glanced at the bloody fissures in his leathery skin, and saw the murderous look in his eyes. She tried to match this visage up with the man who had walked out of the hardware store with a can of paint.

Ray put his hands on her arms. "Kat—"

She recoiled from his touch. "What is he? What is . . ."

Kat felt it then. Panic, fear, and anger had all been roiling inside her, and now the anger surged upward in a wave of malice. She snapped around to glare at Ray and her lips peeled back in a snarl. His eyes widened in alarm and he stepped backward, but she pursued him, swinging a fist. Ray tried to block, but too slow. She struck him in the cheek and heard the bone crack, then followed up with a left to the gut that sent him reeling across the grass.

She ran her tongue over her teeth and felt their sharpness . . . and their number. Horror seized her. Thick drool ran out over her bottom lip and dribbled down her chin. Raising her hands to lunge at him, she saw that her skin had darkened and split, and she understood, but Kat could do nothing to stop herself. She grabbed a fistful of Ray's hair, and she laughed as she dragged one yellow fingernail across his cheek, opening up a bloody furrow.

When the gunshot rang out and the bullet punched through her back, she felt only relief.

* * * *

Kat woke with a groan. Her throat felt parched and she ached all over. When she shifted on the hard cot, bright pain seared a place on her back just below her left shoulder blade. She rolled onto her side and opened her eyes to see metal bars and flickering fluorescent lights.

A jail cell.

She shifted on the cot and saw Ray leaning against a desk out in the room beyond her cell. *Village jail,* she thought. *Police chief's office, one cell. Fucking Mayberry.* Sitting up, she felt like she might pass out again, but she forced herself to sit there and she stared at Ray . . . at this man who had been her friend under fire. More than a friend.

"It started in Iraq," he said quietly.

"Say again?"

Ray gestured toward the door and whatever lay beyond it.

"That. Out there," he said. "It started in Iraq. Since then, I've done some research. Different stories come from different parts of the world, Greece in particular, but the name translates pretty much the same in Arabic as in Greek. Both call it 'the Bad Hour.'"

Kat tried to clear her head. "Are you making zero sense or am I just not—"

"You remember the day I lost it?"

She stared at him, a hard knot in her gut. Images slid through her mind of a shattered door and a dead family, a grandmother with her head caved in, two little bloodstained boys full of bullet holes, and a grief-mad mama shot for trying to take revenge. Kat had seen worse in her time in Iraq, but not at the hands of a friend, someone she trusted. After that day, it had been weeks before she had let Ray touch her again.

"I remember."

"That wasn't the only time something like that happened. Just the only time you were there to see it." His voice was a guilty rasp. "A couple of days before the incident you remember, Harrison picked me for a squad to search a little enclave on the outskirts of Haditha for insurgents. Local informants told us the place was off-limits—nobody ever went there and nobody ever left. Merchants brought supplies up from the city and left them at a drop point. People from the enclave came out to get them after the delivery men had gone."

Kat blinked, alert now, remembering her walk into Chesbro and the sign she'd encountered at the roadblock. The parallel was not lost on her.

"I don't know if we got intel that insurgents were hiding there or if we just figured what better place for them to hide than somewhere considered off-limits, but we went in hard," he continued.

Ray stared at her, his eyes so damn sorry. She remembered those eyes well, even that look, and she hated him for making her remember how she'd felt on those dark nights in the desert.

"What you saw out there with Bonner?" he said. "We saw it with everyone in the enclave. Killed every last one of them because once they went rabid like that, killing them was the only way we could stop them. When it was over, Harrison told us the rest of what the locals had fed him, the story about the enclave and the Bad Hour. It's like an infection. You let yourself get too angry or too emotional in general, and it just . . . takes over. The people around Haditha said the Bad Hour was a demon, that once it touched you, it stayed with you always, ready to take over if you couldn't control yourself."

"Bullshit," she whispered, the weight of the story crushing her. If she had heard about it before coming here, she'd never have believed it. But now?

"They also said it was contagious," Ray went on. He closed his eyes and breathed evenly, and she recognized the effort he made to stay calm. Remembered him doing the same earlier, and Bonner as well.

The ice in her gut grew heavier. Kat stood and grabbed the bars of her cell. "Let me out of here, Ray."

"In a while."

She smashed an open palm against one of the bars of the cell. "Let me out, asshole. I can't stay here!"

Ray pushed away from the desk and walked toward the cell. He stopped a few feet from the bars and studied her with those I'm-sorry eyes.

"You can't leave, Kat. We'll let you out in a little while, but the Bad Hour's in you now. Harrison's squad killed everyone in that enclave, but we brought it out with us. Some of the guys in that squad are dead. Others are probably out there infecting people the way I did in Chesbro. I didn't mean to. Even after the times I lost it in Iraq, I chalked it up to the war. PTSD, maybe. But once I came home . . . once I was in one place long enough . . . I started to see it happen to other people."

Kat remembered Bonner's face, the way he'd changed, and the strength and rage that had filled her when she had turned on Ray. Then she remembered the day she had seen him go berserk, the day he'd killed that family.

"When you lost it, you didn't look like Bonner," she said. "Yeah, you were a fucking lunatic, but—"

"At first, none of us looked any different when it came on. The way I've got it figured, once the Bad Hour takes root in a place, it gets stronger. The people in the enclave looked like Bonner when they went rabid—"

"But I . . . This *just* happened to me. If you don't look like that at first . . ."

Ray grabbed one of the bars. "I'm explaining this badly. It's the Bad Hour that's getting stronger, taking root. Maybe it's one demon or maybe it's a bunch of little ones, like parasites, but it gets stronger. Doesn't matter if it's your first time giving in to it . . . it's the strength of the Hour that matters. Not always an hour, either. The stronger it gets, the longer it can hold on to you."

Kat laughed softly, but it wasn't really a laugh at all.

She rested her forehead against the bars. Impossible. All of this was simply insanity. For a moment, she wondered if she had fallen asleep on that northbound bus and still sat there, dreaming with her skull resting against the window. But that was mere fantasy.

"What you're talking about . . . it can't be," she said softly.

Ray wrapped his fingers around hers, him on one side of those bars and her on the other. "I've seen the way you can rein in your fear, Kat. You can do this. You have to."

Kat began to tremble. She pressed her lips together, trying to stay in control, but tears welled in her eyes.

"You don't know what you're saying. I have to . . ."

Ray squeezed her hand sharply, and she snapped her head up and stared at him.

"Stop. You know what will happen," he said. *"Calm down."*

Kat pulled her hand away and wiped at her eyes. She nodded, took a shuddery breath, and straightened her spine. Another deep breath. Terrified of the Hour taking her over again, that madness . . . She didn't want to believe, but she could not erase from her mind the things she had seen. The things she had felt.

"I'm all right," she told him firmly. "But you can't keep me here. I have to go home, Ray."

"Kat—"

"I have a daughter."

He frowned, staring at her.

Kat inhaled. Exhaled. Felt that familiar battlefield chill spread through her. This was an altogether different sort of combat.

"I have to leave," she said, "but I get it, Ray. And I'll come back."

Ray held onto the bars from the outside as if worried he might fall over if he let go. "How old is she? Your girl?"

Kat embraced the combat chill in her bones. Met his gaze. "She's four."

"Four," he said, a dull echo.

"I wanted to raise her myself," Kat said. "You were my friend, but I'd seen what kind of man you could be. What kind of father you might be. I thought it would be better—"

"You started writing to me," Ray said, gaze pinning her to the floor inside her cell. "Then when I stopped replying, you came looking. If you didn't want me to know—"

Kat approached the bars again. This time, it was she who put her hands over his.

"At first, I just wanted to reconnect. I guess I figured someday I'd tell you. Then later . . . I needed to talk to you," Kat said. Breathing evenly. "Her baby teeth started falling out at the beginning of this year. That's early. *Really* early. The new ones have been growing in ever since . . ."

She breathed. Steadied herself.

"Tell me," Ray said through gritted teeth, and she saw that he was doing it too. The both of them just breathing. Slow and steady. In control.

But they couldn't stay in control every second of every day. Not forever. Nobody could do that. Especially not a toddler.

"The new teeth are coming in and she has too many of them, Ray. They're tiny things, sharp and black, and there are too many—"

"Kat, no."

She let the cold fill her, stared into his eyes.

"And, Ray," Kat said. "Your little girl has such a temper."

WHAT IS LOST,
WHAT IS GIVEN AWAY

JOHN LANGAN

I

My ten-year high school reunion, held in the fall of 1997, was a disappointment. This should not have been a terrible surprise, but I'm afraid I had bought into the scenarios played out in endless movies and TV shows, the ones where all the old animosities, the divisions between jock and nerd, popular and outcast, are put aside, and the former classmates discover that their similarities outweigh their differences—as, of course, they always had. What I found instead was that a decade had not been sufficient time to alter much beyond hairlines and waistbands. I learned other things, too.

The reunion was a two-night affair, with an informal meet-and-greet at the bar of the Castle, a local restaurant, on Friday, and a formal dinner at the Poughkeepsie Tennis Club on Saturday. In between, those who wanted to rekindle their school spirit brighter still could attend Our Lady of Fatima's homecoming game Saturday afternoon. Starting Friday, I had the sense that the weekend was not going to live up to my hopes for it. For one thing, no one recognized me. To be fair, I had changed more than anyone else there. When I graduated, I was six feet tall, one hundred and fifty or sixty pounds if I was wearing a heavy coat. I had gained another sixty pounds in the intervening years, as well as a beard that was the same light brown my hair had darkened to in my early twenties. None of my old classmates had deviated as dramatically from their former appearances, so it was perhaps to be expected that they would not know me. They were not prepared to.

All the same, I found this disconcerting. I walked past people paired and grouped as they had been in the halls of Fatima, and their gazes slid over me without catching on anything. While I had not been the class president, or captain of the football team, or even the class clown, I had been in the drama club, acting the part of the villainous Jonathan in the senior class production of *Arsenic and Old Lace*; I had lettered in spring track (hurdles) twice; I had played an active role in discussions and debates in our English, social studies, and religion classes. Especially since our graduating class numbered one hundred and thirty-two, I assumed I had made some depth of impression on the people I had spent four years with. This did not appear to be the case.

After an hour of sitting at the bar, nursing a Corona and watching the room fill with people exchanging hugs, handshakes, and backslaps, I decided to leave my stool and introduce myself to my former classmates. Standing directly in front of them, I extended my right hand, calling them by their names and reminding them of mine. Yet even so direct an approach did not yield the look of pleased recognition, the firm handshake, the repetition of my name followed by an exclamation of pleasure. Instead, the men and women I greeted took my hand hesitantly, their faces confused, as if, while familiar, my name was not one they could immediately place. After uttering a platitude about how great it was to see me, they resumed the conversations whose breaks had allowed me to make my introduction. The forty-five minutes or so it took to complete my circuit of the room left me disheartened, depressed, and back at the bar. I had come on my own, so there was no point to ordering anything stronger than another beer. I poked the wedge of lime jutting from the bottle's neck down into it, and toasted my reflection in the bar's mirror. *Here's to obscurity.*

To my left, a voice said my name. Mood instantly lightened, I turned on my stool, and saw Joel Martin—*Mr. Martin*, I couldn't help thinking. Junior year chemistry, senior year physics, assistant coach of the boys' junior varsity football and varsity basketball teams. Disgraced in the closing days of my senior year for an affair with Sinead McGahern, one of my classmates, which left her pregnant and him out of a job at which he had been a favorite. He looked terrible. His hair, thinning when I had sat in his classroom, had largely deserted his head, except for a few spots here and there where he had allowed it to grow long. The lenses of his glasses were scratched and scored, opaque in some places. The heavy five o'clock shadow that had always darkened his jaw had thickened to a heavy beard, which he appeared to have maintained without the benefit of a mirror. Never a big man to begin with—I would have put his height at 5'5", his weight at one forty—he seemed smaller inside his shapeless black suit, shrunken. A martini glass, full, stood on the bar in front of him.

I was stunned. In the weeks and months after graduation, Joel Martin's situation had gone from scandal to ongoing catastrophe, ending with him in jail, first in Argentina, then locally. During my first couple of years of college, when I still met some of my high school friends at winter and summer breaks, the latest chapter in the ongoing saga of Mr. Martin and Sinead McGahern was among our immediate topics of conversation. As his actions had progressed—or declined—from the questionable to the out-and-out criminal, so had my mental image of him transformed from intense, affable science teacher to something darker, a seducer, a humiliated and desperate father. To encounter him here, looking different, yes, yet more threadbare than sinister, was a scenario I would not have anticipated. Which may have been why, when he held out his hand, I took it. His flesh was gritty, as if he had come directly from the beach without washing. I wondered if anyone else had identified him. Was Sinead here? I wasn't sure. I hadn't seen her, but had I seen everyone?

"How've you been?" he said.

"Good," I said. It was the answer I would have given had any of the people I'd tried to talk to posed the question.

"What're you up to these days?"

"Teaching," I said. "I teach college."

"Oh, yeah? Whereabouts?"

"SUNY Huguenot. Across the river."

"That's great," he said, his voice full of its old enthusiasm. "What do they have you doing?"

"English," I said. "Freshman writing, mostly."

"Very nice. Say, you know what I've been sitting here trying to remember?"

"What?"

"The prank you guys pulled when you were juniors. Well, maybe 'prank' is too strong a word. No one got hurt or anything. Do you know what I'm talking about?"

I did. "The 'What the hell is that?' routine."

He snapped his fingers. "That's it! Who came up with that?"

"No one. I mean, someone saw it on TV—*Saturday Night Live*, I think— and we decided to do it in school."

Joel Martin was laughing now, albeit quietly. "What the hell is that?" he said. Keeping his hand close to his chest, he pointed at a spot above the bar's mirror. "What the *hell* is that? What the hell *is* that? *What* the hell is *that*?" He lowered his finger. "You remember the time I joined you guys?"

I nodded. It had been our most successful staging of the bit.

"Long time ago," he said. "Long, long time ago."

With sudden and uncanny certainty, I knew that the man who had gotten me through both Regents Chemistry and Regents Physics was on the verge of broaching topics I had no desire to discuss. An emotion halfway to panic gripped me. I decided to forego finishing my beer and depart the reunion early. I was pretty much done already, wasn't I? Joel Martin saw me withdrawing a ten from my pocket to cover my drink and tip. His eyes widened, but before he could open his mouth, I said, "I have to go. Have a good night," and slid off my stool.

Excusing and pardoning myself, I navigated the groups and couples standing between me and the front door. The room had grown hot, stiflingly humid. The sports coat and turtleneck I'd opted for were too tight, constricting. I glanced back to see if Joel Martin was still at the bar. I couldn't tell; there were too many people crowding the space.

Outside, the night air was blessedly cool. I pulled off my jacket, tugged my shirt out of my slacks. My car was in front of the restaurant, at the concrete divider separating the parking lot from the main road. I was unlocking the driver's-side door when I heard my name shouted. I looked toward the Castle's front door, and there was Joel Martin holding it open. I raised the hand holding my jacket in what I hoped was a noncommittal wave. From within the doorway, he called, "See you there tomorrow?"

I motioned with the jacket again, ducked inside my car, and almost broke the key off jamming it into the ignition. I was positive I was going to hear a tap on my window and see my former teacher's smiling face leaning toward me. When I stole a look at the front door, however, it was, though still open, empty. It was as if I had just missed Joel Martin stepping away from it to return inside. I had the impression of something within the lighted rectangle, a cloud of dust or sand, but I was too relieved at my good fortune to pay much attention to it. I shifted into gear and drove out of the parking lot.

II

The following night, I spent the car ride from my apartment in Wiltwyck to the Poughkeepsie Tennis Club narrating Joel Martin's fall from grace to Linda, my date for the evening. She was a former girlfriend who had broken up with me in order to pursue a relationship with one of her professors at NYU. They had split when she became pregnant, and now she was the mother of a two-year-old daughter, Elaine, whose father had visitation rights alternating weekends and two weeks during the summer. She managed a bank in Wiltwyck and lived with her dad, a retired cop who spent his days watching his granddaughter. Long past our post-relationship bitterness, we had lunch every few weeks, trading news about our latest romantic prospects and complaining about our respective jobs. After my most recent relationship petered out, Linda had agreed to accompany me to my reunion dinner as, she said, a psychological investigation into the forces that had shaped me. While she might have anticipated a certain level of pre-event nervousness on my part, she was unprepared for the agitation that had hold of me—that had not released me since the previous night. We hadn't been on the road two minutes when she said, "All right. You better tell me what's going on with you."

The first part of the story was related quickly enough. Having lived her own version of it, Linda was less shocked than she might have been. "I take it things didn't work out between this guy and the student," she said.

"To put it mildly," I said. "From what I understand, Sinead's parents wanted to press charges against Martin—statutory rape, contributing to the delinquency of a minor. The problem was, she had turned eighteen the previous December, and both of them swore nothing had happened between them until the end of January. I think her mom still wanted to go after him, legally speaking, but her dad was less gung ho. This was the father of his first grandchild, and Martin was saying all the right things, how sorry he was, how much he loved Sinead, how he intended to do right by her and the baby. Plus, Sinead kept insisting she was in love with him. Eventually, her mom cooled off, especially when Martin proposed to Sinead at the end of the summer. That was the news in the fall, when I was home for Thanksgiving break. Mr. Martin and Sinead McGahern were engaged, with a wedding planned for sometime in the spring, after she'd had the baby and regained her shape. Martin had a job at a gas station, which sounded like a bit of a comedown after having taught high school, but maybe not. Supposedly, he was saving to rent a house for them."

"I want to say they didn't go through with the wedding," Linda said.

"No, they didn't. Sinead had the baby the day after Christmas, a little boy, Sean. Apparently, Martin was in love with the kid the moment he laid eyes on him. I heard that was part of what broke them apart. One look at his child—his son, right?—and he's all ready to settle down with Sinead and start working on baby number two. Her, not so much. She'd been accepted to Penrose, and they'd agreed to defer her admission for a year. This was something she was not willing to give up."

"Plus," Linda said, "the bloom was off the rose, for him as well as for her. You start seeing someone in secret like that, someone who's off-limits to you, who embodies, I don't know, a certain kind of authority for her, a certain kind of youthfulness for him, and let me tell you, it's pretty heady stuff. Forbidden fruit and all that. It doesn't take long, though, for the fruit to spoil. What they had was a fling. Their mistake was in trying to prolong it—which, I understand, they did because of the kid. They would've been better hiring lawyers and drawing up a custody agreement. Did they?"

"Eventually. By that time, things between them were pretty dire. Her second year at Penrose, Sinead moved into an apartment with the kid. It was near the college. Apparently, Penrose offered pretty good childcare for its students and faculty, and this was where little Sean spent a lot of his time. Too much, according to Martin. He accused Sinead of dumping the kid at daycare or on her parents. Said that, half the time, he didn't know where his son was. On one occasion, he showed up to collect the baby, and Sinead was out; she'd left her new boyfriend in charge of Sean."

"Ouch."

"Yeah. Martin took her to court, but her parents hired a nasty lawyer for her, sicced him on Martin the way Sinead's mom had wanted to in the first place. From what I understand, he shredded Martin into tiny pieces. I guess the judge was pretty sympathetic to Sinead too. The upshot was, Martin's custody of Sean was limited to every other weekend; plus, he was put on the hook for all kinds of expenses in addition to child support."

"Could have been worse," Linda said.

"I'm sure," I said, "but Martin didn't see it that way. I don't know if he honestly believed Sinead wasn't taking proper care of their child, or if he was stung by losing the court case."

"Or both."

"Or both. Whatever the reason, he couldn't let things alone. So he came up with a plan. He bought a dime bag of weed—"

"He didn't."

"Yeah, he did. Sinead had a habit of leaving her car unlocked in front of her apartment. He intended to drop the bag under the driver's seat. Then, the next time she brought Sean to his place, he would just happen to notice the drugs. He would call the cops on her and, ultimately, gain leverage when it came to the kid. Unfortunately for him, Sinead's boyfriend looked out of the window at the exact moment Martin had her car door open and was bent down inside it. She called 911. There was a police car close enough to show up before Martin had driven away. A big scene ensued. The pot was discovered. Sinead and the boyfriend accused Martin of planting it, said they weren't into that kind of stuff. I gather they told the cops they could search the apartment if they didn't believe them. Martin still had on the gloves he'd worn to ensure he left no fingerprints. Combined with him having been seen inside Sinead's car . . . The cops took him to the station. I'm not clear what the charges were. Nothing too major. Sinead, though, used the incident to haul him back in front of the judge and have his contact with Sean reduced to one weekend a month."

"Well," Linda said, "this isn't the worst story I've ever heard."

"There's more."

"More?"

"This part I didn't learn about until a few years later. For about a week, it was front-page news. One or two of the TV stations out of the city covered it. You would think Martin's brush with the law would have taught him a lesson—scared straight and all that. It didn't. Or it did, but the lesson he learned wasn't a good one. Since his more modest efforts at rectifying the situation had failed, he decided it was time for drastic action. The legal system had shown it was no friend to him—or that he couldn't manipulate it the way he wanted—so it could be ignored. He started doing research online."

"This isn't some kind of murder-for-hire deal, is it?"

"No," I said. "What Martin had decided to do was take his son and flee the country. He spent months setting it up. Fake documents, fake IDs, fake passports, not to mention enough money to tide him over until he could find a job. Finally, when Sinead needed him to take Sean for a long weekend, he put his plan into action. He left his apartment pretty much as it was except for his computer. He removed the hard drive, wiped it with a magnet, microwaved it, and dropped it in the Dumpster outside the building. He drove to Stewart, where he took a flight to Orlando. He made sure to tell anyone who would listen that he was taking his son on his first trip to Disney World.

"The two of them actually spent a day in Florida, but only so he could make himself up to look like the photo on his new passport. From Orlando, Martin and Sean boarded a flight to LAX, where they passed most of another day before catching a flight to Buenos Aires, via Miami.

"Once they were in Argentina, he hung around Buenos Aires for a week, until he talked himself into a position as a tutor for the children of a cattle baron somewhere in the south of the country. That was where he was when the cops caught up to him three months later. He had done a good job at disguising himself and even the kid, but he was still a single man traveling with a young child. As soon as the cops figured out his new appearance, it was mostly a matter of sifting through hours of video from airport security cameras to reconstruct the route he'd taken. The way the papers presented it, he didn't try to escape when the police arrived. He knew they had him. Sean was taken to Buenos Aires, where Sinead and her parents were waiting for him. Martin was thrown into an Argentine prison; although he lucked out—a little, anyhow. The guy whose kids he'd been tutoring liked him and had enough connections to have his sentence reduced from five years to nine months. The minute Martin was released, however, he was back on a plane to the United

States, where his actions earned him another eighteen months behind bars."

"Holy shit," Linda said. "What happened to him after?"

"I don't know," I said. "I assume he got out and went about trying to put his life back together. From the way he looked last night, I don't think that's gone so well for him."

For a long moment, the two of us were silent. On either side of the street, large, well-kept houses signaled their owners' wealth. We were almost at the tennis club.

Linda said, "The things we do for love."

"Or revenge."

"You don't think he loves his son?"

"I'm sure he does. I'm also sure he hates his son's mother."

"Hmm. Was she there last night?"

"I don't think so. I didn't see her."

"Do you know if she'll be at this thing tonight?"

"I haven't the foggiest. We weren't exactly close in high school."

"All of a sudden," Linda said, "things have become much more interesting."

III

The second night of the reunion was in many ways like the first, with better food and with everyone in semiformal wear. At the entrance to the ballroom in which the dinner dance was being held, the reunion committee had set up a long table on which name tags had been laid in alphabetical rows. In addition to our names, the IDs of my former classmates and me bore wallet-sized reproductions of our senior portraits. As I pinned mine to my jacket, I let my eyes drift over the remaining badges but did not see Sinead McGahern's. There were also name tags for a handful of former teachers, but Joel Martin's name was not among them.

Linda and I were seated with a group of people with whom I had been friendly during senior year. One of the guys had taken over the family business, a sit-down Chinese restaurant at which his wife had been a hostess. Another guy was not long out of the Air Force, and not long married to the young woman with him, who kept expressing her concern over their daughter, who I gathered was only a couple of months old and being watched by his mother. I asked the restaurateur if he'd kept track of a few of my favorite teachers; he said he wasn't positive, but he thought they were dead. I asked the ex–Air Force guy what he was up to now; he said he was managing a Radio Shack in eastern Massachusetts. During these exchanges, something that had occurred to me the previous night became clear. Of the people with whom I would have considered myself especially close during my four years at Our Lady of Fatima, not one had opted to attend our reunion. Who knew where they were? (I tried the restaurant guy; to each of their names, he said he wasn't sure, but he thought he'd heard of a number of personal catastrophes including drugs, prison, serious injury, and devastating illness.)

This left me at an event like a restaging of my senior prom, complete with all the songs and dance moves that had not aged particularly well. Linda actually seemed to be enjoying herself. She had managed a Chinese place in Albany at one point, and her father had been in the Air Force, so she was able to maintain conversations with both of my former class-mates. About halfway through the event, the DJ—a local celebrity who anchored the morning show on the classic rock station and had been a couple of years ahead of us in school—announced that it was time to read the memories people had written on the slips of paper provided at each table. (I had chosen not to.) In the midst of recollections about specific teachers' classes, and sporting victories, and trips here and there, some-one contributed a note that read, "I had sex with one of my teachers." I felt as if someone had thrown a bucket of ice water over me. I'm not certain what response I anticipated from the rest of the audience, but the most the confession received was a scattering of laughs and a couple of approving howls. Linda gave me a significant glance. Had someone else slept with Joel Martin? Or, God help me, had one of my old classmates had an affair with another teacher? Yes, it was naïve to be this shocked, but so what? Apparently, I hadn't left my younger self as far behind as my appearance might have suggested.

I was not expecting Joel Martin to show himself at this night's festivities, not really. It was one thing to chance slipping into a room packed with people busy with one another and sitting with your back to them while you sipped from your cocktail. It was altogether another to stroll into a ballroom whose tablefuls of your former students would have little trouble identifying you. All the same, when I turned from the urinal in the men's room and saw him standing against the door, the phrase that almost escaped my lips was "Of course." It was as if that anonymous admission had summoned him here. I couldn't imagine what he would want with me. I crossed to one of the sinks and washed my hands.

"Nice place, this," he said.

"Yes," I said, "it is."

"You ever been here before?"

"No. First time."

"I was. Years ago. One of the senior classes a few years ahead of you guys had their prom here. I was a chaperone; brought my girlfriend at the time. This was—you would have been a freshman. Yeah, freshman."

I finished drying my hands, dropped the paper towel in the trash. "I should be getting back. My date—"

"I guess you heard about my . . . troubles," he said. "Yeah, you did. Who didn't? Especially after they were all over the front page of the Goddamned papers."

He was right; there was no point denying it. I nodded. "I did."

"Do you have any kids of your own?"

"No."

"Let me tell you, once you do, you will not believe you could love anyone that much. You look at this little wrinkled creature, its arms and legs still tucked up from being in the womb, and it is love at first sight. There is nothing you will not do for this kid. Your entire focus shifts from whatever bullshit you thought was important to making sure this child—your child—is okay. All the things you couldn't imagine doing— changing dirty diapers, dealing with spit-up, waking up in the middle of the night to rock them back to sleep—become the order of the day. Do you understand what I'm saying to you?"

"I do."

"Everything I did, every last bit of it, was for my son, to keep him safe, to give him the kind of life he deserved. I have always wanted what was best for him. Always. I never stopped wanting that, even when I was locked up in Argentina, or when I came back here so they could lock me up some more. My son's mother had taken him and left. She didn't leave word where. Didn't ask for child support from me, in case it allowed me to trace them. Was that fair? I ask you, was any of that fair?"

"I don't know," I said. "I guess she felt—"

"It doesn't matter," Joel Martin said. "While I was in prison in Buenos Aires, I met a guy who let me in on something that is going to get my son back and make certain no one takes him from me again."

"I'm not—"

"Do you know who Borges was?"

"The writer?"

"This guy I met was a friend of his. That's what they called him, the other prisoners, the Friend of Borges, *el amigo de Borges*. He'd hung out with Borges when he was younger, at university. He was a mathematician, into some pretty exotic stuff. There was this one story Borges had written, 'The Aleph'—have you read it?"

"The one about the point that lets you see all other points in space and time."

"Exactly. The guy was fascinated by that story, by the math underlying it. Poincaré theory—how well do you remember physics class?"

"Not at all."

"That's disappointing," he said, "but it isn't important. The conversations with Borges took the guy only so far, but the writer put him in touch with one of his friends at the university, who gave him the name of another person, and so on, until he met with a group who were familiar with the theory underlying the aleph, and a lot more besides."

"Okay."

"You don't get it. That's all right. Do you recall me telling you guys that everything was just math?"

"Yes."

"You thought I was talking figuratively—if you gave it any thought at all. I wasn't. The group the Friend of Borges met understood this. They comprehended it. They were part of a . . . tradition of scholars who had been working with this exotic math for a long time. Like, longer than you'd believe."

"I'm not—"

"These scholars had figured out all kinds of applications for the material they were studying. They had worked out how to employ it, using combinations of words and sounds and . . . mental images, you could call them."

"It sounds like you're talking about magic."

"What you call it isn't important. What's important is that it works."

"Then why was this guy—the Friend of Borges—in prison? Couldn't he just magic his way out of there, teleport or something?"

"He was in hiding," Joel Martin said. "Or, that's not it, exactly. He'd had a falling-out with the other members of his lodge, and he had decided to secure himself within Unit 1."

"Couldn't he have found a better place to hide out?"

"That doesn't matter!" he shouted. "You're missing the Goddamned forest for the trees. I'm telling you I met the modern-day equivalent of fucking Merlin, and you want to know why he isn't staying at the Hilton. Jesus!"

There was no doubt in my mind that my former teacher had traveled far, far around the proverbial bend. I raised my hands, palms out. "Okay.

I'm sorry. You met the Friend of Borges, and he told you about this weird math. Did he teach any of it to you?"

"A little. You can appreciate, the conditions weren't ideal for this kind of instruction. What he did was to tell me where I needed to go once I was free to travel again. Which took a while, and I had to work a bunch of shit jobs to save up the money, but in the end, I got there."

I couldn't help myself. "Where was it?"

"Quebec."

"Quebec?"

"Quebec City. That's where the nearest lodge—the nearest school is."

"And they took you in—accepted you as their student."

"They did."

"So now you're one of them, a . . . mathematician."

"Basically."

"But—why are you here? If you have access to the aleph, or whatever, shouldn't you be using it to track down your son?"

Joel Martin's face drew in on itself, to an expression it took me a moment to name: embarrassment. He looked down at his shoes, stuffed his hands into his jacket pockets. "There's been a slight complication."

Here it comes, I thought, *the escape hatch, the detail that allows the fantasy to exist yet remain ineffectual.* "Oh? What kind of complication?"

"I'm imprisoned. The master of the lodge guards his knowledge jealously. He doesn't introduce you to new material until he's satisfied that you're ready for it. I had passed all the basic tests with flying colors. Everyone said I was one of the best students they'd taught in years. They—the master wanted me to wait before studying anything more advanced. I was sure I didn't need to. I was eager—I could feel time slipping away from me. Every day, and my son is getting older, whatever memories he has of me growing fainter. Have no doubt, his mother and whoever she's with are doing all they can to erase me from his life. I needed access to the aleph now. I pressed the matter with the master. He wouldn't budge. Things got heated between us. I made some . . . intemperate remarks. The master invited me to act on them. I did. It didn't go well. When the dust settled, he trapped me in a place . . . It's kind of a place between places. He said if I could figure my way out of it, I might be ready to start learning again."

"You're in prison," I said.

"Imprisoned," he said. "Again. It's more complicated than the other lockups I've been in. There's a limited amount of energy sustaining the cell. I can draw on it, but every time I do, the space constricts. If I had accepted my sentence, I could remain here indefinitely. But I told you I can't do that. I have to get out of here. I tried reaching out to one of the other students at the lodge, someone I thought was sympathetic to me. I was wrong, and I shrank the prison. I decided I had to think more creatively—outside the box, ha-ha. It occurred to me that your ten-year reunion was coming up. I was able to find out the times and locations without making the cell too much smaller."

"Wait," I said. "You're in this cell."

"Correct."

"Yet you're standing here talking to me."

"This," he said, removing his hands from his pockets to gesture at himself, "is a simulacrum. It's as if you're talking to me on a videophone."

"Okay," I said. "Couldn't you appear to your son, then? Why waste time with me?"

"Because I don't know where he is. I was able to draw on your memories— your class's combined memories of me to locate this spot and assemble a version of myself. I reached out to you in particular because we'd gotten along when you were my student. I hoped you would be willing to help me."

"How could I help you?"

"I have a storage unit on Route 9, down by the malls. There are a couple of things in there, a book and—"

"Mr. Martin," I said. "Joel." At the sound of his name, his head jerked, as if I had slapped him. I said, "I don't know what's going on with you, exactly, but I wonder if maybe you need to talk to someone who could help you with all this."

"What do you mean?" he said. "That's why I'm—oh." His eyes narrowed. "I get it. You think I'm delusional. Paranoid schizophrenia, right?"

"It sounds as if you've been under a tremendous amount of stress," I said. "Things with your son—"

"Don't you understand? There are no 'things with my son.' I don't know where he is. As long as I'm stuck in this prison—"

"Stop. You're in the men's room of the Poughkeepsie Tennis Club. You are not in some kind of magic jail."

"You have no idea," he said. "You have no Goddamned idea. This place is a blank. It isn't a place, properly speaking. It *isn't*; do you understand? It's the white between the letters on the page. Most of the time, it's all I can do to keep myself coherent. And on top of that, it's getting *smaller*. It may have reached its limit. Any more loss of energy, and it's going to collapse and take me with it. I am not shitting you when I say that you are my last chance. I'm doing everything I can to hold on, but time is running out."

A tremendous pity rose in me. I had been in here much too long. "I have to go," I said. "I'm sorry." I walked toward the bathroom door.

"What? Hey, hang on." He put his hands up.

"Please get out of the way."

"Wait—"

I was expecting Joel Martin to move to the side. If he didn't, I had a good half a foot and probably seventy-five pounds on him. Should it prove necessary, I had no doubt I'd be able to muscle past him.

When his outstretched fingers touched me, however, there was a sound like a houseful of windows shattering. Something like a blast of air shoved me across the bathroom, into the wall. Stunned, I looked at Joel Martin. The air around him appeared to have dimmed. He seemed to have lost substance, to have flattened. As I watched, he began to crumple, as if he were made of paper and a pair of giant hands were crushing him between them. His mouth was open; he was saying, "No, oh, no no no no," over and over again. The words sounded as if they were reaching me from across a vast gulf. He tried to reach out in my direction, but the force that was compressing the rest of him collapsed his arms against him. Eyes wide with pain, he alternated his noes with his son's name. His shoulders gave; his legs folded up to his torso. "Wait!" he shouted, his voice further away still. "Wait! Wait!" His body bent inward, condensing itself. As his face began to crumple, he screamed, a howl of rage and frustration.

Then he was gone, and the air was full of swirling dust. Coughing, I raised my hands to my face. My eyes teared. It seemed I could hear Joel Martin screaming still, or maybe that was only the whine of the fluorescent lights. I coughed so hard, it doubled me over. The dust had triggered an asthma attack. I pulled myself up on one of the sinks and saw in the mirror a man whose scarlet face was streaked with tears and dust. For a moment, I remembered standing beside Joel Martin, the two of us vibrating with barely suppressed laughter, as we pointed at a corner of the hallway ceiling and said to one another, "What the hell is that?"

Before the dust had finished settling onto the fixtures, the floor, I fled the bathroom, half running down the dark hallway back to the ballroom. Everywhere except the dance floor, the lights had been lowered. On the dance floor, men and women wearing the disinterested expressions of funeral statuary swayed and shuffled to the Talking Heads' "Road to Nowhere" thundering from the speakers like a demented march. Those seated in the shadows bobbed their heads in time to the beat.

Another round of coughing shook me. No one could hear it over the music. Hand covering my mouth, I stumbled to my table, where I was relieved to find Linda seated. She smiled when she saw me, but her brows lowered as I leaned over for a fresh bout of coughing. My head was spinning. I straightened, listed to the right, and Linda was there to steady me. Leaning close, she shouted, "What is it?"

I managed to say, "Asthma," loud enough for her to hear.

She nodded, said, "Do you have an inhaler?"

I shook my head.

"Is it bad?" she said. "Do you need to go to the emergency room?"

I shook my head again.

"Do you want me to drive you home?"

I nodded.

"Okay. Let me tell everyone what's going on."

This Linda did, drawing concerned looks and waves from the rest of the table. I returned the waves, but kept my distance. On the way out of the tennis club, we passed a man and a woman arguing. He was severely drunk, seated on the lowest of the front steps, his tie yanked to one side, his shirt half unbuttoned. She was standing in her stocking feet, using her flat pocketbook to punctuate the points she was making. The two of them had been among the popular crowd at Fatima, not homecoming king and queen but certainly part of their court. I was grateful another round of coughing took me as Linda and I walked by them, so I could pretend I wasn't aware they were enacting what appeared to be a fairly regular drama.

By the time Linda pulled into the parking lot in front of my apartment building, the worst of my asthma attack was over. It had prevented much conversation on the ride back, except for me to say that it had been triggered by something in the air in the men's room. As she handed me the keys, Linda said, "Are you going to be okay by yourself? Because I can stay over if you need me to."

"It's all right," I said. "I'll be fine. Thank you."

"Call me if you get worse."

"I will, but really, I'm fine. I'll use my inhaler the second I walk in the door."

"You'd better."

I did. And since I knew there was no chance of me falling asleep anytime in what seemed like the next several days, I took down the bottle of Talisker from the top of the refrigerator and poured myself three fingers, whose effects I did not feel. I carried the bottle and glass into the living room, where I set them on the side table and found the TV remote. The nighttime channels were full of all manner of weird and pathetic programming, but together with the scotch, they were almost enough to keep me from dwelling on Joel Martin's expression while his prison crushed him, on his calling his son's name, on his final plea for a reprieve that was not granted. Eventually, I drank enough of the whiskey for it drop me into a black, empty place.

IV

When I received the e-mail invitation to my twenty-fifth high school reunion, I'll admit I considered responding to it. Enough time had elapsed for me to hope that my classmates and I might finally have moved beyond our differences. Instead, what I discovered, after a couple of messages to old friends found again through social media, was that there were two reunions being planned, one for the former elites of my class and the other for the rest of us. I was sufficiently disgusted by the news to delete my invitation, washing my hands of the business of high school reunions for at least another quarter-century.

My decision was influenced as well by information that came to me at almost exactly the same time via the same social media connections. One of those old friends sent me a message asking if I'd heard the news about Sean McGahern, the kid of Sinead McGahern and Mr. Martin. I replied that I hadn't. She forwarded me a link to a story about the tragic death of the young singer-songwriter whose first album, *Possession with Intent*, had won him critical acclaim and a Grammy nomination. The record chronicled his life growing up as the child of a narcissistic mother, an uninterested stepfather, and a father who appeared to have vanished off the face of the Earth. (I thought about that locker on Route 9, the one I'd considered checking into but never had.) Emotional and psychological difficulties had led him to experiment first with pot, then heroin, to which he had become addicted. For a brief period of time, while he was working on his album, he seemed to have put his addiction behind him. The pressures of touring to support it, however, combined with those of producing his follow-up effort, had sent him back to heroin. He had died of an overdose; there was some question whether it was an accident or suicide.

After closing the link, I had to stand up and walk away from the computer. I had to leave my office, within the buzz of whose fluorescent light I heard another sound, high-pitched, impossibly distant: Joel Martin, screaming—still screaming—for all he had lost, all he had given away.

—*For Fiona*

NOW AND FOREVER

D. THOMAS MINTON

Elise sits endless vigil over our daughter, and my boy is nowhere to be found.

"I heard the door a while ago," Elise says, cool rag in hand. "I thought it was you."

I know immediately where Owen has gone. If I don't get there in time, he'll be dead. Like the others.

I grab the nail gun and my O₂ breather, but there's no time to don my skin-suit. The ribbon of nails bounces against my thigh as I sprint between dark rows of soybean and quinoa. The garden's grow-lights have yet to cycle on. Through the dome overhead, the Milky Way wraps across the great dark like a diamond-studded noose.

Fool boy! Twelve, and he thinks he can kill the Fiend, when forty-six others failed.

I reach the edge of the garden and stumble onto the metal decking. I barely hear the thud of my feet on the metal plates over the rasp of my breath. The first door, welded shut and barricaded with a field cart, emerges from the darkness, bathed in red light from the night lamp above it. I've guessed wrong.

I fly past, on to the other door.

The cool air burns my lungs. The heat exchangers are failing; every day it gets a fraction colder in the dome, but those who could repair it died long ago.

Ahead, in the next ruddy halo, Owen takes a pry bar to the door. He's already broken the welds on the lower half and works feverishly to snap those across the top. Air hisses out where his efforts have warped the metal.

As I near, Owen must hear my breathing; he puts his weight behind the bar and the last weld pops. The door swings open, but a pressure differential sucks it shut.

The pry bar clatters to the deck as Owen stumbles back.

The door cracks open. Fingers pale as lice wrap around the edge. They have nails like needles, hollow and filled with toxin. The Fiend can project them like darts. That's what put Daphne to bed and Elise into her vigil.

The nail gun is hard to steady as I run faster. . . . Nails ping against the metal door, the frame, and finally, the stream of metal zings through the crack. I throw my shoulder against the door.

The Fiend's fingers crunch and are sheared off by the sharp metal. They plop to the deck, still wiggling like a half dozen severed lizard tails.

"Dammit, boy! You want to die?"

Through the pounding of blood in my neck, I hear the clicking of the Fiend's mandibles.

"Give me the pry bar." I kick at the fingers inching across the deck toward my foot. They'll keep crawling toward anything with warm blood.

Owen's face is ashen, his eyes locked on the wriggling fingers.

The door bounces out of the frame, but my weight is enough to slam it back into place.

"Owen—the bar!"

The boy is frozen and worthless, his stupid courage drained away by reality.

My toes hook the curl of the pry bar, and I drag it to me. I wedge it under the door—it barely fits—then drive it fast with the heel of my boot.

The trencher that had blocked the door sits to the side. I clamber behind the controls and press my thumb against the ignition scanner, and it whirs to life. I slam its back end against the door, and drop the cutter against the deck for added leverage.

From a bottle I keep under the seat, I squirt accelerant on the fingers and scrape sparks from a lighter onto them until they flare into blue flame.

Owen hugs his knees to his face and hides his eyes behind them. His knuckles are white.

I'm too afraid and relieved at the same time to have room for anger. If I had been five seconds later . . . What's gotten into him, thinking he can take the Fiend by himself? This isn't the first time either. I've always stopped him, but each time, he gets a little closer. I don't know what to do with him. I can't lock him up, and I can't talk sense into him.

The Fiend's scratching grates my nerves. Even with the metal door, it's too close, too dangerous. I think it can sense us, even through the pressure door. Like it can smell our blood, or maybe our fear.

I pick up my boy, frail in my hands. His shaking doesn't stop.

"Please, please, don't ever do that again. I can't protect you out there."

Owen nods his understanding into my shoulder.

We were four years out, not even to the halfway point of our transit to Echelon Colony, when the first body turned up riddled with pinprick holes and strung up like an animal being bled. We thought we had a murderer on board, but the doctor assured us that no one on the ship was capable of that level of savagery.

But people are capable of a lot.

Then the sightings started. A pale creature lurking the corridors of the engineering module. Scrapings on hatches. Clicking sounds from air ducts. How it got aboard, we didn't know. You'd think something like the Fiend couldn't hide on a ship so small, but it was like a splinter of nightmare driven into the flesh of our reality.

After that, the bodies began to collect like regrets. Smart and deadly, the Fiend was a relentless killer.

Attempts to hunt it failed, so we launched the SOS beacons and retreated to the garden because it was two acres of open ground with limited entry points. We sealed everything up, but still it found ways in and picked us off one by one. Iulian . . . Traci . . . Michal.

We decided to kill it by disabling the environmental systems in the rest of the ship. Four of us shut them down, but the Fiend found us in the dark corridors, and I was the only one to make it back.

Now it's just me and my family. And the Fiend.

I make sure Owen is secure in his room. He's scared and unharmed, his courage drained away. Elise is where she always is: sitting at Daphne's bedside. I lean against the door frame, exhausted after the adrenaline rush has faded.

Elise sings gently to our daughter, a lullaby we used to sing when nightmares ripped her from peaceful dreams.

I can't remember how long ago Daphne was attacked; the days run together. She had been harvesting peas in the far field when I heard her scream. By the time I got to her, the Fiend had pulled her halfway into a duct. The pop of nails from my gun made it drop her and retreat.

Elise arrived, crying, and scooped our daughter into her arms.

I stared at the open vent, the unbroken grate on the deck. How could I have missed sealing it?

Daphne's arms twined weakly around Elise's neck. Her voice, a whisper I could barely hear, pierced my heart like a needle. "It hurts. . . . I'm cold. . . ."

By the time we got her back to the house, Daphne had slipped into unconsciousness.

As her father, it was my job to keep her safe. I failed.

Elise startles when she notices me in the doorway. Her face is all shadows, and where her eyes are supposed to be are dark pits, like holes in a skull. She never sleeps, best I can tell, and it's pulled her essence into something insubstantial like spun sugar.

"I didn't mean to scare you," I say.

"She's burning up and we're out of medicine."

I check the cabinet.

Elise stands in the doorway to Daphne's room like she's unable to cross its threshold. "She needs medicine."

My stomach curdles. The only medicine is in the infirmary.

I check the cabinet again, and all the other drawers in our small house. Elise watches me, arms crossed.

Nothing. My knees weak, I collapse into a chair. How can we be out?

Elise turns her back on me and retreats to Daphne's side.

I wring my hands. The fingers are cold and numb. It's my fault. That's hard enough to live with, but every day, I see the accusation in Elise's face.

Saying nothing, I pull on a skin-suit and slide the hood over my head. It'll keep me warm in the habitat module, and its compression bands will keep the blood from pooling in my extremities in the low pressure.

I pick up the nail gun and decide against taking a second belt of nails. If I get into a fight with the Fiend, I won't survive long enough to use it, so why lug the extra weight?

"I want to come."

Owen's voice startles me, and I nearly drop the nail gun.

Sepia light leaks from his room, casting his face into a jigsaw of black and grey.

"I need you to protect your mother and sister in case . . ." I work my mouth but find no moisture. "You need to take care of things until I get back."

He digs his trembling hands deeper into his pockets. I can't tell if he's relieved or not.

I want to hug him, but I can't do it. I'm not ready to say good-bye to any of them.

"You better come back," he says, his voice chopped off as I pull the door closed behind me.

I jog along the decking on the edge of the soybean field. Overhead, stars spin in the great dark. I arrive at the door and need to sit for a moment.

My mind is a jumble of regrets. My inadequacies threaten to paralyze me.

The first of the grow-lights come on, simulating dawn. The garden, once quiet and beautiful, is our prison.

I visualize my route to the infirmary and back. In my head it takes me only seconds, but I know if all goes smoothly . . . "Five minutes," I whisper to myself.

I clip the O_2 cannula against my nostrils and concentrate on slowing my breathing.

I press my ear to the door.

All quiet.

I move the trencher just enough to allow me to squeeze through without damaging my suit, and prop the pry bar near the door.

My body trembles, and I will my hands to stop shaking. I leave the garden.

The door shuts behind me, pushed by the outflow of warm air.

My breath crackles as it crystallizes. I breathe through my nose, drawing warm oxygenated air through the cannula.

The circle of light from my headlamp plays down the walls and across the floor. Ice rimes the conduits snaking along the ceiling and the metal support struts that rib the corridor. On the floor, a black line smears off into the darkness. Dried blood.

I move quickly from intersection to intersection, picking my way through the dark toward the infirmary. Even with my light, it's black as a grave, and the cold bites hard into my fingers and nose.

A clang shivers through the metal floor, and I freeze. Metal groans.

Quiet settles again.

I'm breathing so hard now, the O_2 enricher labors to compensate.

I hustle on; several turns, and I'm there. With the power out, my thumb chip won't cycle the door. The manual release is frozen fast with condensation.

I flash my light down the corridor in both directions. Shadows scatter away, but otherwise, it's empty.

I slam the butt of the nail gun against the release. A dull thud rings out. I hammer the lever a second time, and the ice gives with a loud crack.

I listen into the dark, but it's hard to hear over the pounding in my chest. I swing the hatch aside and pull it closed behind me, but there's no lock to secure it.

The infirmary is a jumble of overturned furniture and medical supplies spilled onto the floor from rifled cabinets. Glass and metal crunch underfoot, a carpet of broken surgical tools, syringes, and vials. I can't remember which cabinet held the medicine, so I search haphazardly. Nothing.

The front room, the clinic, has been thoroughly ransacked. The door to the surgical theater doesn't open, but a blow to the handle with the end of the nail gun gets me inside. The cabinets here have been ripped open too. I search the debris on the shelves, the countertop, and the sink, finding sutures and bandages, broken glass, gauze, tubing, but no vials.

I throw my hands up, spinning, but see nothing except my failure.

A small bottle glints in my light as it skitters across the floor and under the surgical table. I drop to my hands and knees and peer underneath.

"Where are you?" I mutter, maybe out loud, maybe in my head. Either way, it's loud in my ears.

I move my head lamp around so I can see between the cables and struts of the table's hydraulics. I see it! I can't read the label, but it's the only medicine I've seen, and anything is better than nothing at this point.

I work my hand into the narrow space. My fingertips touch the curve of the bottle, but I can't get enough purchase on it to roll it toward me.

"Dammit. Dammit."

The sound of crunching glass freezes me. I don't move, not even my eyes, as I strain to hear. Maybe my mind is playing tricks, but I still can't bring myself to take a breath.

Crunch. Louder this time, coming closer, slowly.

Crunch.

I can't move, paralyzed by my fear.

Crunch.

At the door to the surgical theater. It'll be on me in seconds.

My bones compress as I force my hand into the tight space until I can get my fingertips around the backside of the bottle's curve and tap it so it rolls closer to me. Extracting my hand, I gash my thumb. Blood drips onto the floor and steams, but fortunately, my hand is numb enough that I don't feel it. I scoop the bottle into my pocket without looking at the label.

The glass crunches on the other side of the surgical table.

I scramble away, tearing a hole in the thigh of my suit on the debris. The gun *thunk*s as nails blur through my headlamp beam, clattering off the table edge and flying into the blackness.

A high-pitched scream. Slender arms flash through my lamp beam as a small person rolls away from the stream of nails. Glass crunches as Owen scrambles back into the clinic.

"Owen!" I leap over the surgical table. In the front room, the door to the corridor hangs open like a black maw. I sweep my light around, whispering my boy's name and praying he hasn't run into the corridor.

I find him curled up in an open cabinet, shaking but unhurt. I kneel next to him. Set the nail gun on the floor. He tries to squirm away, but I get him into my arms. "It's okay," I whisper. Eventually, he turns into my shoulder and hugs me. His warmth spreads into my limbs.

"I wanted to help you. I wanted to help Daphne."

"I know," I say, then shush him. I should be angry, but all that matters is he's safe, and that I keep him that way. "Let's get out of here."

I pick up the nail gun as Owen climbs out of the cabinet. At the door, we pause while I peer down the corridor. "You know the way?" I ask.

He nods, and we head off.

I keep Owen behind me but within arm's reach. We stop at the first intersection. I hold my breath as I peek around the corner. A series of metallic clangs echoes in the distance.

Owen's eyes are large and glow white in the blackness. "What was that?"

My finger shakes as I hold it up to my lips.

The noise stops. As we dash through the intersection, I look down the corridor, but my headlamp doesn't cut the darkness deep enough to see anything. The Fiend is close. I sense it, as clearly as I sense my boy laboring a step behind me.

At the next intersection, we don't stop—nor the one after that—but fly through like panicked dogs.

The garden is near.

The gash on my thigh aches and my muscles burn.

I run harder. Owen's ragged breaths fall behind me. I slow as I approach the last intersection and turn to find my boy. He materializes at the edge of my lamp beam, his skin pale and translucent as a specter. His eyes widen; his mouth stretches open to scream, but only a terrified rattle comes out.

I spin. My light glares off the Fiend's milky skin and the smooth dome of its head, shiny like the carapace of a beetle.

"Run!" Nails spark off the ceiling and walls. The gun echoes in the tight space. We must have surprised it as much as it surprised us, because it falls back into the dark.

I run without looking back, my headlamp wiggling such that I can't see where I'm going, so I run on instinct.

I catch up with Owen as he's slipping through the crack in the door.

"Go, go, go!"

Behind me, the Fiend comes clicking up the corridor. I fire the nail gun, hoping to hold it off long enough for Owen to get through. The nail belt is almost empty. Firing one-handed, I dig the medicine bottle from my pocket and push it into Owen's hand. "Get this to your mother."

My last nail zings into the darkness.

I push Owen's shoulder, and he squirts into the garden. The door slams shut with the finality of a coffin lid.

Behind me, the Fiend squeals angrily. I don't look back; I don't want to see it.

Warm piss runs down my leg.

I throw my weight against the door. It opens wide enough for me to get a shoulder and arm through. I topple over, half into the garden. The empty nail gun pops from my hands and clatters out of reach.

Fingers wrap around my ankle.

I kick at the claws with my free foot, but the hard blows don't weaken its grip. Any second, it will rip my leg off and feast on the bloody muscle.

I grab the pry bar from next to the door and stab through the opening, hoping to hit the Fiend's arm. I strike my own leg. Pain burns up into my gut, but I don't stop, swinging again and again until finally the Fiend's claw releases me.

I drag the rest of my body inside.

The door snaps shut.

I lie there, drawing labored breaths. Out of the corner of my eye I see the medicine bottle on the deck. In his panic, Owen has forgotten it. I roll over and grab it. Pain shoots up into my hip and across my groin.

I see now my leg is in a bad way. The Fiend's claws have peeled the flesh down on the front of my ankle. Blood soaks my shoe and the tattered pieces of my skin-suit.

My stomach betrays me, but there's nothing in it, so it only convulses painfully.

The door clangs into the back of the cart. The Fiend chitters and clicks in frustration. I nearly black out scrambling away.

How I get back to the house, I'm not certain, but I stumble inside, weak and light-headed. I leave a trail of blood smeared across the tiles.

I've no feeling in my foot. From the floor where I have fallen, I drag a rag off the table and wrap it around my ankle. The blood soaks through before I can tie the knot.

"Elise." My voice is just above a whisper.

I know she's in Daphne's room, straining to hear the smallest rustles of our daughter.

My vision blurs. I won't die in my house like this. "Owen."

The boy comes out of Daphne's room. His eyes widen, and I know now it's as bad as I thought. He covers his mouth and steps back.

The look of terror on his face bites into my heart.

"The medical kit," I say.

Owen backs down the hallway, dissolving into the shadow.

Don't leave me, boy. I need you.

Outside, something rustles near the door. Claws scrape over the lever.

With a cold lump in my belly, I realize the nail gun isn't with me. There's nothing in the small room—no club, no knife, nothing I can wield against it. I curse my stupidity.

I struggle onto my good foot. The adrenaline masks the pain.

The door latch lifts with a click loud enough to shatter my eardrums. I charge, but my foot cannot hold my weight, and I crash to the floor. The Fiend descends on me like the hunter it is.

I scream, driving strength into my limbs, and thrash around trying to buck it off me, but it's too heavy. It claws at my arms and head, chittering and squealing.

"Run, Elise! Run, Owen!"

A needle drives into my leg. Weakness spreads through me as the toxin works its evil.

"Elise . . . Owen . . . run." The words come hard and quiet across my lips. I hope they escaped out the back and find a place to hide until it drags me away.

But how long will they last without me? Owen is not ready to protect even himself. Elise is wrapped in a shroud of grief, and Daphne—I've already failed Daphne.

A click and a hiss of air.

With effort, I turn my head.

A woman in an environment suit shakes out her short hair. She sets her helmet on the table and touches a small boom hugging her cheek. "Request medical assistance at my location." She does not take her eyes off me, and all I can do is stare into them.

"My name is Nadia," she says, kneeling next to me. "We found your SOS beacon." She has strong bones in her face but a soft nose and lips. "I've given you a sedative, but you need to lay still. I don't want you to hurt your leg more than it already is." She takes my thumb and presses it to a scanner pad on the wide wristband ringing her left forearm. She reads the information that scrolls up the band's display.

I try to move, but my body is slow, like I've spent an hour in the sauna making jelly of my muscles. "It killed everyone. Have to—" My head spins and threatens to float away.

"You need to stay still, Paul."

I don't immediately recognize my name; I haven't heard it in a long time.

Two more environment suits arrive. They crack off their helmets and set the domes on the table next to Nadia's. One of them kneels over my injured ankle.

"Delman's going to fix you up," Nadia says. "You're safe now."

I reach out toward her. She takes my hand and finds the medicine bottle wrapped in my fingers.

"My daughter," I say. "She's sick."

Nadia looks at the bottle. Her brow pinches into a vertical line. "What happened here, Paul?"

"My daughter . . . the Fiend . . ." Why can't they understand me? "First door on the left."

"Try to relax." She pats my shoulder, then goes to confer with the standing man. Snippets of their hushed conversation reach my ears, but I can't piece them together, because my attention is absorbed by the outer door, which they've left unlatched.

Elise peeks out from Daphne's room. I call out loudly, attracting everyone's attention. When that happens, Elise quietly backs into the shadow.

Nadia returns to my side. She repeats my name several times, gradually drawing my attention back to her. "Timmons will check on your daughter." She continues to talk at me while the man goes into Daphne's room. I strain to hear anything, but Nadia is speaking too loudly.

"—ship records say your daughter was injured in an equipment accident—"

No, no. The Fiend hurt her.

"—and put into a medically induced coma—"

I crane my head, trying to see around the kneeling woman. Down the hallway, Owen's door is ajar. Through the narrow crack, his eyes glitter with fear.

A soft chittering outside the window drives a spike of fear into me. My breath leaves with a force that spins my head. "It's coming," I say, the words insubstantial as fog.

"Just a minute more," says Delman, tearing a strip of tape from a roll.

But there isn't a minute. It's coming.

Timmons returns from Daphne's room, his face grim. He pulls Nadia to the side.

A shadow darkens the crack under the unlatched door. My breaths come shallow and rapid, but no one seems to notice.

"Two of them," Timmons says softly. "One in a chair; a child in the bed. From the looks of them, they've been dead for years."

Nails like needles scrape the lever.

"I found these lodged in the skull of the one in the chair." Timmons hands Nadia gray slivers of metal.

"What the hell is that? Nails?"

The latch moves.

"It's here! Oh, god, it's here!" I kick away from Delman, surprising the medic and knocking him over. Nadia lunges at me, but I scramble under her hands. Behind me, the door bursts open, and the Fiend rushes in, chittering insanely. I don't look back but claw my way across the floor to Daphne's room. Furniture tumbles behind me. Nadia and Timmons scream, but their words are swallowed by the staccato of the Fiend's clicking mandibles.

I slam the door and fumble the lock into place.

The Fiend screams.

Fists pound on the door, but I push my back against it, even though I know the lock is strong.

"Paul! Let us in. Paul!"

Elise cowers in the chair at Daphne's bedside. Owen stands in the corner, his back to me. In the darkness, he looks like a standing lamp covered with a black sheet, but I am relieved that he's here and that he's safe.

"Paul!"

I shove my fingers into my ears. The noise outside is horrific and it echoes painfully inside my head.

Elise's lips move silently in the shadow of her face.

"I will protect you," I say. The dull thuds of fists on the door slow. Everyone in the room is still and quiet like shadows in the night as we wait for the Fiend to finish its grisly work and leave. Then we will go on, like we always have. Now and forever.

#CONNOLLYHOUSE
#WESHOULDNTBEHERE

SEANAN McGUIRE

Boo Peep @boo_peep • 19:42
Hello boos and ghouls, and welcome to a very special episode of
Go For Ghosts, the Internet's BEST, TOTALLY UNSTAGED ghost-
hunting show!

Boo Peep @boo_peep • 19:43
For the live camera feed, go to goforghosts.com. Be sure to follow
@screamking @screamqueen and @deadhot for CONSTANT UPDATES.

Boo Peep @boo_peep • 19:45
We have permission to explore one of the most INFAMOUS haunted
houses in all of Maine: the Connolly House on Peaks Island.

Boo Peep @boo_peep • 19:47
If you are unaware of this terrible MURDER PALACE and its
HORRIFYING HISTORY, we have resources linked at goforghosts.com.

Boo Peep @boo_peep • 19:50
The current owners of the house, Harry and Jenna Connolly, have
agreed to this UNPRECEDENTED ACCESS because the house . . .

Boo Peep @boo_peep • 19:51

. . . which was the site of SEVENTEEN BRUTAL MURDERS in 1903, is to be torn down at the end of the summer.

Boo Peep @boo_peep • 19:52

We will be the first and last people to film there. And it begins in EIGHT MINUTES. Follow #connollyhouse for all the terrifying details.

Boo Peep retweeted
Scream King @screamking • 19:55

Ha ha can't wait to see you run out of there in tears.

Boo Peep @boo_peep • 19:55

@screamking oh please you're totally going to be the first to snap. :) :) :) @screamqueen and I will be first in/last out. #horrorgirls

Boo Peep retweeted
Scream Queen @screamqueen • 19:56

You tell 'im! GIRL POWER 4EVR.

Boo Peep @boo_peep • 19:57

@screamqueen You know it girl. ;) You + me = the TRUE ghost hunters.

Boo Peep @boo_peep • 20:01

HERE WE GO! #connollyhouse #thebigscare

Boo Peep @boo_peep • 20:03

Front porch. Cold—too cold for July. Lots of dead leaves. No spiders. Sort of weird. Rest of the island is WEBBED. #connollyhouse

Boo Peep @boo_peep • 20:04
Key doesn't want to work. What, @deadhot, have you never unlocked a door before? #connollyhouse #haha

Boo Peep retweeted
Dead Hot @deadhot • 20:06
Bite me. I got it open. #connollyhouse

Boo Peep @boo_peep • 20:08
WOW. I hope you're following the video feed, horror fans! You can FEEL the cold in the living room. #connollyhouse

Boo Peep @boo_peep • 20:09
The porch was chilly but this is FRIGID. I can see my breath. Definite paranormal activity here. #connollyhouse

Boo Peep retweeted
Scream Queen @screamqueen • 20:10
Don't call it that I think the movie people trademarked it. #connollyhouse

Boo Peep @boo_peep • 20:10
@screamqueen LOL #connollyhouse

Boo Peep @boo_peep • 20:12
Getting serious now. @screamking setting up PKE meters, thermostats. If anything comes through here, we'll know. #connollyhouse

Boo Peep @boo_peep • 20:13
There's a feeling of palpable menace in this room. I so believe that seventeen people died here. #connollyhouse

Boo Peep @boo_peep • 20:15
I think the roof is sagging a little. There's something weird about the corners. #connollyhouse

Boo Peep @boo_peep • 20:20
OH MY GOD TELL ME THAT CAME THROUGH ON THE VIDEO. #connollyhouse

Boo Peep @boo_peep • 20:23
Fuck. Video didn't pick up noise. Everyone here heard it. Like fingernails on crystal. Eerie and LOUD. #connollyhouse

Boo Peep @boo_peep • 20:25
Fifteen minutes in the entryway. House hasn't told us to get out yet. Shall we go deeper? #connollyhouse #yes #yesweshall

Boo Peep retweeted
Scream King @screamking • 20:27
We need to split up. @boo_peep, you take @deadhot. I'll take @screamqueen. #connollyhouse

Boo Peep retweeted
Scream King @screamking • 20:27
@boo_peep @deadhot @screamqueen We'll meet up here in half an hour. #connollyhouse

Boo Peep @boo_peep • 20:28
@screamking Aye aye sir! #connollyhouse

Boo Peep @boo_peep • 20:30
Since @deadhot has our camera, I get to keep the text feed going! Aren't you lucky, followers? #connollyhouse

Boo Peep @boo_peep • 20:32
The hallway is even colder than the living room. Feels like we're walking into a freezer. I want a coat. #connollyhouse

Boo Peep @boo_peep • 20:33
There are pale patches on the walls where pictures used to be. The wallpaper is patterned with little white flowers . . . #connollyhouse

Boo Peep @boo_peep • 20:33
. . . and scratches that look like writing, but not any language I know. Ugh. So creepy. No wonder the Connollys snapped. #connollyhouse

Boo Peep @boo_peep • 20:36
While @deadhot gets some good atmosphere footage, here's a little history: the Connolly family built this house in 1843. #connollyhouse

Boo Peep @boo_peep • 20:38
The Connollys lived on Peaks Island for sixty years. They were well liked. Good neighbors. Until the day . . . #connollyhouse

Boo Peep @boo_peep • 20:40
. . . when they invited all the neighborhood children over & slit their throats in a ritual that has never been decoded. #connollyhouse

Boo Peep @boo_peep • 20:42
Since that day, neighbors have reported strange sounds, sightings around the house. No one has lived here since the deaths. #connollyhouse

Boo Peep @boo_peep • 20:43
And here's the best part: the Connollys themselves, Shawn and Sarah, were NEVER FOUND. #connollyhouse

Boo Peep @boo_peep • 20:44
Maybe their ritual worked, and they have gone to join their demonic masters. Maybe we'll find out today. #connollyhouse

Boo Peep @boo_peep • 20:46
CAMERA FEEDS ARE ONLINE! The video can't convey the sense of frozen menace in this room. #connollyhouse

Boo Peep @boo_peep • 20:48
Everything looks normal. Outdated, but stuff you might find in your grandparents' house. But it's not normal. #connollyhouse

Boo Peep @boo_peep • 20:50
I know that's so Blair Witch of me—there is an evil here oooOoooOoo—but it's true. This room isn't normal. #connollyhouse

Boo Peep @boo_peep • 20:51
It's like it still remembers what happened here, and hasn't forgiven, or maybe it hasn't stopped waiting. #connollyhouse

Boo Peep @boo_peep • 20:53
Waiting for it to happen again. #connollyhouse

Boo Peep @boo_peep • 20:55
Ha ha ha woo that was sort of off the rails, wasn't it? That would be a story for our competitors. "Boo Peep cries boo hoo." #connollyhouse

Boo Peep @boo_peep • 20:57
But I think it says something that none of our competitors asked if they could come here. They knew this was the real deal. #connollyhouse

Boo Peep @boo_peep • 21:01
Sometimes it's easier to chase fake ghosts than real ones.
#connollyhouse

Boo Peep retweeted
Dead Hot @deadhot • 21:02
Uh Peep you wanna lighten it up a little? LOL you're so dramatic.
#connollyhouse

Boo Peep @boo_peep • 21:03
@deadhot Bite me, fanboy. You feel it too. #connollyhouse

Boo Peep @boo_peep • 21:04
Something is really wrong here. #connollyhouse

Boo Peep @boo_peep • 21:06
Something is wrong with the way the walls fit together. I can't . . .
I can't explain any better than that. #connollyhouse

Boo Peep @boo_peep • 21:10
WHOA BREAKING NEWS. @deadhot opened what he thought was
the pantry, found stairs to basement. #connollyhouse

Boo Peep @boo_peep • 21:12
Air coming up from basement actually WARMER than
air in kitchen. Maybe somehow connected to outside???
#connollyhouse

Boo Peep @boo_peep • 21:13
SHOULD WE GO INTO THE BASEMENT OF THE
MURDERHOUSE?! Tweet me, Y or N! #connollyhouse

Boo Peep @boo_peep • 21:16

. . . wow, that was fast. I guess the choice is easier
when you're not the one in the murderhouse. :/
#connollyhouse

Boo Peep @boo_peep • 21:18

@screamking @screamqueen Hey we found a basement & put it
to an audience vote. #connollyhouse

Boo Peep @boo_peep • 21:20

@screamking @screamqueen Long story short it looks like
we're going to go down. #connollyhouse

Boo Peep @boo_peep • 21:22

@screamking @screamqueen Want us to wait
for you??? #connollyhouse #strengthinnumbers
#somethingiswrong

Boo Peep retweeted
Scream King @screamking • 21:23

you go on ahead @screamqueen and I found something up here a
library #connollyhouse

Boo Peep retweeted
Scream King @screamking • 21:25

all the books are still here so many books I have to know what
they say #connollyhouse

Boo Peep @boo_peep • 21:28

@screamking LOL okay I guess I should've known we'd lose
you if you found any weird writing. #connollyhouse

Boo Peep @boo_peep • 21:29
@deadhot I guess it's just you and me. Let's get this party started. #connollyhouse

Boo Peep @boo_peep • 21:30
Here we go. @deadhot is starting down w/camera and flashlight, I am following. #connollyhouse

Boo Peep @boo_peep • 21:32
Walls almost warm to touch. The bannister feels slick, slimy, like running hand along a giant salamander. #connollyhouse #somethingiswrong

Boo Peep retweeted
Randy Kaufman @rkaufman • 21:33
Why do you keep using hashtag #somethingiswrong? This rocks!!! #everythingisright

Boo Peep retweeted
Ivy Odell @climbinivy • 21:33
I don't get the #somethingiswrong thing—what gives?

Boo Peep @boo_peep • 21:34
Where does that tag keep coming from? Technical glitch? NOTHING IS WRONG. This is AMAZING. #connollyhouse

Boo Peep @boo_peep • 21:35
We are so privileged to be here. No one has breathed this air in decades. #connollyhouse

Boo Peep @boo_peep • 21:37
Not that it's not terrifying in here. The walls are wrong, and too slick. The air tastes like pennies. #connollyhouse

Boo Peep @boo_peep • 21:40
I thought the water table was close to the
surface on the island, but we're still descending.
#connollyhouse

Boo Peep @boo_peep • 21:46
That noise again from behind us, somewhere far
behind. Like nails on hard crystal. Makes my teeth hurt.
#connollyhouse

Boo Peep @boo_peep • 21:50
How are we still descending? How is this possible???
#connollyhouse

Boo Peep @boo_peep • 21:53
Stairs are angled oddly. Feels almost like we're climbing. LOL not
possible. Basement must be v. deep. #connollyhouse

Boo Peep @boo_peep • 21:55
Getting warmer. Glad I don't have a coat. #connollyhouse

Boo Peep @boo_peep • 21:58
This isn't right. #connollyhouse

Boo Peep @boo_peep • 22:00
@deadhot Does it feel like we should have reached the bottom by now?
#connollyhouse

Boo Peep retweeted
Dead Hot @deadhot • 22:00
I guess they built this place on the bedrock. We're probably below sea level. Creepy. #connollyhouse

Boo Peep @boo_peep • 21:59
. . . good thing Maine isn't known for its earthquakes. #connollyhouse

Boo Peep @boo_peep • 21:58
@screamking @screamqueen You guys okay up there? Basement is weird. Seem to be going UP. #connollyhouse #somethingiswrong

Boo Peep @boo_peep • 21:56
@screamking @screamqueen We've been going downstairs for half an hour, still not at the bottom. #connollyhouse

Boo Peep retweeted
Scream King @screamking • 21:54
no no everything is good everything is wonderful we have it under control. #connollyhouse

Boo Peep retweeted
Scream King @screamking • 21:52
don't come to the library my sister is resting right now you might wake her shhh. #connollyhouse

Boo Peep @boo_peep • 21:50
@screamking Um, okay, naptime in the haunted house? That's a little hardcore for @screamqueen. #connollyhouse

Boo Peep retweeted
Scream King @screamking • 21:48
she can eternal lie. #connollyhouse

Boo Peep @boo_peep • 21:45
@screamking Whatever that means. #connollyhouse

Boo Peep @boo_peep • 21:42
Something weird with time stamps. Can't focus on it much. Walls here
DEFINITELY warm to touch. #connollyhouse

Boo Peep @boo_peep • 21:40
When I hold a light up to the wall, I can see same weird
scratch marks as in wallpaper upstairs. #connollyhouse
#somethingiswrong

Boo Peep @boo_peep • 21:39
It looks more like writing here, in the dark. It looks like
it makes WORDS. #connollyhouse #somethingiswrong
#helphelphelp

Boo Peep @boo_peep • 21:36
Okay there have GOT to be technical issues. My time stamps are
wrong, & those are not my hashtags. #connollyhouse

Boo Peep @boo_peep • 21:35
IGNORE THE HASHTAGS THEY ARE LYING TO YOU.
#connollyhouse

Boo Peep @boo_peep • 21:33
Stairs continue to slant down, but feel so much like we're going up.
Doesn't make sense. #connollyhouse

Boo Peep @boo_peep • 21:30
Feels like we have been walking for a long time. @deadhot feels same
way. #connollyhouse #weshouldntbehere

Boo Peep @boo_peep • 21:25
WHAT WAS THAT SOUND. #connollyhouse #weshouldntbehere

Boo Peep @boo_peep • 21:23
Something is SCREAMING up ahead in the dark HOW CAN
ANYTHING BE IN FRONT OF US. #connollyhouse

Boo Peep @boo_peep • 21:20
@screamking We need you can you come down to the basement
please it's getting weird down here. #connollyhouse

Boo Peep retweeted
Scream King @screamking • 21:19
sorry can't too much to do up here but sent @screamqueen to help you.
#connollyhouse

Boo Peep retweeted
Scream King @screamking • 21:18
she should be there soon don't worry nothing to worry about.
#connollyhouse

Boo Peep retweeted
Scream King @screamking • 21:16
she wasn't happy about being woken up just fyi. #connollyhouse

Boo Peep @boo_peep • 21:15
Okay. Okay. So @screamking is busy and his sleepy sister is coming.
#connollyhouse

Boo Peep @boo_peep • 21:14

But that's cool. @deadhot is with me, and we are GHOST
HUNTERS EXTRAORDINAIRE. #connollyhouse
#somethingiswrong

Boo Peep @boo_peep • 21:10

I ain't afraid of no ghost. #theclassics #connollyhouse
#weshouldntbehere

Boo Peep @boo_peep • 21:08

Something on the stairs . . . wet. Sticky. Maybe
we're finally reaching the bottom. #connollyhouse
#somethingiswrong

Boo Peep @boo_peep • 21:05

Not sure how much longer I'll have service. Stairs seem to go on forever.
More of that wet, sticky stuff. Looks like tar. #connollyhouse

Boo Peep @boo_peep • 21:00

@deadhot hold up a second I want to figure out what this stuff is.
#connollyhouse

Boo Peep @boo_peep • 20:53

OH GOD OH GOD OH GOD. #connollyhouse #getoutgetout
#getoutwhileyoucan

Boo Peep @boo_peep • 20:50

BLOOD IT'S BLOOD THERE'S BLOOD ON THE STAIRS.
#connollyhouse #weshouldntbehere

Boo Peep @boo_peep • 20:49

HOW DOES BLOOD EVEN GET DOWN HERE. #connollyhouse

Boo Peep @boo_peep • 20:45
OK. OK. I am taking deep breaths. I am a professional ghost
hunter. It's just . . . it's a rat. There's a dead rat down here.
#connollyhouse

Boo Peep @boo_peep • 20:44
a dead rat that bled a lot. do rats have this much blood in them?
#connollyhouse

Boo Peep @boo_peep • 20:42
we should go back we shouldn't be here @deadhot let's go back.
#connollyhouse

Boo Peep @boo_peep • 19:40
. . . where, where did he go? He was just here. WHERE DID HE GO?!
#connollyhouse #somethingiswrong

Boo Peep @boo_peep • 20:39
@deadhot @screamqueen @screamking HELLO IS ANYONE THERE I
AM FREAKING OUT THIS ISN'T FUNNY. #connollyhouse

Boo Peep @boo_peep • 20:38
@deadhot @screamqueen @screamking if this is a joke IT ISN'T
FUNNY come get me WHY ARE YOU DOING THIS. #connollyhouse

Boo Peep @boo_peep • 20:37
oh god I can't stop tweeting I'll be alone and I can't tell which way is up
both ways feel like up. #connollyhouse #somethingiswrong

Boo Peep @boo_peep • 20:35
I think . . . I think I hear something. I think I hear @deadhot. OK. I'm
going to be OK. #connollyhouse

Boo Peep @boo_peep • 20:33

How did he get behind me? These stairs are narrow. It doesn't make sense and I DON'T CARE. #connollyhouse

Boo Peep @boo_peep • 20:31

Going to backtrack to catch up with him. #connollyhouse

Boo Peep @boo_peep • 20:19

no no no no no no no no no no no no no. #connollyhouse

Boo Peep @boo_peep • 20:15

NO NO NO NO NO NO NO NO. #connollyhouse

Boo Peep @boo_peep • 20:11

I DIDN'T SEE THAT I DIDN'T SEE THAT THAT DIDN'T HAPPEN NONE OF THIS IS HAPPENING. #connollyhouse #getout #nowwhileyoucan

Boo Peep @boo_peep • 20:09

oh god oh god no I can't I can't this isn't real I #connollyhouse

Boo Peep @boo_peep • 20:02

OK. #connollyhouse #somethingiswrong

Boo Peep @boo_peep • 19:57

Sorry about that, horror fans. I thought . . . I saw . . . something on the stairs. Something that wasn't really there. #connollyhouse

Boo Peep @boo_peep • 19:54

I'm better now. I know it was just nerves talking. #connollyhouse

Boo Peep @boo_peep • 19:50
I know @screamqueen is still upstairs in the library. She's
not skinless and standing in front of the pantry door.
#connollyhouse

Boo Peep @boo_peep • 19:48
Besides, we went down for half an hour. I can't have gone back up that
quickly. See? It's impossible. #connollyhouse #butisawher

Boo Peep @boo_peep • 19:45
Just like women without skin, standing in front of the pantry door, are
impossible. #connollyhouse #shesaidmyname

Boo Peep @boo_peep • 19:40
I think I need to go down again. I can find @deadhot. He'll tell me this
is all a prank. #connollyhouse

Boo Peep @boo_peep • 19:38
I'll even forgive him. #connollyhouse #itsnotaprank #getout
#timeisbroken

Boo Peep @boo_peep • 19:25
I think I'm back to where I was when we got separated. I'm going farther
down. #connollyhouse

Boo Peep @boo_peep • 19:20
The scratches on the walls are getting denser and denser. I can almost
read them. I almost know what they say. #connollyhouse

Boo Peep @boo_peep • 19:18
I . . . I don't think I want to know what they say. #connollyhouse
#weshouldntbehere

Boo Peep @boo_peep • 19:13

who would write such terrible things o god the things the walls are saying to me make them stop. #connollyhouse #somethingiswrong

Boo Peep @boo_peep • 19:10

dont make me listen to the walls I cant I cant I cant I #connollyhouse

Boo Peep @boo_peep • 19:00

OK. I'm back. I'm . . . I'm sorry. I just lost track of myself for a little while. #connollyhouse

Boo Peep @boo_peep • 18:57

Something is wrong with the way the corners are shaped. They have too many angles. Or maybe not enough? #connollyhouse #somethingiswrong

Boo Peep @boo_peep • 18:53

I don't think corners are supposed to change when you stop looking at them. I think that's against the rules. #connollyhouse

Boo Peep @boo_peep • 18:50

please someone reply to me why isn't anyone replying are these even making it out of here. #connollyhouse

Boo Peep @boo_peep • 18:45

maybe they're all queuing up won't that be fun when I come back into a service zone. #connollyhouse

Boo Peep @boo_peep • 18:41

why is the camera on the ground? We don't get footage when the camera is on the ground. #connollyhouse

Boo Peep @boo_peep • 18:35
I have the camera now. It feels solid. Reassuring. This is a real thing that we brought in with us. #connollyhouse

Boo Peep @boo_peep • 18:33
It has the right number of angles. It won't change, even if I look away. #connollyhouse

Boo Peep @boo_peep • 18:25
Everything is clearer through the night scope. Even the writing on the walls. #connollyhouse

Boo Peep @boo_peep • 18:19
I don't know why I was so scared of it before. It's just telling me the story of the house. #connollyhouse #somethingiswrong

Boo Peep @boo_peep • 15:15
OH MY GOD IT'S THE BOTTOM OF THE STAIRS. #connollyhouse

Boo Peep @boo_peep • 10:11
I didn't think they would EVER end. #connollyhouse

Boo Peep @boo_peep • 09:50
The basement is very large, and has no walls or corners, but only blackness, which is silly. #connollyhouse

Boo Peep @boo_peep • 09:48
Every room has walls. Every room has corners. You need edges to make the world seem real. #connollyhouse

Boo Peep @boo_peep • 08:50

There is a circle on the floor. There is something in the circle. Something dark and wet. #connollyhouse #dontlook

Boo Peep @boo_peep • 08:42

What the hell is that? What is it? How can it be there? It shouldn't be here. #connollyhouse #dontlook

Boo Peep @boo_peep • 08:37

That sound again. It's almost pleasant now. It's familiar. I'm approaching the circle. #connollyhouse #DONTLOOK

Boo Peep @boo_peep • 08:12

Whatever the thing inside the circle is, it looks solid like nothing else in the basement does. It has edges. #connollyhouse

Boo Peep @boo_peep • 07:59

It has eyes. #connollyhouse

Boo Peep @boo_peep • 07:58

o god o god I think I found @deadhot #connollyhouse

Boo Peep @boo_peep • 07:50

how #connollyhouse

Boo Peep @boo_peep • 07:31

what the fuck what the fuck WHAT THE FUCK IS GOING ON WHAT THE FUCK IS HAPPENING WHAT THE FU #connollyhouse

WHAT THE #@&% IS THAT?

Boo Peep @boo_peep • 07:06
Wait who's talking? Oh god WHO IS DOWN HERE WITH ME.
#connollyhouse

Boo Peep @boo_peep • 07:03
I can't find them where are they why won't they stop oh God.
#connollyhouse

Boo Peep @boo_peep • 07:00
IT'S MY VOICE IT'S MY VOICE AND I'M SAYING THE THINGS
FROM THE WALLS AND I CAN'T STOP. #connollyhou

Boo Peep @boo_peep • 06:20
WHY CAN'T I STOP WHAT AM I SAYING WHAT DOES IT MEAN

Boo Peep @boo_peep • 06:03
IT'S NOT JUST A STORY THE HOUSE LIED TO ME HOW CAN A
HOUSE LIE

Boo Peep @boo_peep • 05:12
the thing in the circle the thing in the circle it's not @deadhot anymore
it's not PETER anymore IT'S MOVING IT SEES ME

Boo Peep @boo_peep • 04:07
NO NO NO NO NO NO NO NO NO NO NO NO NO

Boo Peep @boo_peep • 03:06
no

Boo Peep @boo_peep • 02:05
make it stop no I cant see this I cant no

Boo Peep @boo_peep • 01:04
no

Boo Peep @boo_peep • 00:03
it has no shadow IT HAS NO SHADOW it is the shadow IT IS THE
SHADOW AND IT NEVER ENDS IT NEVER NEVER ENDS

Boo Peep @boo_peep • 00:02
how

Boo Peep @boo_peep • 00:01
no

Boo Peep @boo_peep • 00:00
. . . oh

Boo Peep @boo_peep • 00:00
Sorry about the fuss. I was confused before. Old house + stale air =
hallucinations. No big deal. #connollyhouse

Boo Peep @boo_peep • 00:00
I'm back upstairs now. Everyone is with me. @deadhot
and @screamking and @screamqueen. We're all fine.
#connollyhouse

Boo Peep @boo_peep • 00:00
We just found some surprises the original owners left for any
unexpected guests, that's all. Like party favors. #connollyhouse

Boo Peep @boo_peep • 00:00
The house was just so happy to see us, it didn't know how to contain
itself. #connollyhouse

Boo Peep @boo_peep • 00:00

Joke ha ha. Houses aren't alive. That would be silly. #connollyhouse

Boo Peep @boo_peep • 00:00

The owners should be ashamed of how they've let the place go. This proud old lady deserves so much better. #connollyhouse

Boo Peep @boo_peep • 00:00

I think I'll live here now. I think we'll all live here now. #connollyhouse

Boo Peep @boo_peep • 00:00

You should come live here too. I can show you what the shadows showed me. How they bent away from the truth. #no #connollyhouse

Boo Peep @boo_peep • 00:00

Come to Peaks Island. Come let me show you the truth. #no #stayaway #itsmakingmelie #connollyhouse

Boo Peep @boo_peep • 00:00

Come. #helpme #killme #dontleavemehere #connollyhouse

Boo Peep @boo_peep • 00:00

Come. #please #please #please #please #connollyhouse

Boo Peep @boo_peep • 00:00

Come. #dontleavemeinthedark #connollyhouse

Boo Peep @boo_peep • 00:00

Come. #theyweremyhashtags #itriedtowarnmyself #connollyhouse

Boo Peep @boo_peep • 00:00

Come. #ifailed #youllfailtoo #connollyhouse

THE HOUSE THAT LOVE BUILT

GRADY HENDRIX

"That sunrise is God setting his world on fire and we're born anew out of the ashes," Angela says. "Every day begins with the promise of the Resurrection."

Angela is always saying stupid shit like that. Jesus loves you. He is risen. Judge not lest ye be judged. It's why I fell in love with her. Angela trusts that the world is a rational place built according to God's plan. She can't imagine anyone might want to hurt her.

"I love you," I say.

"So sweet," she says. "What time are you leaving?"

"Few minutes."

"I'll miss you every second," she says. "Daddy told me they're opening a Boeing plant down by Charleston. It'd mean no more traveling."

I hear the door open behind me, and a yawn.

"Brrr," Karen says. "It's fucking freezing."

"I love it out here," I say, not turning around.

Karen drops into the chair on my right, hands shoved into her armpits, boots unlaced, wearing one of my flannel shirts.

"We wouldn't have to move," Angela says. "It's only a forty-five minute drive."

"It's a Nicole Kidman morning," Karen says, hauling out one of her old jokes. "Pretty to look at but frosty as fuck."

"I've heard that before," I say, careful to make sure I'm always talking to them both.

"One of the churches I speak at has some guest apartments in Hanahan," Angela says. "You could stay there if you're ever too tired to drive back."

"Think your material's so fresh?" Karen snaps. "I've heard your jokes so many times, I'm about ready to stab you in the balls."

I smile.

"Trying to get rid of me so soon?" I say to them.

"Oh, sweetheart, no," Angela says, leaning on my shoulder and resting her hand on my heart. "I'm going to miss listening to this every night."

"Hell, no," Karen says, cupping my crotch with one hand. "Your balls are the only part of you I like."

These are the moments that make my delicate situation worthwhile.

"Want to go upstairs?" I ask. "Say a real good-bye?"

Karen traces the edge of my ear with her tongue. Angela buries her face in my chest and gives a shy nod.

"Let me run to the little boy's room," I say. "Meet you there."

Then I take my coffee cup and leave the two of them on the deck, watching the sun come up over the trees, completely oblivious to each other. I wash my mug and put it on the draining board, then I take a piss, brush my teeth, head for the bedroom.

The sex puts a pepper up my ass and makes fire shoot out my dick. I can't remember having it any other way.

My first jump is from Charleston to St. Louis with a load of generator enclosures. Whenever JT has something over-width, over-height, or over-weight, they have me haul the load because I'm a careful guy by nature. Still, they've been pressuring me to take a partner again. This time, Danny tries to sweeten the pot by offering me a thousand dollars to train a codriver.

My sanity is worth more than a thousand dollars. Being on the road is the only time I'm alone. When my phone rings, it tells me if it's Karen or

Angela before I put her on speaker so I can relax and talk natural. I'm not giving that up for no one.

Driving long haul suits me. I like systems. I like organization. Every eleven hours I take a mandatory ten-hour break. The computer notifies dispatch every time I turn the key. There's a governor on the fuel line that won't let me go above sixty-nine mph. My Qualcomm lets me look at speed, routes, mileage, every single bitty detail. There aren't any surprises.

Back when I first met Karen, I loved surprises. I was wearing my whiskey-face and throwing punches with some sailors on shore leave in a honky-tonk outside New Orleans when I saw her crawling across the floor on wallet patrol, scooping up cell phones and cash that fell out of our pockets. When the police arrived, I headed out the back door, where I discovered Karen having an intimate encounter with a familiar wallet.

"Finders keepers," she said.

I pointed out that while her philosophy was punchy, it flew in the face of several hundred years of jurisprudence. She invited me to suck her dick. One hour later, we were in bed, and while I tried my hardest, eventually we gave up and she sucked mine instead. By the time I hit the road again, I was forty hours behind, which isn't a problem if you're willing to gobble speed and fake your logbook, which I was happy to do in those days.

I'd never considered myself a one-woman man, but when that haul was over, I found myself back in New Orleans. Life with Karen involved a whole lot of whiskey and a whole lot of fucking. My work schedule was the only fly in our ointment. While I was on the road, I knew that it was highly unlikely she was sitting in front of the TV sewing buttons on my shirts, and consequently, I became overly sensitive. Soon, the time we spent fighting was eating into the time we should have spent fucking, so I went down on one knee and made an honest woman out of her.

With my first big trucking money, I'd bought a piece of land way out past Walterboro and built a house that had sat lonely for the better part of

WHAT THE #@&% IS THAT?

eight years. I moved Karen there, and the novelty of buying furniture and playing Holly Homemaker kept her happy for a while, but before long, the same questions came back to torment me.

"Self," I would ask, "what does a young woman of Karen's inclinations get up to in Walterboro while you're on the road?"

Self did not have a satisfying answer, and soon, the only time we weren't fighting was when we were blowing rails or I was on the road, and after I failed a piss test, I wasn't on the road anymore. Our situation quickly deteriorated. Soon Whiskey-Face was joined by his friends Coke-Face, Pill-Face, and Vodka-Face. We'd start fighting early Monday morning, and by late Friday evening, we'd still be fighting.

It all came to a halt one day when I woke up at the crack of dawn, cold and naked in the woods behind my house. At some point in the night, I had apparently burned my pants for warmth, been pleased with the results, and then piled the rest of my clothes on the fire. This must have been a bridge too far for Karen, because she was nowhere to be found. Instead, there was a note from her on the living room wall that read:

EAT SHIT

Impressively, she'd written it in actual shit.

I had to repaint the wall, but then it didn't match the other walls, so I repainted them, too. That made the rest of the house look drab, so I repainted the entire place. Before I knew it, I'd ripped out the cigarette-scarred carpets, replaced the busted-out balusters on the stairs, hung a new bathroom door to replace the one I'd kicked down in a fit of romantic enthusiasm, and hauled all my furniture to Goodwill. Two months later, I realized I hadn't had a drink in weeks and I didn't much want one anymore. When I finished, my house was clean and empty and so was my mind. I got my CDL back in shape, found a job on probationary status with JT Trucking, and hit the road again.

A few years later at a Christmas oyster roast, Danny the dispatcher told me that I was a social misfit who needed a woman to make me less awkward to be around. He suggested his sister and that's how I met

Angela. A year later, Karen came back home without a word, and I've been juggling the both of them ever since.

Unloading takes forever because all the docks are overbooked, so when I pull up to my house, it's past three in the morning. I call it Schrödinger's House because when I'm present, my wife seems to exist in two states simultaneously: as Karen and as Angela. I cut my headlights and roll into the driveway real quiet-like so I don't wake either one of them up.

Key in the lock, take off my boots, tiptoe into the living room where Karen's curled up on the sofa, an empty six-pack of Michelob Ultra on the coffee table, TV advertising some kind of rejuvenating cream.

"Hey, baby," she says, all sleepy. "Missed you."

Her body is warm and all her hard angles are soft and it isn't until we're about to begin round two that I hear Angela on the stairs.

"Robert?" Angela calls down softly. "Is that you?"

She starts walking downstairs as I pull my pants on. "Love 'em and leave 'em," Karen says.

"I have to take a piss," I say.

"I hate that phrase," Angela says as I walk into the hall. "Can I get a kiss first?"

I give her a good one.

"Someone's excited," she says.

Then we go upstairs. I know there'll be hell to pay in the morning for ditching Karen, but after two weeks on the road, I'm not really thinking much about consequences.

"I think our house is haunted," Karen says.

"Do you still love me?" Angela asks.

Karen is cutting her toenails on the couch, which is one more thing I'm going to have to take the rap for if Angela finds any stuck to the carpet. Biological byproducts tend to get noticed once they're separated from the body, and I've had some close calls because Karen is not a big fan of flushing toilets. Angela is folding the laundry, which I'm going to have to pretend I did if Karen wonders how all my laundry wound up back in my drawers.

I ignore them both and keep reading. Ever since Karen came back, I've discovered that reading is the perfect pastime. No one demands an answer from a guy who's got his nose stuck in a book.

"I said," Karen repeats, snapping off another toenail. "Our house. It is haunted."

This nail lands on my thigh and I pluck it off with distaste and put it in my pants pocket. It's thick and yellowed. My father had toenails like this, minus the flaking red nail polish.

"Why do you think that?" I ask them both.

Angela bows her head and studies the interior of the laundry basket. Tears are sliding down her nose and plopping onto my clothes.

"You're drinking again," Angela says. "I found the cans this morning. And last night in the living room, I heard you pleasuring yourself. I know I must be doing something wrong as a wife for you to be so unhappy with me."

"First thing," Karen says. "I was wearing your red flannel the day you left. I dumped it on the floor by the bed after we fucked, and then half an hour later, I found it hung up on the hanger. Second thing, that spooky Jesus picture on the dresser in the bedroom. The second you leave, I turn it around to face the wall. Later, it's facing the bed again. That freaks me out, so I put on the alarm and go stay with Clem and Louis. Almost every night you're gone, the motion detector goes off and ADT has to call me. They woke me up five times."

That's bad. Normally, the two of them sort of glide past each other like ships in the night. Karen buys a bottle of Popov, and Angela reaches around it for the cereal. Angela hangs an inspirational Christian painting and Karen assumes I must have put it up before I went on the road. One of them thinks I'm a secret drinker, the other assumes I'm a Jesus freak. But Angela shouldn't be setting off the alarm. Something's changing.

"Why do you think that is?" I ask.

"I think it's a fucking ghost," Karen says. "I think there's a ghost in this house, flushing toilets, cleaning up after me like my fucking mother, turning pictures around, setting off the alarm."

"There's a dark presence between us," Angela says. "You're always distracted. You're always thinking of someone else. I only get half of you."

"You know that's not true," I say.

"The fuck I do," Karen says. "I'm getting rid of this ghost, and you can either lead, follow, or get out of the way."

"Half the time, you don't even look at me when you talk to me," Angela says, crying harder. I hate seeing her cry. She's always been an ugly crier.

"Don't be like that," I say, and they both think I'm talking to them.

Karen announces she's going to consult Clem and Louis, her gay friends, on how to get rid of our ghost, since their gayness makes them experts on everything. This gives me a chance to comfort Angela, who is becoming hysterical. I'm in the front hall saying good-bye to Karen while Angela runs upstairs and slams the bedroom door.

"Did you hear that?" Karen asks, pointing at the ceiling.

I shrug. It's too risky to say anything in the front hall. Sound travels in this house.

"You're such a punk," Karen says, then storms out of the house and slams the door behind her.

I turn to head up the stairs and see Angela looking down at me, hands on the banister.

"I didn't hear you go outside," she says, wiping her cheeks with the flat of her hand.

"I was going to take a walk," I say. "But I changed my mind. I owe you an explanation. Last night, I wanted to split a beer to celebrate with you when I got home, but you can't buy less than a six-pack. Then I got here and you hadn't bothered to wait up, so I guess I felt kind of ignored and I turned on the TV and before you know it . . ."

Carefully, I approach. She lets me put my hands on her frail shoulders.

"What about the other thing?" she asks. I give her my dumb face. "I heard you in the living room, making those sounds. Am I not enough for you?"

"I was frustrated. You were asleep," I say. "It won't happen again. And I'll go to a meeting tonight. I promise."

Soon, I'm rubbing her back and making comforting noises. Karen's probably getting high with her buddies, so I've got plenty of time to turn this around. By the time I'm putting two fingers underneath Angela's chin and turning her face up to mine, she's starting to breathe harder and her lips are parted. She presses herself to my front and slides her hands into the pockets of my jeans. I remember what's in there the second her hand jerks back. I twist away too late as, laughing, Angela pulls out the toenail and holds it up between us.

"Gross," she giggles. "Put them in the toilet, honeybear. Are you saving—"

I'm grabbing for it, but it's too small, and she sees the nail polish, and her face falls.

"It was in the cab of my truck," I explain. "Probably one of the other drivers had himself a lot lizard."

It's not enough. The channels change and all of a sudden she's channeling the wrath of God. Apparently, she had her own paranormal activity while I was on the road. Her picture of Jesus kept turning its back on the bed. The alarm kept getting shut off and reset. ADT came to the house five times in the middle of the night for no reason. She found my clothes thrown on the floor. There was a fifth of vodka hidden in the toilet tank. But her explanation differs from Karen's. Angela accuses me of allowing demonic influences into this house via my alleged infidelity.

I don't like being accused of things I haven't done. I don't like being called a liar. I don't like being put on trial for a crime I didn't commit, so I tell her what I think of her behavior, in no uncertain terms. Perhaps I speak more harshly than I intend.

It takes her a while to get herself under control, but eventually, she tells me she's going to talk to Reverend Gary. She has some serious thinking to do. I tell her I'll clean up the house, and about an hour after she leaves,

I'm getting the laundry put away when Karen walks back in, stoned, a box beneath her arm.

"We're going to solve this spooky shit right now," she says, sliding her tobacco tongue into my mouth. "Lookie."

She shows me the squashed-up box held together with masking tape. OUIJA, it says on the cover.

Karen says the kitchen table is the best place to Ouija since it's in the physical center of the house. The edges of her speech are softened by a beery slur.

"So, now what?" I ask, looking at her over the Parker Brothers board.

"Now we empty our minds," she says, placing her fingers on the planchette.

"Shouldn't be hard for you," I say.

She shoots me the bird. Somehow, I knew she was going to do that. I put my fingers on the planchette and nothing happens. Fifteen minutes of nothing happening later, she breaks out the vodka. I tell her I don't want any.

"Your ghost showing up anytime soon?" I say. "I want to get to a meeting tonight."

"Maybe he's busy," Karen slurs. "Maybe he's hauling a big load of sanctimonious bullshit to his wife in North Dakota."

"Hand me that bottle," I say.

I'll do anything to keep the peace.

Another fifteen minutes pass and nothing happens unless you count getting drunk.

"Let's call it a night," I tell her.

"In a hurry to go hang with your crackhead buddies at AA?" she asks.

"If you're not careful, I'm going to start taking your comments personally," I say.

"Oh, no," she says. "I'd better watch out or the big pussy might actually do something."

We both have a couple of drinks from the bottle while we consider the implications of her comment.

"It's ten o'clock," I say, taking the high road. "We can watch *The Daily Show* and go to bed. Nothing good is going to happen tonight."

"Is that a Christian thing?" she says. "Early to bed, early to rise?"

"Actually," I say, trying to keep things light, "Benjamin Franklin said that."

"Judge not," she says, "lest ye be judged. And all you do is judge, you sanctimonious prick."

"All you do is drink," I say.

Karen and I sit there hating each other until Angela comes in and freezes in the doorway, purse over one shoulder, keys in her hand.

"What is that *thing* doing in my house?" she asks.

The vodka's got me foggy, so it takes a minute to realize she isn't talking about Karen.

"I'm just playing," I say.

"Playing, my ass," Karen says. "You've been judging me for years with your AA, your church, all your shit."

"It's a tool of the Devil," Angela says, her eyes glued to the Ouija board.

"What is it you're scared of?" I ask.

"You're changing," Karen says, and the bottom of her eyes get wet. "And when you realize I'm not changing too, you're going to ditch me for another woman."

"You're inviting evil into this house," Angela says.

"That's not on the menu," I say to both of them. "This is the house that love built. We have our problems, sure, but nothing bad is going to happen."

"You've been drinking," Angela says, noticing the vodka.

"You're full of shit," Karen says.

"Come on," I say. "Let's play. Let's play Ouija together and you'll see there's no call to be scared."

Karen makes a dismissive sound and stands up. Angela turns to go. Sometimes, it's more than I can take.

"Sit right down right this fucking minute!" I shout. "You're going to sit the fuck down and play the fucking Ouija with me and we're going to have a nice fucking time."

Karen freezes. Angela stops. They both look at me scared.

"Please," I say. "Sit down."

Angela and Karen sit down next to each other.

"I don't want to do this," Angela says. "Please don't make me do this."

I look at my two wives sitting across the table from me, their four eyes red and wet.

"It's okay to be scared," I say. "But you have to push past your fear."

Putting my fingers on the planchette, I nod at it encouragingly. Karen crosses her arms. Angela raises her hands, then lowers them.

"Don't be like that," I say, then I raise my eyebrows to let them both know I am not to be fucked with right now.

In one of those beautiful moments of synchronicity, they place their fingertips on the planchette simultaneously.

"Now what?" Angela asks.

"Let's ask the spirit if it has a name," I say.

"No," Angela says.

"Spirit, what is your name?" Karen asks.

The planchette slides around the board on its little felt feet and I can't tell which one of us is steering. It stops on *A*, then it stops on *N*, then it stops on *G*, then it keeps on stopping until it spells a name.

"Who the fuck is Angela?" Karen asks.

"How does it know my name?" Angela asks.

"Ask it," I say.

"Who's Angela?" Karen asks.

The planchette burns up the board, and together Karen and Angela spell out two words:

HIS WIFE.

"What the fuck?" Karen asks the board. "What the fuck?" she asks me.

Angela is pale and her lips are trembling. I hate seeing Angela upset. Karen, on the other hand, she can go fuck herself.

"It's just the subconscious mind of the people playing," I reassure them. "That's all it is. You aren't even aware you're doing it, but your subconscious mind spells out what you're thinking with involuntary muscle contractions. So, if you're scared of something, you spell out what you're scared of."

Karen stands up.

"Your fingers are on it," she says. "Your fingers are on it, so why the fuck are you thinking about some wife named Angela?"

I wish she could be quiet for one minute.

"That's not true," Angela says. "I didn't do that. I didn't move it. Someone else was moving that thing."

"Answer me!" Karen screams.

They're talking too fast for me to figure out a response that'll suit both of them.

"It's just a game," I say. "We don't have to play."

"I always thought something was fucked up," Karen says. "What man lives in an empty house with no furniture? What man doesn't have any friends and is either in his truck or sitting on the sofa reading a fucking book all the time? Did you kill Angela? Was she your first wife? Or just some truck-stop whore you picked up? Don't tell me I'm lying. There's a female presence in this house. I been feeling it for weeks!"

"There are no evil presences," I say. "There's no one here but us."

"You invited something in here," Angela says. "Your self-pleasure, and your drinking, and I know you haven't been faithful to me. You let something dark in here with us. You've let a demon of lust and addiction into our home."

These two start carrying on and they have no idea of the pressure I'm under. They have no idea what it feels like to be pulled in two different directions all the time. They have no idea what it's like to watch every word you say.

"Pray with me," Angela says, reaching across the table and gripping my wrists while Karen stalks the kitchen, ranting. "Pray with me. There's something in this house. We'll pray, then we'll burn this thing in the backyard."

"Think I'm stupid?" Karen shouts. "Think I've bought your bullshit? I know you been cheating on me from day one, but so fucking what? I can cheat on you anytime I want. You murdered your first wife? I'll put your ass in prison if you so much as touch a hair on my head. I'll lock you up, motherfucker!"

Finally, it all gets to be too much.

"I didn't kill Angela!" I shout.

And I know I've made a mistake. Angela's face crumples, Karen's eyes light up.

"Why would you say that?" Angela asks. "Why would you say that about me?"

"Then why do you keep talking about her?" Karen asks, and storms out of the room.

I hear Karen slam the door of the downstairs bathroom. Angela jumps.

"What was that?" she asks.

"Wait here," I say.

I check the bathroom door in the front hall, but Karen's locked it from the inside. Angela stands in the living room doorway, watching me.

"It's jammed," I explain.

"It's locked, you bastard," Karen shouts from behind the door.

"I'm leaving this dark place," Angela says.

"Let me explain," I say. "There is a perfectly logical explanation."

But before I can gather my thoughts, she's backing away from me, shaking her head, hands feeling behind her for something to put between us. My own wife is scared of me, and this isn't what I meant to have happen at all.

"There's something in this house," she says.

"No, it's nothing—"

"Nothing except a giant cheating asshole who murdered his wife," Karen screams from the bathroom.

"It's you," Angela says. "These things only happen when *you're* here."

I get down on my knees and clasp my hands and say the Lord's Prayer.

"Let's pray together," I say to Angela.

But she's still backing away. The bathroom door opens behind me and I smell wet shit.

"You're a fucking psycho," Karen slurs. "So, let me spell it out for you. We're finished."

She goes into the living room and I swear she has a turd in one hand but maybe I'm drunk? I get there just in time to see that it actually *is* a turd and she's using it to write on the living room wall:

EAT SHIT

Angela stares at it in horror.

"What the fuck is that?" she asks.

I have never, ever heard my wife cuss before. Karen certainly has a knack for the grand gesture.

"It's okay, honey," I explain to Angela. "I can paint over it."

But she's running away, and Karen is shouting again, and I need them both to just hold on a minute. Can't they see that I can fix this if they just stop pulling on me all the time? I get my hands on Karen, or maybe it's Angela, and I admit I've been drinking, so maybe I'm not quite as gentle as I ought to be, because she's screaming at me, or maybe Karen's screaming at me, as if this situation is somehow my fault.

Everybody just needs to calm down for a minute and let me think.

I'm outside burying something in the treeline, and thank God I brought along that vodka to keep me warm. Karen's shit is smeared all over my clothes and there's no way I'm putting these filthy pants in my new washing machine, so I light them on fire, then sit down next to the flames and drink vodka and nod off as I watch them burn. It's cold out here, but any second, I'm going to get up and go inside and wait for my wife to come home. It's like Angela said: every day begins with the promise of the Resurrection.

WE ALL MAKE SACRIFICES:
A SAM HUNTER ADVENTURE

JONATHAN MABERRY

-1-

I looked up from the business card to the lawyer seated across the desk from me.

I said, "Mister, um, 'Douche-weasel'?" pronouncing it the way it looked in the expensive raised printing.

He gave me a weary look. The kind of look that said two things. First, that he's been through some variation of this conversation ten times a week his whole life. The second is that he expected just exactly this level of maturity from someone with rates as low as mine.

"DuSchwezel," he said slowly, saying it as "DEW-schwee-ZELLE." Emphasis on both the first and last syllables.

"Okay," I said.

"Okay," said Mr. DuSchwezel.

A moment passed, taking its time. My office was quiet. He sighed. "You're still thinking it's pronounced 'douche-weasel,' aren't you?"

I held my thumb and index fingers an inch apart. "Li'l bit," I said.

"Tell me, Mr. Hunter, don't you get annoyed when people make jokes about your name?"

"What's wrong with my name?"

"'Hunter'? Seriously? And you're a private investigator?"

"Hunh. Never came up," I lied.

Another moment limped past.

"We're not off to a very good start, are we?" he asked.

"Not a fan of banter?"

"Not as such, no."

I put his card down on my desk blotter. "Okay, so let's try it from a different angle. Why are you here?"

"To see about engaging your services."

"Uh-huh."

"You are for hire, are you not?"

I nudged the card with a finger. "Almost always."

"So—?"

"It's just that I don't get why *you* want to hire me."

"Why not? My money's good, isn't it?"

"That's just it; you're a Main Line estate attorney. I couldn't afford to park in your garage. You probably paid more for a thousand of these cards than I've spent on rent for this dump. Lawyers like you have investigators on retainer, and none of them have offices in this part of town."

He said, "Ah."

"Ah," I agreed. "So, why does a guy in a two thousand–dollar suit schlep all the way here to hire a guy like me?"

"The suit," he said, "cost eleven thousand dollars. I paid two thousand just for the shoes."

"First," I said, "that was a very douche-weasel thing to say. Second, fuck you."

He smiled at that.

After a moment, so did I.

DuSchwezel picked up the briefcase he'd stood next to the client chair, placed it flat on a corner of my desk, and popped the locks. The case was positioned so that he could see the contents and I couldn't. He removed an envelope, considered it for a moment, and then reached out to lay it on the blotter next to his card.

"What's that?" I asked.

"Look and see."

It was unsealed, so I folded back the flap and removed a long, blue-green slip of paper. That exact color was probably sea-foam or some shit like that. Very heavy stock, high linen count, expensive printing. It was a check drawn on a personal account rather than something corporate. It had his name on it. Arnold Tyro DuSchwezel. It was made out to me for the amount of five thousand dollars.

I nodded appreciation at the numbers, which were some of my favorite numbers, and placed the check on my desk atop the envelope.

"This a bribe to make me say your name the right way?"

"Cute," he said, "but no. This is me giving you a check to retain your services."

"For what?"

"That's complicated, but first, I'd like you to give me a check for one hundred dollars."

I smiled. "And why the fuck would I do that?"

"To retain *my* services."

"You lost me."

DuSchwezel said, "In order for us to proceed, you will need to retain me as your attorney so that everything we discuss is covered under the blanket of attorney-client privilege."

"You working for a drug cartel or some shit? Local Mafia?"

He spread his hands. "The five thousand dollars is a gift. You are not legally or morally required to engage my services. If you want to tell me to go away, then I will and you can keep the check. It will not leave you beholden to me in any way."

"Bullshit."

"Not at all," said DuSchwezel. "We have discussed no business, and nothing that's gone between us could be construed as a binding verbal contract. Go to your bank and cash the check if you want. I'll wait here. Or I can come back. Do this in whichever way makes you feel comfortable."

"If," I said, "I decide to write you that check, what's the other shoe? I don't need a lawyer."

"You probably do, but that's a general opinion based on your lifestyle."

"You fucking with me?"

He grinned. "Of course."

I grinned too. Mine was forced.

"If you accept my check," I said, "and suddenly become my lawyer, is there more of this?"

"That would be when the other shoe would hit the floor, yes," he admitted.

"Will I like it?"

He pursed his lips. "I doubt it."

"Then—?"

"But really, Mr. Hunter, how many of your more *interesting* cases have you actually liked?"

I said nothing.

"You have quite a reputation in certain circles," said DuSchwezel. "People respect you."

"No," I said, "they don't."

He shrugged. "Okay, then they respect what you can do. They fear you, if that's a better way to put it."

"Not sure there is a better way to put it if we're both talking about the same thing."

"Fair enough," he said.

We sat there for a moment. My office smells like Lysol and Jack Daniel's. The two smells are related thematically in ways that define me, sad to say. The Lysol for cleaning up some of the messes I've had to make. The Jack Daniel's for helping me try to forget. Cliché? Sure. Fuck it.

DuSchwezel sat back and crossed his legs. Even through the stink of booze and cleaning products, I could smell him. I have a very good sense of smell. Better than yours unless you're like me. He'd used some kind of superfatted soap, probably Camay. His shampoo is scented with tea-tree oil. Cologne was one of the Polo varieties. Blue, I think. Deodorant was

Old Spice Sport. There was a hint of chlorine about him, which suggested he swam his laps today and showered at the gym. There was also a subtle aroma of something else. No, two things. A little fear sweat and a little blood. Hard to wash those away completely. Hound dogs can sniff them after a shower. So can people like me.

I opened my desk drawer, took out my cheap green checkbook, and wrote him a check for one hundred dollars. He watched me with genuine and obvious interest, then accepted it with a nod. DuSchwezel took a moment to study it, though I think he did that to collect his thoughts. There were a few beads of fresh sweat on his forehead. Then he folded the check and tucked it into an inner pocket of his jacket.

We sat for a moment.

"Anything we discuss from here out is protected," he said.

"Yup." In the movies and in poorly researched novels, private investigators often hide information from the cops by claiming client confidentiality. Yeah, that's a myth. Only lawyers and shrinks get that protection. Now we were sealed and square.

"Mr. Hunter," said DuSchwezel, "I would like very much for you to kill someone."

-2-

So, yeah, okay. That just happened.

I sat there, looking at him. I think I was smiling. Or something.

His face was slightly flushed.

"You're fucking with me," I said.

"Actually," said DuSchwezel, "I'm not."

"Then give me back my check and try not to take it personally while I throw you the fuck out of my office. I may knee you in the balls, but that's just a professional courtesy."

"This isn't a joking matter," he said.

WHAT THE #@&% IS THAT?

My smile got wider and probably stranger. "Sounds like it to me."

DuSchwezel's smile faded away. "Do I *look* like I'm joking, Mr. Hunter?"

"You'd better be. You just asked me to commit a contract killing."

"It's not as simple as that."

"I'm pretty sure that I don't give a flying gopher fuck how simple or complicated it is," I said. "And, tell you what, why don't you stand up and assume the position so I can make sure you're not wearing a wire. Entrapment is an ugly word and it'll probably hurt when I shove it up your ass."

I started to get out of my chair, but he stood up more quickly, hands raised as he backed away.

"No! Listen to me, please. If you want to pat me down, that's fine, but please listen to me."

"Pat first, listen later. Hands against the wall."

Before he could react, I snaked out a hand, caught him by the shoulder of his eleven thousand–dollar suit, spun him, and slammed him into the wall, kicked his legs wide, and frisked him. Before I was a P.I. here in Philly, I was a cop in Minneapolis. I worked enough vice cases in my day to know how to check someone for a wire. There are nice ways to do it, and there are ways that can really fuck up a person's month. I went somewhere in the middle. When I was done, his clothes were a mess, he had very little personal dignity left, he was panting with mingled fear and anger, but he was clean.

I pointed to the chair. "Sit," I ordered. He sat and watched while I rifled through his briefcase. Lots of file folders, which I ignored, but nothing else. I took a tuning fork from my desk drawer—a little trick I learned from a cop friend in Pine Deep—banged it hard and touched it to the handle and any part of the briefcase dense enough to conceal a mic. If anyone was listening in, they'd be shopping at Miracle-Ear by the end of the day.

The case was clean.

So, I sat on the edge of my desk, arms folded, and looked down at DuSchwezel. He plucked out his pocket square and dabbed his forehead and upper lip.

"You're an asshole," he said.

"Blow me," I said. "Tell me why I shouldn't throw you out the window."

DuSchwezel held the pocket square in his lap, and I could see his hands tremble. Son of bitch was scared, but I don't think it was because of me.

"People think that when you're rich, you can do anything you want," he said, coming at this from around a corner. "That's not true. Not really. Sure, there are things we can do, and things we can get away with, but we're not invulnerable. Everyone has a weakness, Mr. Hunter."

I said nothing.

He looked up at me. "I am not a very nice person."

"I'm not your therapist."

"No," he said, "I'm not looking for understanding. I am a bad man. I do bad things."

"Yeah, well, I'm not a priest, either."

"I'm not seeking absolution," said DuSchwezel. "I'm making a statement. This is confidential and I need you to understand who and what I am. I represent very rich people in the Philadelphia area. People who use my services and those of my partners to make sure that the law always bends to whatever angle they need. I am a magician when it comes to twisting regulations, soliciting illegal compliance from judges and politicians, dispensing bribes, and hiding large amounts of cash in dummy corporations. In short, I facilitate corruption in virtually every way that does not involve direct violence."

"Well, to be fair," I said, "I already thought you were an asshole when you said you were a lawyer. This doesn't slide you that much further down the crapper."

"This isn't about me," he said, "this is about my daughter, Olivia. Beautiful girl. Smart."

I said nothing.

Two tears suddenly dropped down his cheeks, and whatever was left of his professional calm and poise collapsed like broken scaffolding, dragged down by the weight of why he was really here. He said, "She was eighteen."

Ah . . . fuck.

Was is such an ugly word.

When it's laid against the age of a daughter, a kid, it's beyond horrible. It disfigures the moment.

Mr. DuSchwezel put his face in his hands and began to cry.

I did not pat him on the back and tell him that it was okay, that it was all going to be okay. I'm not that much of an asshole, and I had no reason to lie to him. Whatever this was, it was already not okay. *She was eighteen.* No, it wasn't ever going to be okay.

I went around to my side of the desk, sat down, let him cry. Waited. Tried not to own any of his hurt. Tried really hard.

She was eighteen.

Was.

Goddamn it.

-3-

He got his shit together and told me the story. It was long and he rambled. Short version is this. . . .

One of the biggest clients he represented was a man named Fenner, and Mr. Fenner made his money by providing transportation, storage, and distribution for large lots of stolen merchandise. We're not talking a couple of microwaves that fell off the back of a truck. We're talking about entire trucks, or at least the cargoes of trucks that are hauling either illegal freight like untaxed cigarettes and unstamped booze, or the contents of hijacked trucks. There's a lot of money in that. One of his specialties was stealing the contents of cargo containers at the docks and placing them in his own cans elsewhere in the same freight-yard. And he made sure that his stuff always had the proper paperwork. Lots of steps to his organization, lots of checks and balances, lots of money for everyone involved. Tens of millions per year, just in the dockyard scams. Twice that much for stuff he hauled up from meth labs in the south.

Mr. Fenner wasn't the problem.

His son, Erik, was.

Erik was so cliché, I almost laughed as DuSchwezel described him. Twentysomething, good-looking, perfect teeth, deep-water tan from spending so much time on boats off Miami, rich, arrogant, vicious, petty, grabby, violent, charming, and all of the other adjectives that describe a child of wealth and power who was the only heir to a crime fortune. You can order the cocksucker from central casting. You know the type, the kind who genuinely believe that the world exists to help him get high, get laid, and have fun. The kind who drops twenty grand on a weekend out with his friends and won't let anyone else pay for anything, because he needs to be seen as the one who *owns* the fun and has everything covered. And because his dad is who he is, doors get opened, he never waits in a line, he always gets a table, he gets more ass than a porn star, everyone grins at him like he's the king of the jungle, and to that crowd, he *is* the king of the jungle. But what they're really doing is kissing his ass in order to kiss his father's ass.

Like I said, you've seen this a million times. Every single grade-B cop movie, every modern gangster movie, blah blah blah. In those movies, he's the one who usually does something so heinous that it causes the action hero to cut a bloody swath through the criminal empire his father has taken so long to build.

The thing that really torques my ass, though, is that this particular cliché is reinforced by the fact that there are hundreds of real-world assholes exactly like that. Maybe thousands. I ran into some of them when I was a cop in the Cities, and I've brushed up against a few—even dented one or two—since I hung out a shingle here in Philly.

Unfortunately, they are usually very well guarded, and their asshole parents do everything they can to spoil them and enable the very worst behavior. In the movies, the action hero goes in guns blazing and does some chop-socky and racks up a body count that makes cancer look like a third-string killer with no running game.

That's the movies. Liam Neeson, Denzel Washington, Keanu Reeves, Bruce Willis, and Jason Statham manage to outfight and outgun whole mobs of wiseguys. That, as they say, is Hollywood. The bullets aren't real, the bad guys in those flicks can't shoot worth a damn, and heroes seem to be able to do complex, extended fight scenes even after taking gunshot wounds, stab wounds, falling off balconies, getting thrown through plate glass windows, and getting wailed on by fists, elbows, and feet. Special effects, baby. Fake blood, rubber knives, stunt men, and guns firing blanks.

I pointed all of this out to Mr. DuSchwezel.

"And so I came to you," he said simply.

"Sure. But why? Last time I checked, there was a shit-ton of cops in Philadelphia. They've organized now. Call themselves a 'police department.' Maybe, you being a lawyer and all, you've heard of them."

"I'm a mob lawyer," he said.

"And you told me you have connections out the wazoo. Judges in your pocket and such."

"Whose money do you think pays for those judges, Mr. Hunter? If I filed a formal complaint against Erik Fenner, who do you think would enforce it? Even *I* don't know who owns whom in this town. Erik's father has other lawyers, too. We don't share all of the details about bribery and corruption while we braid each other's hair."

"There's that," I conceded. "You're afraid that leveling charges against Erik will backfire."

"I have two other children," said DuSchwezel. "And a wife, a mother, cousins, nieces, nephews. Just in the Philadelphia metropolitan area, there are over twenty members of my extended family. How many of them do you think Mr. Fenner would hurt or kill to protect his only son?"

"Balls," I said.

"Do you think I'd come to you if I had anywhere else to go?"

Not sure if he was trying to be deliberately insulting, but what the hell.

He had a point. And besides, I was still thinking of him as Mr. Douche-weasel.

"What's all this have to do with Olivia?"

Even though this was why he was here, my question hit him like a punch. He cleared his throat and said, "You spend a lot of time at Heaven Street Diner."

A statement, not a question, but I nodded anyway.

"Do you remember a dark-haired girl who worked there for a few weeks last fall?"

"Sure. Livvie something."

And something went *clunk* inside my head. Livvie. Short for Olivia.

"Oh," I said. "Fuck."

"Yes. Livvie was always troubled. She ran away from home half a dozen times. Last fall, she got a fake ID that said she was nineteen, and she moved into a roach-infested apartment near the diner. Got a job working tables at Heaven Street."

"I remember her," I said. It was true. Livvie was a pretty little thing. Thin, pale, rocking a goth look. Never said much and I don't think she ever waited on me. When I was at the diner, the counter waitress, Ivy, always took care of me. Ivy and I go way back. "She seemed like a nice kid."

It was a lame comment but it was all I had. I doubt we ever swapped more than a "hello" two or three times. Like a lot of diner staff, she came and went and then was gone from my memory until today.

"I had another investigator look for her," said DuSchwezel. "He found her and brought her home."

"But she ran away again?"

"In a way. I had a party at my house and the Fenners were there. Erik saw Olivia, and I could tell right away she fell for him. He's very good-looking, and he wears his father's money like a suit."

I nodded, knowing the type.

"They started seeing each other," he said. "I tried to warn her off, to tell her that he was dangerous, but . . ."

"But that probably made her more interested."

"Yes."

"Aside from the obvious, why was Erik dangerous? I mean, you took a risk telling her, when if she was so into him, she might have told him what you said."

His hands still gripped the pocket square. Twisting it, clutching it with white-knuckled fingers. His eyes kept meeting mine and falling away. Over and over.

"Okay," I said, "you're not paying me enough to play games. Tell me what it is or buzz off."

He took a fortifying breath and said, "There are rumors about Erik."

"Ah, boy. . . . Tell me."

"Erik is into some strange stuff. His father told me about some of it because he knew I was having some issues with Olivia. His father wanted advice on finding a good therapist."

"When you say 'strange' . . . ?"

"Erik was into supernatural stuff."

"So what?"

"No," said DuSchwezel, "not as a hobbyist. I'm not talking about him being into monster movies and Stephen King novels. No, I mean he was *into* the supernatural. He believes in it. He . . . sought it out."

"How and in what way?"

Again his eyes flicked away. "I'm not sure how it started. He's always had unusual friends, particularly another boy whose father is with the Kirikov family. Do you know them? Russian Mafiya."

"They're dead, right? Turf war over the uptick in the heroin trade between here and New York. Both sides killing family members?"

"That was the cover story, sure. But it went deeper than that. I'm pretty sure that the Kirikov boy was not killed by their rivals in that particular line of commerce. I'm almost certain that Erik killed him and made it look like it was done by the rivals of the Kirikov family. The resulting drug war was the usual escalation of payback."

"Why would Erik do that?"

"Because he needed a blood sacrifice."

I stared at him. "You're going to have to explain that one."

"I . . . don't have all of it together," he admitted. "And, quite frankly, I'm not even sure how much of it I believe. But I managed to put someone inside Erik's circle of friends. A promising attorney right out of law school who looks younger than he is. He ingratiated himself into Erik's crew and . . ." He stopped and shivered. Actually shivered. "He said that Erik is insane. Erik doesn't just want to be like his father; he wants to eclipse the old man and become something much bigger, something much more powerful. He wants to be feared."

"He has a lot of thugs who will shoot people if he asks. Pretty sure he's already feared."

"No," said DuSchwezel, "you don't get it. This isn't the kind of power-hunger I see all the time among my clients and their sons. No. When I said Erik was insane, I meant it. I think that he was crazy—clinically psychotic—to begin with, but the more he got into whatever supernatural stuff the young Kirikov shared with him . . . well, I think it pushed him into a whole new shape. Mentally, I mean."

"So, he's making blood sacrifices now? To whom? Or to what?"

"To what Erik thinks is the patron god of his family."

"You're shitting me."

"I shit you not."

"And who exactly is the—and pardon me if I grin while I say this—patron 'god' of their family?"

"Well, see, that's one of the main reasons I came to see you," said DuSchwezel. "You specifically, I mean. 'Fenner' is an Anglicized version of the family name. They're Scandinavian and their real name is—or at least *was*—Fenrisúlfr."

I said nothing. My mouth dried right up.

DuSchwezel nodded. "You know that name, don't you?"

I nodded. "Fenrisúlfr," I said hoarsely. "It's another name for Fenrir."

"Who is—?" he asked, making sure I knew.

"The wolf god of the Vikings. Fenrir is the father of the wolves Sköll and Hati Hróðvitnisson, is a son of Loki, and is foretold to kill the god Odin during the events of Ragnarök."

"Yes," said DuSchwezel. "Erik is trying to invoke a dark god who he believes—really fucking believes—is going to help bring about the end of the world. And, god help me, Mr. Hunter, he sacrificed my little girl to try to make that happen."

His words seemed to be painted on the air between us in dark red letters. It took me a while to figure out how to reply to something like that.

"Even so," I said slowly, "why me? If Erik is a psychopath and a serial murderer, and you can't trust the cops to take him down, what you need is an assassin. I'm not a button man. I don't do contract hits, and 'revenge killer' isn't on my business card."

"No," said DuSchwezel, "but 'monster' is."

-1-

Bang.

There it was.

"No, it's not," I said. Which was true in the literal sense. My business card said, INVESTIGATIONS AND PERSONAL PROTECTION. But I could see it in his eyes. He knew.

Maybe he didn't know *what* I was, but he knew I wasn't Joe Normal.

"Who's told you what?" I asked, keeping my voice casual. "And if you try to play the client confidentiality thing, then I'll tell you in advance to fuck off and go away."

He considered that for a moment, then nodded to himself as he decided to play his cards faceup.

"Ivy," he said.

Ivy. She was one of the few people who knew who and what I was.

A year or two back, she tapped me to help out a friend of hers with a problem no one else could tackle. I've never been exactly certain how Ivy figured it out, but she asked me for help. A friend's little son was being attacked in his sleep by something that came out of his closet. Yeah, I know. Monster in the closet is a standard kid thing. Except this time it wasn't. And it wasn't a sequel to *Monsters, Inc.*, either. There was something big and bad in the closet, and Ivy asked me to go in there and see what I could do.

It got weird and it got messy.

Bottom line is that there's nothing left in that closet that's ever going to hurt anyone again.

So, sure. Monster. Not exactly inaccurate. Not entirely unfair.

Ivy knows that.

"She shouldn't have told you," I said.

This time, his eyes didn't dart away. He gave me a long, hard, sad, broken, desperate look. A father's look. A look that was filled with all of the grief in the world.

"Ivy thought the world of Olivia," he said. "She knows that I loved her. Really loved her. Olivia was my little girl."

Saying that broke him.

And, damn if it didn't break me, too.

-5-

Which is why I went to see Erik Fenner.

There are some cases where I spend days or even weeks running down clues, doing background checks, tailing suspects, building a case. And then there are some where I go right up to a door and knock. I don't get many of that second kind. If it was easy, they usually wouldn't hire guys like me.

Except, in this case, it was easy. Finding Erik, I mean. And there *are* no other guys like me. Not for something like this. I mean, sure, I've got cousins and aunts and all who are like me, but that's different. None of them live in Philly. Most of my relatives are either in the Cities or in Europe. We *benandanti* go back a lot of years. I can name every family member going back to early sixteenth-century Friuli, Italy, and my Aunt Violet can name them going back to Etruscan times.

Benandanti.

The "good walkers."

The hounds of God. Which is a pretentious nickname, but someone else hung it on us.

I wonder if DuSchwezel did his background check. Probably. If you want to stop a psychopath trying to invoke a wolf god, hire a private investigator who has some skin in that game. Not the Norse crap, but you get the picture.

So, yeah. I took the case. Ivy told him the right things about me. He knew I'd take it.

Maybe I did too. That "was" word still burned in my head. The man may have been an asshole, but he had a daughter and he loved her. Maybe he thought he failed her, too. Probably did. Mob lawyer and all. Kid has no one to look up to, so she starts looking down.

And sees a handsome monster looking up at her.

-6-

I drove out to Bucks County, to a sprawling estate near New Hope. DuSchwezel gave me the address and the code for the front gate. I told him I didn't need the code. Wall was only twelve feet high. I mean, c'mon.

Erik's father was in South Philly, overseeing one of his dockside concerns. DuSchwezel had made sure that nobody but Erik was home. Well, besides a couple of servants, and three or four bodyguards.

I parked my car under some trees on a side road a quarter mile from the house. Walked the rest of the way as the sun was tumbling over the trees toward tomorrow. I don't need darkness, and that whole full moon thing is pure bullshit. Moon's got nothing to do with it. On the other hand, sunlight makes it easy for witnesses, and who needs that bullshit.

Was I here to do a contract killing?

Not really. I gave DuSchwezel his check back.

This was for a teenage girl who didn't know better than to walk into one of the outer rings of hell. DuSchwezel couldn't actually tell me what happened to her. I doubt any father could force those words into his mouth. Instead, he handed me a copy of the autopsy report.

That she had been raped was horrible enough. It wasn't the worst thing that had been done to her. We don't need to go into all the details. Even I get nauseous sometimes. Her body was found in a wrecked car, but the extent of her wounds wasn't consistent with the amount of damage to the vehicle. The car had rolled and burned, but that didn't account for the dismemberment. It didn't account for her eyes and heart being missing. And the pathologist determined that the victim was not alive when the car caught fire. However, on reflection, the pathologist recanted and decided that all of the injuries had, in fact, been sustained in that crash.

Five weeks after the autopsy report, the pathologist put a down payment on a mini-mansion in Newtown. You can connect the dots however you like.

I found a nice little blind spot where the Fenner security cameras couldn't see through some thick rhododendron. I stripped out of the sweats I'd worn and went over the wall in a way that left claw marks on the brick.

On the other side, I dropped down and ran on all fours. I usually stay on two feet except when I need to move fast. My senses are better then, too. DuSchwezel had given me a scarf that used to belong to Erik. Olivia had kept it as a token of her love.

Still had his scent on it. Useful. Before I went over the wall, I took a big enough sniff that I could have found him halfway across the state.

In the end, it wasn't even all that hard.

He was sitting by the pool, wearing a pair of skintight Speedos, Wayfarer sunglasses over his eyes, a beer resting on his belly. He did not have three bodyguards with him. There were six of them. Or maybe three worked for his dad and the other three were part of Erik's mini-cult. They all had wolf tattoos on the sides of their necks. Very stylized—Fenrir with his jaws wide to swallow Odin on the day the world ends.

Even the guards had that.

They all looked blown out. Couldn't tell right off if they were hammered, high, stuffed from a big meal, or just a bunch of lazy fucks who were dead tired this early. Or some combination of all of that.

There was an iPad plugged into a Bose speaker dock and Kanye was yelling some bullshit that I didn't want to hear. They had it on too goddamn loud, too. The asshole club was sprawled all around the pool. No women around, which is odd. Usually, these clowns have all kinds of arm candy, and often it's paid for in one way or another. Cash, drugs, access to power, whatever. But not now.

Good. That simplified things.

I circled the pool area, following the blood scent to its source. It was the pool house. It had been converted into something else. Not sure if the word "church" would apply. Temple, maybe. Shrine. Something like that. The windows were all blacked out, and inside, someone had gone completely ass-fuck nuts. The walls were painted with magical symbols from at least a dozen religions and twice as many phony cults. Inverted pentagrams, representations of goat-headed Baphomet, symbols of evil. Such bullshit. Some of this crap I knew for sure was from old monster movies that had no actual connection to real beliefs.

The blood was real, though.

There was a lot of it. Old and new. Many sources. Not just Olivia—and I could smell her scent here, too. There were others. As I stood in the doorway, I took in at least fourteen separate female scents. Two of them were prepubescent. These fuckers had killed little girls, too. That's worse. I'm not sure how exactly, but it is.

Fourteen dead girls and women.

There was an altar and Erik had laid them upon it and he and his wolf pack had done terrible things. I didn't need to see pictures to know what had happened there. My senses fed the information to my mind. When I was a cop and we learned about forensics, there was a saying that every contact leaves a trace. Now imagine what traces were left for senses like *mine* to find.

I could smell the pain, the horror, the death. I could almost hear the echo of voices screaming for mercy that was not theirs to have, just as I could hear the laughter of those sons of bitches out by the pool.

Were they true believers? Or was this part of some kind of shared madness inspired and perpetuated by Erik Fenner?

I don't know and I didn't much care.

As I stepped into that room, my focus was drawn to the altar. To the smell of blood that washed down from it.

So potent.

So fresh.

"What the *fuck* is that?" I breathed, and my words came out twisted because my throat was not a human one.

The answer to my question was there to be read, and my senses never lie.

That's when I knew I was too late. That's when I realized why those pricks out at the pool looked so logy and sated.

I'd waited until sunset to come here. My caution made me too late to save somebody else's little girl. Or sister. Or wife. Or whatever. There was blood on the air and smeared on the altar. Female, young. Dead.

And, if my senses were reading it right, not just dead.

No.

Fuck me. There are certain smells flesh makes when it interacts with saliva and digestive juices. I smelled the stink of a feast only recently finished. It was the smell a pack of wolves made when they were gathered around a deer they'd just torn down.

I turned and prowled to the doorway to the pool area and looked at the seven of them.

And I *knew*.

They had crossed way over the line from making human sacrifices to a wolf god to trying to *be* wolves. Or become wolves.

The wolf in me wanted to attack. Right then. To kill them all as they slept. The wolf was vicious but he was not cruel.

That's why I changed back to me.

You see, I can be cruel.

Sometimes, I want to be.

Sometimes, I need to look into the eyes of certain people because I want to see understanding. Maybe I hope for a flicker of regret or remorse. Not that a moment of repentance has saved anyone who I've gone after. Fuck it, I'm not a saint. I'm not even a very good private investigator.

I'm a hell of a hunter, though. And, yeah, sure, make a joke about the name. It was picked as a joke by one of my ancestors, so the joke's on you.

When I take on a client—or in the case of DuSchwezel, a proxy client, because I was here for Olivia, not for her dickhead lawyer father—then that person becomes part of my pack. Wolves protect their packs.

Oh, yeah. We do.

So, it was in my own shape that I walked out of the pool house, strolled over to Erik Fenner's chaise lounge, raised my leg, and heel-kicked him in the Speedo.

Real fucking hard.

He screamed and grabbed his balls and fell out of the chair.

The screams woke everyone else up. The three bodyguards came out of their chairs like they had springs up their asses, and suddenly, there were guns in their hands. The other three sprang up too. One of them had a gun; another produced a knife from god knows where. The third one grabbed a beer bottle and smashed the fat end off it.

Six of them in a ring around me, with Erik screaming on the ground while his face turned an amusing shade of puce.

And me standing there. Short, skinny, twenty years older than any of them. Naked as an egg with my dick hanging out.

"Who the fuck are you?" screamed one of the guards.

This was the kind of moment when you really want to put a button on it by saying something really cool. Witty. Like the one-liners those action heroes always use.

But goddamn it if I couldn't really come up with anything snarky.

What I said was more expository than colorful.

I said, "Fenrisúlfr isn't real, assholes. Fake god from a dead religion. Not even sure the Vikings believed in him."

They stared at me. Part surprise that I was even dropping the name Fenrisúlfr, and partly wondering who the hell this naked crazy guy was. Even Erik paused in his shrieking to stare at me.

He said, "W-what—"

"You fucktards think you're becoming wolves?" I asked. "Is that it? I mean, is that what this shit is all about? Some kind of superstitious ritual bullshit?"

Erik managed to get to his knees. His face was dark with pain and he still cupped his mashed balls, but there was fury in his eyes.

And . . . something else.

Maybe it was the darkening sky or maybe it wasn't, but I saw his pale Scandinavian eyes change from an icy blue to a red that was brighter and bloodier than his face.

All around me, I saw the eyes of the others begin to change, too.

"Well, fuck me," I said.

The shape of Erik's mouth began to change. He suddenly had way too many teeth and his lips almost couldn't form the name of his god. "Fenrisúlfr."

I don't know how they managed it, but holy shit. They were actually turning into wolves. All seven of them. A wolf pack transformed somehow by blood sacrifices and the savage slaughter of the innocents, all in the name of a god whose mythical status I was very quickly having to reevaluate.

I said, "Oh . . . shit."

They laughed, but the laughter sounded like snarls.

Like growls.

So, I figured . . . what the fuck.

They were wolves. Okay, I have to accept that. Werewolves, I suppose. Of a kind.

But they were new at this game. I've been playing it a long, long time.

They say age and treachery will overcome youth and skill. Take that to the bank. And another aphorism. Experience is the best teacher.

These pricks have only ever sunk their teeth into innocent flesh.

Fighting another werewolf is different.

Fighting a *benandanti* werewolf is even harder. It's a death wish. Ask anyone I've ever gone up against.

Oh, yeah, wait: You can't.

These young monsters changed.

I changed faster.

-7-

While they still could, they screamed for mercy.

Didn't help.

They screamed for their god.

He didn't show.

They screamed.

And screamed.

And screamed.

I was okay with that.

-8-

I let a couple of weeks go by and then met with DuSchwezel in a booth at Heaven Street Diner. Couple of the regulars were there, but nobody disturbed us. It's that kind of place.

We worked through a cup of coffee each and he pushed his apple pie around with a fork before we got to it.

"Terrible what happened," he said. "The fire. Those poor boys."

"Yeah," I said. "Makes you think."

He nodded. Lifted some apple glop, looked at it, set it down.

"I went to Olivia's grave the other day."

I said nothing.

"There were flowers on it. Not expensive but lovely."

I sipped my coffee.

"Any idea who put them there?"

The clock on the wall ticked through half a minute. DuSchwezel nodded.

"Thanks," he said.

"For what?" I said. "I never did anything for you. We have no understanding other than the fact that I paid you a hundred bucks to answer some legal questions. You cash that check, by the way?"

"Of course. It's a matter of record now."

We sipped our coffee.

"Hunter," he said, "can I be frank with you?"

"Funny question for a lawyer to ask, but sure."

He almost smiled. "I went to law school to be the kind of lawyer I became. Seriously. I never had aspirations of being Atticus Finch. I never wanted to do anything but make money pretty much the way I do."

"Congratulations," I said.

"Go ahead and sneer, but I'm trying to say something here."

"Be my guest."

"In my line of work, I only meet bad people. Fathers and sons, like the Fenners. Hangers-on. Gangs in expensive suits. You understand what I'm saying?"

"I do."

"I don't ever get to meet good people. When I do meet someone who's supposed to be stand-up, I'm immediately figuring the angle to break them down and turn them. You understand? I'm always looking for a way to make them like me. In one way or another."

I said nothing.

"In all of my dealings," he said, "I've never met anyone like you. The people with whom I work always talk about honor and all that, but it's talk. The deference people show to them is totally out of fear or greed. Never because these people have earned their respect."

"If you're driving in the direction of a point, man," I said, "take the next exit."

He said, "You are a third- or possibly fourth-rate private investigator working out of what is arguably the seediest office it has ever been my displeasure to visit. You smell of cleaning products and old booze, and you are not a very nice person."

I leaned back. "Gosh, thanks. I—"

He cut me off. "But you may be the only honorable man I have ever met."

Before I could figure out a way to respond to that, he stood up and tossed a twenty down to cover the tab.

"Olivia would probably have liked you."

And with that, he turned and shambled out.

I sat in the booth and drank my coffee. I ate his slice of pie and stared out the window at the night.

GHOST PRESSURE

GEMMA FILES

"How d'you like it here, Gran?" young Kristle was forever asking her, to which Gavia Pratt ("Not *missus*, just *miss*, or *nurse*, if you prefer") would only reply, "Doesn't rain enough." Which it didn't, by a long shot, though the days were certainly overcast, air water-heavy and gray, sinus pressure forever shifting like the beginning of the bends. Still, a lake wasn't the sea, and couldn't be; she missed Blackpool, the pier, cold wind and sting of salt, always bracing even with bad tourist karaoke bawling in the background, plus the sound of amusements-with-prizes going off in the distance every thirty seconds like a layered choir of tiny electronic car alarms.

She'd been in Toronto almost six months now, sent by the Hermes Lifequality head office to help structure their primary Canadian outreach, a task which mainly consisted of vetting care-workers, matching them with assignments, coaching debriefers, or debriefing them herself. It was a tight-knit group thus far, funded through a mixture of benefactor donations and fees from global pharmaceutical companies looking to test new pain-management product variations on subjects unlikely to complain if anything went wrong; eggs and omelettes, all that. Did get the job done, though, which was more than she could say for her staff, on occasion.

"What you have to remember is, palliative care's not all about *you*," she told them, what felt like over and bloody over. "Can't be, not if it's going to

work the way it has to. So, be present for *them*, and keep all the chat about your own fine feelings for me, thank you very much—it's what I'm here for, isn't it? One way or t'other, these things do come with a time limit; you'll make yours, you just try hard enough. Or if not, I'll rotate you off-site and find someone else who can, no harm, no foul. That's guaranteed right in the contract, case you didn't think to look before you signed it."

They were main soft, this lot, most of 'em; you'd think they'd never seen anyone die at all, 'less it were on the telly. But they did tend to have these very specific *ideas* about the process, nevertheless—touchy-feely, broad-base "spiritual" without benefit of church, all candles and incense and white light, total Serenity Prayer faff. Some even preferred to be called end-of-life doulas, if you could believe the cheek; exit midwife, was it? These young girls. Nothing ever good enough.

Like a lot of her peers back home, Gavia'd rotated through a gross of other counseling services before eventually settling at Hermes—Samaritans, Adfam, ElderCare. Everything from emotional distress to right-to-die work for Exit International, though that was on her own time, of course. Her NHS background stood her in good stead, along with the experiential legacy of those wild teenaged years that'd seen her saddled with Kristle's father before she reached the grand old age of nineteen. And now, thanks to the same lovely girl's fine practical judgment about whether or not it was worth reaching for a rubber after a drunken night out, she was a great-grandmother at barely fifty: tall, gray, and grim, striding 'round this silly city with her coat barely buttoned, sweating like a human hot flash. Probably would've had to be here anyhow, but she could've stood not to have to change nappies on her off-time nevertheless.

Right at this moment, though, her phone said 4:05; time for . . . Jaiden, if she recalled correctly. One of the better sorts, a butch little number who dressed like Elvis circa "Heartbreak Hotel." She got out the file.

"So," Gavia began, "this makes a month you've been with Mister Zukauskas, by my count. How're you getting on?"

"Uh, pretty well, I'd say. He's got late-onset Alzheimer's and stage four lung cancer, so it's all about keeping him happy, at this point—or less *un*happy." Gavia nodded. "Stopped eating last week, so we have him on a drip, and we moved from transdermal fentanyl patches to oral morphine; added haloperidol to stop the nausea and vomiting. But now we're past the first three days we're just on a prophylactic laxative to clean him out, and I discontinued that today."

"You're day-shift, yeah? And that starts when?"

"Five a.m."

"So, you're off early today."

"I . . . asked the night-shift guy to come in early, to cover for me—Sayyid. Because I wanted more time to talk to you."

"Oh? About what?"

Jaiden paused for a moment, seeming to think; Gavia felt the urge to tap her pen, mark off however many seconds it took, but resisted it. Her AA Agnostics twenty-year was coming up fast and she'd been feeling the pull all week, cycling through various coping techniques till she could get back to her original sponsor rather than rely on one here, though she took as many meetings as seemed useful in the interim. Tonight's was at that odd little Heritage building church sandwiched between the DoubleTree by Hilton hotel and the Eaton Centre, but Gavia didn't think she could make it before needing to get home and relieve the babysitter she'd arranged for instead of chipping in on rent, so Kristle could work that ridiculous "acting" job she'd gotten and pretend she was still paying her own way. . . .

"You know much about Lithuania, Miss Pratt?" Jaiden asked finally. Gavia shrugged.

"Used to be Soviet, now it isn't; next to Latvia, I think, or Poland, or both. Why?"

"Well, Zukauskas is from there—his family snuck out around 1952, after the war, when he was like twenty. Came over with his mom, his little brother, and his brother's wife, so he's been married sixty-plus years. His dad died in a camp. And I know all this 'cause he told me, right, 'cause he talks *all* the time, like pretty much nonstop, except for when he's asleep. . . ."

"Old people do tend to, yeah, even when they're not dyin'."

"Which I get; I remember that from the prep course, the materials. But . . ." Another beat. "Then, last week actually, right before he went all liquid diet, he starts telling me different stuff—weird stuff. Like folklore, fairytales. Except he's not telling them about once upon a time, or some sh—crap; he's telling them about him*self*. His life. His . . . wife."

"What about her?"

"Well, that she's like—a nightmare. By which I mean she's not a person? Like, not even human. That she's this *thing*, called a Slogutė or a Naktinėja . . ." Jaiden pronounced the words carefully, almost phonetically, with a hint of what Gavia could only assume was the old man's accent: *slow-GOO-teh-eh, nacktee-NEH-EH-yah.* "This creature that, like, comes through the keyhole and oppresses people while they're sleeping. How his mom used to tell him he had to protect himself by getting into bed sideways, like a crab, or she'd sneak into their house and sit on the youngest person in the family till they died—"

"Sounds like classic night terrors to me, with a little bit of cats suckin' baby's breath thrown in for good measure."

"Yeah, I thought so too, at first. So, I just nod and smile and go 'uh-huh,' basically, same way you taught us to. But—he just won't stop, keeps going on and on. And the *really* creepy part is that his wife? She's in the *room* while all this is happening. Like, right there, in the corner."

"Does she hear what he's tellin' you? Can she even speak English?"

"I don't *know*, Miss Pratt. I mean, I've tried to talk to her, but she never says anything back, not even hi, hello, good to see you . . . she's just always *there*. I actually don't think I've ever seen her anywhere else in the house, or seen her leave the room, either. Just sits there knitting the whole time, never even looks up."

"Odd she isn't mentioned on the intake form." Off Jaiden's look, Gavia sighed, and spun her the document. "See? Nowhere."

"Well, I don't know what to tell you. She's about his age, and little, like this high—" She sketched a figure whose head might come up to Gavia's armpit, at best. "Looks nice, normal. Old lady with her hair pulled up under a scarf. Nothing remarkable about her at all."

"A nightmare," Gavia repeated, and was slightly heartened to see Jaiden smile, at least a little: sidelong, self-deprecating. Like she couldn't quite believe she was still going on about all this.

"It *is* normal, y'know—*this*," she told her, comforting as her basic personality would allow for. "Clients start flushin' out their heads, by the end; doesn't mean anything, no more than froth from something bein' boiled. And eventually it's all boiled away, froth as well, so you can wash the pot out and start over."

"Uh-huh."

"I mean, if it's really bothering you, I *can* see about gettin' you moved—"

"—'cause that's in the contract, right, I know, but . . . I don't; I'm not . . . That's, uh, not what I'm trying to . . ."

Here she ran down for another few moments, face contorted, puzzled. As though she was sounding her next words through in her head, or trying to decide how the whole thing made her feel. Continuing, finally—

"Mister Zukauskas says he had three little brothers and sisters, to begin with, and she—the Slogutė, his wife—killed them all, or that's what his mom said, at the time. And granted, things were really bad in Lithuania back then, so it could just as easily have been, like, pneumonia, or starvation, or freakin' typhoid fever from drinking water with sewer waste in it, or whatever. But one night, he stayed awake while everybody else was asleep and he watched the keyhole, and he saw her come in through it, twisting in the air like a ribbon. And when she tried to wrap herself 'round the bed where his little brother was, he caught her in a trap he'd made out of pages from an old Bible, so old it still had the Book of Tobit in it. And he told her if she didn't agree to leave his family alone, he was gonna throw the whole thing in the stove-fire and burn her up, and then she'd just be gone forever—no heaven, no hell, no nothin'. But then she said she'd only agree if they got married, for who the hell knows what reason. And I guess he said yes, 'cause they've been together ever since."

"Now, Jaiden—"

"So, he's telling me this, right? And then he says he's happy he's dying, finally, 'cause no matter where he ends up, there's no way she can follow him; says all this time he's been suffering, she's waited till he's asleep and then pressed on his chest, given him awful dreams and suffocated him till he can't sleep anymore so he's had chronic insomnia for over sixty years— and *that*, that *is* in the file; I know, 'cause I checked." Words spilling out, faster and faster, and the more they did, the more Gavia was inclined to simply let 'em till Jaiden ran herself down—sit back a bit, narrow her eyes, and watch her go on as long as she needed to. "But he feels bad too, right, 'cause then she'll be free to start doing what she was doing before, back when. So, he says to me, 'Can you take her?' Like, 'I know you like women. She can be beautiful, she can be whatever you want. It's a hard bargain, but there are rewards.' And I'm just . . ."

"Sounds like clear grounds for a sexual harassment suit, you ask me."

"No, I mean—I don't think he means it like that. It's just . . . I'm getting afraid, 'cause now *I'm* having these dreams, almost every night, and I feel like I'm going to wake up one morning, go into work, and find out he died during the night, and then she'll just *be* there in my apartment when I come home, you know? Like she's come to stay with me, forever, and I never even got the chance to say no before she starts in *pressing* on me—"

Gavia raised her hands, then, fingers spread. Told her shivering charge, voice gentle as it ever went, "Jaiden, love, breathe. Just take a minute. *Breathe*, yeah? It's hardly the end of the world, y'know."

"No?"

"No. Not by a long shot."

Two hours later, Gavia was finally on her way back to Kristle's, still debating the best way to deal with Jaiden's odd troubles. 'Cause it really was *not* about her so much as it was about the case: Zukauskas's final process, with its built-in time limit. If Jaiden was still able to see that through—and nothing she'd told Gavia truly gave her to understand the opposite—then there was no problem. The man was terminal, had no heirs to complain about her behavior, let alone his; pretty soon he'd be gone, and all this'd be gone too, along with him. Meaning that though her most cautious instincts might say to move Jaiden on, this current situation wouldn't *last* unless Jaiden let it.

Working with the soon-to-die was upsetting, after all, inherently so. Reminded people of their own mortality—the ghost inside, their flesh's frailty, senescence in action. Entropy. Universal pressure wearing away at 'em all, same's the sea did the shore, visible in every mirror. Couldn't penalize the poor bint for reacting to *that* cold revelation, could she?

Well, in every strictly legal sense, yeah, she could; had a perfect right to, right there in black and white, uncontestable. But in this particular instance, she wouldn't.

Stopping on the corner of Kristle's side street, Gavia cast a slightly longing look over the local dive bar's way: classic all-day drinkers' haven, the type she'd spent a good deal of her twenties in. Had a moment's clear impulse to go in, order a gin and tonic, then sit there looking at it till some poor sod came over to chat her up, at which point she'd simply get up and leave him there with it as a donation for wasting his time. Last occasion she'd put herself through that rigmarole, playing it out like a ritual from some long-lapsed religion, had to 've been . . . five years back, at the very least. So, she supposed Jaiden's little fairy tale must've had her feeling a trifle fragile on some level, not that that necessitated doing anything about it.

Felt a cold wind at her back all of a sudden, and not from the weather, either. But, *Aw, get on with you, old woman,* she told herself scornfully. *Never anything in the dark weren't there in the light, and no mistake.*

So, up she went instead, feeling for her keys.

The sitter, Karen, was curled up on the couch with one of Kristle's books, some twenty-quid fantasy soap opera hardback big enough to kill a rat with; she uncurled herself slowly, yawning. "Hi, Miss Pratt," she said. "Kristle called to say she's gonna be late again—they've got her walking lights for setup, or something like that."

"Oh, aye? Don't s'pose she's bein' *paid* for her trouble, at least."

A shrug. "Minimum wage; still, industry work, right? So, that's something."

"Hm, yeah. How much she owe you, exactly?"

"Two-twenty?"

Sighing a bit at the expense, Gavia paid her, saw her out, locked the door carefully behind. Then went into Gavin's room to peep in on the poor little mite, fast asleep and snoring with his chubby fists up in the air, like he was boxing God. The name had been a nice touch on Kristle's part—almost as though she'd been coached in it, already knowing Gavia would need to stop over for a good chunk of the year, chequebook in hand. Which, by turns, only served to remind Gavia how in some ways, her ever-so-respectable schoolteacher son could be very much like that feckless bloody "entrepreneur" bugger of a father of his indeed; not that she'd more than barely allowed the two to know *of* each other, let alone bond. She still saw the latter up and down the pier sometimes back home, flashing the charm and cadging cash out of punters with a chippie on either arm, looking more like some Vegas preacher than the gangly young rockabilly thug she'd once fallen pregnant by. . . .

But enough of that; tea, then paperwork, then sleep. Tomorrow started early, like always.

Waking to dreaming was a dim slide, barely perceptible, like floating to sinking. Then the dark behind Gavia's eyes bloomed up, became a door whose keyhole hung perhaps waist-level, perhaps lower, through which a feeble, dreadful light of no discernible hue leaked like poison—and soon enough, something fluttered behind it, visible only from the corner of her eye, giving her to know she was not alone, for all she might dearly wish to be. The knowledge, washing overtop her in one choking wave, that someone—something—sat beside and a trifle behind, unbreathing yet undeniable, with all its considerable focus kept trained at one itchy point on her back: not her spine nor the rhomboideus next to it, neither trapezius above nor serratus below, and not quite her shoulder blade's bony wing, either. Some cluster of nerves, perhaps, unfurling like a knot made from pain to catch and hook, spiral itself deeper, unstring the various parts of her like pegless puppet-pieces. And hurting, hurting, all the way through: colder than undertow or tide, than barely melted ice, than frozen gut-blood slurry off the decks of fisher-boats. Colder even than her own long-dead father's heart, when he waited all night in the maternity ward for her to wake up after her caesarian, just so's he could tell her to her face how no bastard's bastard would ever set foot in *his* house, Gavia Jane Pratt. . . .

Something plucking at her now, filtering down through fathoms, a too-bright skewer popped in and twisted, over and over again. The squeal of a thousand pigs. Or, better yet—

(the bloody phone)

And up she came again, like a popped cork. Back out into the real world, brow wet, arm already flailing for the receiver.

"Yeah? Gavia Pratt, this is, from Hermes Lifequality. Who? Oh, Sayyid— he's one of mine, yeah. Put him on, please." A second of silence to let both breath and pulse slow as she waited. Then Sayyid's Arabic lilt, more exasperated than upset: "Sorry to disturb so early, Miss Pratt—"

Reflexively, she glanced at the red LEDs of the clock radio: 5:45 a.m. Could be worse. Then memory clicked. "Jaiden left you to cover her shift again? Might've let the switchboard know. . . ." Trailed off, suddenly thinking, *But that's not like her, really—not after today.*

"I do not think it matters if she arrives or not, very much. Mister Zukauskas is dead."

That set her back. She'd never had much use for the typical euphemisms— "passing on" or "away"—but they were taught not to be so blunt, 'specially in front of other people; then again, that first voice had had an EMT's impersonal professionalism, or a cop's. "What happened?"

A sigh. "I checked on him at three thirty; he was still breathing at that point, his wife in her chair as always. I thought she had gone to sleep. Made sure the call button was under his hand, then went downstairs, where I . . . also closed my eyes, but only for a moment; that was my intent. When I woke, it was a few minutes past the hour, and when I went upstairs, he was gone."

"The wife?"

"Gone as well. I called paramedics, as per S.O.P.—"

"Wait—not in the house? She's much the same age, Jaiden said; not likely to wander off, I'd think."

"Quite old, yes, but nevertheless. An emotional break? Nothing seems taken, so I've no doubt the lady will return, but Jaiden knows her better than I do, to a degree. Perhaps, if and when she arrives . . ."

A shadow moved in the hallway, sliding down the wall towards Gavin's room. Gavia shrugged it off, sure it must be Kristle going to check on the boy—then stopped, all at once realizing she could hear Kristle's snores from the main bedroom.

What the fuck is *that?*

"'Scuse me a moment, Sayyid," she said, voice low, and put the phone down sideways 'cross the cradle, not quite hanging it up.

Been a long time gone since she'd gotten herself in (or out of) trouble, but fear's spike brought all the old tricks rushing forward. She grabbed up that brick of a book Karen'd left behind on the end table—do for a club to the face, in a pinch—and slid soundless off the couch, stalking quiet, balanced on the balls of her feet. Gavin's door'd been shut—she'd done that herself, but it now stood open. Fingers clenched 'round the book's spine, aching with effort, Gavia lifted it high and was 'cross the threshold in one quick stride, poised to strike at whatever she might find—

But all that greeted her was a woman, completely unfamiliar, plain gray coat belted under her high little breasts like an Empire gown and neither young nor old at first glance: small-framed yet upright, hair hung down dark in a double curtain, soft as smoke. She stood there staring down into Gavin's crib, transfixed, as though he were something far less ordinary, more precious, than a mere sleeping baby—at least till Gavia made some small noise, alerting her to her presence. And even then she didn't *turn*, per se; just cocked her head, birdlike, to glance back over her shoulder and smile very faintly.

"Such handsome boy," this creature told Gavia, accent vaguely Baltic. "*Such* lovely place you have here, with family, even so far from home—*so* very lucky you are, *mažai močiutė*. Your life here is pleasant dreaming, surely."

Her grip failing, muscles gone slack, the book Gavia clutched came wavering back down, abruptly too heavy to hold; that black wave swept back up and over in one vertiginous rush, frost and tide and pain, a scraping, keening rush of sound. Memory, swirling headlong into words; Jaiden's voice, cautious but driven, once more telling her how *I'm afraid I won't even get the chance to say no, before she just starts in to pressing on me.* . . .

But, "Who're you?" Gavia husked, or tried to—abruptly gone all vowels, throat constricted thick with indignation. "What d'you—what y' *want*, here? Whuh, whaaah . . ."

The woman shook her head, however. Put one scar-white, nailless finger to her own lips—one of six, Gavia now saw, on either delicate hand—before reaching out to lay it on Gavia's instead, bisecting her mouth in mid-protest like a sharp downward cut, a needle-thrust, a still-burning brand.

Not fair, she might well've complained, if only her tongue would allow it; why *her*, for Christ's own sake, of all people, to be selected for recompense—she who'd never even set foot in Zukauskas's house, let alone heard him boast of his ancient crime? Why not Jaiden, who'd worked the contract and listened to the stories, who already knew this fast-unravelling shell of a thing—this pretty nightmare, this swan-queen refeathered, this selkie without a skin—by sight?

Salt in her lungs, a wet gasp, swallowed under fathoms; pain in her chest, her heart, light and hollow, dank and deep. Kristle'd find her drowned on dry land by sunrise, no doubt, with Gavin suffocated in his sleep nearby and no possible hope of a swap even were she able to beg one out loud, no last-minute offering up of old for new. For nightmares, Gavia well knew, were rarely so logical, and cruel by default.

Better by far to try to fail than not to try at all, though. She could do *that*, at the very least.

Letting go book-first, skeptic and practical Gavia Pratt fell by slow degrees, a tree toppling, doing her level best to broadcast, all the way to the floor, *Not him, me, take me. I'll even marry you, that's what you're lookin' for again; marry or burn, either way. Falling down down down, with no attempt at protest. . . .*

Whilst the woman, in turn—Zukauskas's wife no longer—only let that smile of hers widen in return till the whole front of her head fell open, a hole of stars through which only a dim black beach could be glimpsed, far away in the distance: some empty world, stretched out dead and cold under a faint white sun, irregular-shaped and pale-shining as the top of a baby skeleton's soft skull.

THE DAUGHTER OUT
OF DARKNESS

NANCY HOLDER

The Daughter Out of Darkness
by Dr. John Seward

With an addendum provided by his wife
Transcribed from wax phonograph rolls found among the
belongings of the former Mary Holder, ancestress of Nancy Holder
SEWARD ASYLUM
LONDON
JANUARY, 1906

Some hold that there is more darkness in women. That they are the daughters of Eve; they are weak and easily seduced by the tantalizing power of evil. Some say that is why Dracula was able to scale the walls of my asylum and make Mina Harker his own. The darkness, the invitation to invade, churned within her and she surrendered to its siren call.

Thus, the argument runs that the weaker sex requires the guidance of strong, moral men to keep their faces toward the light. It is through our strength of character and wisdom that we temper love with patience; when we fail to correct, we fail them. One sees this in the tens of thousands of unfortunate women teeming the streets of London—depraved, lost, wretched. Soulless. They have no men on whom they can depend, and so they are scattered to the winds like rotten leaves.

Does that mean, then, that we men were not strong enough to thwart Dracula's seduction of Mina, our fair sister in all but blood? Not sufficiently moral to keep the monster at bay?

Was it my own weakness that drove my first wife mad?

Do I have the fortitude to combat the evil in our midst tonight?

These are questions I must answer now, for in this palace of madmen, we are under siege. I stand between disaster and triumph, and I must remain resolute.

Though I did not know it then, the path to destruction began six months ago. As the solstice sun descended and our small estate was cloaked in shadow, Elizabeth Louise Thornton, the woman who had divorced me five years previous, shrieked an eldritch chant that compelled my complete attention. Over and over, a hundred times, a thousand, she called out the same refrain. Fascinated, I copied down the syllables that ripped from her throat: *"Ygnaiih! Ygbaiih!"*

Did *she* summon *him* with those words? Is that how *he* found my Mary?

"Jack!"

It is Mary who calls me now. Mary Holder, now Seward, once my head nurse and now my wife, struggles at the door, which I have locked. She beseeches me. *She* summons *me*. I am speaking this into my phonograph diary in darkness, for I dare not light the lamp. They must not find me here. They must not know my grim purpose. And it is this: I shall kill everyone in this fortress to modern psychiatric medicine. My cure rate is formidable. Alas, though, for Eliza, she has grown worse. Now I know why: she carries within herself another voice, and is forced to commune with nightmares.

My brow is wet, my hands cold and clammy. The cylinders of that other, horrid nightmare—our pursuit of the dread vampire king Dracula—were destroyed when the first Whitby Asylum burned to the ground. Eliza found those rolls after we had married, and after listening to them, she left me, believing me a madman or a demon. She believed that my spoken diary contained either delusions or horrible, debased truths that I had kept from her before marrying her. She raged at me, told me that I should have shared all before her ring was on my finger, so that she could have judged more prudently my suitability as a husband.

I countered that how could I have initiated an innocent, pure angel into a world that had such creatures in it? She called me a coward, and that I do now own. Though I swore to her I remained silent because I did not dare fret her heart, I carried on my soul the terrible question that plagued me night and day. *Had we killed the vampire? Was he, as Dr. Van Helsing would say, true dead?*

I believed that she was correct to leave me; that this was the curse that hung over me like the Sword of Damocles, and *I* had no cause to draw her beneath that sword. I had loved selfishly, with no thought of her protection, nor that of children should we be so blessed. I had thought not of her at all, only of my loneliness among the madmen and women in my care. Tormented souls! Now I share their descent into hell. . . .

For Mary Holder brought with her a dread secret of her own, which she did not disclose until this very night. I knew some of it: I knew that she had lied, and stolen, and left in the night with the reprobate Sir George Burnwell, who would have made her a fallen woman, but married her at the last.

But I did not know that she had committed murder.

Hours ago, as the snows swirled and eddied in the leaded windows of our great hall, cutting us off from tonight's thin crescent of light, an echoic pounding rumbled through our hall. My assistant, Peter Duinsmire, went to answer and I trailed after, for it was uncommon for us to receive visitors at such an hour. Into blackest pitch the door opened with a squeal.

Were our fates sealed then?

I recognized the figure who stood before us, as Mary had kept the newspaper articles detailing his many peccadillos and scrapes with the authorities. Tall Sir George Burnwell was, and dressed like, an aristocrat in a greatcoat and top hat. His bones were stacked precariously on his frame, with little tissue between them, the musculature withered. His fingers were claws of bone. His face shone gray and green from the grave, and his eyes were not his. *They were not his.* They blazed with an evil I never dreamed of, although I had reconciled myself long before to his villainy and cruelty when Mary disclosed to me the facts—but not all the facts, I was soon to learn—of her first marriage.

But among all these revolting facts of his appearance, one surpassed them in every way: his mouth hung open as happens in death, and I saw inside a dark, frenzied whirlpool of worms and beetles where his tongue should be. Then words issued from that mouth, although the hinges of his jaw were dislocated. They poured out as if from a phonograph recording, and he said:

"I am the legal husband of Mary Burnwell, née Holder. If she is under this roof, I demand that you give her to me at once. Then we shall leave you in peace."

A triple bolt of lightning illuminated the doorway, and I saw that the cadaverous Burnwell was not alone. Another stood beside him, and although his appearance was less hideous—he seemed to be a member of the Egyptian race, wearing a fez above a black-hued face, though the dark features were entirely Caucasian—a miasma of such depravity issued from him that I took three steps back and slammed the door before my accustomed civility allowed them entry.

I turned . . . and beheld my Mary. She wore an apron over her dressing gown, her hair was askew, and there was a fresh scratch on her cheek from which bubbled droplets of blood. As she stared at the door, she gathered up the folds of her apron between her fists, uttered a cry of horror, and collapsed to the floor.

Duinsmire stood guard whilst I lifted my unconscious wife in my arms and hied her out of the room, down corridors, directing the securing of gates and doors at every juncture. At last she was in our apartment in the madhouse. I lay her down on our bed and applied spirits of hartshorn. She roused with a start and uttered a horrible scream only equal to Mina Harker's shriek after the vampire had forced her to drink his blood.

Just then, as the room lit up with St. Elmo's fire, a loud wail vibrated through the stone. It was Eliza, screaming her mad syllables: *"Ygnaiih! Ygbaiih! Y'btbn . . . h'ebye-n'grkdll'lb . . . Iä! Iä! Iä!"*

Mary clung to me and cried, "Jack, Jack, what is happening?"

I answered her question with my own question. "Mary, what the deuce was that thing? That was your husband, yes? And another?"

Her face was a ghastly white. She began to weep, and said brokenly, "I brought this upon us. I am cursed!"

Then she told me all. She had killed the bounder when he had attacked her, he intending, I believe, to use her in some dark rite. She described to me an octagonal room filled with hideous paintings on the walls and a statue of a creature composed of eyes and tentacles. Unholy, blasphemous, repugnant. She had thwarted him by pretending to fall into a swoon, then bashed his head in with a smaller statue that she could not describe. She had left him dead in their villa. Of that she had been certain.

And the thing outside *had* to be dead. It could not be a living man.

Eliza was screaming again: *"Ygnaiih! Ygbaiih!"*

Mad Eliza. My fault.

In 1901, after my asylum had burned, Mary and I moved to Texas, and eventually Dr. Van Helsing joined us. Three years later, Eliza's wealthy uncle wrote me, revealing that my former wife had gone quite mad, and that he laid her affliction at my door. Like her, he believed that the very air of my asylum carried the contagion of insanity. That it was a disease that one could catch. I doubt that she shared with him the secret of my diary, for how, in that case, could he ask me to care for her?

As congress with you has utterly overset her, I charge
you now to return to England and minister to her. I

WHAT THE #@&% IS THAT?

shall set up a small asylum for you to run, with but a few patients, and in return, she shall be your primary concern. I do this to prevent further scandal. I will not brook a refusal on your part. It was I who arranged for your divorce, and I understand that you have remarried. Thus, you owe Elizabeth and me a double debt.

It was so, and to my astonishment, Mary insisted that we conform to the man's wishes, and so we returned to London. And we have cared for her all this time, my new wife attending my mad wife. Surely you who are listening know that it is impossible to obtain a writ of divorcement in England. I wonder then, if her uncle knew that she was weak-minded, for one *can* divorce by reason of insanity. Perhaps he had done it so that I could not claim that legal relief when her affliction could be hidden no longer.

"Jack," Mary calls to me again through the door. In my mind's eye, I can see the deep scratch on her cheek, sustained when Eliza wounded her while struggling in vain to pull the bars from her windows.

After Mary had confessed, we rushed together to Eliza's room. The door, of course, was barred and locked. Mary had the keys and I ordered her to stand aside whilst I opened it, fearing an attack from the madwoman within. But the door itself fought against my efforts, and it was not until I had called for Duinsmire to assist me that we succeeded in forcing it open.

A dervish of wind and rain assaulted us from an enormous hole in the wall opposite! Colors—green and purple and a noxious ochre—whirled from the center, and as we fought to reach it, I thrust Mary behind myself and shouted to Duinsmire to remove her from the place. But she would not go, clinging instead to my hand, and we staggered forward en suite, the three of us.

Then I was filled with a dread certainty that something lurked *behind* us, and I instinctively ducked, pulling my dear wife down with me. But

Duinsmire was not so lucky, and I beheld the corpse of Burnwell bringing down the blade of his sabre—and he cleaved my poor assistant in half!

"So I will do to you!" he bellowed to us both.

Then Coates, the new head nurse, hung in the doorway shouting, "Sir, sir! There is a devilish man in the wards!" Her gaze fell upon the grisly, dripping remains of Duinsmire, now tossed wildly by the gale, and she began to scream.

The colors spun and I charged grimly ahead, but I saw no sign of Eliza. My mind informed me that our enemies had breached my home, but how, I did not know. The hole was in the outer wall; the door, locked. Where was the inmate? She, whose purity I had sullied, whose mind had been lost?

The colors . . . they danced before me. . . . I do not know if I stopped in my tracks, rooted in the tempest; I do not know what happened to me. But my mind spun; I lost all purchase on my surroundings; my mouth hung open in astonishment. I thought I saw stars, and a vast city of monoliths, blocks of granite covered with runes; I hovered hundreds of feet above a vast, surging landscape and a boiling sea. And I longed—how I longed!—to caper with the strange, shadowed creatures whose forms I could only glimpse from the corners of my eyes. I felt as if I were beholding a great truth; that I was privileged to commune with a purity of being I had not dreamed of.

"*Women hold darkness,*" came a voice. And I *knew* that voice: it belonged to the one who had walked with Burnwell. I knew him: great Nyarlathotep, Messenger of the Gods, the Crawling Chaos. The Egyptian who walked silently beside him. Who had raised his loyal servant, Burnwell, from the dead.

My voice raised in praise: "*Ygnaiih! Ygbaiih! Y'btbn . . . h'ebye-n'grkdll'lb . . . Iä! Iä! Iä!*"

"*They hold more darkness.*" His voice, filled with authority, and promises. I searched for him, lifting my eyes toward the fervent heavens. I saw . . .

Oh, I *saw* . . .

I saw that what I have called "madness" is transcendence; what I labeled "good" was weakness. Men cannot guide and correct; only the gods can. And they *wish* to. They desire to return and to raise and ennoble us; to make us more than we are now.

No. That is utter madness. That is my own weakness of mind, addled from my delusion. I feared insanity when Mary came to me; I was descending into a black voice of guilt and despair, and culpability. I feared that I should never be free of the dreams about Dracula and the unscientific threat he posed to my certainty of an ordered world. I suffered endless nightmares—that a *vampire* had walked among us—until Mary sat down with my phonograph diary, and listened, then bade me listen with her, a witness to the knowledge that there are more things in heaven and Earth than are dreamt of in our philosophy. I *know* that she turned me back to the light of rational thought, and science. She was rock, anchor, and beacon. My angel.

Murderess. Thief.

She was on the run for years, and when she came to my asylum, she lied to me, *lied,* put me in harm's way, from this Burnwell creature and his god—

Great Nyarlathotep of the Thousand Incarnations, who has shown me a miracle!

"He is in the wards!" Mary shouts through the door. Lightning crackles overhead and the building is shaken to its foundations. I see colors everywhere. Beautiful light. Clarity.

"The monster! The thing!" she cries.

I shake myself from my stupor. Yes, the thing. It is not a god. It is a supernatural being, like Dracula. Can be killed, like Dracula.

"Jack!" she cries. "They are coming! I hear them. *I see them.* George, oh, dear God, have pity! Have mercy!"

She is pounding on the door. I rouse myself. What am I doing, speaking into my phonograph? When the world is ending outside my door, and my beloved is in mortal jeopardy?

I throw open the door.

Mary falls forward, into my arms. I catch her awkwardly, burdened as my hands are. Then I look past her distraught form to the end of the corridor and I *see*—

—Eliza, eyes wide and unfocused, covered in blood from head to foot, her garments, her hair, her face; and behind her, not walking, but *floating* two feet off the ground: Burnwell, or what is left of him. Grave sheen covers him; his right arm has pulled from his body; his lips are gone. What he walks beside I cannot tell, for it is all light, but I *know* . . .

I drag Mary into the room and slam the door. Her arms go around me; her face is pressed against my neck; the gold of her hair casts a halo and I can almost see her gossamer wings. She came to me as an angel.

But I know better. Women hold more darkness. And it is this darkness I must cleave out. She will draw me down, and away, and if that happens, I will not walk with Him.

I have the sword that Burnwell sundered Duinsmire with; it is in my right hand, very heavy. But not too heavy. I am a man, vigorous and strong. Moral, and knowing.

Eliza chants:

"Ygnaiih! Ygbaiih! Y'btbn . . . h'ebye-n'grkdll'lb . . . Iä! Iä! Iä!"

As I raise the blade, a thought flashes through my mind: *This is all a lie. I am being tricked. I must not do this.*

But the light is shimmering off the blade as the Messenger glides through the door with his servants on either side. As he compels me: *Women hold more darkness.*

And before that darkness takes me, I must cut it out.

I must cut it—

I must—

I

Iä! Iä!

And thus you have witnessed my client's chief defense, my lords; for Mary Holder Burnwell Seward had no choice but to defend herself against the madman her husband had become. It is not suspicious but tragic that two gentlemen, charged with the protection of the fairer sex, both abrogated that responsibility and instead attempted to kill this poor lady. She has done nothing to deserve the gallows; indeed, she merits the collective apology of the sons of Adam for abandoning her to such darkness. Thus I say to you, you must acquit her and set her free. She has not seen the sun for seven months, and it is monstrous that her trial has lasted this long.

And in conclusion . . .

What is this? What has happened to the lights? They are so bright!

Mrs. Seward, what are you doing?

What the devil is that?

> *Never cross us. Do not trouble me or mine. I walk*
> *with a god, vengeance shall be mine.*
> *I am the haunter of the dwark, the shadow over time.*
> *Mary Holder I have been;*
> *now I exist beyond your ken.*
> *The brightness of our light burns out your eyes, it is*
> *the color out of space;*
> *it is the darkness of your future and the end of*
> *your race.*
> *Iä! Iä! Iä!*

Discovered in Nancy Holder's attic October 14, 2014,
San Diego, California

FRAMING MORTENSEN

ADAM-TROY CASTRO

Once I had become wealthy enough to buy miracles, I used one to obtain the living head and shoulders of my longtime enemy, Philip Mortensen.

The news services reported that a prominent attorney working behind closed doors had just been found dead in his favorite chair, intact up to the wound that ended his torso just below the collarbone. His two severed arms were found fallen to the floor at either side of him, forming parentheses. An autopsy revealed that all these remaining parts had been completely drained of blood, but was unable to determine what tool had been used to amputate everything above his collarbone. Some stories managed to report that not a single drop had escaped to stain his lush burgundy carpet.

This would no doubt go down in crime history as the most spectacular and baffling unsolved murder of all time, not just a whodunnit but a *how*dunnit.

Nobody, not the police, not his wife, not his children, and not his secret mistress, would ever know that it was not a murder but a kidnapping.

Mortensen's head and shoulders became the prisoners of what looked like an oil painting, portraying some jowly, balding man with thin strands of hair floating above the round arc of his skull like cirrus clouds. It was the face of a well-fed man, a contented man . . . even, if you believed Mortensen's public image, a *good* man.

It made little logical sense for the landscape behind him to be a stark image of arctic wastes and that nineteenth-century sailing vessel the *Erebus*, stuck in ice during its journey to discover the Northwest Passage, but I wanted him to begin his time in my possession aware of being cold and alone in a place far from home.

I hung the framed image over the fireplace, in the private study that neither my household staff nor my wife were allowed to enter. I had an excuse for declaring the room off-limits to anybody besides myself. Among my many enterprises were certain highly sensitive projects for the government that required me to keep particular documents of a sensitive nature at home; I even apologized, in full humility, for the necessity. Everybody understood. I was not some capricious tyrant who made that demand lightly. The routine maintenance of this one room, all on my own, was a small matter. Thanks in no small part to early financial reversals fomented by Mortensen's enterprises, I had spent many of my early years poor enough to need to perform such chores all the time.

The miracle had not cost my soul, an artifact that the provider of miracles had no interest in. The price had been legal tender, cash, a sum greater than the annual budget of some fair-sized cities. It's a given that I shuddered when I first heard it, an equal given that when I had a little time to contemplate the purchase further, I found that it was a price well worth paying for power over the piece of garbage who had been my chief competitor for so long. Later, I might choose to pay that price again, for a second miracle and maybe even a third—as simply being able to exercise such power over the physical universe had been pleasurable all by itself—but right now, it was difficult to imagine any other I might even desire. I had my health. I had more wealth and power than any man could possibly use. I had a beautiful and obedient wife thirty years my junior, who by contract had to remain married to me for at least five more years in order to escape with alimony. I had a big house, a fine position in the community, a sterling reputation as a captain of industry, and now, a passion: being the personal Mephistopheles to my worst business rival's eternally damned soul.

A busy schedule prevented me from initiating my fun for a few months, but I did make a point of a weekend aside, late in the fall. That night, I was able to give my beautiful wife a break from the responsibility to pretend that her skin did not crawl at my touch, by telling her I would be working in the study all evening, and indeed that she should not be concerned if I remained in seclusion for several days. She left the house with the credit cards and a visible air of relief. I locked myself in the study, set a fire in the hearth, settled into my most comfortable high-backed chair with a snifter of brandy, and spoke the words that would, by prior arrangement, restore my enemy to awareness of his predicament.

"Hello, Mortensen."

The figure in the painting blinked, in the stupid way men have when they're first returning to consciousness and have yet to know that they've been taken to a place absent of hope. It was a look I already knew from the faces of any number of other associates facing their last hours in darkened rooms; though their fates had been significantly more mundane than the one Mortensen faced, the principle was the same, and I was able to follow the rapid evolution from confusion to concern to genuine dismay and fear with ease despite the less than five seconds it took the damned man to travel it. "Hello?" he said. And then, rising to a cry: "Hello! Hello! Is any-body here? Hello?"

I reached into the painting and slapped him twice, once on each cheek. He gasped. I pulled back my hand and registered not just the pleasant sting of flesh against flesh, but also the impression of the great, indeed inhuman cold of the place where I had trapped him: the kind of environ-ment that would drop an unprotected man in seconds.

I said, "Hello, Mortensen. Can you hear me?"

I had asked the dealer in miracles to arrange for my voice, as heard by the trapped man, to possess the distant but resonant and echoing tones that motion pictures of a certain sort attribute to the Lord God. This was not because I'd ever possessed any fantasies of playing God, but because I'd wanted to amuse myself by seeing whether Mortensen's first explanation for his plight would involve any of that religious rot.

In this small matter, I was doomed to disappointment. He did jerk as if stung, but a certain animal craftiness entered his eyes as his petty little mind began seeking some means of controlling whatever happened to him. He said, "I . . . I know that voice. I've heard that voice. Recently."

"Please, sir. Until now, we have not been in the same room for five years."

"Oh, my God. Perkins? It's you, isn't it? It's you, you son of a bitch! What have you done to me? Why can't I feel anything below my shoulders?"

I grinned at him. "You certainly do have a great number of questions, my good fellow. But I will attempt to provide all the necessary intelligence as expeditiously as I can. First, you are right. I am your old friend, and as for where I've taken you, it's a place that I control utterly. You cannot feel anything below your shoulders because there is no longer anything to feel. I do hope these answers prove a comfort to you, because they are the last comforts you shall ever know."

He began to scream.

I can afford to be clear on this. I have witnessed any number of enemies taken to dark subterranean places for vicious treatment. I relegated all of them to that fate out of business necessity, rather than the kind of personal animus I harbored for Mortensen. He evaded my wrath for as long as he did because I'd put off dealing with him for the day when I could find means that fulfilled the bottomless depths of my malice for him. But I'd learned a great deal about screaming from the others. I'd determined that screams of anticipatory fear like these were best permitted to go on for however long it took the subject in question to exhaust himself and come to terms with the knowledge that none of this melodramatic fulmination had profited him one iota. This epiphany can arrive in minutes. I've seen it take days.

Sometimes, it's more productive to cut it off at the start.

I went to the dartboard that had until recently been my chief recreation in this room, and plucked one of the darts from the bull's-eye. It was gratifying to learn that I was still as skilled at the pastime as I had been in college. The dart flew true and embedded its point in the center of Mortensen's forehead, right above the bridge of his nose.

His reaction to this was instant, disbelieving silence. Blood flowed freely from the point of the puncture, forming a rivulet that split at the bridge of his nose and followed the line of his cheeks toward his jaw. His gaze moved upward, struggling to make out what had just impaled him, just barely managing to pull the stabilizing fan of the tail-feathers into focus. His response reeked of disbelief. "A dart."

"Yes. And don't get your hopes up, my old friend. It shan't kill you. Nothing I will do to you in this room, tonight or in any of the other long nights to come, will kill you. You will stay alive for as long as I wish, enduring all the ways I shall twist your present form to the cause of my own amusement."

"You're insane," he said.

I had, of course, expected precisely that banal observation, precisely this early in our evening together.

"I suppose, on the subject of you, I am. I must confess it, Mortensen. I loathed you from the very first moment I set eyes on you. I loathed you more every time we spoke, every time your enterprises ran into conflict with mine. For decades now, I have had few ambitions that excited me more than the prospect of ensuring that you experience more suffering, at greater length, than any living man has ever known. You have no idea how many plans I've discarded because they were not elaborate enough. You don't know how many times that's saved you for another day, another year." I chuckled. "Of course, I am so glad that I held out. This is so much more satisfying than a simple assassin garroting you in the dead of night."

"But you can't!" he cried. And then, another sentence I'd known he would get around to, sooner or later. "You'll never get away with it!"

I laughed again, this time with genuine affection. "Oh, Mortensen."

I readied a handful of darts.

"You don't know how fully I intend to test that hypothesis."

*   *   *   *

The outside world continued to turn in the manner it always has. Empires rose and fell. Mortensen's supposed death became one of those notorious mysteries that vanish in the tabloid press when new atrocities arrive to supplant them. I arranged various entertaining fates for his wife and children, and brought the news back for Mortensen to enjoy. Some of the details would have been enough to drive most men in his predicament mad, but there was no pleasure to be had in tormenting a shattered soul. I'd therefore denied him the respite of madness.

My associates took note of how much time I spent ensconced in my study. My wife, acting out of the need to document that she'd noticed, remarked that I hadn't spent any time with her in three weeks. My board of directors told me that I needed to attend more corporate functions. My friends said that they missed me at the club. I obliged the wife with a night plying her erotic trade and an increase in her allowance sufficient to mollify her for what I expected to be a number of additional months of neglect. I fired three members of the board and gave the others a detailed business plan for the next year. I went to the club and spent a fine evening trading industry gossip that included extensive speculation over the leftist conspiracy behind the strange assassination of poor Mortensen. I did a quick run around the world and returned to the one room in my home—and by extension, the one place in the entire world—that held any interest to me.

Outside my study windows, it was the height of summer, the golden rays of the sun casting their blessed light on a countryside overflowing with life's wondrous bounty. Inside the frame, it was still arctic wasteland, the air so frigid that if I did not use the paints I'd been provided to maintain the image as only I could, Mortensen's skin turned black with frostbite, and his eyes froze shut beneath blindfolds of pure ice.

Have I mentioned that I was once quite the talented painter of portraits, in my university days? It never took any real time at all to retouch his skin and undo whatever the climate had done to him, restoring to his jowly features to the very pink of health . . . which, of course, the frigid air never wasted any time ravaging again. This did, of course, involve more and more effort the more time I spent away, and on this particular occasion, I'd just returned from a two-week industrial conference in Rotterdam. The wind-rotted fissures in the flesh of his cheeks had grown so ravaged that it was now, in spots, possible to see the teeth behind them.

I removed his painting from the wall and set it against my easel. "You're not looking well, Mortensen. You should take better care of yourself."

"P-please," he begged. "Enough . . . is enough. In the name of decency, please stop."

"I told you, my old friend. In a relationship such as ours, begging only increases the pleasure taken by the one wielding the power." I dabbed my brush in some jet-black paint and touched the bristles to his forehead. A few simple movements and I had added a tick to his forehead: a swollen, gruesome, blood-saturated blot of a thing, with a proboscis sunken deep into his flesh. It was my will that the thing be venomous, and so the flesh around the spot began to pucker, to swell, to grow rank and infected. "For instance, *that*. Do you have even the slightest idea how satisfying I find that?"

"What do you need me to say to you? I'm sorry, dammit! Stop!"

Of course, I would not. I had grown quite adept at adding and subtracting elements from his tightly circumscribed world. I had subjected him to plagues of ants and scorpions, to needles peeling his skin from his skull, to broken glass in his eyes, and to a great number of foul substances erupting from between his lips; I had also recast his features in the most delightfully comic ways, blacking out his teeth or adding pendulous tumors to his cheeks or creating unbroken expanses of skin where his mouth or his eyes should have been. Always it had been delightful to watch him writhe in full awareness of his obscene new incarnations before I demonstrated divine mercy by restoring the portrait to its prior, unsullied state.

The only time he had ever come close to endangering me was one occasion when I had been having some fun covering his lips with leeches. He had clamped down his teeth and managed to catch the tip of my index finger. I'd cursed, pulled away, and for the rest of the day, visited upon his eyes and forehead cruelties that I would have thought beyond even my motivated imagination. Since then, I'd taken special care when touching up his mouth.

In any event, the tick was just a warm-up for today's fun, the first stage of a brand-new project.

"Do you know, Mortensen? I have found that I have empathy for Satan's dilemma."

The swelling had spread to his right cheek, making his voice sludgy. "Go t' heh!"

"That," I said warmly, "happens to be a most germane suggestion. Because this is your personal Hell, and I your personal eternal demon, I am forced to contemplate the difficulty all such demons must face not long into their stewardship of such damned souls as yourself: to wit, just how much novelty can one keep bringing to the task of rendering any given soul's torment unendurable, even when the power at hand is infinite and the possibilities for fresh punishment limited only by the boundaries of one's imagination. To a horned imp inflicting all the horrors of the nether regions on some sinner of merely human capacity to feel it, is it not an occupational hazard to run into the torturer's equivalent of creative bankruptcy? To have reached the limits of one's personal imagination and find that all that remains is derivative hackwork?"

The venom must have spread to Mortensen's airways, because he was no longer attempting to answer me but instead purpling as he struggled to breathe.

I applied paint remover to the tick, repaired the physical damage to Mortensen's face with some dabs of paint appropriate to his skin tone, and gave him time to recover.

Once he had breath again, I said, "So, where was I?"

"You said . . . you were running out of ideas."

I chuckled and painted an oozing sore on the tip of his ear. "I'm an imaginative man, Mortensen; I have enough ideas to keep this going not just for the rest of my life, but also for the lives of the talented artists of the grotesque I had hoped would take over your punishment after I'm gone."

His next suggestion was a pathetic effort to be helpful. "You could wish for extended life for yourself."

"Oh, I could. And I have. You will be happy to hear that you and I will now live in health, or what passes for health in your current condition, decades longer than I ever would have expected. Beyond that, the price of the miracles necessary to keep me going increases past what even I could afford. In fifty years or so, I may need to renegotiate.

"But it occurs to me that even if I live forever, or secure your fate as a commissioned legacy lasting generations, then the creative well will still someday run dry; the ideas will stop coming, or the will to continue will fade to nothing.

"So, what I need, really, is a way to make the process self-perpetuating for all eternity.

"I need a demon."

I mixed my pigments until I found myself with the perfect shade of awfulness, and touched the tip of my brush to the canvas. This time, unlike any of the previous times, I didn't make any adjustments to Mortensen's face or figure but instead applied my skill to the landscape behind him, where the ship remained frozen in arctic ice.

Mortensen flinched as I drew near, realized that nothing was done to him directly, and turned his eyes as far as they would go, but no will he could muster could turn his head all the way around and grant him what he most feared and craved: a clear view of what I was adding to the background art.

He cried out, "What are you doing?"

I began to hum Beethoven's Fifth.

"You son of a bitch! You sick, sadistic son of a bitch! Tell me!"

I hummed the symphony in its entirety while continuing to work.

Another year passed in this fashion. It is remarkable how much I learned of the fine art of oil painting in that time, how much further I was able to refine the skills that turned a few swabs of pigment into nightmares beyond Mortensen's imagination. Of course, business continued to make its serial demands on my time, and I sometimes had to leave the poor soul unattended for days or weeks, with nothing to do but contemplate ominous scraping sounds behind him—but that, I found, added a delicious additional dimension to his plight; alone in the cold and dark, savaged by the elements, he was left no alternative but to deeply miss me, both the company I provided and the first aid my brushes administered. His demeanor, whenever I returned with apologies, often included a pathetically grateful measure of relief, relief that I took care to betray with grotesque adjustments to his features before I left him behind and turned my attention back to the evolution of the growing awfulness behind him.

Near the end, I grew so enamored of the work that I abdicated my other responsibilities in order to work on the painting all my waking hours. I granted my wife a divorce along with a settlement grand enough to ensure that I never needed to see her again. I resigned the board and sold off all my shares in the enterprises. I stopped sleeping in the bedroom and instead took my rest on the couch in the study, leaving that room only to bathe and to eat. The servants thought I didn't hear them whispering that the old man had gone mad. I cared not. For the first time in my life, I understood the obsessive quality that can overtake an artist working on his masterpiece. The view out the window revealed winter, then spring, then summer again, but the work on the grand picture continued, the awful sounds of grinding teeth and rumbling growls grew louder, and finally came the day when I put my brush aside and said, "Mortensen?"

He said, "What?"

"This is magnificent. This is absolutely bloody magnificent."

He seemed less than enthused. "Oh. Please. Don't."

Even constant pleas for mercy can become rote. For some time now, Mortensen's had become almost sarcastic.

I forced some jollity into my tone. "Oh, come now, you don't want to be like that! You were always an intolerable oaf, even on your best days, but I always credited you with a modicum of intellectual curiosity. You have to be wondering what I've been working on for so long! The need to know must be burning in your breast!"

"I don't have a breast."

I was mildly surprised. "What an excellent point."

"I don't have anything," he said. "Not family, not friends, not even life. Nothing but my hatred for you."

"Also an excellent point."

"Better than you think," he said. "Because if I have nothing, neither do you. Look at what you've done to your own life. You've thrown it all away so you can spend all your days and nights harassing me. You've made yourself a prisoner too, even if you don't know it."

"Perhaps," I said. "But I can always leave this room when I tire of it. I can always find myself another wife, start myself another company. What choices do you have, Mortensen? Nothing but stoic endurance . . . and I'll soon be taking even that from you."

"Fine. Put me out of my misery, then."

"No such luck. I've had too much fun painting you into it. Here. Let me make it possible for you to look."

I brushed out his eyes and began to construct something else in their place, something that would be capable of the perspective he needed: a pair of long, prehensile eyestalks that were able to loop about and snake around the curve of his hated fat head to garner a clear glimpse of what would soon be coming. I amused myself by making them each a meter long and giving them the muscularity of pythons, so that they had to be coiled on his shoulders like springs, before I bothered to add eyes to the end of them: eyes without lids, that he would not be able to close in order to shut out even the most terrifying sights.

The stalks flailed about in front of his face, some of them emerging from within the boundaries of the frame into the warmer air of the study. "I won't look, Perkins. You can't make me look."

I grinned at him. "Really? Offhand, I can think of about a dozen ways I can force you to look. But I don't have to. You'll look within seconds."

"Never!"

"Really. You're still human, even if you only possess the pathetic half-life I choose to give you. And human nature works the same way it always does. I know that you've heard the inhuman scraping noises behind you. I know you've sensed the presence looming in all its awfulness behind you. I know you've felt the chills race down the segment of spine you have behind you. Every instinct you have demands that you look. Every moment of the fun we've had together dictates that you don't dare. I'm perfectly willing to sit here and wait for as long as it takes for you to fail the same test that destroyed Lot's wife. Why not get it over with?"

The trembling of the eyestalks grew more violent. "Because I know it won't be anything good."

"Oh, that's a given. But does that even make a difference?"

For several additional seconds, he kept the eyestalks focused at me, to the exclusion of whatever filled the landscape behind him . . . but for I who had spent so much time orchestrating his misery, it was easy to discern the faltering of his will, the bargaining with the inevitable, the first moment when he thought he could get away with the briefest of all possible glimpses, that and no more. Almost on schedule, the will left his iron features, the defeat defined the set of his jaw . . . and the stalks whipped about to grant Mortensen his first unwilling look at what loomed behind him.

He managed to scream, *What the hell is that?* before all reason fled.

What I'd done was paint him a companion; a creature of limitless imagination and limitless malice, who once freed would be able to devote its immortal existence to tormenting him in a manner far more imaginative than any I had ever been able to muster. I had started, well over a year earlier, by painting a simple multi-tentacled horror of the sort I remembered from the pulp magazines of my youth; and believing those early efforts had not been extraordinarily impressive, I had devoted every day since then to refining its awfulness, adding additional layers to its bottomless evil, putting more intimations of power in shadows that surrounded it and the way the air itself turned unholy colors wherever it moved. It was a sprawling thing too; the ship in the ice, once its home, was now dwarfed by it, a fragile toy in the grip of a god. Even the landscape itself was too small to contain it, as its furthest extensions appeared to curl over the horizon itself, like a veritable mountain range of malice. I had given it a mind of truly limitless intelligence and no agenda other than creating a universe of endless suffering for the tiny human speck before it. I had also ensured that it could not reach Mortensen, not quite, not yet. But one of its tentacles, a quite horrid thing dripping goo from razored barbs, had been straining for his neck for months now.

No subsequent sound that came out of Mortensen's mouth was at all recognizable as a word. It was just shrieking, anguished and damned and horrified and wonderful: the sound of a man who would never make any other sound, not even if the thing he beheld succeeded in reaching him. There was simply nothing else left. The fear had chased everything else he was from his skull. The tremors rippled up those serpentine eyestalks in waves, almost like somebody had cracked the whip on one end and watched as the reverberations traveled up the line to the other.

I leaned in close, rested my fingertips on the corner of the frame, and whispered, "Beautiful, isn't it?"

Alas, I never should have equipped him with anything so prehensile.

His left eyestalk seized the opportunity to whip away from the horror behind him and leap at the horror in front of him, lashing around my wrist half a dozen times before I had any chance to move.

I tried to pull away, but the coils were stronger than I was and were able to yank my right arm, up to the shoulder, into the frame. Only my exposed hand and the top of my head were able to feel the bitter cold, but it was worse than anything I had ever felt. It was like being flayed with razors. I yelled and the other eyestalk, sensing the opportunity for revenge, whipped around and encircled my neck, cutting off my air and silencing me.

I kicked and the easel went down, painting and all. I was pulled down after it, now waist-deep in the painting, only my legs still thrashing in the real world of the study. Behind Mortensen, my ultimate demon roared in delight at having two treats to anticipate instead of one.

I punched Mortensen in the jaw and he went down—not in the way a full man falls to a powerful blow, but in the way a floating head and shoulders fall when they have long levitated at the height of the man but no longer have the fraudulent perspective of a viewer outside the frame to support them. He landed amputated-side down, his grip on my neck and arm pulling me even farther into the painting.

For a few seconds, I was able to keep my shoes hooked on the frame and maintain a handstand by bracing myself against ice so cold that it felt like fire against my flesh. I was unwilling to fall, because I had no way of knowing if I'd be able to find the frame again, let alone climb back to my study through that window.

Then he snarled at me and yanked harder.

My feet came loose of my shoes and I fell, my skull colliding with Mortensen's with a force that stunned us both.

His grip on me abated. I fell back against the ice, feeling a terrible cold that the fabric of my pants did nothing to insulate. The sensation ripped all remaining breath from me. I blinked through eyes that were already beginning to freeze up and caught a quick glimpse of Mortensen's head bobbing toward me at knee level on eye-stalks that he had already adapted for walking.

I had just enough strength left to lunge, grab one of the eyestalks with both hands, and use it to swing his head like a cudgel. Three times, four, I whipped it about at the end of its prehensile ocular chain, building up momentum. Then I let go and it sailed away from me in an arc, slamming into a patch of ice not at all different from any other patch of ice in the arctic waste that surrounded us. I don't know what I would have done if it had popped back up and started scurrying toward me again, but it made a very loud crack when it hit and then did not move again at all. In seconds, the only sign that it had not been there forever was the redder color of the ice where it had landed.

I stood, hugging myself with both arms, the thin fabric of my socks not preventing the cold of the glacier from piercing all the way to the bone. I saw no sign of the portal back to my study. Perhaps I could find it, given time, but if I did not, I'd be dead in minutes, and the search seemed a minor consideration in light of the tableau that now faced me, in the direction opposing the one in which I'd hurled Mortensen: a sprawling, unspeakable mass of flesh the scale of a mountain range, that was even now dragging itself across the waste to get at me. Perhaps it was able to manage some progress. Perhaps it did not and it only seemed that way, because it was so overwhelming to see it from the perspective of a prey animal on the ground that I could not stop myself from taking a step toward it out of sheer appalled awe.

I did not know what would happen to me now.

But I did know that I was far too talented a painter.

THE CATCH

TERENCE TAYLOR

The boyfriend was too easy.

He had died slowly, painfully, protested all the way, as they always did. Before I was done with him, the big beefy blond beach boy had wept copious tears, hysterical, and begged as he offered sexual services he would never have considered under any other circumstances. None of which ever appealed to me. There had been nothing original that told me anything new. He'd been the same as every dumb jock I'd slit open in secret since college, long before I'd built my home surgery. All the butch boys bawled like babies, no matter how big a bully. This one hadn't looked like the brightest bulb in the box when I had surreptitiously watched him and his girl at the restaurant as they fumbled their way through what looked like a first date—and not later as I followed them to their car with my twin Tasers, duct tape, and nylon cable ties.

Even so, he'd been a disappointment.

How many victims had there been? How many of these macho ass-holes had I silenced by now? There had been a time when I kept a careful list of every instrument used on every last one, details of the stalking, capture, and kill. I had film, videotape, then digital files of all the sessions here in my hidden basement room, carefully organized on paper or hard drives, even an assortment of anonymous and untraceable souvenirs, all rigged to self-destruct in a variety of ways if handled by anyone but me.

Meaningless. I'd grown past that.

It wasn't about records or numbers anymore. I only cared about what each individual act told me. Killing wasn't so much an art or obsession now as it was religion, a spiritual quest. Taking life from others as slowly and methodically as I can has become a search for something deep within myself, for the reason I do this if nothing else. I know I'm a monster but still don't understand why.

I can't blame my parents. They were a saintly couple with no idea how to handle their young son's frequent night terrors as I woke screaming from dreams of steely surgical tables and sharp, thin blades—much less any knowledge of where that had led me as I grew to manhood. They were affluent academics able to afford their own home near my mother's teaching position at New York University, with room for my father's studio. His paintings weren't the most daring of his day, but they'd been popular and sold successfully for long enough to afford them an upper-class bohemian lifestyle—idyllic until I came along to cast a pall over their happiness. My poor, dear, innocent parents . . . No, what drove me to do what I did had to be in me alone, something solitary and unique, whatever the cause.

Whatever that was, I haven't found it yet.

I turned my attention to the girl. She'd lain there quietly, facing in my direction, had watched silent as I meticulously vivisected her date throughout the long night. Making the girls watch was usually part of the fun, to let them anticipate what was to come next as I stripped flesh and muscle from their boyfriends. I'd studied anatomy over the years like a medical student, from the same textbooks—mastered where to cut to avoid veins and arteries to minimize bleeding, rinsed away what blood and fluids were released as they rose from muscle tissue. It was a remarkably slow but clean process, one designed to maximize suffering while prolonging life as the meat of the body's extremities was sliced into layers, thinner and thinner, gradually pared to the bone. My methods had evolved over the years to what I considered to be their utmost effectiveness, and had become routine. The only variation I ever sought was in the infinitely individual responses of my subjects.

The girls usually stared in rapt horror, shrieked as best they could through their bright red ball gags, whimpered long after they'd gone hoarse, knowing that when I was done with their date, it would be their turn.

But not this one.

She had watched me calmly, quiet, almost analytical, more like a curious colleague observing a surgery than my next victim. I walked around her partner's remains neatly arranged on the long stainless steel autopsy table next to hers, stood between them without obscuring the girl's view.

"Hello, pretty-pretty," I said softly, stroked her cheek with the back of my rubber-gloved hand, still wet with the boy's blood. She didn't flinch, locked her eyes on mine, as if able to communicate with that cool gaze alone.

Her eyes never blinked. They were a dazzling deep green, almost emerald. I touched her auburn hair, such a perfect complement to the rest of her coloring, picked up a pair of sharp shears, and cut her date-night clothing from her body with a tailor's precision.

I felt like I could almost hear her voice in my head, low, soothing, like a lover's whisper in my ear, encouraging me. Of course, that was just my imagination—the usual siren call of death and dismemberment, to continue until I was done, until my search was complete, until all hope I would find whatever it was I looked for was gone. Hope that only came again when a new couple posed the same eternal question anew in my mind, and provided new bodies in which to search for the answer.

When the girl was completely naked, I gathered the ruins of her wardrobe in my hands, a multicolored bouquet of fabric scraps, and stood at the foot of the table like a bridesmaid to see my handiwork. Her pale white skin was smooth as Michelangelo marble. Though my interests were more surgical than sexual, she had just the right amount of everything to satisfy me, fuller in figure than most men prefer today. Nearly too good to be true, too much what I look for when I go out trawling for prey. She was an almost-exact replica of the first girl to trigger my more violent appetites, even though no one could possibly know that but me. I'd thought so earlier when I spotted the couple at the mall. She was not a perfect woman, by any means, but she was oddly perfect for me.

Almost like bait for the catch of the day.

The thought made me shudder. My father had fished for sport and often took me with him as a treat. Fly-fishers know how to use custom-tied lures to attract what they want. Why did this one feel like it had been designed to accommodate my particular tastes? Why did I suddenly feel the hook in my mouth, a tug on the line? I looked around the room against my will, felt foolish to fear I was being watched by unseen eyes. The only cameras here were mine.

The girl still stared at me. Her eyes followed mine like those in a haunted mansion portrait, implacable as ever. Nary a blush crossed the surface of her exposed flesh. There was still no struggle against her bonds, the bright yellow nylon ropes that bound her securely to the steel table in a trident, arms bent up, tied at the wrists and elbows, at the waist, knees and ankles, legs together, one last double bond at the throat. I felt a hot flash of anger as she gazed at me calmly.

This one would be a challenge.

I sat in front of my big flat-screen TV with dinner on a freestanding tray in front of me, looking forward to a night of *CSI* on my DVR. The girl and her date's bloodless body were secured downstairs in the basement behind my hidden room's secret door. Their car was in the garage in front until I drove it to a predetermined spot in New Jersey. There, a fence I contact only by burner phone would pick it up and strip it down to parts for sale across the country, the garage left empty for my next guests' car.

When my parents' Greenwich Village townhouse had been willed to me, I quickly decided to modify it to suit my own purposes, far darker than their famed Sunday brunches and Christmas parties. It had taken years after their completely natural deaths for me to finish my soundproof little slaughterhouse, equipped with spray hoses and drains to clean blood and other waste from my clinically correct work space, acid baths, and a crematorium for disposal of remains. It had taken patience, but that had only increased my anticipation of how perfectly the concealed chamber would suit my needs when done. My playroom had been perfected with discreet but regular use over the last decade. The latest addition I'd made was installing wireless cameras to keep an eye on it.

The girl's image was crystal clear on the retina screen of an iPad Air that sat next to me. I flipped through DVR choices displayed on my TV with the remote. There was a new *CSI* now, set in New Orleans. My own experiences gave the lie to most of their cases, but I enjoyed outsmarting them in my living room. It was what I did instead of Sudoku or other puzzle games, a cheap way to stay sharp.

I glanced at the iPad screen again.

She was still firmly bound, the flayed male body on the table next to her left to keep her on edge, all fluids washed neatly down the drains of the stainless steel table. Except for that, I never cleaned up the remains until I was done, preferred to work in a room that looked like the abattoir it was. Usually, the girl was in shock by now, either staring at the corpse beside her in mute horror or weeping quietly, eyes squeezed shut against the sight. This one seemed to see the camera I used to observe her, stared directly into the lens as if into my own eyes.

I clicked a control on the screen to select another view. A scant second after the image on my screen changed, so did her gaze, as it moved to the new camera to meet mine. I repeated the experiment, went through all five cameras I had hidden in the room, and each time, her eyes moved with mine. I had covered all the lights on the cameras, the lenses were concealed, there was no way she could know where they were or which was active, and yet she seemed to. I was tempted to go down and try to figure out how but resisted, certain the explanation was not in my equipment.

I finished my dinner, washed the dishes, then dried and put them away, as I thought all the while about the mystery downstairs. *Could she be telepathic enough to know what I'm doing?* I'd read of stranger things. There were enough ESP studies on record to indicate the possibility. I smiled. If she could get into my head, she'd find no solace there.

As I dried my hands and rubbed them with moisturizing lotion, I considered going downstairs to continue, but I usually waited twenty-four hours. No need to vary my routine on her account. That would only give back some of the power I'd gained since abducting her. *Can't have that, now.* I changed into soft fleece pajamas and retired, iPad propped on my bedside table, the gentle glow of the girl's pallid skin as my nightlight. I hesitated before I closed my eyes, knew that she only looked at the camera, not into my room, but still felt an odd tingle of observation, as if I was really the one being watched.

Work was mildly distracting; the usual run of students and professors kept me busy enough to take my mind off the peculiarities of the guest in my basement. I work as a reference assistant at the science desk of New York University's Bobst Library. There's no real financial need, but once I was of college age, I had been expected to satisfy my parents that they weren't leaving their modest but still substantial estate to a ne'er-do-well. My inquiring methodical mind lent itself to library research. My chosen field also gave me every opportunity to pursue odd explorations undetected, including all I needed to build my playroom. Over the years, my position had the added advantage of making me a familiar fixture in the neighborhood, another invisible cog in the machinery of the university, convenient for a killer.

My desk was flanked by a pair of long tables in the center of the ninth floor, with a couple of phones, a computer, and a tranquil view across the central atrium through the front windows onto the trees of Washington Square Park. The building was a shining gem of seventies architecture, its interior an open area twelve stories tall, lined with soaring central stairs and stacked symmetrical floors filled with bookcases and tables, behind a gilded floor-to-ceiling aluminum lattice that made it seem like the inside of a giant cybernetic brain.

Over the first decade of the twenty-first century, for some students, the vertiginous view from the top looking down on the hypnotic stereogram pattern of the floor below had been an incentive to suicide. It started in 2003 with two in a single month. Plexiglas barriers were installed, but when a third student climbed over them to his death, the metal panels went in. I'd seen all three bodies fall past my desk. Shocking for most, but for me it had been oddly thrilling to witness deaths that weren't my responsibility.

Inevitably, my mind wandered back to my captive and I looked for answers to her odd behavior, but research was fruitless. I had no idea what to look for, what I really needed to know. A cursory search on recent ESP research was pointless. I sighed. Whatever she was doing, however she did it, was moot. She would be dead soon, the puzzle ended.

Every now and then, I slipped off to a bathroom stall where no one could glimpse what I was doing, to see on my phone what was happening at home. With hours left on my shift, I decided to check on her again. I stood to go to the men's restroom, put out my BACK SOON sign. A voice spoke up behind me. Only the steely nerves of a lifelong serial killer kept me from being startled.

"Are you okay, Neal? Been hitting the . . . break sign a lot today." Kathy stood behind me, a reference assistant from another department, overly perky with lush blond hair and glasses. I knew she paid too much attention to me but also knew it was prompted by affection, not suspicion. Still, I'd let her little crush go on too long; the flames had recently fanned into an uncomfortably warm blaze. I shrugged and grinned back wanly.

"Got takeout Thai last night, but I fear their rating may not have been accurate. I must check those things before I order delivery." Agreeing with people made them feel perceptive and avoided further questions. Though I lack any real empathy, psychopathic charm and research on how regular people react to stimuli helps me seem plausibly normal. She patted me on the shoulder, sympathetic, and went on her way with a stack of books. I fled to the bathroom before I could be interrupted again.

The restrooms were public, for staff and patrons of the library. Inside, I had to wait, impatiently, for an empty stall. Once one was vacated, I entered and latched the door, flipped open the cover on my phone, and unlocked the screen. I opened my secured basement feed to see the girl standing over the body of her dead boyfriend as she gazed down in silent contemplation, red ball gag still in her mouth.

My jaw dropped open as she lifted a scalpel from its tray, used it to probe the depths of one of my more complex cuts. She stopped and looked up at me, gazed into the lens as I stared back, frozen. The girl replaced the scalpel as smoothly as she had raised it, walked to her table, and lay back down, slipped her feet and legs, head, hands, and arms into her bonds.

Her body parts seemed to elongate to accommodate the tightness of the rope loops so that she slipped into them easily and then reformed her flesh to fit. She maintained eye contact through all of this, even after she was securely tied in place again. The arms and legs I could explain away by stage magic tricks, but her *head* . . . ! The rope had been tied tightly around her neck, less than half the diameter of her skull, and was again.

I almost dropped the phone.

My skin was suddenly covered by a thin sheen of cold sweat as my stomach heaved. The image I saw now was the same as that I'd seen all day, all last night. Had I imagined it? Could I really have just seen her free of her bonds and exploring my handiwork like a curious tourist at a hands-on science museum? Her eyes were as unblinking as always. When I switched cameras, they still followed my electronic gaze.

Enough. It's time to end this. If that stunt was staged to get me home early, it worked. I flushed the toilet and washed my hands after I left the stall to avoid suspicion, then walked out to ask my supervisor if I could leave early, pleading food poisoning. Kathy chimed in enthusiastically when she overheard us, backing up my claim. I know I looked green enough, sick for entirely different reasons, so my level of distress was apparent enough for me to be excused immediately.

*   *   *   *

WHAT THE #@&% IS THAT?

The basement room was exactly the same as I'd left it but now looked new to me. I entered with a high-powered Taser in hand, saw it all as if for the first time, searching for any trace of anything out of place, some trap laid—some sign of danger. The girl was still in place, naked as ever, green eyes wide. I was suddenly afraid for the first time since I was a child, when I woke screaming from bad dreams very much like this. There was some small excitement at feeling fear instead of inducing it for a change. Was this what I had lacked lately, the thrill of the hunt? Had I become so proficient that I'd lost any real enjoyment in my work, going through the motions like a bored civil servant on the job too long to care? If so, what I'd seen on the screen had destroyed all sense of complacency.

The girl's eyes followed me as I crossed to her side and checked the ropes.

"How did you do that, eh? My little Houdini?" I yanked at her freckled arms, still solidly in place. I wheeled my surgical tools into place beside her. No reason to waste time. Do what the Inquisition did with the inexplicable.

Destroy it.

I lifted a slender knife with a short, thin blade. Her eyes didn't leave me as I raised it over her forearm and slid the razor-sharp tip along the surface of the skin, slipped it beneath.

She didn't even flinch.

I ended the long cut, returned to its top with another, shorter blade to slide under the skin and separate it from the muscle. The edge seemed to move too easily, as if there was no real resistance. I was used to severing a few tendons or hitting gristle, but her flesh parted from the meat of the arm like skin on a pudding. There was no blood; just glistening amber tissue underneath that looked like fat, only tougher. I frowned, tried to pull more skin away without success, and then used the knife to worry it free to reveal more. The elastic substance I'd seen was where muscle should be, surrounding what looked like a more traditional skeletal structure, though made of something that wasn't bone. There were dark lines beneath the surface of the tissue, not red or blue, but golden brown, dully pulsing.

"What the fuck is that?" I breathed. *"What the fuck are you?"* Whatever it was shouldn't exist inside someone who had been walking and talking earlier. Whatever this was shouldn't look so convincingly human on the surface, when what was underneath was so completely not. I held the scalpel still in my hand. Why hadn't the thing stopped me? I looked back into her eyes.

She looked significantly down to the ball gag in her mouth. I almost dropped the scalpel as I rushed to take it off, but kept my blade at the ready in case she slipped her bonds again.

"Don't stop, Neal McConnell," the girl—if I could still call her that—said. "You want to see what I am. How I work. Feel free."

"It doesn't hurt?" I examined my incision, peeled back more skin. "I admit that makes it less interesting."

"This body needs to feel, but pain to warn of damage is unnecessary, as this unit repairs itself."

"What *are* you?" I asked.

"A remote biological drone. What your stories of UFO abduction called 'grays' were more primitive models, developed before we gained interest in your world. They looked good enough back then."

Alien drones? That explained what I was cutting up. . . . Any ordinary man would have been paralyzed with shock at this new development, but not me. There were some advantages to my difference from others, my lack of empathy or most other human emotions. I picked up a new tool, sliced a little deeper, and watched the way the thick tissue seemed to flow back together after I removed the blade. *Was it self-healing? If I closed the wound, would it automatically seal itself?*

"Good enough for what?"

"Research and development."

"Of what?" I pulled up my stool and sat, slit open the girl's abdomen and found interesting organs of a number and kind I'd never seen before. It was all quite incredible. She talked on, oblivious to my investigation of her body.

"You. You're the culmination of a decades-long series of experiments to develop a prototype. One that can do what you do for us, without getting caught or cracking up."

The girl retained the casual conversational tone I'd eavesdropped on earlier in the evening when sizing up the couple—sounded like a more seductive Siri, bemused, with a trace of first-date coyness. It was strange to hear her speaking with a full personality while acting as a smartphone for extraterrestrial invaders. I called it an invasion, even if they hadn't. They were here and busy killing us, had been for years.

That seemed to qualify.

"Cracking up?"

"Some of our more 'productive' models can't sustain their sanity in light of their duties. They break down, go out of control, and are arrested or killed. You've resolved your inner conflicts the best. You survived. You thrived. You killed for us and no one knew."

I frowned. "Why?"

There was a pause, and her eyes glazed, as if I was on hold while a side conversation was held. Her gaze snapped back into focus as she spoke again, which confirmed my suspicions.

"We need stimulation, Neal McConnell. You stimulate us."

"Me?"

"Your race. Its pain. Collected in your brain." She rolled her head to look at the other body. "Your species was deemed too primitive to contact for most civilized worlds, but some of us looked deeper—certain impulses your altered brain produces when you inflict suffering can be collected and fed into ours. It's too complex for your limited mind to understand, but the byproduct of human pain and terror that your brain creates for us affects our systems differently. Some of us—enjoy the sensation."

"Like a drug?" I worked with college students in a building on Washington Square Park. I knew how to handle pushers and junkies.

"Much more than that . . ." Her face softened with pleasure.

"You're just addicts and I'm your connection?"

She shrugged.

"So, you make me kill?" I gestured at the body beside us. "Made me for this?"

"We made many to do this. You are simply the best."

"You implanted me in my mother?"

"No . . . only modified your developing fetus during a vacation trip to Florida. Neither parent remembered what happened on the highway, where they went, or what was done to them." She smiled. "Neither did you as you grew up. None of it . . ."

With those words, images poured through my head from childhood— *not nightmares of steel tables and surgery after all, but real memories of alien infant abduction, off-world office visits to my pediatrician for fine-tuning of my little psycho brain, night after night, as they turned me into their killing machine*—I felt the closest I've ever felt as an adult to an emotional reaction, other than pleasure in my work. *No—not my work, their work . . .*, I thought, and felt it again. It was not an emotion I could define, not having had many in my life, but it was not one of the good ones.

"We cannot read your thoughts, only collect what your brain produces when you torture and kill. We felt a loss of enthusiasm that lessened our enjoyment. That's why we needed to do this."

I worried open what passed for a rib cage, careful not to sever any organs that might be used to make it talk.

"Go on. . . ." I mulled over what I was experiencing.

"You are dissatisfied; you want more. So do we."

"What do you suggest?"

Her eyes lit up. "Kill the Earth."

I can't imagine what she saw on my face.

"Hear me out . . . No more one-on-one. Move on to mass extermination. You tell us how and we give you the means. The terror of a planetary extinction will produce in you the worldwide equivalent of what you induce here. You collect it for us; we store our supply. It won't be as much as you could have provided over time—it'll be less refined, less potent. But good enough."

She smiled, sunny bright.

"Does that renew your enthusiasm, to see your entire race die screaming, any way you choose? It's not essential, but it would improve collection. Give us a better buzz, as you might say."

I thought of Kathy, my boss, all the students and staff at NYU, my neighbors, and everyone else I'd ever met, dead, as horribly as I please, with the rest of the human race. For a better buzz . . . *I am a killer, no doubt of that, a serial killer many times over. Am I capable of being history's last and greatest mass murderer? Is that all I am?*

"No. This can't be real. . . ." I faltered. There was that odd feeling again; had I finally slipped over the edge into complete psychosis? Was I hallucinating? I looked down at my hands, wrist-deep inside the drone's abdomen, and knew I wasn't.

"What's in it for me?" I asked suddenly, not sure why.

"A world to kill, Neal McConnell. No limits, no restrictions, no consequences."

"What's the catch?"

"The catch?" The girl looked quizzical, as if she didn't understand something on the menu.

"You're offering a lot. What's the downside?"

"To total domination over the human race?"

"It sounds awfully administrative. You're talking planetary extinction. That means heavy equipment, staff, paperwork, human resources . . ." I shook my head, realized I was stalling for time as I tried to process what I felt. "And what do I do when I'm done? What's my retirement plan after wiping out mankind?"

"Oh, I don't know; keep a few for your . . . wait."

The girl's operators went into consultation again as her eyes went blank. She raised her head again, looked even more puzzled. "What do you suggest?"

I sat back on my stool, selected another blade, one with serrated edges. "Well . . . the real issue here's the buzz, right? You're not getting as good from me as you want. Maybe the problem is your source material."

"Yes?" She looked cutely peeved. "Your point?"

"Well . . . can't you harvest the impulses of your own kind through me? Can you experience this kind of fear or pain?" I toyed with a new tool.

There was a long silence before she answered.

"What's the purpose of the question?"

"I was thinking that if I tortured one of you to death, it would be much more interesting to me than killing more humans. More exciting. The high could be incredible." I twiddled with some long green stringy things that the new tool had uncovered. "For us both . . ."

The girl twitched. I wasn't sure if it was because of something I'd done inside her or because of the idea. Her face looked thoughtful; a slight frown creased her tanned brow.

"That's impossible. Our environment would kill you. There's no protection that makes you a suitable killer. You would be too vulnerable. We are many times stronger than humans—"

"Yet you can put your consciousness into a perfect human simulacrum. You can't put mine into one like you?"

I could see the storm at the other end of the line play out on the girl's face. She was appalled, excited, angry, aroused . . . but greedy for a better buzz. There was the longest wait yet, then a slow response.

"This is not . . . technically impossible."

"Excellent!"

"You could elicit from one of us what you get from one of these?" asked the girl.

"So much more. I'd be better motivated." I didn't explain why. "You'd feel the horror of your own kind, the suffering of greater minds than ours, far more intense than those of mere humans, even as you experience my pleasure in doing it.

"My people make entertainment of the things I do to them, in TV and movies. There are few surprises for my victims, save that it's being done to them. They bore me. You'd be fresh material, unexplored, a blank page

I will fill with blood. You have all been so safe for so long, so superior. . . . Your terror will be exquisite, your suffering sublime. The high would surpass any and all possibilities left for me here."

I stared down into their biological doll's eyes with a salesman's smile and dangled an abstract internal organ I'd just removed from its thorax before the thing's wide eyes.

"I will make meat of you."

Then I paused and waited.

"There could be a way . . ." Her face looked as pleased as it had when the boy let her order lobster at the restaurant. "Your idea has merit. But we can't let you hunt freely on our world as you do on yours—"

"No, of course not, but surely there are those who are . . . undesirable, for whatever reason. Criminals? Deviants? Those who obstruct the greater good . . . I could pick them off for years before anyone notices they're gone."

Pause. "There are always those. In any society."

"Well, then. Just point me to them. If you guys like pot, you're gonna *love peyote*. . . ." I didn't oversell it, but then, you never have to sell a better high to a junkie.

"Transportation will be arranged," she said quickly. "A host body of our species will be grown and we will provide lessons so you can function in it and in our culture." Her eyes glittered brightly as she smiled broadly. "This is a very interesting new venture, Neal McConnell. We will be in contact."

The eyes went blank, its head rolled to the side, the breath and heartbeat stopped as soon as the drone disconnected. I sighed and started the process of cleaning up my playroom. It looked like I wouldn't be seeing it for a while, if ever again.

Space. Who would have thought?

How many murders had it taken for me to find the real reason I did it? I chuckled at the irony as I cut up what was left of the drone and her dead date, dropped the parts into acid, and burned what was left in the crematorium. The answer wasn't what I'd expected, nor was my final fate.

I'd assumed I'd die in jail or an asylum. Instead, after years of whittling it down, I'd just saved the human race—by being raised to be the best guy for the job of killing it, then coming up with a better idea.

Too bad for my employers that they didn't know there was a catch. I had finally recognized the feeling they'd drawn out of me when they answered the one question that had plagued me all my life. . . . *Why was I a monster?*

The feeling was rage.

Rage over my lost life, for all I might have been without their interference, for all that my tortured victims might have been without mine. They'd taken my life, made me a killer, and then wanted me to murder my world for their weekend fix. I could have lashed out, but thanks to the years of rational thinking and discipline that the aliens had instilled in me, I channeled my rage into salvation for the human race, and some small measure of revenge, enough for now. It would grow until I found my makers and fulfilled my promise to make meat of them all.

My parents could finally be proud of me. I wasn't sure if saving humanity redeemed me for all I'd done, or if it was even a good idea. I just knew that I had an adventure ahead unlike any I'd imagined. I looked forward to my new career of murdering those who made me what I am, with renewed enthusiasm. My heart was back in my work.

Neal McConnell. Savior of Earth.

I can't wait to build my new playroom.

HUNTERS IN THE WOOD

TIM PRATT

"So the idea is, we're supposed to shoot each other, right?" Edgar said.

I nodded. "Looks like it. I don't see anybody else we can shoot around here." I shifted in search of a more comfortable position on the mossy rock, but no matter how much I wiggled my butt, the mossy rock refused to turn into a cushioned chaise longue. "They did the same thing, what, eight years ago? When they chose that married couple to be the Hunters."

"At least they dumped those two on a tropical island." Edgar sat on a log across from me, rifle across his knees, bright orange bulletproof vest doing nothing good at all for his complexion. Apart from the vest, he was dressed in street clothes, just like me, though his shoes were shinier and even less suited to tromping through this heavily wooded wilderness than my running shoes were. "They got to float in the pure blue waters before they tried to murder each other."

"Are we, ah . . . I mean . . ."

Edgar shook his head. "I can't shoot you, Gary. Even if I did, I don't think I could live with myself afterward, not for all the cash and prizes in the world. If it comes to it, you should shoot me. I'd rather have you alive than be alive myself without you."

"You say the sweetest things," I said. "And ditto."

"I mean it, Gary. If it's you or me, I pick you—"

I shook my head. "Nope. That's off the table. Just move on. So, instead, what? We just wait it out, and when the Gamekeeper comes tomorrow morning, we let him execute us both together?"

"Go out holding hands, and kid ourselves that we'll become martyrs or revolutionary symbols or something, the power of love conquering self-preservation?"

We both sighed, simultaneously. Our thoughts often ran along similar lines. It was one reason we'd stayed together after what should have been a drunken one-night stand all those years ago. "At least if we die that way, we're just victims of the brutal, oppressive oligarchy, and not traitors to our own hearts," Edgar said.

"Nice one," I said. Edgar wrote listicles for websites for a living—"9 Ways to Blow Her Mind in the Kitchen!" and the like—so he was good at pithy turns of phrase. I was the more blue-collar of the two of us, which meant I occasionally had to leave my desk to do my work: I serviced Internet connections and made sure the oligarchy's snoopware was running properly.

"You want to just have sex until death comes for us?" I asked. I wondered if that green stuff over there was poison ivy. We never even went camping.

Edgar looked up at the hovering camera-orbs, which were also loaded with nonlethal (and, eventually, lethal) countermeasures designed to keep us from leaving the field of play. "You know I have trouble doing it with people watching. Even people watching through floating cameras. Besides, I don't want to give them the satisfaction, you know? I'd rather my last hours alive not be used to get people to sign up for a gay porn site next week."

"Then we might as well walk around for a while," I said. "We've got almost a full day. Who knows, maybe there are a couple of off-the-grid hermits living in these woods."

"We can dare to dream." Edgar rose, cradling his rifle awkwardly. "Where do you think we are, anyway? The northwest zone?"

"Mmm. Maybe. The air's pretty crisp, though. Probably part of old Canada, or maybe—what was it called, Alaska?"

"Probably not a lot of hermits around here, then," he said. "They'd die the first winter."

"Oh, well. It's been ages since we went hiking."

"It's not a bad way to spend the last day of your life." He spat in the direction of one of the floating orbs, and it bobbed out of the way. "At least we can make sure the show is boring."

We set off, neither of us expecting to find an innocent human being to kill, but hoping.

Edgar liked to trade for those old dystopian novels at the swap market. He liked to laugh at how much worse things really were, in some ways, than what those writers had imagined. Me, I always thought they were implausible, all the convoluted explanations they'd come up with to explain why the government would send a bunch of teenagers to murder each other on an island with automatic weapons, or send a bunch of teenagers to murder each other in a high-tech arena with bows and arrows, or send a bunch of teenagers to run from genetically engineered monsters in a maze, or whatever—there was always some kind of reason. Like, the games were pacification measures to keep the oppressed peoples in line, or the result of some ancient pact with dark forces, or a way to fund a cash-strapped prison system with baroque live executions, or whatever.

When the real reason the people in charge make games of life and death is so much simpler: because they *can*, and because it *amuses* them.

So, a few times a year, two Hunters are chosen, snatched out of their beds, given a hasty briefing, and handed weapons—anything from machetes to flamethrowers. They're dropped in the middle of *somewhere*—a major city, or one of the lawless zones, or a hidden rebel camp. (They're never as hidden as the rebels think.) If the Hunters get dropped someplace where there might be real resistance, they probably get full body armor. If they're dropped on a soft target, like a resort for mid-level bureaucrats or a vocational school for the plebs, they get stab-proof vests or something.

The rules are simple: as a Hunter, you can kill *anyone*. And as a Hunter, you *have* to kill at least one person. If you don't kill someone before your time limit runs out, the Gamekeeper—whichever minor media personality the oligarchs appoint to host a particular show—appears and kills you in some baroque way, often sobbing uncontrollably during the process, since minor media personalities aren't usually stone-cold emotionless killers. That way, the audience got to see *something* entertaining, even if the Hunters don't play along.

Except the oligarchs don't actually care about the audience; they just care about amusing themselves. My department monitors all web traffic, and ratings are actually a lot lower than you might expect, at least if you get your ideas about human nature from the sort of books Edgar liked to read. It turns out most people *don't* enjoy watching snuff films—the incidence of psychopaths in the general population just isn't that high. (The incidence of psychopaths among the oligarchs, on the other hand . . .)

So, when Edgar and I were roused in our bed in the middle of the night, we had a brief flare of hope that it was just a murderous home invasion but were swiftly brought around to the reality that we'd been chosen as Hunters. We talked about it in the downtime between briefings, and surgeries, and transport—about whether we'd be able to go through with it, whether it would be okay if we picked people who were really old or something—and came to terms with the reality that we would have to kill to live.

Then we were given bright orange bulletproof vests, rifles, and hunting knives, and dumped in the middle of the woods seemingly days away from anyone, and we thought: *Fuck it*. Maybe doomed token resistance was the best we could do, but it was better than the alternative of turning on each other.

"Wait." Edgar grabbed my arm and crouched down behind a fallen log, pulling me with him. We both awkwardly tried to keep our rifles pointed away from each other and ourselves. I stared into the trees, looking for whatever he'd seen, but all I saw was the occasional flash of a bird—

Then a figure emerged no more than a dozen yards away, leaning with one hand against a tree, head hung low, as if breathing hard. He—if it was a he—looked to be dressed in rags and leaves, and stood with his back to us. I lifted my gun, shakily, and started to lay the barrel across the log to keep it steady.

"Wait," Edgar said. "If you shoot him, that saves you, but I'd still get killed."

I was more eager to fire than I would have expected. "What do you suggest instead?" We had a victim in the hand here, and I didn't want him to slip away.

"Follow him. Maybe he's part of a camp of off-the-grid resistance fighters or something, and we can kill a couple of them and save us both."

Our weird woodsman didn't look like the social type, and I was about to point that out when the figure moved . . . and I saw his tail, four feet long, wrist-thick at the base and tapering to a point at the end, the color of moss, curling and uncurling as he walked away.

"Is—did you—what the fuck *is* that?"

"Guy with a tail," Edgar said thoughtfully. "Wonder if it counts as a person for Hunter purposes?" I noticed the switch from "he" to "it" and approved. It's a lot easier to kill an "it."

"The genetically engineered weirdos in that nightclub three years back counted," I said. "That girl with the eyes on the back of her head, remember?"

Edgar nodded. "Let's try to follow it." He pulled off his bright orange vest, and after a moment, I did too. The thing we were following didn't look like the gun-toting sort—more like pointy stick at best—but it was still hard to give up the protection, though if we were going to have any shot at being stealthy, being a color other than bright orange made sense.

We crept through the woods, and I'm not going to lie: it wasn't easy to track the thing. Not because it was stealthy—in fact, the only reason we kept up at all was because it didn't try to be stealthy at *all*. It took lots of breaks to rest, broke lots of branches, even gabbled to itself in something between human language and the chittering of a squirrel. We tried to trail it from a respectable distance so it wouldn't notice us, and we did a pretty good job. Every so often, it would stop to pick a mushroom, but otherwise it moved in a pretty straight line.

After an hour or so—our phones had been taken, so we wouldn't know exactly how long we had until we were going to die, because the oligarchs thought it was funnier that way—the woods changed. There were . . . decorations. If you've ever seen a backwoods murder cult horror movie, you know the sort of things I mean: mobiles made from bones dangling from tree branches, animal skulls on sticks, half-rotting taxidermy monstrosities, like squirrels with bird wings sewn on the back. Edgar and I looked at each other, wide-eyed, holding our rifles at the ready, and he was probably wishing we'd had more than half an hour of practice on the gun range that morning, just like I was.

The thing we were following lurched forward more slowly, as if reluctant to reach its destination. I was thinking about shooting it, just to break the tension, when my ankle hit the trip wire.

I didn't get jerked up in the air by a rope. A big spiked log didn't fall down on my head. There was no explosion. Instead, I hit the wire, and it pulled loose a big string of bells and tin cans and spoons, making a noise of jangling metal they probably could have heard all the way back in civilization.

A harsh voice shouted, "Intruders! The ritual must continue!" and then the thing we were following whirled around to face us.

We'd never seen it from the front before. Edgar whimpered, and I'm sure I did too.

We'd assumed it was a bioengineered freak, but if so, it was the weirdest one I'd ever seen. Its head was entirely faceless, blank as a gourd, topped by a thatch of filthy hair. Instead, it had a face in its torso—eyes the size of pie plates, black-irised and bloodshot, where the nipples should have been; two ragged holes for a nose below that; and a wide gash full of yellowed triangular teeth all the way across the belly at navel level.

The thing ran toward us, arms outstretched, making more of that horrible gabbling noise. One of the hovering camera orbs swooped in to get a better look, and the thing reached out, and—

I don't know how to explain what its arm did. It reached out, and I want to say it *extended*, but that's wrong. It seemed to . . . zigzag, curving in a way that would have been possible if it had possessed a dozen elbows, only parts of the arm seemed to *vanish* and then reappear. It was like watching the reflection of a reaching arm in the shards of a cracked mirror. (Edgar muttered something about "non-Euclidean motion," and I don't remember much of high school geometry, but I think I know what he meant.) The hand snatched the orb from the air, retracted in a fraction of a second, and then the thing shoved the orb into its mouth and swallowed it. (Was the stomach right behind the mouth? Did it even have a biology that makes sense? I have no idea. Maybe its innards were non-Euclidean too.)

Apparently, the orbs enraged it more than we did, because it reached one impossible arm up into a tree and swung through the branches like some kind of nightmare ape, and its other arm and its tail both lashed after the remaining camera orbs, eating one and smashing the other to the ground, where it sparked and sizzled. The cameras should have been crush-proof, melt-proof, altogether indestructible—every other year or so, a Hunter went nuts and tried to wreck them, without success—but the one on the ground looked pretty well destroyed.

The cameras weren't watching anymore. For a moment, I thought, *We can run*, but then I remembered the trackers they'd embedded over our hearts. We could try to cut them out with our hunting knives, maybe, but I was squeamish about the idea—what do we know about doing surgery? We don't even cut *meat*; we're vegetarians.

While I was pondering escape and tracking devices—in other words, while I was in denial—Edgar was dealing with the present and the actual. He lifted the rifle, took careful aim, and shot the thing in the head. Or the bulb that would have been a head on a human. The blank knob exploded like a watermelon smashed with a hammer, and the thing fell out of the tree, howling from its vast mouth. By then, I had my gun up, and I shot when it got to its feet, managing to take it right in one immense eye. The thing fell back, all its limbs twitching, but at least in a totally Euclidean way, with no weird disappearing movements.

"So, I guess that's your kill," Edgar said.

"I'm not sure that counts as a human. The way it moved . . . unless the Gamekeeper is pumping hallucinogens into the atmosphere . . . there's no body-mod that lets your arms do that. It's dead, at least. Should we be worrying about the ones who screamed 'intruders'?"

"Maybe they're more like humans." He nudged the sparking camera orb on the ground. It looked oddly melted on one side, where the thing's tail had struck it, and I took a step away from the still–mildly twitching body, wondering if its touch did peculiar things to reality. "Assuming we even get credit for kills now that we aren't being watched."

"They'll have us on satellite view or something, won't they?" I said, then looked up at the heavy tree cover.

"Or they might have surveillance devices implanted on us as well as the tracking devices. I did wake up from the surgery with a wicked headache. Maybe our eyes are cameras now."

We flipped off each other, simultaneously, and grinned. "Suck it, people watching at home," I said. "Let's go see if there's anyone else we can shoot."

I wasn't sure what the point of stealth was and, frankly, was a bit surprised that nobody else had attacked us . . . until we reached the clearing. The people there had plenty on their minds. Siccing that thing on us had probably taken all the attention they could spare.

Five people dressed in ragged robes of moss stood equidistant around a hemisphere of some glittering black rock as big as a picnic table. The stone reminded me of volcanic glass, but it had strange blue highlights, which looked almost like fireflies moving under the surface, and I instinctively felt the rock came from *elsewhere*—that it had fallen from space, or someplace even stranger. The people had their arms raised up, and they were *vibrating*, as if every one of them had touched a live electrical wire, and there was this weird hum, low and tooth-rattling, coming from the stone or the figures or both. I moved around to get a better view of the stone—something about it drew the eye—and saw a man sitting on top of the rock, cross-legged, totally naked, staring up at the open circle of blue sky above the clearing.

Suddenly, the humming stopped, and the five standing figures lowered their heads, the vibrations done. "The way is opening," the man on the rock shouted, in the same voice that had called us intruders.

The men in the ragged moss robes—one was a woman, and one appeared to have spiraling goat horns, but most were men—turned toward us, and Edgar started shooting them.

I was afraid he was panicking and wouldn't leave any for me, so I lifted my own rifle and shot the one with antlers and one of the men. The other three, Edgar got. They all fell, dead or dying or groaning . . . except the one with horns, who seemed to dissolve into the ground, horns becoming broken tree branches, flesh becoming mossy slime, robe indistinguishable from the forest floor.

"No!" the man on the rock screamed. "Stop! Heart's blood must touch the stone or the way will not—"

Edgar shot him in the head, which wasn't that impressive from such close range, and the naked man fell off the rock.

"I don't think we get extra credit for killing more than one apiece," I said.

The gun fell from Edgar's hands and he sat on the ground, then put his face in his hands. His shoulders shook as he wept.

I didn't feel like crying. I felt numb. (That lasted for a while. It's wearing off now.)

I looked at the sky, the one patch of blue over the clearing, only it wasn't blue anymore: there was a hole in the sky, about the circumference of a full moon, with a burned look around the edges. Beyond the hole was blackness. "Heart's blood," I said, and didn't know why.

Edgar found the book. A grimoire bound in human skin with a screaming demon face on the spine would have been more appropriate, but this was a battered three-ring binder full of everything from wide-ruled note-book paper scrawled in blue ink to ancient parchment that might have been written in blood. A lot of it was in languages we didn't read—Latin, Greek, weirder stuff—but about half of it was the journal of the leader of this group . . . the naked guy, probably.

They weren't rebels or revolutionaries, at least, not exactly. They were "seers of the unseen," among other things. The leader described rituals and sacrifices, and talked about peeling off the skin of the world, calling up the ancients, overthrowing the hegemony of man. It would have seemed like nonsense . . . but he talked about summoning the "akephaloi," which Edgar was pretty sure meant "headless ones," and about calling forth a "goat of the woods," and those sure sounded like the other-than-human things we'd encountered. If these people could do *that*, call up things like *those*, then who knew where the edge of plausibility was?

"Did the oligarchs send us here on purpose to kill them?" Edgar said. "Like the way they drop Hunters on rebel camps sometimes?"

I shook my head. "I think if the oligarchs knew there were things like this, with power like that, they'd drop rocks on them from orbit. And now that they've seen them, from before the cameras were destroyed, or through our eyes now . . . I bet that's what's going to happen. Any time now. Fire from heaven."

"No cash and prizes," Edgar said dully, flipping a page in the binder.

"No being shunned by our friends because we murdered some people and got PTSD, either," I said. I was thinking, but the thoughts were far away. My inner landscape had become frozen tundra. "That thing in the sky, Edgar . . . That hole. The naked guy said the way was open. What does that mean?"

"The last pages of the journal talk about a ritual," he said. "To summon up . . ." He ran his finger along a page and recited. "'Gods of nature beyond our nature, vast in comparison to mankind, who will tread on us as care-lessly as we tread on grass, cold but not cruel, as indifferent toward the mon-uments of man as a tornado is to the farmhouse it destroys, or the running deer to the spiderweb it disturbs."

"Indifference," I said. "That doesn't sound so bad, compared to the oligarchs. To be stepped on by *accident* is better than to be stepped on because somebody thinks it's funny."

Edgar climbed up on the rock, holding his hunting knife. "We're going to die, aren't we?"

"I mean . . . yeah." I didn't feel much about it one way or another.

"Okay, then. I'm glad I got to be alive with you for a while, Gary."

I saw what he was going to do, and got to my feet, but I was too slow. He plunged the knife into his chest. His eyes went wide, and he gasped, bubbles of frothy blood spraying from his lips. Edgar wrenched the knife out of his chest, and blood spurted across the black-and-blue stone.

The humming came back, louder than before, like trillions of flies descending on a world-sized corpse. I looked up, where the circle of darkness burned and spread and burned and widened. I started to feel something then, like an ice floe breaking up in my chest.

I pulled Gary's body off the rock, and sat down beside him, and started writing this in the journal with the dead man's pen. Maybe someone will be left, to wonder why the world changed. I don't know why, but this is how.

The whole sky is black now, full of blue sparks, and there are structures growing in the darkness.

I'm going to close the journal now and wait for the next thing to happen.

WHOSE DROWNED FACE SLEEPS

AN OWOMOYELA AND RACHEL SWIRSKY

When she comes into the loft, she glares at me with the bright-eyed, serpentine resentment of the dead. In the dry attic, water drips from her hair and pools at her feet. Her lips pull back. I'd forgotten that I used to grimace like that—teeth bared like an animal's.

I'm not her and she isn't me. When I say "I," I might mean either one of us, but that's not precise. I have no past, so I took her memories. I have no name, so I took her name. I had no body, but I have hers now, and she's the one languishing in a puddle, snarling, hungry, and hating.

She went by R. I go by R. R names us both.

I'm still sorting things out.

This is a murder story. It's the story of how I killed myself.

A memory, before I made these memories mine:

I walked into a life-drawing class and there she was, Selene—more comfortable in her naked skin than I was in my jeans and bomber jacket. She sat on a table in the center of the room. Her legs were held tensely together, but her shoulders were relaxed. She sat with her head thrown back so that I could see the foreshortened lines of her face: the way the point of her chin angled up to her cheekbones, the flash and flutter of reddish lashes over hazel eyes.

After class ended, she shrugged into a robe and walked a circuit of the easels as the students packed their things. I tried not to watch as she made her way past one sketch and then another, but even with my focus firmly on my charcoal pencils, I knew the instant she neared. I held my breath until she approached me. Or possibly it happened in reverse; she began to approach and nervousness stole my breath.

My lines were clumsy and architectural, slicing Selene's figure into angular planes. I'd used a gray stripe to replicate the slant of illumination that the skylight cast across her. I wanted to capture something of the building we were in, its mood if not its essence: the old walls, the clouded glass windows, the crown molding that belonged in a more prestigious university.

None of my angles were as sharp as Selene's. Standing there, she looked like a brass detail. Hard-edged and honed.

Without speaking, she put out her thumb and smeared the charcoal under the triangle I'd drawn for her left breast. She worked the smudge down the line of her stomach and hip, blending my lines into effortless chiaroscuro.

One gesture and the meaning of the work changed. Object became artist. "There," she said with a nod.

She gave me a stare edged with challenge. She was prodding me, I thought, seeing if I would just let her get away with the casual violation of my page. Part of me wanted to meet her gaze with equal strength, to assert that even though she was the one who'd initiated contact, I was still equally in control. The bulk of me, however—the part that was nineteen and unsure—barely managed to meet her gaze at all.

"You've caught something real, I think," she said. "I'm Selene."

"R," I said automatically. "I go by R."

"For . . . Rebecca? Roseanne? Radioactive?"

R for "Are you going to stop asking me that?" I would have said to someone else. "Just R." As an afterthought, I stuck out my hand.

She glanced at it; shook her head. "Left-handed."

I switched immediately. She took my left hand and held it hard, leaving a smear of charcoal over my wrist.

Someone told me once that wedding rings go on the left hand because it's the most direct arterial path to the heart. I've read that slitting the wrists kills you because the hands are hungry for blood: all that fine motor control, fed by little capillaries, drinks a mortal quantity. I used to rest my fingers on my pulse point as a child, to experience the thrill of my own fragility. I'd scare myself with the thought that I'd crush my arteries if I pressed too hard.

That childhood obsession left me with a few odd tics. I always needed to be able to see my wrists, to know my blood was safe. I couldn't stick my hands into dark places or opaque containers. I needed clarity.

"You remind me of someone," Selene said. "Coffee?"

"I don't—" I started, then I said, "Sure."

Whether it was because of her confidence, or the aphrodisiac of art, or the ghost sensation of her fingers on my skin, I took a chance on her. I took a chance in the café a block away from campus, sitting beside her on a worn red leather loveseat, inhaling the smoke embedded in the walls. She took her coffee black, and I scanned the menu for a drink I could see through, all the way to the bottom.

She pushed a napkin and pencil in my direction. "I like your style," she lied. "Draw for me."

I call it a memory from before my time, but is it?

Memory, they say, is more like notes scribbled in a journal than a video recorded for playback. One part of the brain jots notes in shorthand and leaves them behind. Later, in the process of recall, another part of the mind reads the notes and constructs a scene to fit them, conjuring or editing details at its convenience.

If I trawl *her* mind (my mind) for notes written long ago, and then turn them over to *my* mind (her mind) to be staged as vignettes, whose memories are they? Do they belong to her, who drew the original charcoal strokes, whose wrist really trembled beneath Selene's touch? Or to me, who, for all I know, could have confabulated that grand old hall to replace a real, unromantic, cramped classroom?

Everyone's brain is a liar. Mine (hers, mine) is more duplicitous than most.

This is a ghost story. Did I say that?

No. It's a love story. But all love stories become ghost stories if you watch them long enough.

Now:

James's footsteps pound on the stair and I look up in time to see him leaning over the railing. "Hey, sweet," he says with a leer. "How about making me some coffee?"

"Sure," I say.

I don't ask how he takes it. James is predictable. That's why he tells me anyway.

"Black as the devil," he says, drawing his eyes up and down my skin. "And hot as hell."

That girl, who called herself R and vanished years ago, wouldn't have liked this any more than I do. She told the world to fuck off with her bomber jacket and shit-kicking boots.

Me, I wrap my chest in compression bandages, buy baggy T-shirts that come in plastic-wrapped three-packs, and wear my loose painter's jeans from the days I did house painting for cash. First things I did in this body were crop my hair short and throw away her long-lasting mascara.

All that, and James still pushes his eyes into me, still has to remind me that under all my clothing is a body he wants to control.

Likes to brag, James. Likes to brag about how many lesbians he's fucked. How they dance a different jig once they've had a ride on his cock carousel. All talk. I've seen him pick a girl I know he's never seen before and spin a tale for his buddies about how he pushed her against the bed and made her beg. Four shots and he'll brag about me even when I'm in the room. *This black maid girl living in the house? Suh-weet, isn't she? Bro, lemme tell you. You don't even know.*

Free rent is free rent, even from a douche.

I go into the kitchen and displace the morning's dishes from the counter to the sink. The coffee pot has yesterday's dregs in it and I don't care enough about James' comfort to rinse them out. I just dump out the old grounds and dump in the new, toss a couple of mugs' worth of water into the tank, and jab the thing on. The maker pisses black. It's as dark as Selene's coffee but bitter. I imagine both of them drinking down the impenetrable murk. Anything could be hiding there, sliding anonymously into their stomachs, invading their organs, their skins.

James is sitting at the coffee table when I return. "Hey, take a look at this," he says, and turns his laptop so I can see the screen.

A woodcut of the devil stares back at me, grin ghastly in oil-slick skin. Naked witches cavort around him. His huge erection casts a shadow the length of a witch's arm.

"Black as the devil," he repeats. His gaze trails me, searching for signs he's made me uncomfortable. He glances down at the devil's enormous cock and then back at me again, hoping to see me flinch.

I put the mug down beside him. "Coffee." I turn back toward the kitchen. He yells something after me and laughs, but I don't bother to make it out.

Take a goddamn joke, why don't you, he probably said.

Or *Do you fuck your girlfriend with a strap-on that size?*

Or *Come sit in my lap and I'll show you my devil.*

The black liquid that remains in the coffee maker roils as if something is swimming through it. A woman's hand, I think, and imagine I can see fingers breaking through the surface, *her* old pulse still hidden in the dark.

Memories of Selene:

Starving artist, thinned to the bone, a beauty of fragile and skeletal proportions. She was an apprentice tattoo artist. While everyone else in the shop wore leather and torn denim, she dressed in scarves and diaphanous skirts, and wore her hair waist-length. Unless you slid your hand along that smooth forearm, nudged the lacy sleeve upward to reveal the iron of her bicep, you'd never know she had the strength to hold a tattoo gun for an hour.

Tattooed on her inner right thigh: a serpent.

On her inner left: a devil.

Between, she was Eve, tempted and temptation.

She could open me up like a gate with fingertips that had been trained to a needle's precision. She drew pleasure in shapes I imagined as the tattoos I'd seen from her sketches: coiled dragons, cherry blossoms, angel's wings.

When she wrapped herself around me, I imagined she was the boa of her ink, all smooth skin and constricting muscle. A woman like that unhinges her jaw and swallows you down.

"I," Selene would whisper, "can take you places you've never been before."

I was too robbed of breath to whisper back, *You wouldn't understand the places I've been.*

Memories. Not entirely mine:

I used to have dreams. Cocooned in blankets like a spider's brood, I dreamed of the entryway, the basement, the overgrown hedges in the yard.

The house where I grew up was palatial. Four stories of niches and hideaways and secret treasures and doors I could never remember. But it was a demon-haunted palace, with windows that admitted the arid night, and dust that had resided there for generations, and the growling of a furnace that could no longer keep the building warm.

In the basement, one whole wall was dominated by the painting of a train tunnel. Garish ambient light sparked across the tracks. The hint of a vast shape lurked in the far, dark distance.

If I wedged my hand behind the frame and felt behind the painting, I could locate a handle that pulled the whole wall aside, revealing a space behind it as large as a warehouse. It was populated by forgotten things: rocking horses and broken dollhouses, old claw-footed bed tables and rolled-up rugs.

Water—stale and clouded with mud—pressed down on the room, threatening to rupture the walls and drown everything. Somewhere, that vast and vague presence from the painting swam through it, always moving nearer.

A dream, I think: impossible, set against the reality of plots of land and blueprints. And how could I have watched my hand disappear beneath the frame as I searched for the switch? I, who couldn't even drink tea?

Still, I have more memories there than of most real places.

A memory that isn't:

Waiting on the outside, listening through the water, pushing nothingness through nothingness, feeling and seeing only the *forward*, only the *toward*.

When the brain senses a void, it struggles to fill it. Where there are no shorthands for memories, it will jot some and then forget their authorship, aver their authenticity.

Do I remember water and waiting?

I may be wrong.

Now, in the kitchen:

James comes down with his heavy tread. "Jesus Christ. Might as well be eating out of a toilet for all the shit lying around."

He picks up a bowl I haven't yet moved from the counter and throws it into the sink so hard that the pile of dishes beneath it jumps. I keep my attention on the even sweep of the broom across the tile.

I like having a broom handle in my grip when James comes through. He likes to scare people. Best to put him in his place.

A girl comes out of the game room in the back. She was there for the party last night, one of the ones who're always there at the parties. The red glaze in her eyes implies she was probably too drunk to drive home. She goes for the purse lying on a barstool. James catches her wrist and presses her against the wall, holding her there with the full weight of his body. He laughs as she tries to push him off. She complains about the smell of his cologne and how she's got to be somewhere, and he just stands there. Even when she giggles and tries to play it off as a joke, he keeps her pinned, until she finally droops.

He presses harder just for a second before he lets up. "There you go, Linds."

She rubs her wrist. "Thanks."

He has never done that to me.

He will never do that to me.

Lindsay starts opening random kitchen cabinets in search of a coffee mug. No matter that she was in a hurry to leave the house while James was holding her, she pauses to wrinkle her nose at the work I'm doing. "She's really your maid?" she asks, flashing a look at James.

"Yes, ma'am," James says with a put-on Southern accent.

"Like, she has to do all her chores or you'll spank her?"

James's grin widens, but he's not drunk enough to answer with a bald lie. His sober self knows just enough to be wary of me and my broom handle.

Both of them are watching me to see if I'll get upset, but I keep on sweeping with perfect measure.

Lindsay says, in a voice as sweet and malicious as a drugged daiquiri, "Think you'll get all that done?"

"I finish my work," I say. And I will.

The deal was light housekeeping, cooking dinners, and handling the administrative business of the house—intercepting calls from the landlord, scheduling service and maintenance—and I could live in the unfurnished attic and use it as my studio for a while. The deal didn't include the seven parties James had thrown this month. Didn't include his insults and humiliation. Didn't include picking up the panties of the girls he'd bullied into having sex with him, and listening to his trash talk the morning after.

James and Lindsay head out. When the sweeping's done, I open the corner cabinet and regard my supply of mason jars filled with vinegar. If James asked, I'd say they were natural cleaners. They are, too—I keep a piece of citrus or a sweet-smelling herb in each one to make the rooms smell good after scrubbing. But their real purpose is to camouflage the outlaw jar I hide behind them, the one crammed with habanero. James would notice the smell if he shoved his nose into the cabinet, but that's one thing I know he'll never do. He might pry into every other aspect of my personal life, but cleaning is beneath him.

I take the moment of freedom from James's gaze to go out into the summer sun, squinting against the glass-sharp shards of light tossed at me by the pool. A careless excess in the local drought, but James is like that. Today there's a shadow occluding the turquoise, and I think of the painting of the distant train, and the water pressing on the secret basement room, and what it was like to float and listen. I shade my eyes with my hand and return inside to get away from shadows that don't belong.

Of Selene:

Late night, in the bathroom, walking in on Selene as she gazed, red-eyed and insomniac, into the mirror. "What is it?" I asked, ready to step in, to save her. That was always my mistake: thinking I could save anyone.

She stared into her own eyes. "I don't know if I can love you anymore," she said. "I love you. But you make me hate myself. And you refuse to admit that anyone could hate me. You're so goddamn noble, I can't fucking breathe."

And:

Bitter night when she shoved through the door to my one-room apartment, one scarf over her head and another wrapped around her shoulders. Cold swirled behind her as she sneered at the gallery I'd made of my walls with my sketches, sketches, sketches of her.

"You make me too fucking pretty. Stop dolling me up. You're good enough to make me look real. Stop emulating this bullshit pop-art Photoshop crap."

She grabbed my hand, which already clutched a charcoal pencil, in the midst of creating another version of her. She forced my fist up, down, sideways, slashing her drawn self until it was black with fury.

And:

Blackout swallowing my apartment, no light but our flickering cell phones. Panting, she came, and then collapsed on top of me, breasts slick with sweat.

Suddenly, like the snake on her thigh, she struck. She jammed her thumb into my neck, *almost* hard enough to make me choke. "We'd both be better off if you were dead. Just look at you. What good are you if you can't even see through me?" She leaned close, the lines of her body catching the barely there light. "What the hell kind of person would lead you on, pretend to love you for so long? You're a piece of shit to fall for a piece of shit like me."

Me, swallowing the pain, even as she still pushed on my windpipe.

"Go to hell," she said when I did nothing. "Go to hell and I'll follow. We'll burn together."

What if hell isn't a pit of fire and fumes? What if it's water instead, cold, motionless, and eternally pressing in?

I believed—she believed:

Selene's an addict. A cutter. She burns herself up like a match and throws herself on the ground. I'm stronger than she is. I'm a good person. I can hold her. I can keep her. If I love her enough, all of this will go away.

I believe:

I was once nothing and now I am someone. Let Selene drive herself into frenzy; let James leer and boast; let memories haunt me; let the world's shit pile up in the kitchen where I can demolish it with my broom. I used to be outside and now I'm in. At the end of the tunnel, there was me.

Now:

Should clean the windows today, but there's a free hour when I know James won't be home. I've got to take the time to paint when I can. I can finish the windows after my break.

As I approach the stairs, I feel a sudden tug. I glance upward toward my attic studio, but the pull isn't coming from there. I take a step toward the descending stairs instead, and there it is, a mental string pulled taut.

I put my foot on the top stair and sudden knowledge swims through me: If I walk the stairs, if I go down into the shadows below, I'll find the painting from my parents' house. It will loom over me, orange light grinning over tracks that stretch toward the shadowed leviathan.

Will it smell like old dust and chipped paint and rusting tin toys? Will there be a handle beneath it that will slide away a wall?

No, because I've cleaned that basement a hundred times, and it isn't there. Train tracks don't go with James's tits-and-ass décor.

I will not go look.

I take the stairs up to my studio two, three steps at a time. I push open the red-painted door and it slams shut behind me.

James lets me have the attic loft because it's got no carpet and no insulation, because the window doesn't open, and because the duct from the air conditioner forgets all about it. It's too hot and too humid and my paints turn out tacky and are slow to dry, but it's my space, mine.

My canvases cover the walls, some hanging unframed, others propped against whatever surfaces I could find. Seen all together, they are a blur of blue and brown, loneliness and perdition.

I'm a better artist than she was. *She* was always pulling herself in multiple directions: toward the naïve sentimentality that she couldn't shed, and toward the intellectual abstraction she couldn't emulate.

I paint what I paint. The swirls, the jaws, the geometries, the realistic figures that shade themselves in when I'm not paying attention, the bloody eyes, the listing trees. I close my eyes and paint nothing I remember.

Today, the paintings stand in half a foot of impossible water. It surges around my feet, but my shoes stay dry even as I kick a sodden clod and watch it break apart and churn away. The air tastes like murk: restless, muddy incipience.

Something is coming.

I try to remember what caused it before, what let me through. I've thought on this a hundred times, trying to think of another answer, but there's only one: it was coalescing death.

I remember the habanero in the kitchen. I note which canvases have frames that I can break down most easily into weapons. I mentally inventory every mirror in the house that could yield dagger shards, every knife in its drawer, every hammer and bat and nail gun.

I will not be the one to die.

Memory:

Standing in the bathroom and staring at the bruise Selene's thumb left on my throat.

She's gone this time, really gone. Car missing, phone service dropped, handwriting scrawled across the painting of her that I hung above my bed: GOOD-BYE R, SHOULD HAVE KILLED YOU, I'M SORRY.

I looked into my reflection, bruised and grieving, and I saw

this red-eyed girl
unfamiliar
miserable
half-shattered
pathetic

stranger girl's hands pouring a bath. testing the water to see if it's warm enough. digging through old drawers until she finds a straight razor. laying the metal on the edge of the tub where it glints under the bathroom's fluorescents. she gets in without taking off her clothes. she submerges her wrists. the water quickens to match her pulse as

I look down and I can see all the way to the bottom of the tub. This is good water. This is clear water. I pick up the razor from where it lies beside me. I drag it across my wrist—vertically, I've done my homework—but my hand is shaking and I know it's too shallow before I've even finished the stroke. Pink spills out and I watch it cloud into the bath, making it red and impenetrable and bad.

The sight of myself disappearing shocks me into doubt and I stare at the razor before moving again and

there, like a switch, behind her eyes. now I see my hand (stranger girl's hand) aloft with the blade in it. now I feel the warm water squishing into my jeans (stranger girl's jeans). now I

Two minds suckling at the same senses, two thinkers poring over the same memories and preoccupations and pain.

Diluted blood washes against our submerged body. Someone says, *Help me.*

The other, *I'll take over now.*

What if people—

They'll never know.

Can I? the one asks, hesitant, wary. *Are you sure?*

And the other: *Go.*

Now, in the kitchen:

It's the only middle ground between the impossible painting in the basement and the impossible flood in the attic. I'm drinking ginger ale. I'm pacing. James is not supposed to be home yet.

He is, though, slamming in like a tidal wave, stinking of liquor. When he catches me in the kitchen, his face goes red to purple. "What the hell are you doing? You think this is what I pay you for? Why the fuck is the house still a garbage pit?"

"I needed a break," I say.

I am doing the wrong things. I should put down the bottle and get out of his way. I should go clean something, even if it's already clean, keep him at bay with diligence. I shouldn't stand here calmly by the sink, sipping my drink as if I'm his equal, entitled to my own time and space.

He gives me that lustful, disdainful up-and-down. This time, there are an extra thousand needles in it. His color goes pinker as he smiles, eyes still hard as pebbles.

"I ran into this chick named Selene today," he says.

I answer flatly. "Okay." As if the name doesn't mean anything to me. As if my gut isn't turning to ice.

"Lesbian. Smoking hot. She was wearing this see-through top and you could see this tattoo on her tit of a—"

"And?"

I'm not the one who loved Selene, but the memories are mine. My grip tightens on the bottle. James grins at my tense hands. I've shown that he got to me. Now he'll try to escalate.

"She used to fuck this other chick, called herself R. A black coffee babe. Perfect miniature titties. Good fuck, she said. *Crazy* fuck."

I put the bottle on the counter. It's time to go. I should be in motion; I should be prowling the tracks.

James blocks my way into the hall. "Is R a common name, you think?"

I growl at him. "I need to go up to the attic."

"I told her she should see you now. How hot you are when I've got you bent over, scrubbing the floor. How I bought you this little French maid costume that goes up to your ass—"

I put my hands on his shoulders and shove. "Get out of my way."

"You act like you're too good to fuck anyone. But you sure fucked her." The anger is back on the surface now, his smile a grimace, his teeth too wide and too white. "You think you're too good to be a maid? Let me tell you something. No one else is going to hire a black dyke like you. If you're going to let my house go to shit, you need to come up with another way to pay me."

For months, I've been telling myself, free rent is free rent. He's a douche. He's all bluff. Stupid, stupid.

He grabs for my wrist and I duck under his arm. I jump backward into the kitchen and go for the corner cupboard. He could catch me faster than I could run away, but he thinks he has me trapped.

Stupid.

Mason jars of vinegar clatter as I grab for the one in back. Its lid is loose and ready.

Pepper spray, you can't use indoors. Tasers, he'd grab me before I could stick him. But this is good capsaicin. James screams like a skinned rabbit when it hits his eyes, the whole hot quart of time-pickled habaneros.

He claws at his face, spreading the capsaicin, only making it worse.

I grab another jar. It's not more peppers, but he doesn't know that. "Lie down on the floor," I say. "I'm going to the attic and I'm going to pack and I'm going to go." *Go.* "You're going to leave me alone. Got it?"

James makes a strangled noise of rage and pain. I make a show of loosening the lid on the new jar.

"On the floor," I say again. "Now."

One of us may think he has the guts to kill, but the other actually has. Even though James doesn't know that, some spark of survival instinct must guess. He lowers himself onto the tile.

It wasn't a bathtub. It was a lake. She walked out in the late fall frost, just before the first snow of the year. It was nighttime, which made the waters black, but they were filthy anyway, choked with seaweed and pollution. She wore her shit-kicking boots with their steel toes to help her sink and took one sloshing step into the water and then another until she was buried to the ankle, knee, thigh.

Help me.

It was a bathtub, but the water was cold, ice-cold, and she kept a hairdryer beside it, because she thought it would be artistically beautiful to die as a spark, to make herself into fire and ash. Her hand slid out and her fingers were about to touch the cord.

I'll take over now.

It was the waters beyond the world, which God once divided into the heaven and the Earth, and we were both swimming, and one of us was a ghost and the other one was in love, and our dirty, muddy thoughts hid us in sinister eddies.

Can I? Are you sure?

It was nothing. It was nowhere. These are all lies from my duplicitous brain. The past is a fracture, the future a mist. Only the waters of the present are certain, but even they are so opaque.

Go.

I ended what needed ending. Like a surgeon. That's not the same thing as murder.

I tell myself an awful lot of lies.

The attic. Now:

My things disappear into the duffel I came here with, one after another, and I try to ignore the sucking sounds of the mud-water around my dry feet. The paintings won't fit. I'll leave them. He always said they were crap. If he doesn't give them back, he'll throw them out. I'm not too proud to steal from the garbage. I've stolen worse.

Wood creaks, and a wall bows in, and I stumble back just as the flood bursts through. And there she is, the dark shape resolving into my younger self. She's bloated and discolored as though drowned. Her clothing hangs in wet folds and she reeks of stagnant water, of algae and fish and forgotten things.

Her eyes cast about the room, but it's perfunctory. When she looks back, she only has eyes for me.

"He's going to come after you," she says. "As soon as he talks himself into believing that he's the big, strong man and you're the itty-bitty girl."

"So let me pack," I say, but I stand there, staring at her, not returning to my duffel.

Her eyes want to butcher me and wear my skin, want to steal the air from my lungs and put it back into hers. "You thought you could do better than me?"

I shrug. It wasn't a matter of better or worse. I thought there was life for the taking.

"Did anyone miss me? Did anyone even fucking know?"

"Who?"

She blinks, as if she'd forgotten her isolation, her total reliance on the sun that was Selene. "My parents—"

"I didn't go back."

"That's it? You just let everything die?"

No, I don't say, *You let yourself die.*

"And what the hell have you done with my life? Who am I now? Who is this jackass you're living with?"

"Craigslist," I say. "Free rent."

She scoffs, a wet, choking noise. "You could have finished college. You could have done things. You could have—" She stops, surveying the room again, taking in the paintings this time with her expressions darkening. "What shit is this?"

"You made art," I say. "So do I."

This reference to continuity doesn't seem to appease her. It's clear that she disagrees with my assessment of our relative talents. What did she think? That I would keep tracing her charcoal portraits, frame all her vignettes, draw Selene and Selene and Selene until arthritis got too bad for me to hold a pencil?

She approaches. I hold my ground. Up close, cool air rolls off of her like fog. A long, low, hidden sound echoes up from her throat, as if traveling from another dimension. Vibrations shudder through my bones.

She exhales breath like rotting fish. "You *did* think you could do better. How much better, huh?"

"I'm still alive."

The muscles in her neck bunch. I expect to see her jaw open to reveal row on row of jutting, dagger teeth. "Maybe not for long."

I have years and strength training on my side. I know everything in the room that can be turned into a weapon. "Try it and you'll regret it."

Like you never did? is the question in the air.

There's a crash below us, and then swearing. The echo of James's footsteps is louder than it has any right to be.

"Here comes James," the dead me says conversationally. "Better run."

These are seconds I don't have, but I waste them, warning her. "If you kill me now, you won't know how to fit back in. You'll never get your old life back. You'll be a shambling corpse trying to fit into a life that left you behind."

She grins and the muddy water around her rises, churning. There are more sounds below us, of creaking, straining, foulness rushing in. What will happen to me if she attacks? The younger, dead me probably doesn't care. No more than I cared what would become of her.

Muddy water surges through the attic floor. I grab the half-packed duffel. I'm out of time. I run ahead of the lashing wave, my steps smacking against the stairs as I flee downward.

Suddenly, I'm thrown backward, toward the water pouring from the attic. I stretch out my arms, pushing against the wall to slow my fall. When I blink away the fear, I expect to see R in front of me, corralling me back into her domain, but it's James instead, his eyes blood-streaked from rubbing.

"You little bitch," he says. "You think you can just *do* this to *my* house?"

I don't know what he means, but more importantly, I'm not sure what to do. I can't back up into the water, and James is a wall of rage between me and the bottom of the stairs. He may be stupid, but he's stronger than me, and I only have one weapon I can think of.

I draw back the duffel to swing at him. Then I see that James's gaze is no longer on me. He's staring behind me, his jaw slack, his red eyes round.

With fear so icy that it cracks his voice, he whispers, "What the fuck is that!"

I turn and see what he sees: the dead me, rising, grinning like the damned.

"It's—she's—" I hear his hands scrabbling against the wall as he braces himself. "It's the devil!"

How must she look to his burning eyes? Dark as the woodcut he showed me earlier, the waves cavorting around her like witches. Black as the devil and cold as hell.

R rears up in a mockery of Aphrodite from the shell. She launches toward us. She and her water pass through me, and I expect the cold, I expect the twinning of our minds, but instead there's nothing but the sensation of rushing and then she's on the other side, roaring down the stairway as if it were a tunnel studded with tracks.

"Jesus *fuck*—" are the last words I hear from James, then a wave reaches upward from below. It smashes him against the stairs, and he cries out in pain. His second shout is drowned as the undertow pulls him down.

Behind me, I can hear the water roaring in the attic. Beneath me, James's swagger sinks below turbulent waves. I'm trapped between oceans above and below, alone on the tiny island of these steps, and I don't know how high the tide will rise.

What made way for me? Turn the question over and over and there's still only the one answer. Someone is going to die.

After I killed myself, I dried my skin and I went to sit by the window in the kitchen of my apartment. It was a small, bleak place, all I could afford.

But outside the window grew a persimmon tree, its leaves limned in sunlight. I stared at the patterns of the leaf-shadows on its bark; I stared at the heavy fruits among the green. I stared at the way a leaf had fallen against the window and stuck there by the fragile adhesive of dew. Its veins were defined like brass details.

I put my hand on the glass and watched my own veins, flowing toward my knuckles, toward my fingertips, all those hungry capillaries.

Glutted on detail, I walked out under the light-polluted skies. I breathed the city air. I strode across asphalt and carpets and grass. I wasn't her, but I was.

* * * *

WHAT THE #@&% IS THAT?

Frozen in place:

I remain while the noises surge below, the crash of waters, and wordless screams whose echoes grow weaker. The dead girl's long, distorted calls hang lonely in the air, twisted by the measureless fathoms she swam through to reach this world.

The tide lowers as the noise quiets. It recedes to the bottom of the stairs, then farther. I secure my grip on the duffel and make my way down.

The ocean has vanished, but the floor is a foot deep in sewage. Real sewage this time. Sewage that sticks to my shoes, that stings with its foul stench. The dead me stands in the worst of it, shit streaking the calves of her jeans.

"You burst a pipe," I accuse her. There's more than a pipe's worth of sewage, but what does that matter to a dead girl?

She smiles a smile I know. A confession.

"He thought I did it," I say. "He was coming after me because of this."

She shrugs. "Did he really need a reason?"

James lies on his back in the water, his face as red as a blister, eyes and nose both leaking. Drying vomit crusts the side of his face.

With shock, I see that he's still alive. I don't know how he survived, but *how* is a strange question at the moment. A breath rattles his lungs. He paddles his arms uselessly, trying to push himself up.

"You could take him," I say.

R raises her lip at me in a snarl. There's nothing in her gaze but disdain for the suggestion.

When R gave her life for Selene, baring her wrists, drinking electricity, stumbling into the lake, she made herself a fragile creature, easy to treasure and easy to break. Now it won't happen the same way. Watching the echo of my past gather herself to spring, her wrists invisible beneath the filthy water, her shoulders hunched like the wings of a buzzard, I think maybe we've both learned something.

The water doesn't take James. Not entirely. He rises back to the surface when she stops holding him down, his body discolored and starting to bloat. The stench of him surpasses even that of the sewage.

There's something missing in me: the space where I should feel joy or satisfaction or outrage or dread is polished smooth and empty. I am like the day I came into the world. All I can see is detail, the intricate spray of droplets as dead-me raises her hand away from his skin, how well-defined the thrashing ripples are around her ankles as she backs out of the water and onto the stairs.

"Did I look like that?" she asks.

"No," I say. "You wanted to go."

She stares at him. "It's so gruesome."

I say, "If it helps, I thought you were beautiful."

She gives me a cold look. She hasn't gotten older, but she's not the nineteen-year-old she used to be. She won't be drawn in by the romance of leaving a beautiful corpse.

"Why did you come?" she asks. "Who the hell were you?"

"I don't remember. Why did you come back?"

She looks up, at the walls, at the ceiling, at all the places where we can both feel the water-not-water pressing in. Goosebumps prickle along her skin, and she slides crossed arms over her chest, trying for warmth.

She won't meet my gaze. "I don't remember either."

And we both know, without saying, that it's the not knowing that's terrible. The water, the cold, they're no more inherently frightening than what's left for us in this world. The serpentine girlfriends who wrap themselves around our throats. The landlords whose bravery comes in whiskey shots. The coldness of being a girl who was once alive and is now dead, or of being a dead girl who's come back to life.

Curious, I reach for her hand. I can do this, can't I? Touch my own skin? Look to myself for comfort?

She startles, and her eyes are angry, but she doesn't break my grip.

Her hand:

Soft in mine, and waterlogged, like a piece of driftwood that's been floating alone too long. I pull her palm toward me in the dim light. I can see her pulse point, the life that was extinguished in her, changed but still there.

"Back?" she asks.

I didn't say it first, but did I have to? What is it but a thought alighting in my mind (her mind, my mind)?

"Maybe," I say, tightening my fingers around her wrist.

We pull each other up with our mutual strength. Before us, the basement stairs stretch downward, drowned in sewage. Simultaneously, we set our feet on the top stair. In the waters that wait, we will swim as leviathans, vast and inexorable, and come to know what death and life and death has made us.

Those few moments, when we were in the body together, when my face was my face and a stranger's face, when my mind was my mind and a stranger's mind—what did they mean? Grief pulled me down. Desire pushed me up.

This is a ghost story. I said that. But we are both ghosts now.

And it's a love story. I said that, too.

I'm still sorting it out.

CASTLEWEEP

ALAN DEAN FOSTER

"The walls weep, but only on nights when the moon is full."

Uh-huh, Cort mused as he cast an amused glance across the folding camp table at Shelly. And the gorillas dance in the clearing while the frabulous chimpanzee thumps out a beat on a hollow log and the black colobus monkeys chorus in counterpoint from their perches high in the odum trees. Shelly's tight grin showed that she was having an equally hard time repressing a laugh. Sharing a knowing smirk with her, he decided, would have to do.

They were up in the northeastern part of the country, where Gabon fades toward the Congo and tempts the inhabitants of that unhappy country to risk an illegal dash across the border for a chance at a life in their more prosperous, less populated neighbor. Cleft by the equator, little in the way of civilization penetrated this obscure, densely forested corner of one of the planet's least-visited countries. Baka pygmies still silently stalked downsized duiker in the depths of soundless jungle while keeping a wary eye out for dyspeptic forest elephants and the occasional fidgety lime-green mamba. If not for the unauthorized loggers and illegal bushmeat hunters, probably no one would come here at all, Cort reflected.

A soft rush of disturbed air as if a small plane was passing low overhead caused him to set his coffee down while casting a casual glance skyward. It was only another spectacular hornbill. He was sick of hornbills and their interminable raucous cries. It was just after noon and not much was stirring in the forest. Soon, it would be too hot even for the mangabeys to move.

You knew you were in the real tropics, he reflected, when you sat perfectly still, did not move a muscle, and sweat still ran off you in rivulets. Every day, his chest became a delta.

Peering across the battered table, he found himself admiring Shelly anew. He had known many attractive women, but she was the first he had ever met who had shown a willingness to accompany him on a trip like this instead of insisting they must go somewhere like Rome or the Riviera. Her predecessors' notions of exploring the tropics rarely extended beyond attending a garden party in Miami. Limiting their horizons thusly caused them to miss out on much that was of interest.

Him, for one thing.

Where his personal appeal was concerned, Cort labored under no false illusions. The substantial trust fund he had inherited only enhanced his attractiveness to the opposite sex. He felt no shame at this unearned wealth. *We are none of us responsible for the conditions imposed upon us by fortuitous origins,* he had often cheerfully reminded himself. Usually while withdrawing money.

Now, as they neared the end of this particular journey, having gone about as far north in Gabon as one could go without running out of road entirely, their driver apparently felt it necessary to conclude their last day with a fairy story.

"Let me guess." Cort winked at Shelly, who had to lower her gaze to hide her smile. "You're referring to a *secret* place, and nobody knows about it but you."

Yacouba looked offended. "Not so, Mr. Cort. Many people know about the place. They just don't go there."

Shelly could restrain herself no longer. "Oh, let me guess." She bugged her eyes and shook her hands. "It's—*haunted.*"

Their guide pursed his lips. He was a small, slightly built man from a coastal tribe but no pygmy. In addition to being a student of local history, he was also an excellent driver, a self-taught 4x4 mechanic, a decent cook, and fluent in English and French as well as an unspecified number of local languages. He was an educated man, having attended college, though family needs had prevented him from graduating. He had revealed to Cort his true dream was to be a historian, but when one had an extended family to support, one took what work was available. Given the man's background, Cort would not have expected him to lend credence to local superstitions.

"You joke at my expense." Yacouba was clearly hurt. "If you don't believe me, ask the Fang."

Cort started to laugh aloud but caught himself. "*The* Fang? Don't you mean *a* fang?"

The driver eyed him patiently. "The Fang are a large and powerful tribe in Gabon. They know the territory of which I speak better than anyone. They know full well what lies hidden among these mountains. But even they will not go to the place I tell you about now."

Cort nodded, sighed tolerantly, and took a swig from the mug sitting on the table in front of him. He'd had just about enough of camp brew and would be glad to get back to Boston and some decent coffee. Such unavoidable impositions aside, he had to admit that he had enjoyed the trip. Even if the principal motivation in embarking upon it had been to provide him with the means to yet again one-up his many sometimes insufferable globe-trotting friends. To the best of his knowledge, none of them had ever been to this part of the world. Naturally, he could not resist the opportunity to beat them to it. Once home, he would regale them with tales of his adventures while delighting in their inevitable expressions of envy.

"I suppose you're referring to some ancient, mysterious relic of a bygone race and age?" he ventured.

"No." Yacouba spoke not as a guide but with the assurance of a scholar. "The place I speak about is only a few hundred years old. It was built by Europeans."

Cort perked up slightly. It was not the response he had been expecting. "Europeans? What Europeans?"

Clearly pleased to share more knowledge of his homeland, the guide continued. "No one knows for certain who came to the place first. Given the age of the walls, most probably the Dutch. But it might have been the French, or the English, or quite possibly the Portuguese. At one time or another, all of them could have had a hand in it."

Cort looked again at Shelly. While informative, their driver was still being evasive. "So, at this place on the night of a full moon, there are walls that weep. What kind of walls, Yacouba?"

"Stone walls. The walls of a castle."

Now, that *was* interesting, Cort decided. Could the ruins of some forgotten British or Dutch outpost lie this far inland, beyond mountains and across forest, overgrown and concealed by centuries of festering jungle? During the great age of exploration and colonization, the Europeans had built and maintained posts all along the west coast of Africa, but until the nineteenth century, few of them had ventured very far into the interior. Still, big local rivers like the Ivindo and the Ogooué offered a route inland, just as the great Congo itself did farther to the south. What lure might have drawn early European explorers away from the coast and into the hellish, fever-infested hinterland?

There was gold in Gabon, and diamonds all over Africa. Had some undocumented explorers found and then lost a diamond mine? As for the "weeping" walls, a full moon might produce just enough of a tidal surge in a pool or river to send its water trickling over the old stone wall of a cistern or two, giving it the appearance of weeping. Or so Cort chose to surmise. He would have been the first to admit that he was no scientist. But it was the best explanation he could think of on the spur of the moment. Assuming an explanation was even called for. Yacouba might simply be yanking his chain.

He gave a mental shrug. Why not check it out? It wasn't as if he had to be back at a job or anything.

"It'll be a full moon in a few days. If you're not just spinning us a tall tale, Yacouba, I think Shelly and I would be interested in having a look at your weeping walls."

Their driver immediately looked away. "No. You are right. It is just a story, m'sieur. A forest fable to amuse children."

Cort grew annoyed. First, because he didn't like the guide's tone, and second, because people did not say "no" to William Edward Cort. But he did not get angry.

"Come on, Yacouba. You tell us this story, you get me to where I'm half believing you, and then when I seek actual confirmation, you decline to provide it."

As the diminutive guide turned to face him, Cort was startled to see that the man's expression was not one of defiance or uncertainty but unmistakable fear.

"I know of this place, Mr. Cort. I mentioned it to you only in passing—not thinking you would ever contemplate actually going there. I know where it is supposed to lie, but I myself have never been there. I will *never* be there." His sudden resolve was startling.

Bored by the discussion, Shelly delicately sipped down the last of her coffee, pondered the cookies set out on a paper plate in the middle of the table, and leaned back in her folding canvas chair. "Go or don't go—I don't care, Cor. One more week of this and then we head home. That was the arrangement. I've put up with these conditions pretty well, I think." Her eyes narrowed. "You owe me a month in London. With shopping."

"I know, I know," he agreed irritably without looking at her. "Can we get to this place in three days, Yacouba?"

The driver looked away again. "One day driving, then two days' walk. Same back out again. Not easy, but it could be done." There was no hesitation in his voice. "But it does not matter. I will not take you there. I am sorry now that I mentioned it."

Cort sighed and leaned toward the guide. He knew exactly what to do, because he had done it dozens of times before and it always worked.

Always. "I paid you half your fee in Libreville." His smile was not unlike that flashed by the crocodiles that inhabited the nearby river. "I'd hate to have to reconsider payment of the rest following our return due to, um, unsatisfactory fulfillment of designated duties."

As expected, the threat shook Yacouba. Not only did he need the money for his family, but Cort knew how the game was played. If a Westerner complained to the Tourism Department in Libreville, Yacouba could lose his official guide's license. In a country like Gabon, it could mark him for life.

Despite all that, Yacouba hesitated for a long time. At last, he cursed under his breath. "I will take you close enough to see. But I *won't* go to the weeping walls myself."

Cort put his hands behind his head, leaned back in his seat, and nodded complacently. "Fine. You stay with the tent and the rest of the gear. That's all we want, is to have a look." He eyed his companion. "Isn't it, Shelly?"

She did not turn back to him. A bird was singing in the trees and she was trying to locate it. "If you say so, Cor," she said absently.

"Then it's settled." Even if they didn't find a lost diamond mine, he told himself as he pushed back from the table, there might be relics of historical value. His bank account would ensure smuggling such artifacts out of the country would pose no obstacle. He might get his picture in the paper back home. The anticipation was delicious as he envisioned the boys at the Club pondering *that* and fuming.

Pain made him wince suddenly. Looking down, he slapped hard at whatever had bitten his exposed calf. Something small, multi-legged, and dull blue in color scampered madly off his leg as it made for the cover of the low scrub beneath the nearby land cruiser. His momentary visitor was not close kin to what one might expect to encounter on, say, the grass of Boston Common.

Central Africa, Cort reflected, would be a far more tolerable place without the bugs.

* * * *

It was a stupid idea. The notion that it had been a stupid idea struck Cort forcefully about an hour after they had left the land cruiser parked at the terminus of a winding, bumpy, near-impassable track that could not by any stretch of the imagination actually be called a road. What kept him going now that they were on foot was not an overwhelming desire to see their guide's conjectured weeping walls, but Cort's sure knowledge that he would look like a prize idiot for having insisted on coming this far only to turn back at the first indication of difficulty.

To her credit, Shelly was complaining no more than usual. At least they were both somewhat acclimated from the couple of weeks they had already spent in the country. But tramping through the jungle, real jungle, was very different from lounging about at places like the Lopé Hôtel, with its fine restaurant and swimming pool and air-conditioned suites.

Dreaming of air conditioning did nothing to improve his mood. Further-more, Yacouba was not only leading them through raw jungle but uphill as well. Cort's tone was cutting as he addressed the guide.

"Wouldn't an outpost, much less a castle, have some kind of road or at least an old trail leading to it?"

Yacouba looked back at him. Though he was carrying the tent and most of their supplies, their guide was hardly sweating. "It has been a long time since anyone has come this way except local people, Mr. Cort. Local people do not need roads, and the forest long ago swallowed any trail."

"You're sure you know where you're going?"

"I am sure. The place of the weeping walls is as well known to the people here as it is little visited. It has been well known for hundreds of years." A bit stiffly, he added, "It is referenced in several books."

We had damn well better find something substantial, Cort growled silently to himself. If not diamondiferous earth, then a couple of hundred-year-old bottles of rum. Otherwise, a certain wise-ass guide was going to find himself handed a pocketful of coins instead of a fistful of Euros when they finally returned to Libreville.

Buttressing tree roots seemed to reach out, deliberately trying to trip them up. Once, they had to freeze and wait for a browsing forest elephant to move out of the way. Later the same day, they had to sprint across swarms of driver ants too extensive to go around. The presence of the ant swarms was further proof they were walking through primary, unlogged, untouched forest. The trick was to imitate a ballet dancer, employ the longest strides possible, and leave only the tiniest footprint while dashing across the restless, ever-moving surface. Despite their best efforts, every time he and Shelly found themselves successfully on the far side of a swarm, a few of the ferocious ants always managed to grab hold of a boot and scurry upward to bite and sting. A couple of frantic slaps was usually enough to finish off the isolated assailants.

"What happens if you just ignore the ones that get on you? They're so small. Do they just sting you and then drop off?" Shelly asked as they plodded onward. Even while grumbling and soaked in perspiration, she still managed to look good, Cort thought admiringly.

Yacouba peered back at her. "You notice how the ants that get on you always climb upward? They are looking for your eyes."

"Oh." She quickly terminated the line of questioning.

As if by way of compensation for the heat of the day, the first night away from the land cruiser and its conveniences proved surprisingly cool, though just as humid as the daytime. Lying on the ground, looking up through the tent's netting, Cort found himself contemplating an endless, tree-framed black sky speckled with thousands of stars that barely winked. After several minutes of this, he turned to reach for the undulating shape lying on the foam pad beside him.

An annoyed Shelly swatted his groping hand away. "Are you out of your mind? Until I've had at least two showers and a full bath, you keep your hands to yourself."

He persisted. "The sweat doesn't bother me."

"Then you're more of an animal than any we've seen." Disgusted, she turned over on her side and away from him. The fact that her back was now facing him was in no wise discouraging, but her words were. He decided this was not the place to push that particular envelope. With a grunt, he rolled over onto his back. Small, fast-moving shapes were scuttling across the ground all around them but outside the walls of the tent. Somewhere nearby, an exhausted Yacouba snuffled quietly in his sleep.

The sultry, oppressive reality of his immediate surroundings, Cort reflected as he lay still, was not nearly as exciting as had been the contemplation of them back home in Boston. Ah, well. Another day would see them reach their mysterious destination. They would have a look around and then they could start back. At least the stinking hike back to where they had left the land cruiser would be mostly downhill. And as luck would have it, it still had not rained on them.

Not only would sightseeing in a tropical downpour be uncomfortable, in the midst of a thunderstorm it would be difficult indeed to evaluate the legend of weeping walls, he mused as he drifted off to sleep.

"This is as far as I go, m'seiur."

Cort glared at the guide; if Yacouba chose to run off, he and Shelly would have a difficult, dangerous time trying to find their way back. Even if they succeeded, if their guide beat them back to the car and decided to take off with it . . .

"No. You're coming with us, Yacouba."

The man's eyes widened. "Mr. Cort, m'seiur, I said I would bring you to the place, and I have done that. But I also said I would not go up to it." He nodded skyward, through the trees. "Soon, the sun will be down. I have to start making camp."

Cort nodded curtly forward. "Then set it up next to one of your 'weeping' walls. Wouldn't that be a good place to camp? There might even be some overhead shelter."

Unsettlingly, Yacouba took a step backward. Cort did not pursue—not yet. He had been quite an athlete in college and he was not worried about the guide outrunning him, not even in the jungle. Especially not with all the gear that was still strapped to the man's back. Especially not if he had any hope of receiving the second half of his payment.

Nor did Cort raise his voice. He preferred to persuade with words rather than violence. It usually worked. It had worked with the girls in college, it had worked at the Club, it would work here. He'd always risen to a challenge.

"Come on now, Yacouba. Be reasonable. Remember the remainder of your fee. I think Shelly and I have gotten to know you a little bit over the past couple of weeks. Surely you aren't afraid of some old ruins? This weeping phenomenon—if it's real, I bet I can explain what causes it. Maybe there's a small spring near one wall. Or a pool of frogs who are more active during a full moon. There are plenty of possible explanations."

Yacouba was not swayed. "No m'sieur, please, Mr. Cort, sir."

Cort's expression hardened. "You don't come with us, you don't get paid. You get nothing more."

Yacouba looked angry enough to fight, but Cort knew he was trapped. The government would never take Yacouba's side in a dispute with a wealthy tourist. And if Cort ended up hurt, none of the promised money would be forthcoming, anyway. Shelly stood nearby, examining a cluster of yellow flowers and ignoring the confrontation. She did not draw the blossoms close to sample their fragrance. Cort had warned her not to touch anything in the jungle—not even pretty flowers.

Yacouba abruptly seemed to cave in on himself. "All right, Mr. Cort. I will come the rest of the way with you. As you put it, I have no choice. But please promise me that we will not stay long. You will look, you will see that I told the truth of this place, and then we will leave, oui?"

"Sure." With a dramatic flourish, Cort stepped to one side. "After you, Yacouba—M'sieur."

His expression grim, their guide resumed the trek forward.

He was as true as his word. They did not have much farther to go. One moment, they were completely surrounded by high trees and thickets of denser brush, and the next . . .

"Well, what the Bingham do you think of that?" Cort halted to marvel. Coming up beside him, Shelly futilely dragged a glistening forearm across her perspiring brow and pushed back her hat as she joined him in staring.

"This is what we hiked two days through the jungle to see? A bunch of rocks?" She was exceptionally bummed.

"Not just rocks." Cort's eyes traveled slowly over the structure that rose before them. "They're walls. Real walls." He glanced over at the visibly apprehensive Yacouba. "You were telling the truth about that much, at least."

"Yes, walls. The castle walls." Fearless in the face of nocturnal prowling leopards and hordes of driver ants, their guide was now unashamedly on edge. "We can go now, oui, M'sieur Cort?"

Cort studied the wall before them. "I don't see any weeping. I guess we just have to wait for tonight's full moon."

It was amusing to see how big the guide's eyes became. "No! We leave now, M'sieur. Cort. Please. You have seen. It is enough."

"It is not enough." Cort was adamant. "Besides, as you so correctly pointed out, it'll be dark soon. Might as well make camp right here. And while you're setting up the tents and starting dinner, Shelly and I will have a look around. Or are you afraid the rocks will eat us?"

"No. No, not afraid of that," Yacouba muttered. Without elaboration and with obvious reluctance, he swung the heavy pack off his back.

"Shelly?" Cort eyed his companion. She shrugged.

"Might as well sweat while walking as sweat while standing."

"Not quite the investigative spirit I was hoping for," Cort said as he started forward.

"You want to see spirit?" She cocked a jaundiced eye at him. "Show me a spa and a salon, I'll show you some spirit."

"In Libreville," he told her. "In a few days. Don't I always keep my promises?" She threw him a look but said nothing.

Though the walls confronting them were formidable, the structure did not resemble a castle in the historical European sense. Fashioned of blocks of neatly cut gray stone that had once been covered by white plaster, the inward-sloping ramparts were now carpeted in green moss so dark, it was almost black. Opportunistic fungi thrust stark white caps and beige tubes from cracks where the binding mortar had crumbled away. Crusted with old rust, the protruding cylinders of heavy cannon jutted priapically from bastions at each corner of the impressive fortification. Eying them, Cort marveled at the effort and labor that must have been required to haul the massive weapons up a river and then overland to this remote site.

Of the heavy double wooden gate that had once barred entry into the inner courtyard, only nails and clasps of failing black iron remained, fallen to the ground where they had been enveloped by eager vines and the questing roots of small trees. The wood itself had long since rotted away, consumed by the voracious, ever-opportunistic jungle. Kneeling to examine the ragged tongues of rusting metal, Cort lamented that he was not historian enough to date them. He would have to query Yacouba later. To his untrained eye, they looked plenty old. Certainly not twentieth century, he assured himself. Heedless of national laws that forbade the taking of antiquities, he thoughtfully pocketed a few of the smaller nails as he scanned the twilit courtyard in front of him. He had not hiked all this way for nails, even if they did qualify as antiques.

Enclosed by forbidding stone walls three stories high, the courtyard boasted several equally overgrown freestanding stone structures. One clearly had contained living quarters while another was just as self-evidently an old stable. They found evidence of a large communal kitchen, storerooms, a meeting hall of some sort, and a church. As Cort and an increasingly disinterested Shelly explored the ruins' interiors, they found remnants of glazed pottery, furniture, and even a few disintegrating, moldy books. The writing in the latter reminded Cort of Dutch, but the pages were so filthy and worm-eaten, he could not be sure. Any potentially valuable artifacts were notable only by their absence. The nearest to anything of worth they uncovered were a scattering of badly corroded silver spoons and knives. As he continued to pull out and ransack drawers in the kitchen, Cort methodically shoved old silverware into a pocket.

"We'll have another look around tomorrow," he told his companion. "It's getting dark and I don't want to step in a hole or something. This wouldn't be a good place to sprain an ankle." As he started toward the doorway that led out of the kitchen, he was careful to step over the labyrinth of roots that coiled their way across the stone floor.

Following close behind, Shelly paused to pick up half a broken plate. It was white with blue designs. "I hope Yacouba has dinner going. I'm starving."

"He'd better," Cort snapped. "I'm not paying him to sit around and pick his toes. I don't like his attitude lately, either." He shoved a chair aside. Largely intact, it might have been worth something if not for the dozens of wormholes that riddled the intricately carved back.

She ran a hand through the blond hair she'd deliberately had cropped short for the trip. "Are you going to pay him in full now that he's brought us to this place?"

Cort kicked aside a tin ewer. It clanged noisily as it bounced across the floor. "*He* certainly thinks so. We'll work it out when we get back to the train station at Ivindo. I'm sure we'll come to an arrangement." He smiled. "Not that he has much choice in what I finally do decide to pay him. Or any leverage."

Out in the courtyard, night overtook the forest like a quiet apocalypse. Here at the equator, the sun did not so much set as plummet below the horizon. Same time every day, day in and day out. To someone used to the gradual sunsets of temperate climes, the sudden descent into darkness could be disconcerting. Cort had a small flashlight on the chain he kept in one pocket, but he knew they wouldn't need it. Yacouba had been ordered to set up camp just outside the main gate. Cort had no doubt that regardless of his superstitious fears, the guide would do as he had been told. The man had too much money at stake to do otherwise.

So, Cort didn't insist they keep going when Shelly declared that she wanted to take a quick look inside one of the portals that beckoned from the inner wall of the fortifications. Several such arching openings formed

WHAT THE #@&% IS THAT?

dark ovals within the overgrown stone. Though clearly intended to allow entrance, they had low lintels just like the doorways in the courtyard buildings. People today were taller, Cort knew, than those who had gone before. The opening she chose stood out because of the elaborate gate that hung half-open on massive, bent iron hinges. The heavy black grate looked strong enough to stop a charging rhino.

"Go ahead and have a look," he told her, "but don't linger. I don't know what you think you'll find in there that we didn't see inside the main buildings. And watch out for snakes."

She smiled reassuringly at him, alluring in the deepening twilight despite the perspiration that streaked her face. "I won't be long, I promise. But we came all this way. Maybe there are some diamonds. Or some antique jewelry. Something like that would almost make it worth coming all this way." She gestured skyward. "Anyway, the light's fading. I won't go any farther than I can see. And I'll be careful."

While she bent low to pass under the opening's lintel, he occupied himself examining the ground. The courtyard was paved with large blocks of the same finely cut stone as the outer walls and interior buildings. Someone had gone to a great deal of trouble to erect this imposing fortress here in the middle of the equatorial jungle. Europeans, certainly. Yacouba had been right about that much. Cort had seen pictures of the walls at Great Zimbabwe, and this looked nothing like them.

The rationale for the fort's construction remained as much a mystery as ever. If its builders had found gold here, or diamonds, the establishment of such a commanding facility would make sense. Or maybe the driving force had been ivory, he told himself. There were still a lot of elephants in this part of central Africa. He could be standing in the middle of an important ivory trading center whose history had been swallowed up by time and the jungle.

Perhaps he ought to have another, more thorough look at the buildings he and Shelly had just walked through. An ivory storeroom might be situated underground, or otherwise carefully hidden. So far, their cursory search had revealed very little in the way of artifacts. It was possible that everything of value had been carried off by various tribes. But, he reminded himself, Yacouba was insistent that locals didn't come here.

Ivory held up well over time. He and Shelly couldn't carry off a hoard of tusks, of course, but if they discovered anything substantial, it might be worthwhile to come back with porters (who would no doubt have to be paid handsomely to convince them to come here). If its age could be verified, old ivory was something for which he might be able to obtain a legitimate export permit. If that was the case, he knew paying off local officials wouldn't be much—

Shelly's horrific high-pitched scream split the thick, inert evening air, and he forgot all about any possible profit that might be gained from the teeth of long-dead elephants.

She was still screaming as he raced out of the central building, the piercing quaver testing the upper register of what the human voice was capable of. It stopped cold by the time he reached the portal she had entered.

A snake, he thought. Sweat made his shirt stick clammily to his back. She had seen a snake. Or, he worried, she'd been bitten by one. Or maybe she had encountered nothing more than a big spider. Except—her screams had not been screams of fright. Those throaty, bladed trills had been full of pain. Something had hurt her.

By now, the corridor inside the wall had filled up with darkness the way a barrel fills with oil. Had she tripped and knocked herself unconscious, Cort wondered? A place like this was likely to be peppered with unmarked cavities. Old open wells, for example. Despite the confidence she had expressed, he realized now he should have insisted that she take the little flashlight.

"Shelly! Shelly?" One hand rested on the corner of the dark portal, the stone damp and cold against his palm, as he tried to peer inside. The inner depths were impenetrable, black as the inside of a cave. Extracting the small emergency light from his pocket, he squeezed it to life.

The beam the twin LEDs cast was narrow but bright. He could not see very far ahead, but he could see clearly. Certainly clearly enough to avoid something as obvious as an uncovered well. Unexpectedly, the path he was following inclined downward. The uneven pavement underfoot was slick with moisture.

It was plain what had happened, he told himself. In the gathering darkness, she had lost her footing on the slick cobblestones, slipped, and hit her head. That was why she was not answering his calls. It was a hypothesis that explained her present silence—but not the preceding screams. One scream, yes. Multiple screams . . .

The corridor widened, turned a sharp corner, and continued to descend. Soon, it had widened enough to accommodate two-way traffic. Heavy iron sconces bolted to the walls showed where torches and later oil lamps had once blazed to illuminate the subterranean maze. Like fossilized flames, sooty streaks rose above each one.

She's crazy, he told himself. Wandering down into a place like this at sunset. What could have driven her to keep going beyond where the fading sunlight reached? Darkness pressed in tight around him while fingers of damp wormed their way beneath his shirt. Without the flashlight, it would have been impossible to see anything.

An iron grate in the ceiling allowed the first hint of intensifying moonlight to illuminate a tiny portion of floor. Until that moment, he had not realized how far he had descended. The grate was at least thirty feet overhead.

Where was he? Despite the twists and turns he had taken, he was certain he was still somewhere within the castle perimeter. Tilting back his head, he found that he could almost see the rising moon. Still gazing upward, he took a step forward and stumbled on something.

"Dammit!" Lowering the beam of his flashlight revealed the chain he had tripped over. It lay on the floor in a haphazard heap, as if it had been dropped or fallen from a cart. The links were pitted and heavy. In the feeble light from overhead, the iron had a peculiar greasy sheen.

As he continued onward, he encountered more of the chains. Many were attached to iron rings that were bolted to the walls, but a fair number lay scattered across the floor itself.

Shifting the beam from side to side as he slowly made his way forward, he was relieved when the flashlight finally picked out the pale brown of his companion's pants. He barely had time to register the fact that the pockets were too high and were facing the wrong way. He didn't scream, but that was because he inhaled so sharply, he temporarily stopped breathing. Just as he stopped moving.

Shelly was hanging from the ceiling, her legs spread wide. Too wide. A worn, rusted, but still unbreakable iron shackle was clamped tightly around each of her bare ankles. As she swung slowly back and forth, blood flowed copiously down her front and back, soaking her shirt, staining her blonde hair dark, completely covering her face with the same slick sheen as oil on glass. Her eyes were wide open and staring. The left one bulged halfway out of its socket from the sheer force of her screaming.

She had been pulled apart, split like a chicken wing, her pelvis cracked and one leg wrenched almost completely out of its socket. The brief but intense screams he had heard echoed through him, repeating in his head like a bad heavy metal track, refusing to go away. In the heat and humidity and the cloying, cramping darkness, he found himself shivering. Something had, something had . . .

He spun in a panicked circle, the beam of his tiny light catching slashing, brief pictures of walls, chains, ceiling, floor. Within the subterranean chamber, nothing moved. Shafting silently down through the iron grate overhead, cold moonlight etched a crisscross pattern on the stone floor. There was no sound save for the steady drip, drip of blood onto the cold rock.

Then he heard it: the slightest of scraping noises. Something moving over the stone. Sliding impatiently across the same pavement on which he stood. A rough, unyielding, inorganic sound. Not footsteps. Not an animal. There was no soft flesh to muffle the noise.

He brought his light around sharply to seek the source, and saw the chain coming for him.

Advancing like an iron serpent, it was slithering across the floor toward him of its own apparent volition. No one was pulling on it; no one was pushing it. Neither was it truly sliding, since it could not slide uphill. In place of a snake head there was a circular shackle of heavy black cast iron. A single bolt held the hinged halves together. Fixed in the beam of Cort's flashlight it rose, cobra-like, to regard him. Ancient caked blood lined the inside of the shackle. The bolt unscrewed and the two halves of the shackle parted, opening like jaws.

What the fuck is that? His eyes widened.

He might have made a sound. In any case, there was no one around to take note of it except the unfortunate Shelly, who was beyond hearing. He stumbled backward, staggering uphill. Something struck at his right calf and a sharp pain shot through his lower leg. Twisting wildly, he looked down to see a second chain starting to wrap itself around his upper ankle. Uttering an inarticulate cry, he wrenched free of the encircling metal and turned to run back the way he had come.

All around him now, the sloping subterranean passageway was alive with the brassy clink and clank of awakening metal. Chains scraped and rattled, jangled and clattered as one serpentine shackle after another shook itself to horrid, metallic life. Cort ran as he had never run, trying to keep to the middle of the corridor and away from the walls, dodging the mamba-like strikes of chains heavy and light, flailing madly at those that lashed out as they tried to wrap themselves around his legs, his torso, his thrashing arms.

Somehow, he made it out without falling, without being dragged down. Though distant and indifferent, the brightening light of the ascending full moon was as welcome a sight to his wild eyes as the flash and flare of the signs in Times Square on a Saturday night. Behind him, the deep, damp corridor that pierced the ground like a junkie's cracked syringe was alive with a rising metallic cackle. Looking back as he struggled to catch his breath in the superheated, cloying air, he saw to his horror that the hideously animate metal Shelly—and now he—had disturbed would not be satisfied with trying to trap him in the stone catacombs below.

It was coming out after him.

Dozens, hundreds of lengths of chain large and small; some with shackles attached, others adorned with draperies of dried blood, came heaving, writhing, and humping like a horde of gray-black worms out of the arched opening, as if a truckload of giant leeches had been dumped into the courtyard. With a cry, Cort rushed toward the main gate, howling frantically for Yacouba as he ran. What the guide could possibly do he could not imagine, but if nothing else, the presence of another potential victim might at least divert some of the attention of the horror that was tracking him. Risking a glance backward, he saw that the metal coils still pursued him across the open stone courtyard.

He shouldn't have looked back.

As a result, he did not see the root that tripped him. It was not animate and did not reach up to grab at his feet, but it might as well have. He went down hard just inside the beckoning gateway. Losing the flashlight as he threw out his hands to protect his face, he managed to break his fall as he slammed forward into the corner of wall where a massive gate had once hung. Slumping to the ground, he grimaced as he rolled over onto his back. The liquid that filled his mouth was syrup and salt. Raising his hands, he saw where he had scraped them against the eroded rock. Both palms were bloody. His lower lip had caught the edge of the entrance and was bleeding as well.

Horribly, he was not alone in his silent hemorrhaging.

Blinking away blood and sweat as he pushed back against the moss-covered stone and struggled to his feet, he saw that the wall he had slammed into was wet. Reaching out, he ran his fingers down the rock. When he drew them back, they were sticky and sopping. Not with water—it had not rained all day, and it had not rained while he had been underground.

His fingers were covered with more blood. Blood that was not his. It was then that he understood. The walls were not weeping.

They were bleeding.

Eyes wide, holding his gore-soaked hand out away from his body as if mere contact with it would irrevocably find him completely coated with the thick, dark, alien fluid, he struggled to his feet. The moon was rising fast, fast enough to enable him to see the courtyard, the central buildings, and the enclosing inner walls without the aid of his dropped flashlight. Everywhere he could see, the ancient, laboriously worked masonry was soaking wet. Every surface leaked dark red fluid. It oozed from crevices between the stones, bubbled lugubriously from pits in the courtyard, flowed in rivulets and pinched waterfalls from the cornices and carvings that decorated the main structures.

Blood soaked the buildings, pooled up in the stable, filled the fissures and clefts in the paving stones. Ancient blood, but not forgotten. It was the thick liquid ghost of all the blood that had been shed in this place down through the centuries. As it spread outward to submerge the courtyard in all its salty crimson wetness, the chains continued to hump and writhe their way toward him through the rising liquid. Some continued to rise up like snakes, but others—others formed different shapes.

Behind him, a pair of small shackles near the ground connected by chains to another pair higher up were attached in turn to a much larger shackle in the center where—a head might fit, he realized in horror. That was when understanding struck him through all the blood and noise, terror and night, in which he had become engulfed.

Lives and labor and treasure had not been expended to raise this fortress deep in the jungle to protect trade in gold, or in diamonds, or even in ivory. Castles, the European exploiters and their chiefly native allies had euphemistically called such places. Perhaps to mask the real purpose for which they had been constructed. They had been built to protect, yes. As well as to guard and regulate and look after the most valuable trade commodity of them all.

Slaves.

He could hear the other sounds now. They were soft and subtle and almost imperceptible, but he could hear them. The hopeless whisperings, the agonized moans, the desperate final cries that rose above the clanking and rattling of the pursuing chains. The echoes of the thousands, perhaps tens of thousands, who had been brought this way, manacled together at the feet and at the neck on their long, sad, one-way march to the waiting distant sea. Torn from their villages by war or raiding parties only to be held here until the time came to send them in armed convoy to the coast. There they would be packed aboard ships bound for Brazil, for the islands of the Caribbean, for the south of North America, never to return. Many would never make it. They would perish from disease or malnutrition or overcrowding during the horrific Middle Passage. Many would not even get that far.

Instead, they would die here, crammed together in subterranean pens of stone and iron, asphyxiated by their comrades in the nightmarish heat and the unimaginable stench of the dungeons. No wonder Yacouba had not wanted to come that last half mile. No wonder he had not wanted to walk those final yards. No wonder.

Cort forced himself to turn, to stay upright. Surely Yacouba had not fled at the sound of Shelly's screams. Surely not! Yacouba would still be waiting for him in the camp in the forest. Once he was free of the noisome walls and beyond their suffocating stone grasp, he would finally heed the wise counsel of his knowing guide. They would not stay anywhere near here, proximate to this hellhole of horror and death, but would use the light of the moon to lead them away. Across the nearest river, however far that might lie, yes. There they could finally rest, safely distant from the flesh-crawling moaning and the unyielding iron and the weeping, bleeding walls. Shelly—poor broken, dead Shelly—in the darkness below, she had fallen into a pit and broken her neck, he would tell the authorities. Yacouba would corroborate the explanation. Yacouba would not question. Yacouba would go along with anything that let them flee this place and collect the rest of his fee.

Cort went down for the second time just as he emerged outside the gaping portal.

The shackle that snapped shut around his right ankle was attached to a chain whose individual hot-forged links were as thick as sausages. Whining like a trapped dog, he pulled at it frantically until his already bleeding fingers were torn and raw, and more than one nail hung loose and bloody. As he dug at the first chain, a second manacle clamped tight around his left wrist and contracted, dragging him backward while practically lifting him off his feet. The back of his head bounced when it hit the unyielding pavement.

Vision blurring, he looked up and managed to half-focus on the yellow circle of the rising moon. Something blotted it out. It was a heavy neck shackle, four inches wide and half an inch thick, solid wrought iron, supported in an upright position by a coil of bloody black chain. Below it, other chains extended off to left and right. The silhouette they formed was nearly recognizable as that of a human body, a representation in hovering, twisting, restraining iron that stood as a symbol for the thousands who had passed this way, long ago.

The chain that was now secured to his right wrist pulled hard. Very hard. Cort screamed as his shoulder was dislocated. Rolling, moaning Yacouba's name, he tried to crawl back toward the beckoning gateway. In contrast to the intrusive slaving castle that was a hulking artificial blot on the landscape, the fetid surrounding jungle now seemed innocent, pristine, pure. It tempted him. It smelled of refuge.

Another shackle clamped shut around his left ankle. Chains snapped taut. He felt himself being pulled backward along the ground, across the hard stones, his unwilling passage lubricated by a layer of blood that was not wholly his own. He tried to dig the tips of his raw fingers into the ground, but the rock allowed for no such purchase. The gateway receded in his vision, growing smaller and smaller in the moonlight as his sobbing, desperate form was dragged back into the castle.

From high above, the moon looked down, its soft light glistening off the dark liquid that now pooled freely in the open courtyard, shining on the back of the single screaming figure that was being pulled inexorably across the stones toward a single dark, arched opening in the inner wall. The moon had been witness to such sights for hundreds of years and knew that no one escaped from such a place. One could only be marched out, single file, and that sorrowful spectacle had not been played out beneath its glow for a very long time indeed.

The legs of the figure disappeared into that dark, unfeeling maw. Then the torso, then the head. A last hopeless howl accompanied the disappearance of arms and hands and finally fingers. All movement within the ancient castle walls ceased. Except for the weeping. And the bleeding.

As long as the walls stood, it would never stop.

[Author's note: *The description of northeastern Gabon derives from some time I spent in the Ivindo region of that wonderful, underpopulated country. As for the castle itself, it is based on visits made to actual slave castles in Ghana, particularly Cape Coast Castle. Not so beautiful . . . but instructive. The low entrances, living quarters, chains, shackles, overhead grate, sunless corridors described in the story are, I regret to say, all too real.*]

ABOUT THE AUTHORS

LAIRD BARRON is the author of several books, including *The Croning*, *Occultation*, and *The Beautiful Thing That Awaits Us All*. His work has also appeared in many magazines and anthologies. An expatriate Alaskan, Barron currently resides in upstate New York.

DESIRINA BOSKOVICH's (desirinaboskovich.com) short fiction has been published in *Clarkesworld*, *Lightspeed*, *Nightmare*, *Kaleidotrope*, *PodCastle*, *Drabblecast*, and anthologies such as *The Way of the Wizard*, *Aliens: Recent Encounters*, and *The Apocalypse Triptych*. Her nonfiction pieces on music, literature, and culture have appeared in *Lightspeed*, *Weird Fiction Review*, *Huffington Post*, *Wonderbook*, and *The Steampunk Bible*. She is also the editor of *It Came From the North: An Anthology of Finnish Speculative Fiction* (Cheeky Frawg, 2013), and, together with Jeff VanderMeer, coauthor of *The Steampunk User's Manual* (Abrams Image, 2014).

ADAM-TROY CASTRO's twenty-six books to date include, among others, four Spider-Man novels, three novels about his profoundly damaged far-future murder investigator Andrea Cort, and six middle-grade novels about the dimension-spanning adventures of that very strange but very heroic young boy Gustav Gloom. The penultimate installment in the Gustav

Gloom series, *Gustav Gloom and the Inn of Shadows* (Grosset and Dunlap), saw print in August 2015. The finale, in which Gustav and company complete their quest for his father and their epic battle against the forces of the vile Lord Obsidian, will appear in August 2016. Adam's darker short fiction for grownups is highlighted by his most recent collection, *Her Husband's Hands and Other Stories* (Prime Books). Adam's works have won the Philip K. Dick Award and the Seiun (Japan), and have been nominated for eight Nebulas, three Stokers, two Hugos, and, internationally, the Ignotus (Spain), the Grand Prix de l'Imaginaire (France), and the Kurd-Laßwitz Preis (Germany). He lives in Florida with his wife Judi and either three or four cats, depending on what day you're counting and whether Gilbert's escaped this week.

AMANDA DOWNUM is an American fantasy author currently living in Austin, Texas. She is most known for her Necromancer Chronicles: *The Drowning City*, *The Bone Palace*, and *Kingdoms of Dust*. Her short fiction has appeared in venues such as *Strange Horizons*, *Weird Tales*, and *Realms of Fantasy*. She has been nominated for the James Tiptree Jr. Award and the Spectrum Award.

GEMMA FILES, a former film critic and teacher–turned–horror author, is probably best known for her Weird Western Hexslinger series (*A Book of Tongues*, *A Rope of Thorns*, and *A Tree of Bones*, all from ChiZine Publications). She has also published two short fiction collections (*Kissing Carrion* and *The Worm in Every Heart*), two chapbooks of speculative poetry, and a story cycle (*We Will All Go Down Together: Stories of the Five-Family Coven*). In 1999, her story "The Emperor's Old Bones" won the International Horror Guild's Best Short Fiction Award. Her next novel, *Experimental Film*, is now available from CZP.

ALAN DEAN FOSTER is the bestselling author of more than a hundred and twenty novels, and is perhaps most famous for his Commonwealth series, which began in 1971 with the novel *The Tar-Aiym Krang*. His most recent series is the transhumanism trilogy the Tipping Point. Foster's work has been translated into more than fifty languages and has won awards in Spain and Russia in addition to the United States. He is also well known for his film novelizations, the most recent of which is *Star Trek Into Darkness*. He is currently at work on several new novels and film projects.

CHRISTOPHER GOLDEN (christophergolden.com) is the *New York Times* bestselling author of such novels as *Snowblind*, *Of Saints and Shadows*, *The Myth Hunters*, *The Boys Are Back in Town*, *Strangewood*, and the thriller *Tin Men*. He has cowritten three illustrated novels with Mike Mignola, the first of which, *Baltimore, or, The Steadfast Tin Soldier and the Vampire*, was the launching pad for the Eisner Award–nominated comic book series, *Baltimore*. His graphic novels include the Cemetery Girl trilogy, coauthored with Charlaine Harris. As an editor, he has worked on the short story anthologies *The New Dead*, *The Monster's Corner*, and *Dark Duets*, among others. Golden has also written and cowritten comic books, video games, screenplays, and a network television pilot. He was born and raised in Massachusetts, where he still lives with his family. His original novels have been published in more than fourteen languages in countries around the world.

SIMON R. GREEN lives in a small town in the English countryside, and has written over fifty novels, including the Deathstalker books (space opera), the Secret Histories (featuring Shaman Bond, the very secret agent), the Nightside series (a private eye who operates in the Twilight Zone, solving cases of the weird and uncanny), the Ghost Finders series (traditional ghost stories in a modern setting), and the Ishmael Jones mysteries (Agatha Christie with a weird touch). His first film, *Judas Ghost*, has just appeared on DVD. He's going to take a rest any time now.

MARIA DAHVANA HEADLEY (mariadahvanaheadley.com) is the author of the young adult skyship novel *Magonia* from HarperCollins, the novel

Queen of Kings, the memoir *The Year of Yes*, and coauthor with Kat Howard of the short horror novella *The End of the Sentence*. With Neil Gaiman, she is the *New York Times*–bestselling coeditor of the monster anthology *Unnatural Creatures*, benefitting 826DC. Her Nebula and Shirley Jackson Awards–nominated short fiction has recently appeared in *Lightspeed* ("Give Her Honey When You Hear Her Scream," "The Traditional"), on Tor.com, *The Toast*, *Clarkesworld*, *Nightmare*, *Apex* Magazine, *The Journal of Unlikely Entomology*, *Subterranean Online*, *Uncanny*, *Glitter & Mayhem*, and Jurassic London's *The Lowest Heaven* and *The Book of the Dead*, as well as in a number of Year's Bests, most recently Year's Best Weird. She lives in Brooklyn with a collection of beasts, an anvil, and a speakeasy bar through the cellar doors. Find her on her website or on Twitter at @mariadahvana.

GRADY HENDRIX has written about the confederate flag for *Playboy Magazine*, terrible movie novelizations for Film Comment, and both Jean-Claude Van Damme AND ninja death swarms for Slate. He's covered machine gun collector conventions, written award shows for Chinese television, and spent years answering the phone for a parapsychological research organization. His stories about UFO cults, killer Chinese parasites, Cthulhu dating your mom, and super-genius apes have appeared in *Lightspeed*, *Strange Horizons*, *Pseudopod*, and *The Mad Scientist's Guide to World Domination*. He is the author of *Horrorstör*, about a haunted IKEA, and in 2016 his second novel, *My Best Friend's Exorcism*, will be available.

NANCY HOLDER (nancyholder.com) is a *New York Times* bestselling author (The Wicked Saga) of approximately eighty novels and two hundred short stories, essays, and articles. She has received five Bram Stoker Awards, a Scribe Award, and a Young Adult Pioneer Award. Recent works include *The Rules* (Delacorte, June 2015) and *Demons of the Hellmouth*, coauthored with Rupert Giles (Titan Books, September 2015). She is the vice president of the Horror Writers Association, and a member of the faculty for the MFA in Creative Writing program offered through the University of Southern Maine. A columnist for SFWA and the HWA, she also writes and edits comic books and graphic novels for Moonstone Books. She lives in San Diego. Tweet her at @nancyholder.

JOHN LANGAN is the author of three collections: *Sefira and Other Betrayals* (Hippocampus 2016), *The Wide, Carnivorous Sky and Other Monstrous Geographies* (Hippocampus 2013), and *Mr. Gaunt and Other Uneasy Encounters* (Prime 2008). He has written a novel, *House of Windows* (Night Shade 2009), and, with Paul Tremblay, coedited an anthology, *Creatures: Thirty Years of Monsters* (Prime 2011). He lives with his wife and younger son in upstate New York.

JONATHAN MABERRY (jonathanmaberry.com) is a *New York Times* bestselling author, multiple Bram Stoker Award winner, and comic book writer. He's the author of many novels, including *Code Zero, Fire & Ash, The Nightsiders, Dead of Night*, and *Rot & Ruin*; and the editor of the *V-Wars* shared-world anthologies. His nonfiction books are on topics ranging from martial arts to zombie pop culture. Jonathan writes *V-Wars* and *Rot & Ruin* for *IDW Comics*, and *Bad Blood* for Dark Horse, as well as multiple projects for Marvel. Since 1978, he has sold more than 1,200 magazine feature articles, 3,000 columns, two plays, greeting cards, song lyrics, poetry, and textbooks. Jonathan continues to teach the celebrated Experimental Writing for Teens class, which he created. He founded the Writers Coffeehouse and cofounded The Liars Club; and is a frequent speaker at schools and libraries, as well as a keynote speaker and guest of honor at major writers' and genre conferences. He lives in Del Mar, California.

SEANAN MCGUIRE (seananmcguire.com) is a Californian author of speculative fiction. She was born and raised in the San Francisco Bay Area, resulting in a fear of weather and a deep respect for the sea. Since 2009, she has released more than twenty books, under both her own name and the name "Mira Grant." Most people believe that she doesn't really sleep. Seanan was the 2010 winner of the John W. Campbell Award for Best New Writer, which came with a tiara. In her spare time, she enjoys Disney Parks, horror movies, and trying to summon her vegetable armada to subjugate humanity. We think she's kidding about that last part. We hope. Keep up with Seanan on her website or on Twitter at @seananmcguire.

D. Thomas Minton (dthomasminton.com) recently traded a warm tropical island for the Pacific Northwest of the continental United States, where he now lives a short walk from vineyards and an alpaca farm. When not writing, he gets paid to "play" in the ocean, travel to remote places, and help communities conserve coral reefs. His fiction has been published in *Asimov's*, *Lightspeed*, and *Daily Science Fiction*, and his idle ramblings hold court on his website.

An (pronounce it "On") Owomoyela (an.owomoyela.net) is a neutrois author with a background in web development, linguistics, and weaving chain maille out of stainless-steel fencing wire, whose fiction has appeared in a number of venues, including *Clarkesworld*, *Asimov's*, *Lightspeed*, and a handful of Year's Bests. An's interests range from pulsars and Cepheid variables to gender studies and nonstandard pronouns, with a plethora of stops in between. An can be found online on her website and can be funded at patreon.com/an_owomoyela.

Tim Pratt is the author of over a dozen novels, most recently *Heirs of Grace*, and many short stories. His work has appeared in *The Best American Short Stories*, *The Year's Best Fantasy*, and other nice places. He's won a Hugo Award for short fiction, and has been a finalist for World Fantasy, Sturgeon, Stoker, Mythopoeic, and Nebula Awards, among others. He lives in Berkeley, California, and works as a senior editor at *Locus*, a trade magazine devoted to science fiction and fantasy publishing.

SCOTT SIGLER is the *New York Times* bestselling author of the Infected trilogy (*Infected*, *Contagious*, and *Pandemic*), *Ancestor*, and *Nocturnal*, hardcover thrillers from Crown Publishing; and the cofounder of Empty Set Entertainment, which publishes his Galactic Football League series (*The Rookie*, *The Starter*, *The All-Pro*, and *The MVP*). Before he was published, Scott built a large online following by giving away his self-recorded audiobooks as free, serialized podcasts. His loyal fans, who named themselves "Junkies," have downloaded over eight million individual episodes of his stories and interact daily with Scott and each other in the social media space.

RACHEL SWIRSKY holds an MFA in fiction from the Iowa Writers' Workshop. Her short stories have been published in a number of magazines and anthologies, including Tor.com, *Subterranean Online*, and *Clarkesworld* magazine. Her work has been nominated for the Hugo Award, the World Fantasy Award, and the Locus Award, and won the Nebula Award twice. Her second short story collection, *How the World Became Quiet*, came out from Subterranean Press in 2013. She enjoys writing collaboratively, as she did in this collection, and would like to raise a fictive glass to her cowriter, An Owomoyela.

TERENCE TAYLOR (terencetaylor.com) is an award-winning children's television writer whose work appeared on PBS, Nickelodeon, and Disney, among many others. As an author of fiction, his first published short story, "Plaything," appeared in *Dark Dreams*, the first horror-suspense anthology of African American authors. He was one of a handful of authors to be included in the next two volumes, with "The Share" in *Voices from the Other Side* and "Wet Pain" in *Whispers in the Night*. Terence is also author of the first two books of his Vampire Testaments trilogy, *Bite Marks*, and *Blood Pressure*. After a two-year hiatus, he has returned to the conclusion of his trilogy, *Past Life*. Find him on Twitter at @vamptestaments.

Isabel Yap (isalikeswords.wordpress.com) writes fiction and poetry, works in the tech industry, and drinks tea. Born and raised in Manila, she has also lived in California, Tokyo (for ninety-six days!), and London. In 2013, she attended the Clarion Writers' Workshop. Her stories have appeared in Tor.com, *Shimmer*, *Interfictions Online*, and *Nightmare*; they have also been included in *The Year's Best Weird Fiction Vol. 2*, *Apex Book of World SF Volume 4*, and *The Best of Philippine Speculative Fiction 2005–2010*. Her poetry has appeared or is forthcoming in *Stone Telling*, *Uncanny*, *Apex* Magazine, and *Goblin Fruit*. You can find her on her website or on Twitter at @visyap.

ABOUT THE EDITORS

JOHN JOSEPH ADAMS (johnjosephadams.com) is the series editor of the Best American Science Fiction and Fantasy, published by Houghton Mifflin Harcourt. He is also the bestselling editor of many other anthologies. Called "the reigning king of the anthology world" by Barnes & Noble, John is a winner of the Hugo Award (for which he has been nominated nine times) and is a six-time World Fantasy Award finalist. John is also the editor and publisher of the digital magazines *Lightspeed* and *Nightmare* and is a producer for WIRED's podcast *Geek's Guide to the Galaxy*. Find him on Twitter at @johnjosephadams.

DOUGLAS COHEN (douglascoheneditorial.com) is the coeditor of the anthology *Oz Reimagined: New Tales from the Emerald City and Beyond*. He is a former editor of *Realms of Fantasy* magazine, where he worked for six and a half years. In the magazine's final year, it published its one hundredth issue, won a Nebula Award, and was nominated for a second one. Douglas is also a writer, and his stories have appeared in *Weird Tales*. Additionally, he is the author of *Realms of Fantasy: A Retrospective*, a book collecting his detailed blog entries on every single issue published during the magazine's seventeen-year history.

ACKNOWLEDGMENTS

Many thanks to the following:

Publisher: Joe Monti for acquiring and editing the book, and to managing editor Jeannie Ng, production lead Elizabeth Blake-Linn, and the rest of the team at Saga Press.

Art/Design: Special thanks to Mike Mignola for providing an original cover illustration. You were the only artist we could envision handling the cover and the fact that you took time out of your schedule to make this happen has taken this project to a whole new level. Thanks also to Michael McCartney for adding in the beautiful design elements, and to Matthew Kalamidas for talking to Mike Mignola on our behalf.

Proofreader: Amanda Velosa.

Agent: Seth Fishman, for getting behind this incredibly whacky project midstream and running with it like the superagent he is. To any writers out there, you'd be lucky to have Seth in your corner.

Special thanks: to Jaym Gates, one of the original coeditors on this project. Other commitments forced her to drop out before the anthology found its ultimate home, but her contributions early on should not and will not be overlooked. Jaym, thanks so much for all the time and effort you put into this book. Any other editor would be lucky to coedit a book with you. Thanks also to Theodora Goss and Livia Llewellyn, who were part of the original random conversation on Facebook that sparked the idea for this book. And thanks too to Ken Liu and Ken Schneyer for taking time out of their schedules to pontificate upon legal matters.

Mentors: John thanks Gordon Van Gelder and Ellen Datlow for being great mentors and friends. Doug thanks Jeanne Cavelos, Shawna McCarthy, and Warren Lapine for exactly the same. We couldn't have done this without your tutelage.

Family: John thanks his amazing wife, Christie; his stepdaughters, Grace and Lotte; his mom, Marianne; and his sister, Becky, for all their love and support. Doug thanks his parents, Joyce and Gary, and his brother, Brian, for exactly the same.

Friends: Robert Bland, Desirina Boskovich, Christopher M. Cevasco, Matt and Jordan London, David Barr Kirtley, Nicole Mikoleski, Jesse Sneddon, and Michael Spensieri, for being there for us when we're anthologizing, and for putting up with us when we nattered about the project incessantly.

Readers: John and Doug both thank all the readers and reviewers of this anthology, as well as the readers and reviewers who loved our other anthologies, making it possible to do more.

Doug would also like to extend a special thanks to his coeditor, John. It's always a pleasure working with such a talented and professional friend, but being as you came into this project some months after it was already underway and contributed so many excellent ideas to make this book that much more awesome, your contributions are even more appreciated than usual. Thank you, John. I continue to admire your craft, drive, and dedication.

Writers: And last, but certainly not least: a big thanks to all of the authors who appear in this anthology.